"THE BASTARDS ARE ON TO US! OPEN FIRE! KNOCK THAT GUN OUT!"

Without realizing it, Devane was shouting. The bridge shook as the twin machine-guns on the port side rattled into life. He heard a sharp exchange of fire, the wild whooping of the Russian soldiers as they tensed themselves for the impact. One of the seamen gave a sharp cry and fell to his knees. He was trying to speak, but it sounded as if he were drowning in his own blood.

Devane gritted his teeth. *Now* . . .

DOUGLAS REEMAN

TORPEDO RUN

A JOVE BOOK

TORPEDO RUN

A Jove Book / published by arrangement with
William Morrow and Company, Inc.

PRINTING HISTORY
William Morrow edition published 1981
Jove edition / November 1982

ISBN: 0-515-06638-9

Jove books are published by Jove Publications,
Inc., 200 Madison Avenue, New York, N.Y. 10016.
The words "A Jove Book" and the "J" with sunburst
are trademarks belonging to Jove Publications, Inc.

PRINTED IN THE UNITED STATES OF AMERICA

For George,
one of the Glory Boys

Contents

1

RECALL

Lieutenant-Commander John Devane sat on a plain wooden bench seat and regarded the opposite wall. Grey rough concrete. You could even see where the first layer had been tamped home. The brief professional interest passed just as quickly as it had emerged and he sank back again, outwardly relaxed, but his mind busy with the distant sounds, the feeling of being off balance, lost.

The room was little more than a space curtained off from one of many such corridors beneath the Admiralty building in London. A far-off murmur was like the sea across a scattered reef, but it was traffic—red buses which still managed to make splashes of colour against the dust and rubble of wartime London, and taxis which never seemed to see you when you needed one—and people on the move: endless, restless throngs, many in the uniforms of countries occupied by 'them', as his mother called them. The enemy.

Devane glanced at his watch. Again the movement was easy and without waste. It was eleven in the forenoon, a May day in 1943. But down here it could have been anywhere, any time.

He thought briefly of his leave, the first he had had for many months. He tried to resist the feeling that he was glad it had been interrupted by this summons to the Admiralty after only four days. Perhaps that was what you needed after the blood

1

and guts of the Mediterranean war. Any longer and maybe you were too scared to go back.

His home was in Dorset, or had been in that other, prewar world. It was strange to go back, for, unlike London and other major towns and cities, Dorchester seemed to move more slowly, as if reluctant to accept that change would ever come. His father was still running the family business where he himself had once been employed as a fledgeling architect, although now there seemed very little to do unless it was under some government contract or other. His mother had grown older, but not so much that it caused surprise or pain on their rare meetings.

The curtain was plucked aside and Devane saw a small Wren studying him, her hair shining in the corridor lighting behind her.

'Captain Whitcombe will see you shortly, sir.'

Devane reached for his cap and stood up, adjusting himself for this unexpected interview. He knew Whitcombe from way back, a bluff, red-faced captain who had been in retirement before the war and had been slotted into a desk job to allow someone else to take over a bridge at sea. Unlike some, Whitcombe seemed to have dropped into a niche which suited him perfectly.

Devane fell in step beside the little Wren and wondered if she had a boy friend, if she liked her job underground, what she would say if he took her by the arm and. . . .

She paused by a steel door which was labelled SPECIAL OPERATIONS and waited for Devane to open it. The door weighed a ton, and he guessed she always had to do that.

Another concrete box, with clattering typewriters, harsh lighting, and engrossed Wrens bustling about with signals and files as if Devane were invisible.

A Wren second officer looked up from her desk. 'Wait here, please. I'll tell Captain Whitcombe you've arrived.'

He nodded and ran his fingers through his hair. It was as unruly as ever, and nearly four years of active service had not improved it. He thought about his last commission. The North African coast, sunshine and washed-out blue skies, or the fierce off-shore winds which tore your face with dust and desert sand.

What were they going to do with him? Not back to the Med

surely? Perhaps to the Channel, to the motor torpedo base at Felixstowe where it had all started?

His mother had exclaimed angrily, 'It's not right to recall you so soon, John! There are plenty round here who've never been in uniform!'

Whereas his father, as mild as ever, had said, 'I expect they know what they're doing. Our boy's important.'

Important. Devane smiled to himself. His father had really meant it.

It had certainly been a long haul from those other days when he had started to work for his father. Looking back it always seemed to have been spring or summer. Every weekend down to the coast in the green sports car he owned jointly with his best friend Tony. Sailing their old sloop round Portland Bill, pints afterwards in a pub at Weymouth. And later, more for a bet than anything, when they had both joined the peacetime Royal Naval Volunteer Reserve, he should have seen what might happen. What was still happening. Now the old sloop and the sports car were gone. Tony too, for that matter, killed in a mine-sweeper within sight of the Portland Bill they had both loved so much.

He steeled himself as he heard footsteps and muted voices. So there was someone else in that room. Probably saying, 'You speak first, old chap, while I watch his reactions.'

With a start he realized that the typewriters had all stopped, that several of the girls were looking at him. Naval officers, with wavy stripes or otherwise, were two a penny here. His eye fell on a carefully preserved newspaper which one of the Wrens had taken from her desk. The same one which his parents had at home.

Was it really him? Eyes squinting at the camera, battered cap all awry; some vague, grinning faces in the background with what he knew to be part of the old Maltese battery in the far distance.

The glaring headline still stunned him. DEVANE'S BATTLE SQUADRON STRIKES TERROR INTO THE RETREATING AFRIKA KORPS! THE LAST GERMANS FLEE FROM TUNIS! There was more, a whole lot more.

The voice said, 'Will you come this way, sir.' Even the unsmiling second officer was looking at him differently.

Devane had seen that look on the faces of newly joined

3

officers and ratings. It asked, what was it like? How does it feel to fight the enemy at close quarters?

Devane found himself in the other room without realizing he had moved or that the door had closed silently behind him.

Whitcombe strode to greet him. Still the same, thank God. Good old Tubby.

The other man was in civilian clothes but he looked like a naval officer.

Whitcombe beamed. 'Bloody good to see you again, John.' He jerked his head but his eyes stayed on Devane's grave features. 'This is Commander Kinross of our operations staff.'

Kinross did not shake hands but gave a stiff nod. He looked a cold fish but extremely competent. On the ball. Between them, these two men, whom most people had never heard of, planned each special operation in the Mediterranean like chess players. They probably had irons in other fires too, Devane thought. The world was waiting to see what would happen next. The Germans had been pushed out of North Africa and for the first time were on the defensive. This year the tide would have to go harder against them. Italy and Sicily were obvious beach heads, maybe Greece too. Then, with the enemy divided on several fronts at once, the real one, the invasion of northern Europe, which months, rather than years, ago had been the impossible dream.

Whitcombe was saying, 'Damn sorry about your leave.' He smiled and glanced at the ribbon on Devane's jacket. 'Another bar to your DSC, what does it feel like to be a hero and the public's darling?'

Devane looked past him, at the vast wall map which was a twin of the one in an adjoining operations room. Crosses and flags, dotted convoy routes, and mine fields, sinkings and marks to show approximately where ships had simply vanished without trace.

Feel like? Devane was twenty-seven years old and had been in the Navy since the outbreak of war. But he was a veteran, more than that, he was a survivor, and the two rarely went together in the roaring, clattering world of motor torpedo boats, the war where you saw your enemy, sometimes even his fear, as the tracer cut him down and turned his boat into an inferno.

'I feel immensely old, sir.'

Devane grinned. It made him look like a youth.

They all sat around the littered desk, and then Commander Kinross said abruptly, 'I know your record, of course, your rise from first lieutenant in a Vosper MTB at Felixstowe to command a flotilla in the Med.' He gave a wintry smile. 'That sounds a bit brief for so active a life, but it was when you came to us with your command that I really had the opportunity to study your methods.'

By 'us', Kinross meant the special operations section, and more to the point, the Special Boat Squadron which had achieved the impossible. From running guns to Tito's partisans and landing agents behind enemy lines, they had harried the German convoys and communications from the Aegean to Tobruk, from embattled Malta to the Adriatic. Devane's handful of MTBs, nicknamed the Battle Squadron, had tied down desperately needed patrol vessels and aircraft and, as the man had written in the newspaper, had indeed struck terror into the retreating Germans.

There were only two of his boats left, however, and they were little better than scrap. A lot of good men had gone, and some had been left in hospitals. It was the usual equation.

Whitcombe said, 'Fact is, John, we need you back. Otherwise. . . .' He glanced at the urbane commander, something like rebuke in his eyes. 'God knows you've earned a break, but we're stretched to breaking point. We *need* experienced officers as never before, leaders and not just brave chaps who obey orders right or wrong.' He gave a sad smile. 'But then you know all about that.'

Kinross sounded impatient. *His* war was waiting in the other room.

'This year is the turning point. It has to be. However we invade, northwards through Italy or the surrounding territory, it has to be soon. It's got to be *right*. One real failure now and we'll never get back in a million years.' He stood up and moved to the great wall map, then he pointed at the Mediterranean. 'Everything is regrouping, we have the whole North African coast sewn up and the convoy routes covered by sea and air.' His finger moved up still further. 'France next year, certainly no later, and after that it will be one long slog all the way to Berlin.' He turned and looked at Devane calmly. 'Of course, we'll not have it all our own way. Decisive campaigns are built on small ventures which are often never revealed until after a war. By then, who cares anyway? But who would have

5

believed that weather was as important as fuel and ammunition?'

Whitcombe interrupted uneasily, 'Get on with it, William.'

Kinross was unmoved. 'Last winter for instance, our Russian allies thought they were on the advance, that the German armies on the Eastern Front would collapse in the snow and ice. But they didn't. Somehow the Germans stood firm. Incredible casualties on both sides, millions probably, acts of barbarism which make Attila the Hun seem like a bloody amateur.'

Devane felt cold, as if the battlefield had suddenly penetrated the concrete bunker.

Fascinated, he watched Kinross's finger on the move again. It came to rest on the Black Sea, then on the thrusting Crimean peninsula itself.

Kinross said distantly, 'Brings back memories, eh? *Boys' Own Paper*, the Charge of the Light Brigade, Florence Nightingale, all good stuff.' His tone sharpened. 'Well, now it's the hinge of the whole front. The Germans took it from the Russians, and while they remain there in strength the Russians have no chance of thrusting as far as they must into Europe. They know it, the Americans know it, and so doubtless do the Germans. If Hitler's generals can withstand another winter the Russians will have to begin all over again. We can say goodbye to our own invasion of northern France unless the enemy is completely involved on every front. The defender always has the final advantage, remember that.'

Devane tensed. They were going to give him a staff job. Right here beneath London, hemmed in by charts and filing cabinets. He suddenly felt sickened at the prospect.

Whitcombe said, 'The coastal forces flotillas, MGBs as well as your MTBs, took quite a hammering, so the regrouping and remanning is top priority.' He smiled. 'You have to know sooner or later, John, but the invasion of Sicily is already set for July, so we don't have much time. A special MTB flotilla has been formed and trained, and was sent to the Med a few weeks ago. All brand-new boats, five to be exact.'

'Their senior officer is Lieutenant-Commander Don Richie, right?' Devane saw their startled exchange of glances. 'You know the Andrew, sir, no secrets for long.'

Kinross said coldly, 'Well, that had better be changed, and quickly.'

6

Whitcombe dragged out his cigarette case and lit one carefully.

'Of course, John, you and Richie served together at the beginning. In the Channel?'

'Yes. I know his wife too.' Devane looked away. Why had he said that?

'Well, Richie's special flotilla was put aboard some fast merchant ships, ex-passenger liners, at dead of night, men, torpedoes, everything but the kitchen sink, and whisked away. Through the canal and up to Kuwait. We don't have much trouble with Iran these days after we and the Russians "persuaded" them to get rid of their pro-German Shah.'

Whitcombe and Kinross smiled at each other like conspirators.

It was all getting out of hand. Nothing seemed to be making sense. Richie was the best there was. Another RNVR officer who had been a civilian before the war, he had become something of a legend in the little ships he commanded and led. So why did they need *him*?

Whitcombe glanced at the wall clock. 'Lunch soon, I think. Ask Mary to reserve us a table. She knows where.'

As if he was still attached to the desk by an invisible wire, Kinross left the room with obvious reluctance.

Whitcombe regarded Devane fondly. 'I'll come to the point, John. Those five boats were taken overland and launched into the Caspian Sea. A rendezvous is being arranged for the whole flotilla to be carried overland again.' He looked at the map. 'To the Black Sea. To work with the Russians against the enemy's flank. Five boats are all we can spare, besides which, it will give the flotilla more freedom to move and act. The Russians' one real weakness is on the water. Whatever they do, the Germans seem better at it. The Russians will never admit this, naturally, any more than we would. But they are keen for us to help, although I suspect they are hoping for more aid than we have to offer.'

Devane saw the map through different eyes now. It must be important to attract so much secret planning. Now those five MTBs were up there on the map. In the Caspian Sea. Then about four hundred miles across country to another sea, a different war.

'I want you to command the flotilla, John. It's unfair, it's

7

also unfortunate, but we need someone who is as well known and as respected to these men as Richie.'

So that was it. Don Richie was dead. Whitcombe did not have to tell him.

The tubby captain added slowly, 'When you said you knew his wife just now I got a bit bothered. She was here this morning, just before you, in fact. She had already been told in the usual way, but we felt we owed it to her. After all he did, killed in action seems a pretty small reward, for her anyway.' He looked round as Kinross's voice intruded through the door. 'In fact, he shot himself.' He gave a warning glance. 'Enough said for now.'

Kinross entered, his eyes questioning. 'All done?'

Whitcombe said breezily, 'Early lunch. We can talk some more later.'

Devane followed the others, his mind grappling with what Whitcombe had disclosed. Richie dead. They all expected to die, but not like that. Why the *hell* had he done it?

As the door swung behind the ill-matched trio the little Wren ventured, 'The one called Devane, he looks nice. Different.' She fell silent under their amused stares.

The officer had heard her but said nothing. The little Wren was brand new. She had a lot to learn. But she too found herself thinking of the young lieutenant-commander with the sun-tanned face and hands and the slow, almost shy smile.

One of the Glory Boys, as Kinross had called them. She had seen too many go through that door never to return to become involved.

A messenger brought over a bulky file with Richie's name on the jacket.

'This has just been delivered,' he said.

She looked at the tall filing cabinet in the corner. It was jokingly called the Coffin. But with a man's file in your hands it never seemed so funny.

The little Wren who had only just joined the special operations staff took the file and carried it to the cabinet. Once she glanced at it and the bare wording, KILLED IN ACTION. But she saw only the face of the man called Devane, because he was real, and Richie she had never met.

Devane felt bone dry, which was surprising. They had had plenty to drink, before, during and after the lunch in a small club at the back of St. James's, which in spite of the many uniforms in the bar and dining room seemed to ignore the war.

They had been back in the Admiralty bunker for most of the day. Between them, Whitcombe in his bluff, outspoken fashion, and Kinross with his reserved, carefully formed explanations, had built up quite a picture of the new flotilla.

They sat and watched Devane's face as he studied a typed list of officers in the flotilla.

The names were like small portraits of the men, or at least half of them were. The new flotilla had been constructed from others which had been working in the Mediterranean and Devane needed little to remind him.

One of the boats was commanded by George 'Red' Mackay who had been transferred from a Canadian flotilla based at Alexandria. Devane smiled. Red had a loud, harsh voice and was terrific. Another CO was Willy Walker, who looked and walked rather like a disdainful heron. Faces and names, odd moments of brash bravado and others of sheer, gut-tearing fear. Interlaced tracers in the night, or a German E-boat boiling through the sea with a bow wave like Niagara Falls. Men cursing and firing, the lethal glitter of torpedoes as they leapt from the tubes.

Whitcombe asked gently, 'Approve?'

Devane did not answer directly. 'I notice there are extra people, five to a boat?'

Whitcombe met his gaze. Devane's eyes were what you always remembered after you had met him, he thought. Blue-grey, like the sea. There was no sense in pretending or beating about the bush.

'Yes. Once you are on your own in the Black Sea you'll be hard put to get replacements. So we've made certain you'll have one officer and four key ratings in addition to each normal complement. A tight squeeze, but there it is.'

You don't know the half of it. He asked, 'When do you want me to leave, sir?'

'A few days' time. You'll be told. But it's absolutely top secret, John. I've laid on accommodation for you in London. I suggest you take it easy and report daily to me.'

They all looked at the blue folder which lay on Devane's lap.

'You'll be working with Lieutenant-Commander Beresford, but you've done that before.'

Another face. Intelligent but moody. One of the cloak-and-dagger brigade.

He replied, 'Yes. Pretty good officer.' He grinned at the old joke. 'For a regular, that is.'

Whitcombe seemed satisfied with his reactions. 'Remember this, John, yours is an independent command. You'll have to rely on your own judgement most of the time. Beresford will be there to keep the Russians off your back. He's good at that kind of thing.'

They all stood up. It was over. For the moment.

Devane said, 'I'd better make up some story for my parents' benefit.'

Kinross nodded. 'I can help there.'

He's had plenty of practice, Devane thought grimly. 'I could use another drink.'

The Royal Navy had thoughtfully commandeered a small but elegant block of flats in what had once been a quiet square. 'Nice an' near to 'Arrods,' as the accommodation petty officer had explained.

Devane stood at his window and looked down at the square, his head ringing like an oil drum. After yesterday's meeting with Whitcombe and Kinross he should have left it at that and gone to bed. He never slept well these days, but the gin bottle beside the bed, two-thirds empty, showed that it was no cure either. He was drinking too much, and too often. Devane hoped he had hidden the fact from his parents, especially his mother. His father would say he understood. He had been in France in that other war. But Devane was troubled all the same. He had seen it happen to others, the desperate, feverish faces after the flotilla had swept down on a heavily defended convoy, or when they had been ambushed by German E-boats.

The small green square had been given over to ranks of vegetable patches. Digging for Victory. Even the iron railings had been taken away to be melted down for much-needed scrap. A few civilians were moving along the pavements, small, foreshortened figures, shabby and pathetic at a distance.

But Devane knew differently. Without their tenacity, their British bloody-mindedness, as Whitcombe would term it, the swastika would have been flying over Buckingham Palace long ago, no matter what the armed forces tried to do.

A sailor was standing on one corner, his hand on a girl's sleeve. It was like watching a mime, the sailor, a Norwegian, trying to make friends. The girl, used to being pursued by servicemen, just that bit standoffish. How much worse for the Norwegian than for me, Devane thought. His country occupied, his own world confined to another allegiance, and the hatred of the enemy. *Them.*

Devane had had a light breakfast which had been brought to his bedside by a naval steward. The latter was obviously used to the tide of officers who came and went through the little block of flats.

It was strange how it could relax him. He had vaguely heard two air-raid warnings during the night, but nothing serious enough to drag him to a shelter.

Devane had re-read his folder of intelligence reports during breakast, and the coffee had tasted just like pre-war.

He was going to the Black Sea, to a war he had only seen on the newsreels. To Devane the enemy was sea and sky, U-boats and aircraft, the Atlantic or the Med. He had learned to recognize fear in himself and in others near him. From it he had gathered the necessary hatred to hit back, and to hit hard.

The intelligence pack explained the technical side; about the five boats, all of which were new. They were of the latest British Power Boat design with certain extras. Power-operated guns, twin torpedo tubes, four thousand and fifty horsepower and a top speed of thirty-nine knots. Impressive.

Devane hoped there would be accommodation arranged ashore for the crews when they were in harbour. He smiled. *In Russia.* A seventy-one-foot long MTB, with all the additional gear and ammunition for her extended patrol area, had barely room enough for her seventeen-man complement. Now there would be twenty-two! He could hear the moans already.

But this type of craft was the biggest, according to Kinross's precise notes, which could safely stand the ride overland without first being dismantled from bridge to keel, or without falling apart on the journey. He should know.

Devane re-examined the details of his own command, the leader. His first lieutenant was named Dundas, with a high recommendation. Ex-merchant service, he had come straight from the Royal Naval Reserve. He was twenty-six. The additional officer, the third hand, was a RNVR lieutenant called Seymour. He was twenty-two, with two years in coastal forces. All it said of his earlier existence was the title of journalist. At that tender age it probably meant his local church magazine.

The boat's coxswain he did know. Petty Officer Tom Pellegrine, DSM and bar, who had been Richie's coxswain since the beginning. He was a regular, which was fairly rare in coastal forces. They usually retained regulars for ships and equipment more valuable than wooden MTBs.

But a good coxswain was vital. The bridge between officers and ratings. And packed in that little hull, he would have his work cut out as a peacemaker.

It would be strange to take over a new boat, a fresh flotilla. They must have got used to each other while regrouping and working up. He would have to start as he meant to go on.

There was not much in the pack about German naval forces in the area, except that they were a mixed collection of small craft and, like his own, had been carried across country, then floated down the Danube to their new killing ground.

Information about the Russians was even scarcer. The whole of their naval squadron, listed in the pack as the Azov Flotilla, was commanded by a distinguished officer called Sergey Gorshkov, but the man described as the real link with the British was shown as Nikolai Sorokin, a full captain, who had already made his mark against the Germans in the Baltic.

The liaison part would rest with Ralph Beresford. Devane had spent many hours with him in the Eastern Mediterranean and working on special missions amidst the Greek islands. Most people's idea of the peacetime regular officer. Good-looking, dashing would be a better word, Beresford was an unexpected choice for the new job.

But Devane had seen the other side of the man. Tough, almost fanatical about each operation. He liked Beresford, or what he knew of him, and had tried to tell himself to leave it at that. One thing was certain, Beresford was not just brave, he actually enjoyed the danger and the risks, and pushed his luck to the limit.

Devane studied himself in a mirror, as he would a rating at divisions or behind the defaulters' table.

There were lines at the corners of his mouth, but his eyes seemed steady enough. He pushed a comb through his dark brown hair and sighed. It was no use. He would never make another Kinross.

The thought made him chuckle, and he saw the tiredness and strain fade from his face like a curtain. Was that all it took?

The telephone jangled and he swung round like a fighter. In that split second it was all there. The alarm in the night, the frantic scramble to action stations, the brain taking over, ordering. Demanding.

Devane sat down and silenced the telephone. He must try to get over it. Otherwise his new command would imagine they had some bomb-happy nut to decide on their futures, which were precarious enough anyway.

'Yes?'

'RPO 'ere, sir.'

One of the guardians of the lobby which had probably sported a hall porter in safer days.

'What's wrong, PO?'

He could hear the man's breathing. So it was not Whitcombe yet. Perhaps it was off. It happened in the Navy. You arrived with tropical gear only to discover you were going to Iceland, or the appointment had been cancelled altogether.

'I've got a lady 'ere, sir. To see you.' It sounded like an accusation.

Devane sat bolt upright on the edge of the bed. 'Can you put her on?'

He heard mumblings, then the man said, 'Well—, sir, it's not really proper, I—I mean, this is all 'ush 'ush.' He faltered, his voice less confident. 'But if you say so, sir.'

Devane waited. Somehow he was not surprised. He should have guessed it might happen.

'John? This is Claudia.'

He could see her as if she were right here with him. Dark, vivacious, lovely. She had always seemed so poised and confident, and he was shocked by the thought that she did not know how her husband had died. And he did.

'Hello. I'll come down. I—I heard you were in London.' Half a lie was better than a whole one. 'I'm terribly sorry about Don. Really.'

'Yes. I see.' She sounded as if she had turned away from the telephone or was looking to see if the regulating petty officer was listening.

'I must talk, John. You're the only one I can—' The line went dead.

Devane felt very calm, and without any possible reason. He dialled the special number to Whitcombe's HQ and was immediately told by a crisp female that he was not required to report again until 1500.

Then he pulled on his jacket and jammed his cap on to his head. He patted his pockets to make sure he had all he needed.

He glanced at himself once more in the mirror. Aloud he said deliberately, 'You are being a bloody fool, and you know it! Stop right here.'

Devane strode to the door and ran quickly down the stairs to the lobby.

Claudia Richie was sitting on a padded bench by the doorway, her legs crossed, a cigarette in one hand.

She turned and watched him. Even the movement of her head, her lovely pale neck seemed to make him clumsy, obvious.

Devane took her arm. 'How did you find this place?' He cursed himself as the words came out.

She dropped her cigarette into a large brass shell case which did duty as ashtray or umbrella stand as the occasion demanded.

'Long time ago. With Don.' She looked at him steadily. 'Can we go somewhere?'

They walked into the warm sunlight and down towards Sloane Street. At any other time Devane would have been studying his surroundings, the people who lived or worked here despite the daily bombings, the frugal rations and the endless queues for everything from cheese to dog food.

But he was conscious only of her and the way other men looked at her as they passed. She had not changed, and he could never imagine her giving way to austerity. Even to grief.

She asked, 'You heard I was at the Admiralty?'

'Yes. I feel rotten about it. You don't deserve it.'

She had slipped her hand through his arm, as if to exclude the passers-by, the watchers.

'Don't I?'

Devane said, 'Of course not.' He was getting confused. Her

14

hand on his arm did not help. 'Where are you living, Claudia? Still at the farm?'

She nodded. 'Still at the farm.' She did not hide the bitterness. 'It's being run by conscientious objectors and Italian prisoners of war. Can you beat that?'

She turned her head and looked at him, and Devane could see the pain in her brown eyes. Eyes so dark they seemed to fill her face.

She added, 'But the farm really runs itself. They need all the food we can grow nowadays.'

Devane thought about it. She was the same age as himself. Don Richie had been about two years older. Devane had always thought of him as a typical gentleman farmer. They had quite a lot of them in Dorset too.

She seemed to read his mind. 'Don never took much of an interest in it.'

He shook his head, bewildered. 'I didn't know.'

'No. Your Don and mine were different people, I expect. He wanted to be a winner, he *needed* it. Racing, sailing, everything. To him the MTBs were just an extension of his previous victories.'

Devane glanced at her anxiously. She was wearing a thin blue dress, and her shoes were hardly made for walking for miles. She looked restless and lost, and in some odd way he felt responsible for her.

He asked, 'Where are you staying in London?'

She stopped dead and disengaged her hand. 'Why? Why did you ask that?'

Devane lowered his voice. 'I'm sorry, Claudia. I just thought I'd take you there. I can guess what you're going through.'

Her lip quivered very slightly. 'I doubt that, John.' She put out her hand impetuously. 'I'm being stupid. I don't want to embarrass you.' She put her fingers to her mouth. 'Be a darling. See if you can get a taxi. Quickly.'

Devane looked round, searching for a cruising taxi. She was cracking up right in front of his eyes, and for some reason she wanted to be with him and nobody else.

A taxi idled to the kerb and the driver, a very old man with a walrus moustache, grinned at them. 'Spot of leave, eh, Skipper? Just th' job!'

His casual acceptance seemed to bring the girl to her senses. She said calmly, 'The Richmond Hotel, Chelsea, please.'

Devane opened the door and made to follow her into the taxi.

She turned, her face almost brushing his as she said, 'No. I'm sorry I dragged you out like this. It was stupid of me. I'm certain you've got plenty to do.' She was pulling the door as if to sever their brief contact immediately.

Devane said, 'Don't go. I'd like to talk. It's two years since we last met.' The words seemed to tumble from his lips, but he was conscious only of the fact she was leaving, had changed her mind about something important.

The old taxi-driver was whistling, but not too loudly for him to follow the drama behind his back.

Devane added desperately, 'Can't I call you?'

Her glance settled on him and her mouth lifted for the first time in a small smile.

'If you want to. But what's the point? It's over.' She leant forward and rapped the glass.

'All right, driver!'

Devane stood back and watched the taxi edge into the traffic, oblivious to curious stares of two saluting seamen who had just passed him.

She had wanted to tell him something and had changed her mind. Or lost her nerve at the last minute. But why? The question rang in his mind like a bell.

It was true what he had said. He had not seen her for nearly two years. At some naval party or other in Ipswich. And before that he had known Don as the popular farmer-cum-sportsman in the West Country. His farm, the one now run by Italian POWs and conscientious objectors, was close to Dartmoor. They had often met on their naval reserve training or while competing in some sailing race or other.

Devane glanced at his watch, the moment spoiled. What had he expected, for God's sake? She was probably wondering why a man like Don was dead and he was still in one piece.

He tried to laugh it off. Hurt pride, the fact that he was lonely.

He had always had an eye for Claudia, of course, but who hadn't? She was that kind of girl.

Devane looked round for a pub. A drink, lost in pre-lunch

chatter, might help. One thing was certain, he would take it no further.

Even as he thought about it he knew he was deceiving himself. He would ring the Richmond Hotel. After he had seen Whitcombe. Just a quick telephone call to settle the dust.

He pushed at the door of a small pub but it only opened an inch. A sour-looking man peered out at him and took in his visitor from head to toe in one second.

'We don't open for 'nother hour. Don't you know there's a bloody war on?'

2

THE OTHER WAR

Devane finished buttoning a clean shirt and then stared round the room, feeling lost. The blackout curtains were closed for, although it was still light enough to see the outline of the small square, there was plenty of cloud about. The petty officer in the lobby had said meaningly, 'They'll be over tonight, sir. Good cloud cover for the buggers.'

Devane looked at the telephone. How many times had he done that since he had returned from the Admiralty, he wondered. Perhaps if Whitcombe had something urgent to tell him things might have been different.

But Whitcombe had merely filled him in on a few details about engineering staff for the boats' maintenance once they were delivered to the Black Sea, some titbits too about air cover which the Russians were hoping to put into action when their advance was under way, but nothing very exciting.

Whitcombe had looked as if he had been there all night. Maybe he never went home.

Then he had said abruptly, 'I understand you saw Richie's widow this morning. What did she want?'

Devane had been both startled and angry to discover his moves were being recorded. Even when Whitcombe had added, 'Just routine security, John. All phone calls, in, out and internal, are registered. You should be honoured. A German secret agent used your room a few months back. We thought he was a Polish naval officer,' Devane had still felt resentful.

'Well, I'm not Polish *or* German, sir!'

Whitcombe had changed tack. 'See it this way. The war is a vast gamble, but it depends on little Caesars like me to keep things running without unnecessary losses. You are taking command of a new operational flotilla. It is no secret that all pendant numbers have been removed from the boats and the flotilla will be known to us only by the code name "*Parthian*". Very appropriate, under the circumstances. Your responsibility you already know, and have proved your ability beyond doubt. You have five boats and some hundred and ten officers and ratings, to say nothing of Beresford's shore party and equipment, in your hands alone. A rash act, or some unexpected enemy move, might smash *Parthian* to bits within days of your arrival.

'But the overall responsibility is bigger, even awesome. A mistake now, a break in security somewhere, and everything could fall apart before we can begin. It's the horseshoe-nail syndrome, except that we're talking about the Eastern Front, not the bloody cavalry!'

Devane sat on the bed and played with his tie. Whitcombe had listened without further interruption as he had explained what Claudia Richie had said, or had not said.

Then, surprisingly, Whitcombe had suggested, 'Go and see her, John. Why not? It might calm her down, poor lass. It won't help us in Operations to have her making inquiries somewhere else. Some idiot in high places might check up and spill the beans about Richie's suicide. Questions will be asked, the bumph-war will spread, and I shall have to delay *Parthian* until I can see what's happening. In Berlin, for instance?'

Devane wondered if Whitcombe had just been opening the door for him. Had known or guessed that he had had every intention of seeing the girl again.

'Oh, hell!' He stood up and reached for his jacket. She would probably pitch him out on his ear anyway. She might even have gone back to Devonshire without further delay.

When he reached the lobby he found the petty officer and a naval fire-watcher listening to the news on the radio, and noticed they were both carrying steel helmets.

The PO came round the desk and said, 'You'll not get a taxi now, sir. Some of 'em do ambulance and fire duty after

19

sunset.' He added unhelpfully, 'Be a raid tonight, sir, sure as eggs.'

Devane went out into the cool evening air and paused to get his eyes accustomed to the gloom. A few people were still on the move, but the blackout curtains and shutters made the square look dead, deserted.

The PO was right, not a taxi to be seen. But there was a bus, and wedged between a fat lady with a roll of blankets and a downtrodden youth in a boiler suit Devane managed to convey where he wanted to go to the girl conductor.

There were strips of paper and netting pasted on the bus windows to protect the passengers from blast. It brought this other war much closer to Devane than he would have imagined possible. The fat lady beside him was making her way to some draughty underground station or air-raid shelter for the night, to make certain of a good place. The youth was quite likely on a night shift at a factory somewhere. Working through the raids to make something which Devane and his men probably took for granted.

The girl clippie called, 'That's the Richmond, sir!'

The bus stood grumbling throatily against the kerbside, and then, after taking on a few dark figures, moved on again towards the Albert Bridge.

Some watery searchlights licked out across the clouds, their invisibl   esting them, just in case. Devane saw the reflected glitter on water and knew the hotel was facing the Thames.

It had often been his dream to come and live in Chelsea. Leave his father's old-fashioned firm and start with an up-and-coming company with prospects and ideas. He and Tony had often discussed it. They could have shared a flat and kept the little MG for weekends.

Devane shook himself angrily. It was always the same when he was too long alone. At sea he was too busy to remember and regret. On land, he could only wait to get back again. A sort of madness, with nothing at the end of it. Perhaps that was how Richie had seen it? His number was nearly up anyway. They all said that. If you got through the first few operations you gained a kind of immortality, a confidence that nothing could destroy you. Then it passed. Maybe Richie could wait no longer and had ended it before his desperation had put others' lives at stake.

Whitcombe had made it sound easy. Five boats and one hundred and ten human beings.

It was a pity that men like the journalist who had written those sickening headlines about him could not see what really happened when a man died in combat, without hope, stripped even of dignity.

His fingers groped for a door handle and then he found himself stumbling through some heavy curtains which smelt of stale tobacco.

The lights inside the hotel were coldly bright. It was a combined lobby and lounge, with an oak staircase turning above a small reception desk, and a wall-covering which looked like dark red velvet. There were potted plants, and Devane could imagine there might once have been a small trio to play light music before tea and dinner.

He noticed for the first time that the half-dozen or so people who were sitting at the small tables were all women. With something like panic he thought he had blundered into an hotel which was off limits to servicemen. It would make his retreat even more ridiculous.

'May I help you, sir?'

Devane turned and saw a woman in a black dress regarding him from behind the desk. She had not been there before. Like the pantomime genie, she must have popped up through the floor.

She must have seen his expression and said tartly, 'I've been in the cellar. The *shelter*, that is.' She had omitted the 'sir' this time.

'Sorry. I was wondering if I could see Mrs. Richie.'

He waited but nothing happened. The voices still murmured from the tables, and he heard the clatter of plates and someone singing. The kitchen.

'Are you a friend of hers?'

Devane stared. 'Why? Do I need an appointment?'

She flinched. 'We get a lot of strange callers.' She nodded very slightly towards the women in the lounge. 'Some men, well, you know how it is.' Her mood changed completely. 'It's my turn to apologize. I recognize you from your picture, and on the newsreel at the Odeon.' She added quietly, 'These ladies are in town to receive their husbands' medals.'

Devane made himself turn and look at them. So that explained it. The stillness he had felt, the strange similarity of

21

these women. This was the side you never saw. He was learning a lot today.

At sea, and especially in coastal forces, the companies were mostly too young to be married, and the average age seemed around nineteen. In bigger ships and shore establishments there were jokes in plenty at the expense of those who were married, and little sympathy for the meaningless problems of house mortgages, school fees and the shortage of money which affected all families in wartime. The letters of sympathy which Devane had written had mostly been to mothers, not widows.

I should not have come.

'This *is* unexpected.'

Devane swung round and saw her standing at the foot of the stairway. She was wearing the same dress and carrying a coat over one arm.

'Yes. That is. . . .' Again she made him feel awkward and on the defensive.

She said, 'I was going for a walk along the embankment.' She held out the coat to him. 'You are staring. Hold this for me.' She turned into the coat with the ease of a dancer and studied him curiously. 'It *was* me you came to see, I assume?'

He forced a smile. 'I couldn't just walk away. You were upset. I wanted to help.'

'Walk with me.' As he held the heavy curtain aside she said, 'This place is like death's waiting room.' She said it without contempt or bitterness.

As they crossed the darkened road to the embankment she added, 'I'm better now. Sorry I made a scene. Not like me at all. But I felt sick. Fed up with all the solemn smiles, the evasiveness about Don.'

Devane tensed. 'It's hard to know what to say at times like this.'

'I expect it is.' She turned up her collar and paused momentarily to peer down at the swirling river.

She continued in the same controlled tone, 'There is a woman at the hotel. She's here to collect her late husband's gong from the King or somebody. I gather he got burned to death in a bomber when he stayed with his plane to avoid crashing it on a village. That's what they told her anyway. He might have died seconds after the last of his men bailed out.' She was looking at him now, her eyes hidden in the gloom. 'That's not the point. She said that, if he had to die, it was how

22

he would have wished!' She shook her head very slowly. 'Can you imagine being glad about burning to death?'

He felt her move off again and fell in step beside her. He could even smell her perfume, as he had when they had almost touched by the taxi.

'That's why I wanted to speak to you, John. Someone who knows what it's like. To reassure myself that I'm not going out of my mind.'

'I can't tell you anything about Don's death. Really.'

A searchlight sprang across the sky like something solid, an unending blue lance. Devane saw her face, pale in the glare, the moistness of her mouth.

She said, 'I should like a drink. Very much.' She looked across the road. 'There's a place there somewhere. I don't think I could stand a drink in the hotel. I would probably be branded as unpatriotic, or have my head shaved.'

It was then Devane realized. It was a carefully delivered act. She was frightened of being alone, even more afraid of sympathy.

The pub was exactly right. Small, packed and full of noise and cheerful voices. There were several servicemen and their girls, the former mostly Americans, the latter mainly from the profession. Victorian mirrors, some photographs of a prize fighter, cap badges from a score of regiments, a cartoon of Churchill making a V sign at Hitler. A typical London pub.

The landlord peered through the smoke haze, his glance taking in Devane's rank and the girl's dress and appearance.

'Up this end, sir. Officers only.' He winked, and anyone who was listening laughed at his joke.

There was one vacant bar stool, wedged in a corner. Devane smiled and took her arm to help her on to the high stool, while he jammed his hip against the wet bar.

The landlord, whose face was battered into a shapeless ruin, said cheerfully, 'Two gins, right, sir?'

She whispered, 'He must be the boxer in the photos. Or what's left of him!'

More people pressed through the blackout curtains, and Devane had to shout to make himself heard. He was pressed against her knees but she made no obvious effort to move. It was as if she were trying to lose herself here and could not face the brooding stillness of that hotel.

She said, 'I suppose you're taking Don's job?' She watched

him steadily. 'Don't answer, not that you would anyway. But it doesn't take a genius to put two and two together. Your sort don't grow on trees. Don always said you were the best.' She touched her lip with her tongue. 'Next to him, of course.' She pushed her empty glass towards him and Devane signalled to the landlord.

Devane said, 'When you go back to Devon. . . .' He got no further.

'I don't want to talk about it.' Her voice softened slightly. 'Sorry. Gin talking. I'm bad company. Especially for you.'

She swallowed the gin in almost one gulp and Devane saw her grimace at the taste.

She said directly, 'You've not married, I hear.' She nodded as if in agreement. 'Don said you'd wait. He talked a lot about you, did you know that?'

Devane shook his head, afraid of breaking the spell. She was speaking freely now and one stupid remark could smash it. Down the bar two men were arguing tipsily and the landlord was watching them as he polished a tankard. Outside an air-raid warning had droned for several minutes, but as usual it was ignored. It had become a part of daily life. If it had your number on it. . . .

Devane had not known Richie that well. Another flotilla, and later a different sort of war with fresh faces and new problems to contend with had kept them apart. But when he thought of Richie, here in this crowded bar, he seemed more the way she had described him than he remembered him. *He wanted to be a winner.*

She leant forward and brushed something from Devane's sleeve. Her hair, almost jet black, fell across one cheek, but she did not seem to care.

'He told me once that you were always looking at me. That last time, at the party, after we had been married for a few months. That was when he went on about it.'

'I—I didn't know.'

Devane tried to think rationally. Perhaps he had made some indiscreet remark which Richie had clung to.

He added, 'It would be a lie if I said I didn't look at you. I doubt if anyone but a blind half-wit could pass you without his heart taking a few jumps.'

She put her shoulders against the wall and studied him thoughtfully. 'Tell me. Is it true that every time you go into

24

action you have to clear your mind, wipe it clean so that you can cope? That's what Don said. Several times.' She put her hand over his on the bar and tightened her grip in time with her words. 'I should like to know.'

Devane felt vaguely cheated. He must be crazy. What did he expect?

'It's true. There's so much happening all at once.' He could not take his eyes from her hand on his. It was small and beautifully shaped, and seemed to be listening to what they were saying. 'Vigilance is everything. One moment of carelessness or complacency and it can cost lives, other people's as well as your own.'

She nodded as if satisfied. 'I needed to hear that. From you. Because if anyone in this damnable war knows about it, you do.' Once more she nodded, the movement listless. 'Thanks.'

Devane took her other hand and held it carefully. 'Tell me, Claudia. What is it?'

'Don is dead. It's over.'

There was a long pause, and Devane knew that some of the others nearby were watching them, fascinated by their behaviour.

Then she said in a tired voice, 'We had a blazing row, a real beauty, on that last leave before he went off to. . . .' She took her hand from his and wiped her cheek with the back of it. Like a child. 'He'd been at it too long, but would never admit it. He had to do better. To be *the best!*' She spoke the last words so loudly that several people had stopped talking to listen.

'I wanted to hurt him. To get back at him. I told him I was having an affair.'

He stared at her, seeing Richie with the pistol in his hand as if he had been there.

'That was how we parted. The last time I saw him.' She gave a shrug. 'So you see, John, he was most likely killed because of me. That's what I had to ask you.'

The landlord's battered features loomed over the bar. 'Everythin' okay, sir?' He glanced anxiously at the girl. 'She looks a bit dicky.'

Devane's mind was frozen. He must get her out of here, but something was holding him back. The faces and noises which ebbed and flowed around their private corner were meaningless. Somewhere a woman was shrieking with laughter, and a soldier had just dropped a glass on the floor.

25

Devane pushed himself from the bar and seized her by the shoulders, seeing her despair giving way to surprise, then sudden alarm.

There was no time to explain. To say what he knew.

He shouted, 'Hold me! For God's sake, hold on!'

For a split second longer he felt her pressed against him, and then came the explosion.

It was more of a shock than a sound. He was falling and choking in dust and smoke, aware only that they were still clinging to each other and that the whole place was in darkness.

Only the woman's laugh remained, but it had changed into a terrible, unending scream.

As Devane's senses returned he tried to free himself from the pressure of wood and brickwork across his shoulders and spine. It was hard to draw breath without retching, or to know which way he was facing.

A bright column of fire spouted from the other side of the bar, and he guessed that either a gas main had caught fire or the kitchen stove had exploded.

Voices yelled and echoed around him like souls in torment, and he heard screams mingled with desperate cries for help.

He found her by the wall, and as his hands explored her shoulders and bare throat he knew that her head had fallen forward.

He gasped, 'Claudia, for God's sake!' He pulled her slowly to her feet, so that she hung against him as if lifeless.

It was even worse standing up. In the dancing blue flames he saw reeling figures, the glistening reflections of blood and torn limbs, broken glass and rubble everywhere.

Someone was calling, 'My eyes! My bloody eyes! Help me, please *help me!*'

An American lurched past dragging his companion through the upended furniture, his face a mask of blood.

Devane held her firmly but gently and then lifted her chin. She was breathing. She must have been stunned by the blast.

A man blundered against him and Devane shouted, 'Go to the hotel along the road and send for help.'

The man, wild-eyed and staring, yelled back, 'Who are you giving orders to?'

'*You!*' He saw the man fall back. 'Do as I bloody well tell you!'

26

He searched his own feeling. There was nothing. Just concern for the girl. Like she had said of her dead husband, he had been at it too long. After the first tour of operations you accepted it. Or went under.

He began to lift her over a broken beam, or was it the front of the bar?

The landlord was lying face down in broken glass. There was blood everywhere.

It must have been a direct hit, probably on the rear of the pub. The floor seemed to have leapt up to meet the falling roof, so the bomb had most likely exploded in the cellar.

Devane peered down at her and saw that her eyes were wide and staring.

He said, 'We're getting out. You're safe now.'

He saw one hand touch her forehead as if to assure herself she was still alive. Then as her understanding returned she tried to turn her head, to see the smoky destruction, made worse by the dancing flames, the terrible screaming.

Somewhere a bell rang loudly, and Devane guessed that ambulances and fire-engines were on their way. *Just another raid*. The bombs could have hit anywhere.

Two policemen crunched through the broken doors, their torches reflecting on their steel helmets.

Devane called, 'In here. Six or seven still alive, I think.'

The first policeman paused to peer at the girl. 'She all right?'

She whispered to Devane, 'Don't let them take me any-where. I want to keep with you. Don't let them. . . .' She fainted again.

The policeman said to his companion, 'Here we go again, Tom. Ready?'

The other man was staring past him, his face screwed up to withstand what was to come, what they must do amongst the carnage.

Devane stooped down and slipped his arm beneath her legs, then, carrying her very carefully, he stepped over and through the collapsed doors and into the cool air.

The place seemed to be full of people. Voices called instructions, and he heard the clatter of spades and picks as rescuers searched amongst the wreckage for survivors.

Devane walked amongst them. A woman with her hair in curlers was tying a bandage on a man's head. A fire-engine was backing down the pavement with more men unloading lifting gear and stretchers. Devane looked at them. Amateurs, ordinary men and women who were behaving with the skilled precision of guardsmen. Like his own companies, he thought vaguely. Newspaper boys and fishermen, barristers and house painters. The war soon honed away any kind of amateur status.

She said huskily, 'Put me down, please.'

He lowered her to the pavement and she exclaimed, 'I've lost a shoe!' Then she began to laugh, but no sound came, and Devane had to hold her against him until the paroxysm had stopped.

She whispered, 'Thanks. Very much. Near thing.'

When he picked her up again she put her arm round his neck and peered at him. 'All my fault.' She rested her face against his cheek and he felt the dust rub between them like sand. 'I saw you back there. How you coped.' Her arm tightened across his neck. 'Don't leave me. Not yet.'

An ambulance flashed past, its gong ringing frantically. Across the river there was a bright glow in the sky, also a solitary column of sparks like a giant firework.

'I won't.'

He had to kick the door of the hotel before anyone came to open it.

The woman he had spoken with at the desk exclaimed, 'My God! Is she hurt?'

Someone else switched on a small torch and Devane saw blood on the girl's leg. But it was unmoving and already drying under a coating of dust.

Devane said, 'I'm taking her to her room.' He met the woman's stare. 'If you have no objection?'

The woman shook her head jerkily, like a puppet. 'N-no. Number eleven.'

Devane started up the stairs and realized that several heads had appeared behind the counter which concealed the entrance to the cellar.

What a sight we must be, he thought, and it was then that his body began to tremble as if he had a fever.

He clenched his teeth together until the ache steadied him. It was always the same. He had made it. One more time. He looked at the girl's bowed head. And it *mattered*.

The room, like the hotel, was old and musty. All different shades of brown. He sat her gently on the edge of the high bed and took her ankle in his hand.

She said shakily, 'There's some Scotch in the cupboard.'

Devane stood up and paused to collect himself. It had been a near thing.

He heard himself ask, 'Scotch? Who do you know in the black market?'

She was watching him fixedly, her hair plastered to her forehead, her dress stained and crumpled as she tried to match his mood.

'I brought it to bribe someone at the Admiralty.' She tried to shrug but winced and said, 'Ouch! I feel as if I've been in a rugby scrum!'

Devane found the whisky but there was only one glass in the room. There would be.

He filled it carefully, expecting to spill some. But although he felt as if every muscle and fibre were quivering uncontrollably his hands looked quite firm.

She swallowed and almost choked. 'Cheers!'

Then she handed him the glass and he took a long, careful drink. On an empty stomach it was like fire water.

She pulled up the skirt of her dress and examined her thigh. There was a cut, but it looked clean enough.

Devane dabbed the dust away from the blood and felt her leg stiffen. He dared not look at her, but the touch of her skin, the feeling that they had somehow come together from pain and near-death was like a living force.

She said, 'I'll just wash it and put a plaster on it. You have a drink. I'll not be long.' She took down a dressing gown and paused by the door, her voice pleading. 'The bathroom is just two doors away. If the bombers come back you'll. . . .'

'I'll come and get you.' He saw her smile, the way she rubbed the back of her leg with a bare foot. 'No matter what the management thinks!'

He sat down in the solitary chair and poured another drink. He could not leave her, but he should not stay.

Another gong went clanging past the hotel. Some poor wretch cut down by flying splinters or dug out from under his house. It made the war at sea seem clean, even practical, he thought.

The door opened and closed and she moved lightly to a wardrobe and hung her dress on a hanger. She was wearing her robe and her skin looked pink and fresh.

'A drink?'

29

She shook her head. 'Do you want another?'

Devane stood up and took her carefully in his arms. Her hair was damp, and the smell of her freshness drove away the stain of what had happened.

How long they stood like that Devane did not know or care. It was as if the world had stopped spinning for them. The hotel was completely silent, the residents probably down in the cellar again. Some of them were no doubt thinking of the naval officer with the girl in his arms. Like a war film. While they only had the brutal reality to live with, and a medal to sustain them.

She said unsteadily, 'I should like you to kiss me.'

Devane held her more tightly, half afraid he would hurt her or that he might spoil the moment.

As their mouths met he felt her body lift and press against his, heard her moan as he opened the robe and caressed her until he thought his mind would burst.

Then she slipped free of his arms and let her robe drop unheeded to the floor. She lay on the bed, her eyes never leaving him as he tore off his clothes, nor did she speak until he was kneeling above her, her body taut under his exploring hands.

She whispered, 'Take me now. I don't care about tomorrow.'

They made love until they were completely spent, sparing each other nothing in their need and their awareness.

When the final All Clear wailed across the London river Devane lay with her pressed against him, one of her legs thrown carelessly across his body. He listened to her breathing, slow and gentle, then turned to look at the grey light which filtered around the edges of the shutters.

Another day for each of them. And they were alive. *Alive.*

As London reluctantly awoke to another dawn, men and women faced it with what resources they could muster.

Across the river, a young woman was about early to dress and make up her face with extra care. Her husband, a sergeant in the Eighth Army, was coming home today. It was such a special day. It had to be. For he was coming home with only one arm, and she must show him how much she loved him. That everything was going to be the same.

A mile or so away, another woman was going through her husband's things. The police had called during the night to tell

30

her he had been killed in a Chelsea pub during the raid. She had always loathed his drunken outings, every night with his mates at the pub. And many were the times she had cursed his shaky key in the front door on a Saturday night and wished him gone. But it felt different now, and the house seemed dead, as if *he* had given it life.

Clerks put aside their Home Guard uniforms and shaved before going to work. A housewife was lifted gently on to a stretcher by the heavy rescue team which had been digging through a flattened street for three days. When they anxiously peered down at her she merely smiled. Her world had gone, but only temporarily. She had survived.

Beside a camp bed in a concrete bunker a telephone jangled noisily, and Whitcombe yawned as he pressed it to his ear.

'Yes?'

'Duty officer, sir.' He sounded freshly awake and alert. 'The signal has just come through. *Parthian* has the go ahead.' The slightest pause. 'Shall I inform Lieutenant-Commander Devane, sir?'

Whitcombe stared at the clock, hating it. 'No. Give him another couple of hours.' He thought of the girl with the sad, beautiful eyes, and the fact that Devane had only had four days' leave. 'It's the least we can do.'

3

PARTHIAN

Devane clung to the side of the wildly bucking car and
wondered if he had any bones left unbroken. The car, into
which he had been bustled with a minimum of formality, was
the final link in his bizarre journey from England. Those last
two days, spent mostly in London, had been closely supervised
either by Whitcombe or Kinross, and at the very least by the
taciturn aide who had accompanied him through each phase of
the carefully organized trip. Devane seemed to have spent days
changing from one military aircraft to the next, being signed
for like a piece of registered mail. Small airstrips, or ushered to
some isolated building on the fringe of a larger airfield, he had
tried to keep his mind alert and also snatch a few hours of sleep
whenever he could.

With each hundred or so miles he travelled only the climate
seemed to alter. Bright sunshine, or scalding hot sand whipped
up by a desert wind, as he changed planes somewhere in North
Africa. On and on, into the sun, with his tight-lipped companion giving nothing away to ease the strain and lessen the
demands on his mind and body.

Often he thought of the dark-haired girl, as she had looked
on that last morning, their *only* morning together after the
air-raid. What would become of her? Was it something which

32

neither of them would remember beyond all those other fragments left by the war?

His final departure had bordered on the idiotic, he thought, with a carefully phrased telephone call to his parents in Dorset, about a temporary shore job, with a vague hint of some public relations in the North and Midlands. A tour of the dockyards to boost morale, and that kind of thing. By the time the truth was made known he would have begun what he had set out to do. All the time he had been speaking he had had the feeling that Kinross had been listening somewhere, ready to sever the connection if he had shown signs of departing from his lines.

And now, after all the hectic hustle and bustle, he was on dry land once more. He peered out of the side of the jolting car and tried to penetrate the rolling bank of yellow dust which spewed constantly from the wheels. He was actually in Russia, heading inland from the Caspian Sea as if the devil were after him.

It was not what he had imagined. Like most sailors, he had heard plenty of grim tales about the north Russian convoys, the intense cold, with ships capsizing under a terrible top-hamper of ice. Or of the summer months when the ice edge retreated and the convoys were made to plod further and further north around Bear Island, when there was no night to hide them from the bombers and the U-boats.

But here it was rugged and untroubled. A few villages and several army encampments. Camouflage nets to hide ranks of armoured troop-carriers and half-tracks. Only the soldiers looked alien, even hostile.

There were two in the front of the car, the driver hunched behind the wheel and an army major who never stopped smoking. They spoke no English, and Devane's companion, a lieutenant named Kimber from Intelligence, had already explained, 'Some do, but they don't advertise it.'

Devane tried to estimate where the nearest Germans were. The Black Sea was about seven hundred miles from east to west, and maybe half that from north to south at its widest part. Almost as large as the western Mediterranean, he thought vaguely. The Germans had long ago occupied Rumania and Bulgaria, and were now firmly rooted on the Crimean peninsula as well. Where their naval forces operated to best advantage was a carefully guarded secret as far as the Russians were concerned.

The lieutenant leaned forward. 'Look, sir!' He pointed at a crumbling building which still managed to look majestic among a copse of trees.

'Czar Nicolas II had it built. A halfway residence between the Caspian and Sochi.'

It looked deserted and at peace. It was hard to visualize the Eastern Front from this viewpoint, Devane thought. Millions already dead. Vast armies revealed in layers of mud and slush with the arrival of each summer.

The major twisted round suddenly and said something to Devane's companion. Kimber replied in fluent Russian and just as tersely.

Then he said, 'A few more minutes. Your flotilla is up ahead of us.'

Devane wanted to laugh. He was feeling the strain of the prolonged journey and it was beginning to tell on him. Days of jumping in and out of planes, quick handshakes, curious stares from RAF men, Americans, Free French, then the Russians. No wonder he felt light-headed. There was no sea for miles and miles, and yet this humourless lieutenant had assured him that his flotilla, *Parthian*, was just up ahead. Maybe they were all going round the bend.

A small scout car edged through the dust, a long-barrelled machine-gun swinging round to cover the car as it shivered to a halt.

Devane could see nothing but a few flat-roofed, almost Moorish-looking buildings, some trees and two armed sentries with their hands in their pockets.

More throaty exchanges, papers examined, quick searching glances at the passengers.

Devane said wearily, 'Nice to feel welcome.'

His companion glanced at him. 'Most of the troops around this area are resting from the Eastern Front, sir. They stayed alive by mistrusting everyone but themselves.'

Devane eyed him gravely. 'That sounded like a rebuke.'

'Sorry, sir. But it's like Alice through the looking-glass out here. You work things out, then change them round completely. Then you can think like a Russian.'

Another camouflaged scout car rolled slowly down a slight incline and stopped beside them. It had only two occupants, a squarely built Russian naval officer with an impassive face, and Lieutenant-Commander Ralph Beresford.

They climbed down, and Beresford said cheerfully, 'Glad you made it, John.' He turned to his companion. 'Allow me to introduce you. This is Captain Nikolai Sorokin.'

The Russian stepped forward and thrust out his hand. Like the man, it was square, with strong, spatulate fingers.

'Welcome.' He smiled and displayed strong, powerful teeth.

Beresford added casually, 'Captain Sorokin is in command of local flotillas. We shall be working closely together.'

There was the briefest hint of warning in his voice. Had Devane not worked with him before he might not have noticed it.

Beresford gestured to the scout car. 'Come and meet your chaps.' He shot the lieutenant from Intelligence a cool smile. 'You take care of the gear, right?'

So like Beresford. Casually said, but his tone carried more steel than a rapier.

The Russian captain gunned the engine and the little car bounced round and up the incline. At the top of the rise he stopped again, then turned to watch Devane's reactions.

It was like a giant travelling circus which had paused to set up camp for another show. Vans and armoured vehicles of every kind, with anti-aircraft guns, light and heavy, already manned and pointing at the evening sky.

Soldiers busied themselves on every side, and the air above the great laager of vehicles was smoky with cooking fires and mobile kitchens.

But Devane's attention was riveted on the five MTBs. Out of the water, even a forty-four ton boat looked like a battleship. But here they were toys, incidental to the great motorized carriers which were taking them from one sea to the other.

Beresford nodded slowly. 'I thought much the same when I saw them. But after the first confusion and misunderstandings we got them moving, and here we are. Each of those beauties has got sixty-four wheels, and the only real hazard so far was loading the boats without damaging them. When it comes to organization, we could learn a lot here.'

The Russian captain beamed. '*Da, da!*'

Beresford gave a brief shake of his head. Sorokin understood more than he had so far demonstrated.

Soldiers were already hauling great areas of camouflage netting over the canopied boats and their equipment, and

Devane guessed that when they were finished the whole encampment would look like just another hump of land from the air.

A Lavochkin fighter with bright red stars on its tapered wings droned towards the encampment from the next fold of hills, and the AA guns moved to cover it, as if they were sniffing for an enemy.

Beresford said quietly, 'We've got good air cover. Without it, things could get distinctly nasty.' As the car moved forward again he added, 'Cadged a lift in one of their light bombers two days ago. Did a quick recce over last year's battlefield. I've seen nothing like it since the old pictures of the Somme. Even the shell craters were full of craters! Thank God I'm a blue-job.'

Devane automatically straightened his back, the pain in his spine from the constant bumping, even the earlier fatigue, forgotten. Was it merely automatic, or something he had come to accept? He had known what it was like to go out on a sortie in a boat which had only just been in battle. Men's eyes ringed with fatigue and worse, and the boat still punctured with bullet holes from a last encounter. That was the testing moment. Now here was another.

Five MTBs, their crews and attendant care and maintenance staff had come all this way, knowing only a fraction of the truth, understanding even less of what was expected of them.

A strange country, made more awesome by its vast area. Even when you thought of Russia you pictured it more as a map than as earth and water.

He relaxed very slightly as several figures emerged from amongst the parked load-carriers. The sight of British sailors, especially out here, made all the difference.

He saw a lieutenant-commander in a stained boiler suit shading his eyes to watch the oncoming scout car. That was Buckhurst, their 'plumber', who had put together and patched up MTBs from Grimsby to Alexandria. He was a born fixer, and could make do with almost anything. He was a godsend, provided you could put up with his constant moaning. A lieutenant in battledress appeared smoking a pipe, his bared head like a red mop. George Mackay, the Canadian. With him was Andy Twiss, the maniac who had once taken on five enemy armed trawlers single-handed, and had crawled back to Felixstowe, his boat like a pepper-pot.

It was like entering an encampment of olden days. Inside were the familiar faces, outside were the aliens, watchful and unemotional.

Devane slid down from the car and returned their salutes, shook a hand here and there, and found himself wondering how Richie could have abandoned them, no matter what his personal reasons might have been.

'You've not changed, Red.'

Mackay grinned. 'Hell, no, sir. Though much more of this an' I reckon I'll be about ready for the infantry!'

Buckhurst wiped his hand on his boiler suit before shaking Devane's hand.

'Russians!' He shot Sorokin a murderous glance. 'They care as much for these boats as they do for their bloody sanitation!'

Sorokin ambled across the churned-up ground, still smiling, but his eyes everywhere as he watched the sailors checking the lashings on their individual boats.

Devane studied him. A hard nut. His record in the Baltic had read like the path of a whirlwind.

Sorokin spoke to Beresford, who translated sparingly. 'The commanding officers and ourselves will dine with the Russians tonight, John.' He did not even blink as he added, 'That will mean champagne and caviar until it comes out of your ears. Very passable too.'

Devane nodded. 'Thank you.'

Beresford smiled. 'You will get used to it. They have their extremes, and they can be as vast as their country. From immense hospitality to a cruelty which makes you want to vomit.' He dropped his voice. 'Take Sorokin for instance. He is entirely responsible for the safe delivery of our boats. And yet yesterday he found time to visit a rear-base hospital and give flowers and vodka to the wounded there. I'm told he once needed information from a German prisoner. When the man did not or could not tell him he had him stripped naked, then had buckets of water thrown over him. The German died slowly and eventually froze solid while Sorokin watched. But then, the Germans murdered his wife, so how can we judge him?'

They both saluted as Sorokin drove sedately from the circle of camouflaged boats.

Devane sighed. Champagne and caviar. It was further from Chelsea than he had imagined.

For most of the following day the great caravan of vehicles and supporting armour moved ponderously westwards. If it made good six miles per hour, Beresford appeared satisfied, but there were also long delays while the lashings were rechecked on the boats or air cover was called up by some nervous patrol on the road ahead.

After that, as the reality of war drew remorselessly nearer, the procession moved only when it was dark. Sometimes at night they watched flashes lining the horizon and, although the fighting was many miles away, the clear, bright air made it appear close and threatening.

There were other signs too. Blackened and burnt-out villages, deserted farmsteads, to mark the Luftwaffe's onslaught of the previous year. A few small graves, but mostly communal ones at the roadside, each with a fading red star above it.

The Russian air force had not been able to blanket the whole of the area. During one night a German bomber force had attacked a convoy of supply vehicles on the road, and most of them had been upended or set alight before fighters eventually arrived to drive the marauders away.

An anxious interpreter explained that the road was temporarily blocked for the great sixty-four-wheeled carriers. But Beresford was told not to worry. The necessary manpower was on its way.

Beresford appeared to accept each challenge philosophically. Like Devane's first evening when they had dined with the Russian officers in their temporary mess. An army colonel, his face flushed with champagne, had shouted something from the end of the table, his reddened eyes fixed on Devane. Beresford had drawled, 'He says you are here merely as a gesture. In the Red Army they admire deeds, not gestures.'

Devane had sensed the sudden change of mood around the table, the grim watchfulness after the earlier chorus of toasts and counter-toasts. Then the Russian colonel had toppled backwards and collapsed, and his companions had leapt to their feet to cheer and clap their hands, the momentary hostility gone.

Beresford had said, 'They can change like the wind. So be on your guard.'

Devane and Beresford were sitting on a little hillock apart

from the rest of the flotilla when the promised manpower marched along the road. There were hundreds of them, all in step, their field-grey uniforms showing them to be prisoners of war.

Devane found himself on his feet as the long column of men marched towards the pile of upended and bombed vehicles. They were more like ghosts from a battlefield than soldiers. Thin, unshaven, their threadbare uniforms in tatters, they appeared more dead than alive.

Beresford did not stand up, but said warningly, 'Easy, John. Some of this is for your benefit. They're testing you. They've got fitter men in this column, they had no need to collect these Germans.' He looked up, his eyes slitted against the sun. 'Another lesson, eh?'

Someone called a halt and the field-grey column stood motionless while an NCO reported to some Russians in an escorting armoured car.

The nearest rank of men was just a few yards from Devane. The prisoners were all young, but they looked like old men. One was staring at the massive carriers and their covered loads, and then he seemed to realize that Devane was there. That he was not a Russian.

Devane met the soldier's gaze. One of 'them', as his mother would have said. It was a good thing you did not always have to see your enemy face to face. He knew that if the situation were reversed this column would be Russian, the treatment equally brutal. Too many deaths and too many atrocities by both sides had made certain of that.

Another order was yelled and the column wheeled towards a lorry to collect shovels and lifting jacks.

But just for the merest second the soldier and Devane looked at each other. Then the German gave what could have been a sigh or a shrug of helpless resignation before he marched away with the others. The moment was broken.

Beresford said irritably, 'We're heading for a safe place to launch the boats. Day after tomorrow if all goes well.' Then he stood up, his mood changed to one of restless impatience. 'After that, *Parthian* will move up to the Russian base at Tuapse. I'll be glad to get things going.'

Devane looked at him. So it had touched him too. You never knew with Beresford.

Some of the British seamen gave an ironic cheer as the third MTB came up tautly against her lines some thirty yards from the shore. Once again, the operation was impressive, with vehicles and Russian engineers to manage the final unloading of the boats into their natural element.

Devane stood on the beach and watched. It was like seeing an amphibious invasion in reverse. Men scrambled over the gently swaying hulls, as if eager to free themselves from the land, to give their boats life again. Two destroyers cruised slowly off shore, and there was the distant drone of a patrolling aircraft to show they were still under protection. Devane watched the blunt-bowed fuel lighter chugging towards the first MTB to be slipped into the water. It was just as well they had air and sea cover, he thought. For until *Parthian* reached the Russian naval base at Tuapse, which according to his map lay some one hundred miles to the north-west of where he now stood, they would be unarmed and defenceless.

The fourth MTB, Lieutenant Willy Walker's, edged down the great ramps, guided and controlled by steel warps as thick as a man's wrist. He could see Walker fussing about below her bridge, pointing and jabbing with his hands as if he were shadow-boxing.

A motley bunch. But they had worked and exercised together as a flotilla. In the Bristol Channel and up the Welsh coast, making mock attacks, and acting in cooperation with some commando units for good measure. Until the moment of completing the exercises, most of them had imagined they were getting ready for the invasion of Europe.

Devane tried to relax his limbs as the last of the boats moved slowly towards the ramps. His own. Where he would get to know the mettle of his small company and the strength of the flotilla he would now lead.

He had already met Dundas, his Number One, and what he saw he liked. The new third hand too, Lieutenant Seymour, a slim, willowy young man whose gentle appearance was totally at odds with his Distinguished Service Cross and a hair-raising battle he had fought off Crete to win it.

But Devane was not going to make the mistake of being too friendly from the beginning. He was to lead them, but first he must win their respect.

Dundas had been the only man so far to mention Richie by

name. He had been the one to find him dead in a cabin aboard the fast transport which had carried the newly formed flotilla from the Mediterranean to the Gulf.

Bitterly Dundas had said, 'I never thought he was that sort. He was full of drive. I sometimes hated him for being so damned good at his job.' He had made it sound like a betrayal.

Devane found he had been clenching his fists as the boat came under the control of the line-handling parties and slewed round like a thoroughbred. Set against the shark-blue water which rippled on her flared hull, she was a boat which any man would give his arm to command. With her triple screws and three rudders she could accelerate from eight to thirty-nine knots in about eleven seconds.

He could see Dundas climbing astride one of the eighteen-inch torpedo tubes, beckoning to a seaman to lower a fender outboard as a fuel lighter puffed purposefully in his direction.

Even after her torpedoes had been fired each boat was still a deadly force to be reckoned with. In addition to her power-operated six-pounder forward and twin Oerlikons aft, she also carried a variety of machine-guns and depth charges.

Devane could remember those first lectures at Gosport; it seemed like a century ago rather than three years. A stiff-backed torpedo gunner's mate had lectured the new coastal forces officers on the substance of the boats they might one day command. The irony in his tone was not lost on them. Only half of those officers had come through unscathed.

That same petty officer had lingered over his carefully rehearsed statistics like a salesman. The hulls were constructed of laminated mahogany, with glue and four hundred thousand screws to hold them together, to say nothing of the copper rivets, a mile or so of wire and a few other bewildering items.

The MTB was swinging to an anchor now, and to his astonishment Devane saw that someone had even found the time to hoist a new white ensign at her gaff.

A great engine spluttered into life, and like tired monsters the big Russian carriers began to move up the beach towards the road. Some of the soldiers had gathered to watch the five restless motor torpedo boats, but they gave no hint of their feelings. Envy, contempt, it could have been anything.

Devane heard boots squeaking in the sand and turned to see

41

Sorokin watching the anchored flotilla with professional interest.

Devane spoke carefully. 'I should like to thank you, sir, for getting them here in safety. It must have been a great responsibility.'

Sorokin did not turn his head, but his mouth lifted slightly in a smile.

'I would have hoped for more vessels.' He shrugged. 'But that is not your concern.' His lips came together as Beresford came striding down towards them.

Beresford glanced curiously at the Russian before saying, 'Ready, John? Old Hector Buckhurst has admitted to some *small* satisfaction, so that must mean you can proceed safely.' He pointed towards an elderly launch which was idling close to the ramps. 'That will take you out. I've had your gear sent across. Lieutenant Kimber is coming with the base staff.' He grinned. 'By road. That'll keep the rest of us out of your hair. For the moment anyway.'

Devane nodded. 'Thanks. That was thoughtful.' He had pictured Beresford and the grim-featured Kimber watching his every move, recording each contact with his new command.

He looked up the beach. But for the great tracks there was no sign of the massive vehicles. Devane turned to say good-bye to Sorokin, but he too was already climbing into his little scout car.

Beresford murmured, 'Never mind that one, John. The next meeting you have with him will probably be across a table, taking a bottling because you have done something to offend the Soviets.' He grinned again. '*You* should worry.'

Devane realized that he and Beresford were the only two British people left on the beach. The sailors, like the Russians and their tractors, had withdrawn into their more familiar surroundings.

Beresford said, 'Like a piece of Kipling, isn't it?'

Then he drew back and they saluted each other formally, as if they had just met in no-man's-land.

As Devane walked towards the waiting boat he knew Beresford would continue to his transport without looking back. It was his way.

The five boats were anchored in an uneven line, rising and falling in a slight swell, while their companies rushed from one

42

checkpoint to the next. It looked as if they had never been out of water, Devane thought.

Dundas and Seymour were waiting for him, and in the small open bridge he received a smart salute from Pellegrine, the coxswain. He was a sturdy man with a brick-red face. A mixture of sea-time and drink. Very soon now he would know them all. He had read as much about his own command as he could. From Dundas down to an ordinary seaman named Metcalf, who was apparently a failed candidate for a commission. Even as the lowliest member of the boat, it was to be hoped he had no plans for proving he still had a special gift of leadership to offer. It could sometimes be fatal.

Devane's eye continued to move, his brain recording the reports of readiness as they were called from the deck or came up the various voicepipes.

He pictured the petty officer in charge of the boat's powerful Packard engines. His name was Ackland, before the war a garage mechanic, so he should be all right.

Carroll, the leading signalman, was stooping down to push his flags firmly into their lockers, and another leading hand with leather gauntlets to protect him from snags in the mooring wires was mustering his forecastle party ready to weigh anchor. His name was Priest. Devane was satisfied, names were falling into place already.

Carroll said, 'The senior escort is signallin', sir!' He triggered an acknowledgement with his Aldis before peering at a hastily compiled list of local signals.

'*Are you ready?*'

Dundas asked, 'Shall I call up the flotilla on the R/T, sir? It'll save time.'

Devane slung his binoculars about his neck and tugged his cap firmly over his eyes.

'No. You do it, Bunts. The sooner we get used to a minimum of radio communicating the better.'

Dundas watched him questioningly. 'It's a bit like being all on our own, sir.'

'In a way.' Devane listened to the clack . . . clack . . . clack of the signal lamp. 'I'm told that the Russians don't trust anybody they don't know. Well, maybe they've got the right idea.'

Carroll called, 'All acknowledged, sir. *Affirmative*.'

Devane walked to the forepart of the bridge and looked

down across the top of the chartroom to the easy pitch and roll of the bows. He ran his hand along the screen, savouring the moment, prolonging it as he had in that hotel room in Chelsea.

"Start up.'

With a cough and a savage roar the five boats thundered into life, their hulls partially misted over by a curtain of high-octane vapour. Then as they settled down to a steady rumble Devane said, 'Up anchor. Bunts, signal the flotilla to form line astern and take station on the leading escort.'

There was a clang from forward. 'Anchor's aweigh!'

'All engines slow ahead.' He glanced quickly at the coxswain's set profile. 'Steer nor'-west until we have station on Ivan.'

When next he glanced astern the other boats were following him out in a tight curve, the rearmost one's wake already sloshing across the beach and wiping away the ruts left by the great carriers.

He saw some of his men looking at the land, probably wondering what they had got themselves into. *Never volunteer*, that was the guiding prayer in the Navy. But few ever remembered it until it was too late.

The guns were covered and pointed impotently at the shark-blue sea, and their tubes were empty.

Devane levelled his glasses on the leading destroyer. Toothless they might be, but they were back in the war.

4

ALLIES

Devane sat at his newly acquired desk and surveyed the flotilla's shore office without enthusiasm. It was partially underground and, like Whitcombe's HQ in London, had been constructed from gigantic slabs of concrete. There was no other similarity. The whole place seemed to throb with noises from the adjoining workshop, where Lieutenant-Commander (E) Hector Buckhurst had already set up his benches and drills, and from the strange, cavern-like dock beyond. The latter had originally been designed as a pen for Russian submarines, rather in the style of those built by the Germans along the Atlantic coastline to protect their U-boats from bombing raids.

The smells were just as difficult to live with. Diesel and high-octane, damp and boiled cabbage seemed to predominate.

He thought of their arrival at Tuapse the previous day. On the last leg of the passage from their launching point there had been several unexplained delays, which the senior Russian officer of their escort either found incapable of translating or felt it was none of Devane's business anyway.

They had finally entered Tuapse as darkness had closed over the harbour and dockyard. It had been a depressing sight, with many of the long, finger-like wharves savaged by bombings, and several ships showing only their funnels or masts above water.

The town too, or what they had been able to see of it, was badly mauled, and a drifting smoke curtain had been hanging over it in the wake of some departing attackers.

As one seaman had remarked with some bitterness, 'Christ, even Chatham's better than this dump!'

Beresford had been waiting to greet them, and had been quick to shoot down any immediate criticism from the various commanding officers. No bunks had so far been fitted in the concrete dock area, not even for the engineering and supply staff who had arrived by road. So that meant the MTB crews would have to make the best of it in their already overcrowded hulls.

And there was no mail for anyone either. It had taken a long while to move the flotilla from England to the Med, from there via the Canal to the Gulf. Even during the last part of the journey overland, somebody should have thought about the mail, how important it was to men away from home.

Beresford had hinted that the Russians might be able to help. He had said little more on the subject, but Devane suspected that the Russians considered such matters to be mere luxuries which would have to take second place. As if to prove this, Buckhurst had discovered that all the torpedoes, ammunition and spares had arrived undamaged and in mint condition.

The door opened and Beresford stamped into the room. He had a lively, intelligent face which was now marred by a frown. He slumped in a canvas chair and groped for his cigarettes. Then he sniffed the fuel-laden air and gave a wry grin. 'On the other hand, better safe than sorry!'

Devane asked, 'Any news of our first job?'

Beresford eyed him curiously. 'You *are* keen.'

Devane thought of the passage to Tuapse, the way he had pushed each boat through as many drills as possible whenever the escorts had signalled them to heave to and await instructions.

They were certainly a well-trained bunch, he thought. Only *he* had felt like an outsider. They were raring to go, for the real thing. And to keep them kicking their feet in this dreary dump was bad for morale all round.

He said, 'I don't want it to go stale. You know the score.'

Beresford glanced at his watch. 'I have a meeting today with the base commander. You'll be expected to attend.' He grimaced. 'More vodka and champers, I expect.'

Before Devane could speak he added, 'You've not asked about Richie. That surprised me a bit. Your both coming from the same mould, so to speak.'

'I was told to *say* nothing.' He recalled Claudia's voice on the telephone, the way Whitcombe and Kinross had questioned him about her, suggested they should meet. 'I suppose he had his reasons. Remember that chap in Alex who blew himself up with a grenade because he was caught with his fingers in the mess funds? It always seems trivial to the onlookers, like us."

Beresford smiled tightly. 'You're still the same. Bottling it up. Well, I must say it shook me. I always imagined Richie had more going for him. His wife is a bit of all right too, from all accounts.' He grinned broadly. 'But I see from your expression you know that already!' He held up his hands in mock defence. 'All right! I'm going!'

Alone again, Devane turned his attention to the pile of reports from the other boats, teething troubles which would have to be dealt with when there was time. Right now they were taking on ammunition and stowing extra belts and cannon shells throughout the hulls further to reduce the sleeping spaces.

Dundas entered the concrete box and stood patiently by the desk while Devane made a note in the margin of a report.

'Ah, Number One. What can I do for you?'

Dundas looked like a sailor. Rugged, clear-eyed, he could have sailed with Drake, or smuggled contraband under the noses of the Revenue men of olden days. So far their paths had only crossed in the line of routine and duty, of changing a watch bill, or discussing *Parthian*'s special recognition signals and code names.

It had been Richie's boat, and the men, for the most part, had also served with him before. It made Devane feel like the odd man out, and he was yet to discover if it was accidental or deliberate.

Dundas said, 'We seem to be getting all we need for the boat, sir, and I'm told that we have a separate fuel supply from the other small craft here.' He shivered. 'It's the place, I suppose. No shore leave, the perimeter guarded as if we were POWs. It's not what I expected.'

Devane looked up. 'There have been raids every day. They have their problems. We must seem a bit pampered to them. But I want no friction. We're here to do a job, nothing more.

Our lads will want to make friends, but they won't. Not yet anyway.' He thought of the lieutenant's words in the car. *Alice through the looking-glass.* Then he said, 'It'll get better. . . .' A telephone buzzed in its case and he had to move a piles of stores' returns to find it.

It was Beresford. 'Can you come to the main bunker, John? The meeting's been brought forward.' He dropped his voice so that it was almost drowned by hissing static. 'Bit of a flap on, so chop, chop if you can.'

Devane looked round for his cap. He had felt it in his bones as soon as he had arrived. A sense of urgency, even anxiety, which some people were at great pains to conceal.

He said shortly, 'Tell Red Mackay to take over until I get back. He's due for his half-stripe anyway. This will warn him what it'll be like.'

Dundas said awkwardly, 'I'd just like to say how glad we are that you took over as SO, sir. We all felt a bit lost, let down.'

Devane pretended to search through a drawer. *Here we go.*

Dundas added quickly, 'Could you tell me? How did they explain it to Mrs Richie?'

Devane looked up. Dundas had almost called her Claudia.

'They told her nothing, other than that he died on active service.'

Dundas sounded wretched. 'That doesn't mean a thing, sir. There was a two-ringer who was blown out of a brothel in North Africa, bed, woman and all, and they sent the same sort of telegram to his widow, for God's sake!' He flushed. 'Sorry, sir!'

'I take it you knew her, Number One? Fairly well, would you say?'

'I *wanted* to, sir. But she wouldn't have it. . . .' His voice trailed away.

Devane stood up. 'We'll talk about it again later, if you like.' *We won't of course.* Dundas was trying to find out, to test him about something.

Devane strode through the echoing workshop where Buckhurst and his mechanics were levering open packing cases as if they had come to stay permanently.

A Russian sailor with a machine-pistol slung over one arm was waiting to guide him to the command bunker, and Devane could feel the man watching him, as if to recognize the differences between them.

As he had expected, Sorokin was in the bunker, with several other officers. A sailor was wiping one of the big map tables with a soft brush, and Devane guessed that the last air-raid must have brought down some dust from the roof.

Sorokin saw Devane and nodded companionably, but he looked on edge, and lacked the confident authority he had displayed when they had first met.

Beresford hurried to meet him. 'Glad you got here—'

He broke off as a thin, reedy voice said, 'On behalf of Rear-Admiral Vasiliy Kasatonov'—the man half turned as if to bow to a forbidding figure seated on the far side of the table —'I am to welcome you to the struggle against the Nazi invaders.'

Devane saw it was a lieutenant who was addressing him, a sort of Russian Kimber, he guessed, and was translating for the grim-faced admiral who had not taken his eyes off him since he had arrived.

In the harsh overhead lights the admiral's shoulders glittered with his markings of rank, but all his strength and energy were concentrated in his small button eyes.

Devane tried to remember something about Kasatonov. He was in command of the local defence, of the naval air forces, and had a significant political link with Moscow to uphold his authority. He appeared to be hairless, and his whole presence gave an impression of immense determination.

The interpreter continued in the same sing-song tone, 'The arrival of the British vessels is both a mark of progress and a sign of intent.' He was staring at a point somewhere above Devane's shoulder, as if he was under a spell. 'Further intelligence has been received about the movement of enemy forces in this area, and we have learned that even larger. . . .' He faltered and then said, 'What *you* term "E-boats" have been seen on patrol near Sevastapol.'

Devane let the words settle. He already knew something of the German naval strength in the Black Sea. It was a hotch-potch of small craft formed originally around their local minesweeping flotilla. Gunboats, armed launches, craft captured from the Russians, they had thrown everything into the battle to destroy and demoralize their enemies whenever they saw an opening. A few E-boats had also been reported in the

Black Sea. They had begun their journey from the banks of the Elbe near Magdeburg, then by wheeled transport down the *Autobahn* to the Danube. But this news of larger E-boats in the vicinity had changed things before they had even begun. The bigger, one-hundred-ton sisters of the sort Devane had often fought were in a class of their own. No wonder the Russians were disappointed by the smallness of the British offering.

Devane heard the admiral speak for the first time. A low, abrupt remark which made the interpreter stare at the ceiling as if for inspiration.

He stammered, 'While we have won one crushing victory after another, we have expected, *anticipated*, some sign that an invasion in the west was imminent. And now that the British at least have sent us this small group of torpedo boats we can feel the moment of final assault on Germany is not too far distant.'

Beresford murmured dryly, 'It loses a lot in the translation, of course.' He fell silent as the admiral's eyes settled on him.

Devane did not comment. He was trying to read beyond the trite words, the air of patronizing superiority from a great veteran to some unimportant volunteer. He thought of all the men he had seen die, the ships which had gone down in their efforts to carry food and supplies to Russia. Of the countries which had fallen to Hitler while Stalin had sheltered happily behind his non-aggression pact with Germany.

He realized the room was completely silent, that they were waiting for him to reply. There was no point in trying to describe his own country's record, they knew it as well as he did. *Through the looking-glass.*

He said, 'We are proud to be here. To put our skills, all of which have been gained in hard experience elsewhere, at the disposal of the Soviet navy and people. We will have some misunderstandings. That is common even in families. But we share the same enemy, and that is enough.'

The admiral listened woodenly to the hurried translation and then rose ponderously to his feet.

With a curt nod to Beresford and Devane he strode from the bunker.

Sorokin embraced Devane and gripped his shoulders. 'He loves you, Comrade! You found the *right* words!'

It was impossible to know if he was being sincere or not. He certainly sounded relieved.

Sorokin lit a cheroot and spread his hands apologetically.

'Tonight you will leave harbour with some of my own'—he formed the word carefully—'flot-illa. I will give you later the details. Then we will fight like comrades!' He laughed deeply, as if it was a great joke.

'But first we drink.' He peered at Devane's face. 'To seal our friendship, *da*?'

Lieutenant Roddy Dundas climbed on to the MTB's open bridge and groped his way to the forepart where Devane was peering abeam through his night glasses.

'I've been right through the boat, sir.' He had learnt the knack of pitching his voice against the throaty drone of motors without actually shouting. 'Not a chink of light anywhere.'

Devane let the glasses fall to his chest. It had only been a matter of weeks since he had left his last command, and yet everything felt different. Even the motion, or was that merely because he knew this was the Black Sea and not the Med or some other familiar place?

'How are the lads taking it?'

Dundas sounded surprised, as if he had been expecting a stream of operational questions from his new captain.

'Happy enough, sir. There'll be some fresh kye sent round soon. That'll warm them up.' His teeth looked very white in the darkness. 'Where are our allies?'

Devane thought about the brief, almost offhand meeting they had shared with the Russian flotilla's officers just before sailing. That had been two hours ago, and both groups of vessels had been heading due west since then.

There were ten craft in the Russian flotilla and, although Devane had seen some relics pushed into service in his own navy—paddle-steamers for sweeping mines, ancient China river gunboats doing hazardous supply runs to Tobruk and the like—their consorts took a lot of beating. There were three Italian-built gunboats, rather like small destroyers, two very old minesweepers and the remainder were converted motor launches of varying size. They were crammed with weapons of every sort, even multiple rocket-launchers on loan from the Russian army and known locally as Stalin organs. This mixed flotilla, under its commander, a swarthy-faced officer named Orel, was steering about a mile off the starboard beam, but the night was so dark that true station-keeping was hard to maintain.

Devane could recall exactly his own feelings at that meeting. Orel had explained through the inevitable interpreter that the object of their mission was a small but important convoy which was expected to pass along the south-east coast of the Crimean peninsula in twenty-four hours' time. Intelligence reports, confirmed by agents inside German-occupied Rumania, had stated that the convoy would be carrying valuable equipment and armour-plate for the enemy emplacements along the stretch of coast. When the Russians had been driven from the Crimea the devastation caused by the battles had been immense, and whole towns had been razed to the ground.

The German high command knew that an attempt would soon be made to retake the Crimea, just as they must realize its strategic importance to the rest of the Eastern Front. A swift, well-handled convoy to the closest point of unloading was a far better bet than risking the urgently needed supplies overland, when the Soviet air force would contest every yard of the way.

The two flotillas would head out to sea and rendezvous eventually to the south of the estimated convoy route. The enemy would then be unable to retreat, and could either scatter or continue on course until it eventually ran foul of Russian patrols nearer to the Kerch Straits.

Devane had been irritated by the Russian commander's indifferent attitude. The British, having the faster and more modern boats, would stand to seaward, and attack only if ordered. From Orel's tone, if not his actual words, it sounded as if such an eventuality was considered unlikely.

Even at this reduced speed, which was making the MTBs yaw about uncomfortably in even the slightest swell, it would be a close thing, Devane thought. His flotilla carried enough fuel to allow for a cruising range of some five hundred miles plus. It was two hundred miles to the rendezvous. That did not allow much for a pitched battle and the homeward run. The Russian vessels were slower, but were converted for longer endurance. It was an interesting equation. Devane had said as much through the overworked interpreter, and had stressed the importance of the enemy running to time.

Orel had watched him, his head on one side as he had listened to the interpreter's words. Then he had picked up his cap and chart-folder, had nodded curtly to Devane's officers before murmuring something almost inaudible.

The interpreter had stared at the closed door and then at Devane. He had said unhappily, 'He says that you are not to be afraid, Commander. That his men have done it many times before.'

Red Mackay had exploded. 'God damn his bloody eyes! Let the bastards go alone, I say!'

Even Willy Walker, usually reserved, even mild, had said, 'We'll get it over with and go home. Bloody cheek!'

Devane said, 'We must try not to lose them, unfriendly or not.' He saw Lieutenant Seymour's head and shoulders rising above the rear of the bridge. 'Call me instantly if you see anything.'

Devane wondered briefly what Seymour thought about *Parthian*. By rights, with his experience and record, Seymour should at least be a first lieutenant and in line for a command of his own. But it was surprising how much easier it was with one extra officer. Especially the chore of watchkeeping.

Dundas peered through the darkness. 'Going to turn in, sir?'

Devane nodded. 'It should be secure enough tonight. All tomorrow we'll be staying well away from patrol areas and out of sight of land. This time tomorrow might be livelier, however.'

He glanced up at the sky. Broken cloud, no moon. Should be all right. So what was nagging at him?

Devane groped his way forward and down into the chartroom. It would be quicker from here to the bridge than from the wardroom. Even two or three extra steps could make all the difference.

He heard a gentle snore rise to greet him, and switched on the small blue light beside the chart table to get his bearings. There were at least three sleeping figures already here. Devane smiled to himself. Good old jack. He would find a private nest even in a Carley float.

He sat down on a pile of kapok life-jackets and leaned against the pulsating bulkhead.

In his mind he could see the coast, even an imaginary convoy threading its way through the minefield, eager to unload and creep off just as quietly.

Orel was in charge, and Sorokin trusted him. Sorokin's head would be on the block if anything went badly wrong.

What had Beresford said when the German prisoners had been marched up the road? They had been testing him. Was this another trial he must undergo?

With a sigh he snapped off the light and laid down with his cap over his face.

The German convoys had to be stopped if the Crimea was to be recaptured before the Allied invasion in the west.

Best not to think about it. His head lolled, and he heard a man whimpering in his sleep like a child.

Think about tomorrow and the day after. That was far enough.

When the watch changed and the gun crews were relieved to go below, Devane eventually fell asleep.

'More coffee, sir?'

Devane turned and rubbed his eyes. Where had the day gone?

The coffee tasted good. Scalding hot and as black as a boot. It tasted unfamiliar, and he guessed that the acting cook, an AB named, very appropriately, Duff, had wangled a supply on his way through the Gulf.

That was the best thing about coastal forces, the MTBs and MGBs, he thought. It brought out a man's real worth, it was inevitable with each company being so small. The badges they wore on their shore-going tiddley suits were often at odds with what they really did afloat. A stoker or torpedoman was often a crack shot with a machine-gun. A telegraphist might be better at repairing fuel pipes than any artificer.

He pushed the seaman called Duff from his thoughts and searched abeam for the blurred shapes of the Russian vessels. All ten still there, and the average speed now a miserable ten knots.

It would be dark soon. It seemed to come down like a curtain hereabouts. Maybe that was why it was named the Black Sea.

He shook himself. Must be more tired than I thought, to make a stupid joke like that.

It had been a very strange day. They had seen and heard nothing, although the W/T cabin had kept up its usual listening watch of static and garbled signals in a dozen codes and languages. But for them it was a limbo, a nothing of choppy

54

water and no horizon, low cloud and a strange hazy light. But for the breeze it could be humid, he thought.

Dundas joined him on the bridge and followed his gaze astern. The next boat back there was Willy Walker's, code name *Harrier*. The others were already merging into shadow, losing their rakish identity.

Devane glanced at his watch. Soon now. The Russian vessels would be curving away northwards to close the land. God, he hoped Orel knew what he was doing and was not relying too much on the German obsession for punctuality.

He thought about his own command. Five of the best MTBs available. Between them they could muster ten torpedoes and the firepower of a warship a dozen times their size.

Dundas handed his mug to the boatswain's mate and said, 'This motion is making me dizzy.'

Devane glanced at him. 'But you were in the merchant service?'

Dundas grinned. 'Yes. A million years ago. I'd just got my ticket. Never thought I'd end up in a little wooden box like this!'

'What about Seymour?'

Dundas replied, 'He's going to publish the great novel one day. Used to write for a living. Damn useful to have around. I'm hopeless at writing reports.'

A brilliant light stabbed across the water, and Leading Signalman Carroll said, 'The signal, sir! They're up and away!'

Devane nodded. 'Thanks.'

A second earlier and Carroll would not have been on the bridge, nor was he required just yet. But he had already proved his worth and would make a fine yeoman of signals one day. He had already mentioned that if he survived the war he would try to sign on in the Navy. Dundas had shared the confidence on the passage to Tuapse.

When Devane had asked what the signalman had been before the war, Dundas had replied, 'A baker's roundsman, sir.'

To see him now, glasses trained on the departing Russian flotilla, one of any warship's key ratings, it was difficult to visualize Carroll with a horse and cart, a basket of bread on his arm.

Dundas said, 'Shall I keep the guns covered, sir?' He

flinched as Devane looked at him. 'I mean, there's not much chance of us being pounced on.'

Devane smiled. 'Probably not. But we'll go to action stations as planned. Never mind the grumbles. Go round yourself and check that there are extra magazines for the Oerlikons and plenty of spare belts for the MGs.' He peered over the screen and saw the crouching shape of Leading Torpedoman Kirby groping down the length of the starboard tube. 'Another early bird, I see.' He clapped Dundas on the shoulder. 'You've done a fine job. I'm just going below to look at the chart again. Tell the *journalist* to take over the con, will you?'

He went down to the chartroom, now empty of sleeping bodies, and stooped over the table with its notebooks and pencilled calculations.

Dundas found that he was still staring at the chartroom ladder when Seymour arrived to relieve him.

It was not merely that Devane had congratulated him for the boat's efficiency, Dundas had become good at his job and knew it better than most. But it had suddenly occurred to him that Richie had never praised anyone as far as he could remember.

Seymour asked politely, 'Something bothering you, Number One?'

Dundas grinned. 'Only my wasted youth, David. Nothing important.'

An hour later, as the five MTBs closed up at action stations, Devane said, 'We will alter course now. Steer north by east. Revolutions for twenty knots. Warn the engine room.' He could feel them staring at him through the darkness. 'Tell the W/T cabin to inform the flotilla, separate acknowledgements too. After this we'll keep absolute silence.'

Dundas spoke first. 'But isn't that against what the Russians *want* us to do, sir?'

Devane climbed on to the gratings and gripped the screen with his gloved hands.

'Pass the word through the boat. Prepare for immediate action.'

He heard Dundas's feet clattering down the short ladder from the bridge, a voice yelling orders from right aft.

As the throttles were opened and the bows rose in response to the sudden surge of power, Tom Pellegrine, the coxswain, gripped the wheel and rocked back on his heels as if he were riding and not steering the boat.

Almost to himself he muttered, '*Knew* it. Knew somethin' was bloody wrong!'

5

THE GLORY BOYS

Devane glanced up at the sky and saw the glimmer of stars through some fast-moving cloud. It was colder. He shivered as spray dashed over the bridge screen and pricked his skin. Or was it? Maybe his nerves were playing up.

He turned, angry with himself. 'Stop engines. Do your stuff, Bunts.'

As Carroll blinked his shaded light astern, and the signal was briefly repeated down the hidden line of boats, Devane felt the pressure of the voicepipes pushing against his ribs as the motors faded into silence and the MTB rolled forward for a moment longer on her own thrust.

The motors' silence seemed deafening, while the inboard noises of creaks and groans rising to meet the sluice of water against the hull sounded loud enough to wake the dead.

Devane gripped the rail and held his watch to his eyes. The times he had done this in the past. He could even remember his first commanding officer ordering a shutdown of motors in the North Sea. The oppressive silence. The ridiculous feeling of vulnerability, when to stop and listen nearly always gave you an advantage.

The boat lifted and rolled in protest, the signal halliards and bridge fittings joining in with their own particular chorus.

Here and there a man shifted restlessly at his station, while from aft came the unmistakable murmur as the twin Oerlikons swung from quarter to quarter.

Devane heard the chartroom door open and close, and then Dundas loomed up beside him. Even he dropped his voice, as if he expected somebody to be listening beyond the pitching hull.

'I've checked our position again. Even allowing for dead reckoning, I think we're just about where you wanted to be.' He sounded uneasy, doubtful perhaps of Devane's decision. 'The coast is approximately eight miles to the north of us. The Russians should be nearer and to the north-east. Maybe the convoy didn't come? Or that bloody Orel has lost it?' He sounded as if hoped it was the latter.

Devane did not reply immediately. He was seeing it in his mind, a triangle on a chart. The blacked-out convoy, Orel's ten antiquated vessels, and *Parthian*, stopped and drifting while every man in the flotilla probably thought he was raving mad to hang about rather than obey orders and hold to seaward of the Russians.

There was a chorus of gasps as the sky lit up to a brilliant white glare, followed instantly by faster, more deadly red flashes.

Seymour said, 'They've found 'em.' Even he sounded disappointed. 'God, they've caught Jerry with his pants down by the look of it!'

The sounds seemed to take a long time to reach the drifting boats, and then Devane heard the dull boom of explosions, the vague, scratchy rattle of machine-guns. More star shells drifted eerily beneath the clouds, so that the sky appeared brighter than the sea below.

Devane gripped the screen to contain his nerves. That too was an illusion. Somewhere out there Orel's boats were darting amongst the convoy like wolves, and to them the sea and the careering ships would be like a stark moonscape.

Orel was not having it all his own way, and Devane heard the occasional bang of a heavier gun as the transports' armament fired back. The hollow, lifeless thuds which came against the MTB's wooden hull like padded fists were exploding depth charges. Orel was using them like mines, hurling them beneath the slower moving supply vessels as he surged past.

Dundas raised his mouth from a voicepipe. 'Nothing from

W/T. Orel doesn't need us anyway.' He grinned ruefully. 'And won't he crow about that!'

Pellegrine turned on his heels, his hands still gripping the wheel's spokes as if the boat was sweeping through the water.

'*Sir!*' His voice sounded hoarse and urgent.

Devane moved to his side and touched the coxswain's arm. Another veteran. Pellegrine had understood.

'I know, Swain!' Devane felt the icy fingers playing on his spine, the sudden rawness in his throat.

There it was. The unmistakable *thrum . . . thrum . . . thrum* of heavy diesels. E-boats, a whole bloody bunch of them, coming up fast astern of their convoy, judging to the minute what they thought the most dangerous part of the journey had to be.

They had probably fuelled at Sevastapol or Nikolayev to give them plenty of scope for manoeuvre.

Orel and his mixed collection of gunboats were making such a din they would hear nothing, until it was too late.

Devane saw faces lifting from gun mountings and hatchways, pale blobs as they came to listen to the distant, threatening roar of engines.

All down the line of MTBs they would be listening, searching their feelings, preparing themselves. Unlike most flotillas, there were more veterans here than new volunteers. Even a single year in coastal forces made you a professional.

But sometimes the new hands were the lucky ones, Devane thought. They did not know what to expect. If you had lived through one action after another you could know too much, find too many options.

Pellegrine said in a whisper, 'They're crossin' our bows now, sir. I reckon 'bout two miles. No more.'

Devane nodded. 'Good lad. I agree.'

He spoke over his shoulder, hoping that Seymour was listening. 'Pass the word, David. We shall be attacking in line abreast. Gun action.'

He heard Seymour move away, and added for the bridge's benefit, 'Jerry is stalking his kill, he'll not expect a kick up the backside!'

An unknown voice murmured, 'We *hope*!'

The deck lifted sluggishly, and Devane felt the force of water under the keel like a surfacing whale. The combined wakes of the enemy vessels had reached his flotilla, a miniature tidal wave. So they were well past now.

He said, 'We shall steer north-east. Maximum revs.'

He craned forward, his head turned to catch the last of the sound from the enemy's engines.

Feet shuffled behind him, and on the power-operated six-pounder he heard the clink of steel as the gun-layer tested his sights yet again.

'Right.' Devane held out his hand and felt the leading signalman place the microphone firmly in his palm. Like a surgeon receiving the vital instruments, he thought vaguely.

He glanced at Dundas. 'Start up!'

He snapped down the button and pictured the other four skippers listening for his command.

'*Parthian! Nuts* ahead! Line abreast to starboard! *Tally-ho!*'

The motors, already hot, roared into life, and as Pellegrine spun his wheel, his head bowed to peer at the dimly lit compass, Devane heard the responding thunder from the other boats as they surged forward, swinging steeply from line astern to form up abeam of their leader.

Devane clutched the voicepipes for support, feeling the wind in his face as the torn spindrift came back from the bows like ragged arrows. Everything was shaking and rattling wildly, and he could sense the wildness around him like a rising madness.

Faster, faster. The revolutions were still mounting, and Devane could not imagine how the engineering staff below decks, some bent double like old men, could put up with the din which would blot out any warning of danger.

The clouds blinked in reflected flashes, and Devane saw a combined web of scarlet tracer arching from the E-boats before tearing down towards their quarry. Bright, livid explosions, more tracer going anywhere as the Russians realized what was happening. Fires leapt seemingly out of the sea itself as one, then two hidden vessels erupted into flames, spilling blazing fuel into the night like molten metal.

Devane ignored the quick intakes of breath and Carroll's 'Christ Almighty!'

Men were burning and dying, but his mind was concentrated on the dancing reflections, against which the E-boats stood out as starkly as if it were broad daylight.

He shouted, '*Open fire!*'

61

Carroll yelled at him, 'W/T have received a signal from the Ruskies, sir! *Require assistance!*'

'Right on cue!'

Devane watched the two boats to starboard as they opened up on the wedgelike shapes ahead. The Russians were asking for help, although if he had obeyed Orel's orders they would all have been dead before the MTBs could reach them.

The bridge shook violently as the six-pounder cracked out for the first time, joined immediately by the machine-guns on either side. It was enough to blind and deafen you. The spitting threads of tracer, the drifting fireballs of the cannon shells, all drawing together and tearing at the enemy hulls like saws.

There were four large E-boats, and the one on Devane's port bow was weaving from side to side as if already out of control. One of her consorts was faring even worse, her low bridge and after deck spurting sparks and smoke.

Devane ducked as the weaving E-boat exploded with one tremendous flash. Pieces rained out of the sky, and feathers of spray shot up alongside as some of the fragments bracketed the MTB like gunfire.

Dundas gasped, 'She must have been carrying mines! Hell, what a shambles!'

The two E-boats still unscathed were already coming about, firing blindly, their accuracy hampered by the drifting smoke.

Devane watched a line of tracer balls rising very slowly until as they reached their final curve they swept down towards him like comets. He heard metal hit metal and a man cry out as something smashed into the hull below the port torpedo tube.

To make his challenge the enemy captain had turned nearly one hundred and eighty degrees.

The third MTB, Red Mackay's, roared out of the smoke, every gun firing, as the German presented his undefended side for just two precious minutes. Fragments flew from the E-boat and tracer shells rippled along her hull and bridge, crossing with those from Devane's boat in a tornado of steel and high explosive.

'Stand by, *depth charges!*' Devane clutched the screen to stay on his feet. 'Hard a-port!'

The E-boat was still coming through the smoke, burning in several places, but closing the range until their combined speed was nearly sixty knots.

Bullets and shells ripped past the bridge or ricocheted from gun positions as the MTBs leaned over in a dramatic turn to port.

From aft Devane vaguely heard shouts, the clang of depth charges being lobbed across the enemy's bows. At minimum depth setting they exploded almost under the German's stem. The whole powerful hull seemed to leap bodily from the water, which shone bright orange from the twin explosions, and looked as if it would disdain their puny assault and plunge after them.

But as the din subsided the E-boat continued to rise, so that her bows pointed at the clouds. The depth charges and another internal blast had broken her in half and she was already on her way down. Men floundered in the seething bow waves as the MTBs tore past, others lifted their arms and sank out of sight rather than end their lives on those racing screws.

Devane waited for his boat to resume her course and then peered abeam as they tore through the smoke. The others were still there, their guns momentarily silent as the devastated E-boats fell further and further astern. The unscathed one had swung away to disengage, or to wait her chance to pick up any survivors from *Parthian*'s murderous attack.

Other vessels loomed to meet them, and he tried to identify Orel's gunboat as they swept through and past the Russian flotilla and on towards the convoy.

There had apparently been four ships, one of which had been an anti-submarine vessel. Surprise, speed and the knowledge that they were being supported by the powerful E-boats had apparently been considered sufficient protection. The patrol vessel was already capsized, and two of the transports were burning or listing so badly it was unlikely they would see another day.

The one survivor was stern on, heading for the invisible shore as fast as she could move.

'Half ahead.' Devane wiped the sighting bar with his hand and stooped down to peer at the ship's vague outline. 'Stand by with torpedoes!'

He had seen the red blink of gunfire a long, long way off, but when the shells arrived, preceded by a thin, abbreviated whistle, they were no less of a surprise. A shore battery, probably using RDF to locate their remaining supply ship and pin down her attackers.

Another pair of waterspouts shot up close alongside, and

Devane gritted his teeth and tried not to listen to the motors' pitch as splinters punched into the lower hull.

He held his breath, shutting out the shouts and commands, the sudden rattle of machine-gun fire as a motor boat came around the side of the careering transport. Who were those madmen anyway?

'*Fire*.'

The torpedoes leapt from their tubes, the bows lifting slightly as they increased speed again and began to turn away.

Devane wiped his face with the back of his hand. Both torpedoes running. One of them must have passed directly beneath the motor boat, and Devane guessed they were survivors from Orel's earlier attack.

'*Line astern*! *Steer south-east*!'

Every face on the bridge lit up like waxworks as the torpedoes struck and exploded. A solid wall of flame shot up the vessel's side, picking out tiny details with stark clarity. A lifeboat, hanging in halves from its davits. The ship's scuttles gleaming like eyes in the reflected fires, and then from within as more explosions changed the hull into an inferno.

She must have been carrying fuel or explosives, Devane thought.

He turned to watch as his boat speeded away from the smoke which stank of cordite and burning paintwork.

'All engines, half ahead. Bunts, keep an eye open for a Russian forming-and-disposal signal!'

Dundas was wiping his face and neck with a piece of rag. 'You're not going to ask *them*, sir?' He could not stop grinning, although his hands were shaking badly and not just from the motors' vibrations.

Devane shook his head. 'No. I've had that.' He saw the light paling across the water. 'Call up the flotilla, Number One. I think we're all right, but check for casualties and damage anyway.'

A light blinked across the water and Carroll, who was ready with his special code card, said immediately, 'From the Russians, sir. *Return to base*.'

Seymour climbed on to the bridge, soaked in spray and covered with chips of blasted paintwork.

'What, Bunts, no please or thank you?'

Devane gripped the screen and tried to calm each muscle in turn. But it was not going away. Not this time. His stomach was screwed into a ball and he felt as if he were going to vomit.

He made himself say, 'Very well. Acknowledge.' He peered astern at the pall of smoke, which seemed greater rather than smaller with each turn of the screws. 'Now let's get the hell out of it, shall we?'

He was surprised that nobody turned to stare at him. His voice had had no strength to it, as if somebody else had spoken while he stood stricken, unable to move or think properly.

He said tightly, 'Fall out action stations, Number One. I'm going below for a minute.'

Devane nodded to their grimy faces, their bright, brittle smiles and unblinking eyes. One more time, for most of them. And what about the new hands? Would they be as wildly exultant as he had once been, that first time? Never realizing that it was just as easy to lose a fight. To die.

Dundas watched him until he had vanished through the little hatch, then he said quietly to Seymour, 'Did you see that, David? Here's me, thought I was going to lose my guts back there, and the skipper just shrugs it off.' He shook his head admiringly. 'The Black Sea or the bloody Antarctic, he's the one for me!'

Seymour grinned. 'I thought you liked Richie best?'

Pellegrine eased the wheel over and allowed his body to unwind. Nice and smooth, a copybook attack. The motors and the hiss of water alongside prevented him from hearing what the two lieutenants were saying, and anyway he was thinking about Devane. After the previous skipper it was hard to know what any of them must be thinking at the moment of decision. He would have trusted Richie with his life, any time. A real gent. One of the best. So his suicide had been a let down, something personal which had made them resent Devane as an intruder.

Pellegrine heard the clatter of mugs and knew that the kye, that thick, glutinous pusser's cocoa, would soon be handed round. It gave a man back his guts, it was almost a symbol of survival.

Able-Seaman Irwin, the boatswain's mate, touched his arm. 'I'm to relieve you, Swain.'

Pellegrine released the wheel and was surprised just how hard he had been gripping the spokes.

He snapped, 'South-east. Watch yer 'elm.'

65

He grinned wearily. He did not care for Irwin very much. A stroppy jack-ashore, always being dragged aboard stoned out of his mind by a shore patrol. But, like the kye, he was something familiar, one of the 'family', as Leading Seaman Carroll called it.

With each mile under the keel relaxation grew to fend off the strain and the stark terrors of the moment.

In the small wardroom Devane sat with his elbows on the table, his head in his hands, and wondered why he had not noticed it was happening to him. He had seen plenty of others go under, usually hell-bent on destroying the enemy when, like a gun jamming when it was most needed, every fibre and muscle seemed to freeze.

He pushed himself away from the table and stared at the opposite bunks. It was like sea-sickness. In the Navy there was no allowance for it. He stood up and waited to gauge the pitch and plunge of the shivering hull. Especially out here, in a godforsaken place like this.

Devane jammed on his cap and made himself climb up into the keen air again.

From the W/T cabin, which was next to the wardroom, he heard the busy stammer of morse, and from forward he could smell something frying in the galley.

Another mission completed. Returning to base. No matter where it was.

Somewhere a man laughed and then began to whistle to himself.

By the time he had regained the bridge Devane was outwardly calm again.

He nodded to the men on watch as they sipped their hot cocoa or munched the wedge-shaped sandwiches which Dundas had had the sense to arrange before the action. Ordinary, everyday faces. In a London street, or in a crowded barracks, you would never notice any of them.

He gripped the stained screen and took a deep breath. But out here, they were special. They did not deserve to be let down, by him or anyone.

Seymour was fixing up the ready-use chart table, his lower lip jutting as he tried to find a pencil which had not been broken during the short, fierce battle.

Devane let the returning confidence explore his body and mind like a warm drug.

He said, 'Come up here, David. Tell me about this book you're writing after the war.'

Seymour waved his hand across the screen as if to embrace the flotilla as the other MTBs took shape in the dull light.

'Well, all this, sir. It's important. It should be written about.' He almost blushed. 'One day, I mean.'

Devane nodded. *Parthian* was returning to its concrete lair. The flotilla had fought for the first time together and had won. In a matter of hours Whitcombe would know what they had achieved. So, for that matter, would Berlin.

He thought of Kinross's severe features, and what he called his crews. 'The Glory Boys'.

They had come through. Next time it might not be so easy.

Lieutenant-Commander Ralph Beresford, Royal Navy, son of an admiral, and grandson of another, leant back in a canvas chair and surveyed the flotilla's commanding officers with quiet amusement. If he had been worried that *Parthian*'s first sortie would go wrong, or that the new area of operations might affect the MTBs' young captains in some way, he did not show it.

He looked at Devane and smiled. 'I still prefer the Med, but you can't have everything.'

The flotilla's return had been managed without incident. Russian aircraft and two escorts had covered their final approach to the base at Tuapse and, although an enemy raid had since developed, it did not seem to be a part of their world, or their concern.

Even Hector Buckhurst had shown some warmth at their safe return, or maybe that only two torpedoes had been discharged. His team of mechanics, artificers and shipwrights had got to work immediately, and now the armourers were waiting to replace magazines and ammunition belts as soon as they could get aboard.

Damage had been minimal. In the Channel or the Mediterranean it would hardly have warranted a report. Only one seaman had been injured, and that was when he had fallen down a ladder and cut his head open.

Now, in the hazy, drowsy atmosphere, the pipes and cigarettes were lit, and these professionals, who had once been welcomed to active service as the Navy's amateurs, were going over the operation, searching for flaws which might have been prevented. There had been a few of the usual stoppages on the machine-guns, and one boat's power-operated six-pounder had jammed at the vital moment because some idiot had dropped a wrench into it. Otherwise. . . .

Devane listened to the muted drone of a drill from the small dock, and wondered how the Russians had made out. Orel had lost two vessels, and had suffered casualties. Devane had tried to telephone Sorokin's HQ to break the ice, but had received only a polite acknowledgement from some junior aide.

Beresford was saying, 'I think that a few more hit and runs on the enemy's coastal supply lines will change things completely. We could use a few extra boats though.'

The other officers glanced at one another, each seeing an empty chair perhaps. Any or all of them might have stayed back there in the smoke and blazing fuel.

Willy Walker, disdainful and reserved, his long legs outstretched, sipped a mug of coffee, a yellow scarf still hanging from his neck. He always wore it in combat. God knows when it had started, Devane thought.

There had been that pub in Felixstowe where several of the MTB officers had met in the early days. For some reason the landlord had had a supply of long clay pipes, churchwardens, which he had handed to the youthful officers like talismans. After a bad operation in the Channel or off the Hook of Holland they would all gather and solemnly break the pipe of any of their number who had 'bought it'. The landlord had eventually run out of pipes. Which was just as well, Devane thought, otherwise the pub would be full of broken ones by now.

Lieutenant Sydney Horne, a RNR officer like Dundas, who commanded the boat with the code name *Buzzard,* had been a fisherman before the war, running his own drifter with that of his father. He had quit the life and joined the Navy when he had seen his father's little boat shot to matchwood by a German fighter. He was a broad, outwardly comfortable character, who was good with his men and liked by them in return. But beneath it all, Devane suspected, there was a sense of bewilderment. Hate had brought Horne into active service, the need to hit back and get revenge at the same time. But unlike many of his more youthful companions, he was still a real sailor at heart, and had found it harder than he had expected to destroy ships and leave their hands to drown or burn.

Andrew Twiss, commanding officer of the fourth boat, code name *Osprey*, was a real oddity. He had been an actor, although nobody had ever discovered what kind of theatre he had graced before the war. Even he had admitted in his resonant tones, 'It was often a case of sardines and stale beer for most of the week!' But whatever success he had found or lost, he had certainly discovered it in the Navy. Maybe it was what he had always wanted to do, but Devane suspected he was really acting the part of his life. For Twiss was not just a young, hostilities-only lieutenant, he *was* the *British Naval Officer*. Always smartly turned out, which was almost a crime in coastal forces where battledress and old uniforms prevailed, he stood, moved and spoke like a ghost frum Jutland.

Whenever they had pulled his leg about it, he had turned a haughty eye on them before claiming, 'If we win this war, and with the companions I am doomed to serve alongside it seems unlikely, but *if*, gentlemen, there will be a far greater call for admirals in the acting profession than in the Navy. And I shall be there!'

But Devane knew Mackay the best. All of his company were fellow Canadians, and had been transferred from the same Mediterranean flotilla into *Parthian*.

He was one of the warmest, and sometimes one of the most alarming, friends Devane had made. In battle, at close quarters or fanning across a heavily defended convoy with all hell breaking loose, he was like a rock. You never had to look astern to make sure he was covering your flank, he was sure to be there. When they got back from each sortie, his loud voice and grating laugh were equally forceful.

Mackay's first command had been sunk off Tobruk after being hit by a Stuka dive-bomber. It happened, they said. A moment of carelessness, a time when the worst was just over and all you could think of was getting home to base, to sleep or drink it off until the next time.

Devane had detached his own boat from a patrol area nearby and had gone to search for Red Mackay and any survivors. With fuel running dangerously low and an enemy-occupied coastline rising in the dawn light like a warning, Devane had found them. Six exhausted figures, squatting or clinging to a drifting life-raft, more like corpses than survivors.

Mackay had been one of them, but when the MTB had manoeuvred carefully against the little raft, and some of Devane's men had clambered down the scrambling nets to help them aboard, Mackay had called, 'Not yet, John!'

Devane found he was clutching his coffee mug with terrible force. It was so clear. As if it had just happened. The weary, fumbling figures being lifted and guided on to the MTB's deck, too sick and dazed to say anything, when a glance was all they could offer in the way of thanks, and Mackay just sitting there on the raft, a seaman, no more than a boy, dying slowly across his lap.

It had probably lasted minutes, but to the onlookers it had felt like hours, like watching yourself.

When it was over, Mackay had climbed aboard, refusing helping hands, saying nothing until he had joined Devane on the bridge.

Then he had said bitterly, 'His first trip with me.'

It had been over a month before Devane had learned from someone else that the boy who had died in Mackay's arms had been his kid brother from Vancouver.

Mackay was that sort of man.

Devane came out of his thoughts as Beresford said, 'I should tell you that I received a signal from the Admiralty about an hour before your return.'

They all looked at him. A recall? Another assignment? A rise in the price of wardroom gin? With the Admiralty you could never be certain.

Beresford continued, 'It would appear that our stay in the Black Sea may have to be prolonged.' There were several groans but he ignored them. 'Our Chiefs of Staff have been in constant contact with the Russians, and it seems likely that the proposed assault on the Crimea will be delayed until the beginning of winter.'

Walker exclaimed, 'But surely, sir, that will be *after* any Allied landings in southern Europe. I thought the whole point of the Russians attacking when we did was to confuse and divide the German defences? Now, Jerry will be able to take on one side at a time! Bloody stupid, if you ask me.'

Beresford smiled dangerously. 'I was not intending to, Willy!'

Devane said, 'The Russians must think that an assault on the Crimea in the colder weather will give them an advantage?'

Beresford nodded. 'Something like that. But if Ivan makes a cock of this one, and the Germans are still there next spring, you can cross your fingers for a Normandy invasion, or anywhere else for that matter.'

Devane thought about it. He could picture *Parthian*'s role expanding and becoming more involved as the weeks changed into months. The Russians would throw in everything to drive the enemy from the Crimea. It was not just a strategic necessity for the whole Eastern Front, it was a matter of honour, or would soon become one.

Beresford looked at him. 'I've got a report in depth for you, John, but the rest of you may as well know, their lordships are not too happy about the differences in seniority here.' He kept his face expressionless as they chuckled unfeelingly. 'This operation will be taken over by a senior commander, with the necessary administrative and maintenance staff to support him.'

Mackay frowned. 'Empire building! Just as well we weren't all wiped out the other night, the poor devil would have had nothing to command!'

Beresford stood up. 'That's all, gentlemen. Get what rest you can, and report readiness for sea to your SO.' He beckoned Devane to his side. 'I agree with Mackay.' He lowered his voice. 'We're getting a Commander Eustace Barker, by the way. They obviously don't consider I'm senior enough to stand up to Sorokin. Barker will be just right. Not too lowly to invite bullying, nor high enough to excite accusations that we are trying to control this area or any part of it.'

Devane shook his head wearily. 'Where are we going now?'

Beresford gestured to a Russian seaman. 'We are going to see Sorokin. Remember what I told you.' He glanced at him searchingly. 'You all right?'

Devane shrugged. 'Tired. Getting past it.'

Beresford grinned. 'At twenty-seven? Yes, I suppose most of your lads think you're over the hill by now!'

They found Sorokin behind a massive desk, a cheroot jutting from his mouth, one hand signing a procession of papers which were laid down and removed by a lieutenant and then passed to another officer who was arranging them in a dispatch case.

Sorokin glanced up. 'Be seated.' He looked at Devane and nodded slowly. 'Next, we drink.'

Devane opened his mouth to excuse himself but recalled

Beresford's warning. Sorokin did not make requests, he gave orders.

Eventually Sorokin sat back in the chair and scratched his ample stomach for several seconds. Then he came straight to the point.

'Excuse my language, comrades, but I have too much haste for grammar.' He looked at Devane, his eyes dull. 'My flotilla commander, Orel, told me what you did. That you did not obey his orders.' He held up one massive hand as Beresford made to speak. 'That with your superior speed and weapons you were able to destroy some of the enemy.' He interlaced his thick fingers and added softly, 'Is that correct?'

Devane replied, 'I acted as I saw fit, sir.'

Sorokin glanced at Beresford. *'Fit?'*

There was a brief exchange in Russian and then Sorokin continued, 'Orel lost many comrades. Fifty-one to be perfect.' He gave a great sigh, the sound moving up through him like an echo in a cavern. Then he opened a desk drawer and took out a bottle of vodka. As an aide appeared with some glasses he added, 'Fifty-one, you are thinking, Commander Devane? *Not bloody many* for a country like ours?' He said it as a joke but his words came out incredibly sad. 'It is a great country, but we cannot afford to waste our blood. Orel has courage, but he lacks knowledge of this manner of warfare. On land Russia is invincible.' He spoke each word carefully, so that every syllable seemed filled with emphasis. 'For every soldier killed by the Nazi dogs, two fill his place. We will go on until our land is rid of them. For ever.' He poured three large measures of vodka. 'Now we drink a toast to you, Commander Devane, and your men.' He held up his glass, like a thimble in his great fist. 'And to the *knowledge* we need so badly!'

The vodka thrust through Devane like a hot bayonet.

Devane glanced at Beresford and was surprised to see the concern on his face. He began to see Sorokin's position quite differently. Sorokin was an officer of great experience and reputation. He was big enough to ignore the pitfalls of jealousy and pride, of conflicting beliefs and politics, for one purpose only. To save his country and free it from the invaders.

But by taking such a stand on a short acquaintanceship he had shown his hand. Devane was moved by it, especially as he could guess what it would cost Sorokin if his faith and backing were condemned as misplaced by those more senior.

He could feel Sorokin's eyes boring into him, even as he poured another three glasses of vodka.

Devane said quietly, 'I was thinking, sir.' He ignored Beresford's warning glance. 'It is only an idea, of course.'

Sorokin drummed on the table. 'I wait.'

'In the past, your flotillas have attacked the enemy's coastal convoys, or their longer routes from Rumania and Bulgaria.'

'True.' Sorokin seemed unwilling to interrupt Devane's train of thought.

'I think we should attack the E-boat base, sir.' He held his breath, wondering what had made him say it. Why he had deliberately offered his command like a sacrifice.

Sorokin stared at him. 'On the Crimea? Do you understand what you say?'

Devane found he was on his feet. 'Yes. But it has to be soon. Before the enemy guesses what we are doing here.'

Sorokin looked doubtful, his earlier warmth gone. '*Your* flotilla, *da*?'

'Well, sir, not exactly. I thought that a combined attack. . . .'

Sorokin smiled very slowly. It was like a sunrise.

'Together.'

'Yes, sir.'

Sorokin looked at Beresford's masklike features. 'You have given me a tiger, *da*? Then will it be.' He lurched to his feet. 'Leave now. I must think.'

As they left the room Devane saw the Russian's huge shadow swaying across the wall maps like his own prophesy.

Before they reached the concrete dock Devane said, 'Look, I'm sorry about that, Ralph. I'm not supposed to make suggestions. I didn't mean to interfere with your sphere of operations, especially with the new commander about to descend.'

They stopped and looked at each other. Then Beresford said, 'It's your neck, so why shouldn't you decide how to break it?' He clapped Devane's shoulder. 'Actually, it's not a bad idea when you think about it.'

His eyes gleamed, and for those seconds Devane saw him in another sea at another time. All the old dare-devil enthusiasm was still there.

'Yes.' Beresford threw up a salute to a Russian sentry. 'It

73

might bloody well come off, as Sorokin would put it!' He walked away.

Devane crossed to the edge of the concrete jetty and looked down at the boat alongside, his own. Some new paint, the bright scars on the six-pounder's shield already repaired. Buckhurst's team had worked miracles.

He saw Buckhurst giving a lecture to two ratings beside a torpedo trestle. 'A chock under the joint of the balance chamber *and* its engine room, got it?'

He turned and saw Devane. 'God, you'd think these tin fish cost nothing the way they chuck 'em about!'

He added as an afterthought, 'Some of your lads, sir. They asked if they could paint up a "kill" on the bridge. You did well, to all accounts.'

Devane looked past him at the five resting hulls, rocking gently in the dock's oily water.

Parthian had arrived, but its future now seemed less certain than ever.

'Why not, Chief? Start as we mean to go on.'

6

THE SIGNAL

Beresford leant against one of the MTB's bunks and was careful to keep out of Devane's way as he groped for his uniform and his leather seaboots.

Devane said, 'It's only four in the morning, for God's sake! Couldn't it wait?'

Perhaps the flotilla had been resting in its bomb-proof dock for too long, but Devane had been sleeping much better, so that the hand on his shoulder, his inability to grasp where he was, had made him confused and unreasonably angry.

Beresford smiled. 'No, it can't.'

He glanced round the tiny wardroom, at Dundas's inert shape on another bunk, oblivious to the drama and everything else.

"We'll have to get you fixed up with a billet ashore, John. Hector Buckhurst's mechanics have got quarters now, so it's time *you* had a break, as one of our *senior* officers in Russia!'

Devane sat down on a bunk and tugged at his boots. Beresford was wide awake and maddeningly indifferent to the way he felt. It had been getting like that for days. Ever since they had returned from their first operation and had been told about Commander Barker's unexpected appointment. Kicking their heels, doing drills to fill the hours, but building up boredom and resentment.

He stood up again and said abruptly, 'I'm ready. They'll have to see me without a bloody shave!'

They climbed up the darkened deck, past armed sentries, both British and Russian, and into another of the concrete corridors which linked Sorokin's command like underground tentacles.

It was chill and dank, and as they passed an iron grill Devane heard the rumble of gunfire, unending, like thunder across hills before a storm. That had been going on for days too. Another offensive, hundreds of tanks, thousands of men. Artillery duels by day and night, fighters leaving their telltale trails in the sky, broken repeatedly as a ball of fire fell to earth, and sometimes a drifting parachute.

Beresford said unhelpfully, 'Sorokin's been here for hours.' He shot Devane a searching glance. 'Commander Orel too. So watch your temper, my lad!'

The command bunker was in black shadow, with only a central map table and a few stooped figures around it brightly lit by an overhead cluster.

Sorokin was smoking as usual, one hand on his thick hip like a tanned spade.

Orel was speaking, but fell silent as the two British officers stepped into the glare.

Sorokin nodded. 'Have some coffee.' He peered at the shadows and a small man in a white jacket emerged with a tray and a pot of steaming coffee.

Devane felt his tiredness moving away as certain facts stood out. The coffee helped too. Piping hot and strong.

He noticed that Orel's leather coat was stained with salt, that he was unshaven, with dark rings around his eyes. He looked desperately tired, and yet he was excited, more so than he could conceal, although he was doing his best, Devane decided.

Sorokin looked at Beresford and gave a curt nod. He was weary too, his tunic open to his waist, and there were sweat stains on his shirt.

Beresford said evenly, 'You remember the four E-boats which you engaged, John? Well, two were sunk, and another was badly holed and has been towed round to Sevastopol. Air reconnaissance have been working on it, but it's not known how badly she's been damaged, or if she can be put to rights. They think it's a full dockyard job.'

Devane felt a prick of disappointment. He had stated as much in his report.

Beresford continued, 'But word has just come in that the fourth E-boat was also damaged, did you realize that?'

Devane recalled the zigzagging shapes in the smoke, the crackle of exploding ammunition, and the sheet of fire as one E-boat had been blown apart by his depth charges.

He replied, 'Andy Twiss said he *thought* he had hit the fourth one. But it made off so fast he was not certain.'

Commander Orel moved closer to the map table. With the lights directly above him he looked even more lined and exhausted. He had glossy black hair and a thin, aquiline nose. Like Dundas, a face from another century.

He kept his eyes on Devane as he slid an aerial photograph across the map until he could see it.

Beresford said, 'Russian Intelligence believes that the fourth boat is slipped for repairs. Just enough for her to return to her proper base.' His finger touched the photograph. 'See? Compare it with a previous picture. It must be camouflage netting. It wasn't there two weeks ago when the last recce was carried out.'

Devane leaned over the chart and took a large magnifying glass from the table. He could feel the others watching him, but like the surrounding shadows they did not seem to interfere.

Beresford added helpfully, 'It's a very small island. There are some German troops there and an RDF station. But nothing to excite attention. Until now.' He was trying to contain his impatience. 'Well, what d'you think?'

Devane studied the picture carefully. About the right size. And the fact that the fourth E-boat had not been sighted anywhere else made it possible. He straightened his back and found himself looking into Orel's impassive stare.

If it was the missing E-boat but she was damaged beyond repair it would be risking lives for nothing. But if not, and they could somehow seize her before she could put to sea, all kinds of possibilities would be presented.

He said, 'I'd not risk another air reconnaissance.' He peered at the big map and tried to relate the crude photograph to reality. 'It might make them suspicious. Jumpy.'

Sorokin said something to Orel and after a moment's hesitation murmured, 'Your idea of an attack on the German

77

base, Commander. Would it not be much easier if we could provide a. . . .' He frowned as he searched his mind and then added, 'A Trojan horse, yes?'

Beresford asked, 'What do you think, John? It'll be your pigeon. If you say it's no go, then that's it.'

Devane remembered what Whitcombe had said, how he had described *Parthian*. An independent command. Beresford had made that even clearer.

Then he glanced at Orel and could feel the man's anxiety like a consuming force. His patrols must have begun this search immediately after the battle. No wonder he looked dead beat.

Devane asked, 'What sort of place is it?'

Beresford said, 'Commander Orel has described it as small and easy to defend. It is part of the minefield complex, but the Germans have laid the field so as not to inconvenience their own minor war vessels. So an MTB should be safe enough.' He was thinking aloud. Seeing it happen. 'Captain Sorokin has suggested that a raiding party should be landed by submarine to knock out the RDF station. You could move in as soon as the attack gets going. That is, if you feel it's genuine.'

Devane rubbed his chin and remembered he had not shaved. 'We would need a diversion of some kind. Thirty miles from the mainland, and a long haul home for us. It will have to be good.'

Voices buzzed around the table like trapped bees. Even Devane's carefully measured tone had not hidden his true feelings.

Sorokin leaned on his hands and stared at him, his cheroot jutting like a black cannon.

'The admiral has promised support. An attack on the Kerch Straits from Azov. The Germans will think we are trying to force a landing on the Crimea.'

Sorokin turned slightly, his broad forehead creased with irritation, as Orel whispered across his shoulder.

Then he said, 'My Commander Orel insists he is capable of leading the attack.'

Once again Devane and Orel looked at one another, like fighters seeking an opening for that first blow.

And I would feel exactly the same in his shoes.

Devane said quietly, 'Of that I am certain, sir. But, if this is the E-boat we think it is, could he take command?' He saw his words being fed into Orel's mind and added simply, 'Any more than I could control one of your submarines?'

Sorokin nodded heavily. 'That is good sense.' He hugged Orel's narrow shoulders.

Orel shrugged, his features still giving nothing away.

Beresford remarked, 'It could be costly.'

Devane hardly heard him. No wonder he had never wanted to return to general service, even to destroyers, which compared with MTBs were still 'big ships'.

No recognizable chain of command here, no dockets to be signed, no frustrating delays while some tired old men at the Admiralty debated on the value and the outcome of their schemes. In his sort of war you were trusted to make decisions and live by them. Or, if you were wrong, you were expected to die with equal independence.

He said, 'I think it's worth a damn good try. To capture one of their new E-boats, no matter what use we make of her, would be a real bloody nose for Jerry.' He nodded, and wondered suddenly if there had ever been any choice. 'Yes. We should do it without delay.'

Sorokin wiped his face with his hand. He seemed to be sweating badly.

'Two more days.' His fingers bunched into a great fist and he slammed it down on the photograph. 'Then we go!'

It was past dawn when Beresford and Devane returned to the concealed dock. All five boats were alive with busy figures, the swish of mops and the muted purr of generators.

They stood together and looked at the MTBs. The hornets' nest.

Devane said, 'I hate this place. I need to get out. To find sea-room.' He spread his arms and yawned deeply. 'What would you have said if I'd told Sorokin I wouldn't do it?' He turned and looked at his companion.

Beresford smiled ruefully. 'I'd never have got you out of bed if I'd have believed it.' He turned to go. 'But you knew *that*, of course.'

Devane climbed down the ladder and reached out for the MTB's deck with his boot. In some ways, despite their wide differences of background, he and Beresford were very much alike, he thought. Each had learned to create a problem out of garbled facts and a lot of rumour and had then forced himself to solve it.

That was why they were different from people in other jobs. What Claudia had been wanting to pry out of him the night the bomb had driven them together.

You went on and on until one day the problem had no solution, and the realization split you wide open. What would Richie have said to the Russians, he wondered?

Dundas greeted him beside the bridge. 'Flap on, sir?'

Devane smiled. 'Nothing we can't handle, Number One.' He saw Dundas relax. It was that easy. 'Now, what about some breakfast?'

Parthian's officers sat or stood around the table in the flotilla's newly acquired office and listened in silence while Beresford explained the mission in detail.

Devane listened too, although he had gone over it more times than he could remember, had studied charts and aerial photographs, examined pictures and silhouettes of German warships in the Black Sea until it had filled his brain to bursting point.

He glanced around the concrete office. Even it had changed in the short time they had been here. Now, with duty-boards and garish pin-ups, a half-burnt German ensign which some nimble sailor had managed to hook from the sea during the battle, it could have been in any theatre of war.

It depressed him to realize that already they were taking root, when at first it had seemed to be a quick, one-off operation. But like all sailors they were settling in, making it like home. Wherever that was.

Beresford straightened his back and looked at their intent faces. The thoughtful, experienced expressions of veterans like Mackay and Walker. The unconcealed excitement of Sub-Lieutenant Simon Mitford, who as third hand in Lieutenant Horne's boat was the youngest and newest officer present.

He said, 'The Russian naval forces are making two strikes, one near the Kerch Straits, and later another towards Balaklava. A lot will depend on German reactions, and what forces they move in against these strikes. Admiral Kasatonov is keen to cooperate, but he'll not want to pay a heavy price.'

Beresford looked at Devane. 'It will be much like an Adriatic operation. Move in fast, and pull out before it gets too hot.'

They shuffled their feet and spoke amongst themselves, each commanding officer seeing it differently, how it would affect his boat, the problems of attacking without fighting every inch of the way. The others considered their separate parts and how they would pass the final briefing to their crews.

In their protective clothing and worn sea-going gear they looked more like renegades than naval officers, Devane thought. Except for Twiss, of course, who was as impeccable as ever.

Beresford took their silence as general acceptance. He said, 'I'll get the last details and met reports from Sorokin's HQ before you move.'

He smiled at Devane. 'All yours.'

Devane stood up. 'I'll try not to flannel you. This could be a tough one. The island is no problem but, with two hundred miles there and back, we can expect trouble. To some of you this may seem an unworthy risk, but it is the kind of thing we are here to do. Keep probing and jabbing at the enemy's supply lines and coastal defences, never give him time to rest or increase them. The final battle is a military one, it has to be. But as they call us the Navy's infantry, we must play our part beforehand.'

He thought suddenly of London, the red buses near the park. The air of shabby defiance, matched by a confidence that everything would be all right if they held on long enough.

This was a different fight. Where vast armies had surged back and forth and had destroyed every living thing in their way.

Whichever way you looked at it, there seemed to be no end to it. How many who had led at the beginning were still alive? He felt a sudden despair as he recalled the night he had spent with Claudia. They had been so alike, if only for that one moment. They had been overtaken by war and their lives would never be the same again. Whenever he tried to see beyond the year he could find nothing. Just another operation, more risks and less odds in his favour each time.

He cleared his throat, cursing himself for his self-pity. To them he was the leader of the flotilla, the code name *Merlin* on the R/T, the man who would use his cunning to get them out of trouble.

He said, 'We shall put to sea at dusk. Rendezvous with Russian escorts at midnight.'

Mackay stood up, his unlit pipe in his mouth. 'Are the Ruskies coming along with us, sir?'

'A raiding party. Twenty men to be carried in your boat.' He silenced the groans. 'And another twenty in mine. So tell your people to behave. Jack's sense of humour takes a bit of understanding even *in* the Navy, right?'

They began to leave, folding their notebooks and details of the raid. There was not one of them who looked apprehensive about it. It was just another job. *You shouldn't have joined if you can't take a joke*.

Devane glanced at Beresford. 'When you mentioned Balaklava just now, I thought. . . .'

Beresford stared at the chart. 'Yes. Our people have died there already.'

Dundas slid into the MTB's bridge. 'Communications tested, sir. Ready to proceed.'

Devane adjusted an old towel around his neck beneath the collar of his waterproof suit. Nearby, the other boats rocked and murmured as they prepared to leave the confines of the dock with a minimum of delay. To remain under the twenty feet of solid concrete with the Packard motors spewing out their high-octane fumes was like starting up a big car in a sealed garage.

'Plenty of cloud tonight.' Devane stiffened, remembering what the petty officer had said that evening at the doorway before he had gone to see Claudia. *Stop it right now*. 'It'll be good to get some air in our lungs.'

Seymour was on the forecastle talking with some seamen and waiting to cast off from the jetty. Down in his engine room, Petty Officer Tim Ackland, one-time mechanic and manager of a garage on the Great North Road, watched the gauges and listened to his team tinkering with the resting machinery which within minutes would be doing its best to deafen him with its roar.

Lounging against the wheel, the coxswain, Petty Officer Pellegrine, tapped the compass with his finger and thought about his wife in Gosport. She had been so much nicer to him on that last leave. Usually she was placid, even dull, which was the way he liked her. She had seemed brighter, and he felt uneasy.

Maybe she was having it off with some barrack stanchion, or the local grocer, who seemed to be able to keep her well supplied, whatever the shortages were supposed to be. He would have to get to the bottom of it.

He came out of his brooding as a duffel-coated figure groped over the gratings to place freshly sharpened pencils in the little slot where the OOW could find them. It was Metcalf, the bane of the coxswain's life.

'Come on, lad, jump about! You're supposed to be aft with Leading Seaman Hanlon!'

Metcalf mumbled something and then vanished over the rear of the bridge. In the gloom, with his pale features framed in the upturned hood of his coat, he looked like a furtive monk.

Metcalf paused on the short ladder and watched Dundas talking with the commanding officer.

He felt the tears pricking the corners of his eyes as he relived the humiliation and shame of being turned down for commission. He should be on the bridge as they were, talking like human beings, no matter what risks they were all about to share. They never had to endure the other part like he did. The constant blaspheming, the filthy stories which were passed around the mess deck and retold with relish, even though most of the men knew them by heart.

Metcalf hated the crudity, the limited words and the sudden violence which could erupt in a split second over something trivial like a run ashore or an unfair measure of rum.

He came from a good home, and had been at public school when the war had changed his life. All of his friends were officers, some were already quite distinguished in one or other of the services. It was so damned unfair.

Metcalf was in coastal forces with the firm belief that in a small craft like an MTB he would discover another chance, show beyond doubt that his reversal was only temporary.

Leading Seaman Hanlon, a tough young man from the Liverpool docks, greeted him with, 'Wot's up with you, wack? Lost yer bleeding ma or summat?'

Metcalf ignored him and took his place with the other vague shapes by the guardrails. He almost welcomed Hanlon's constant goading. It acted as a spur as well as a scourge. It was the occasional act of rough kindness he mistrusted. He would show all of them soon.

At the opposite end of the boat, his gauntleted fists hanging by his sides as if resting, was Leading Seaman Ted Priest. He was twenty-two years old and came from Manchester. He knew MTBs like the back of his hand, and prided himself that apart from machinery he could do just about everything it took to keep one in fighting trim.

He had twice lost the hook from his sleeve because of trouble ashore of one kind or another. Brawls and women were meat and drink to him, as they had been since his father had knocked him half stupid when he had found him with a girl in the backyard at home. She had been sixteen, he had been about thirteen, as far as he could remember.

They often said that coastal forces took all the hard cases, the ones which had been rejected by other branches of the Navy, or had failed to find their rightful places. Priest was certainly a hard case, but in a MTB he was happy and knew he was good at his job.

He was listening to the young two-ringer, Seymour, going on again about the book he was going to write one day. It had already become a bit of a joke on the mess deck. The lads called Seymour 'Charlie Dickens' behind his back, although none of them had read him either.

But he wasn't a bad bloke for an officer, Priest decided. Just so long as he didn't try to be too popular with the blokes. It never worked. A pig was always safer to be with than a pansy, was Priest's philosophy.

David Seymour, oblivious to Priest's patient boredom, said, 'We're probably the first naval people to visit where we're going!'

Priest chuckled. 'I can manage without it.' Seymour made it sound like a pleasure cruise. 'Give me Alex every time. Straight to the fleet canteen, a few jars with your mates, and then up the backstairs for a bit o' black velvet!'

Seymour hid a smile. Priest was always trying to shock him, and he knew he should shut him up. But the tough leading hand with the lively tongue and a readiness to use his fists at the slightest provocation would make excellent material, *one day*.

Standing on the gratings behind the screen, Devane heard Seymour laugh and felt easier because of it. With so much on his mind he often forgot what others might be thinking and feeling.

Carroll whispered, 'Looks like Lieutenant-Commander Beresford coming aboard, sir.'

Devane nodded. 'Thanks, Bunts.' He moved to the ladder and wondered what was bringing Beresford here.

He did not have long to wait.

Beresford sat in the wardroom, stale now with its deadlights screwed shut and the air heady with fuel.

'You'll have to stand down, John. I've just had a signal.'

Devane stared at him. There was one thing he hated more than a dicey operation and that was having it cancelled at the last second when he had geared himself for it.

'Why?'

Beresford spread his hands. 'Our new commander is arriving tomorrow. Operations are suspended until further orders.'

'That's bloody ridiculous!' Devane saw the sudden start of surprise in Beresford's eyes. 'We're doing what we came for. That signal makes us sound like the Home Fleet!'

Beresford shrugged. 'Commander Barker is highly thought of, I'm told. Combined Ops, commando planning and that kind of thing, although I've never actually met him.'

Devane barely heard. 'You know what the Russians will say, don't you? That we dreamt up this raid in the first place and then dropped them right in it once the plan was fixed.' He nodded, satisfied. 'I can see you overlooked that.'

Beresford snapped, 'What I think is hardly the bloody point, is it? I had a signal, and I've told you what it says.' He stood up and added, 'I forgot, I'm more used to obeying orders than you.'

Devane smiled in spite of his anger. 'What's the time of origin?'

'It came in here twenty minutes ago. I still don't see. . . .'

Devane shouted up to the hatch, 'Number One! See Commander Beresford over the side, will you?'

Beresford exclaimed, 'You mad bastard! You're going anyway!'

Devane was halfway up the ladder. 'You were too late to warn me. We'll be out of here like a dose of salts!'

Moments later, as he stood beside Buckhurst, the engineer officer, and watched the boats swinging round from the moorings to churn the dock into a cauldron of waves and smoke, Beresford yelled, 'Crazy idiot! Too late with the *signal* indeed!'

But Buckhurst had his hands pressed over his ears as the

concrete cavern quivered in the din of racing engines and did not hear him.

Beresford watched the last of the five boats until she had vanished into the outer darkness of the dockyard and said resignedly, 'Not that it would have made any difference. Not to him.'

Devane levelled his glasses over the screen and watched the endless ranks of choppy whitecaps. The wind had risen quite suddenly from the west and the cloud had thinned considerably. He moved the glasses very slowly, from the blurred purple horizon to the raked bow of the MTB which was steaming parallel some half-cable abeam. Mackay's boat, with Horne and Twiss following astern on an invisible thread.

Devane stepped from the gratings and moved to the after part of the bridge. It was mid-afternoon, the first full day at sea. He saw the Russian assault troops muffled to the eyebrows in their padded uniforms and hung about with the tools of their trade—grenades, machine-pistols, mortars. In spite of the crowded conditions in the boat, they still managed to remain entirely deparate from the sailors.

They showed little interest in what was happening. Perhaps they were saving their energy for the raid.

Devane saw Dundas gripping the guardrail as the boat dipped and plunged through the short, steep waves. Like the North Sea. Dundas was with the Russian officer, Commander Orel, and his interpreter, the same reedy-voiced lieutenant who had welcomed him to Tuapse.

There was nothing reserved about Orel. The sea was his element, and he had spent hours creeping through the hull, had fired question after question at Dundas until his interpreter had all but dried up.

Seymour was standing by the ready-use chart table, his glasses scanning the opposite beam as the boats loped across the choppy water at an economical eighteen knots.

Throughout the day they had sighted nothing. It was as if they had the sea to themselves. Sorokin's patrols had done their work well and, no matter what was happening closer to the land, the five MTBs were left to their own devices.

Devane glanced at his watch. It would be time for another alteration of course soon. One more leg to take the boats round to the north towards the small island where it was hoped the damaged E-boat was still in hiding.

Capture her or destroy her. Each MTB skipper knew his part, but when it came down to the actual moment it could rest on a few seconds understanding, a swift interpretation of the facts which could alter everything.

Dundas followed Orel into the bridge and said, 'Tour completed, sir.'

Orel banged his hands together and moved around the small bridge like a caged animal.

The interpreter said, 'How long to *wait*, please?'

Devane looked at Orel, searching for a break in his rigid defences.

'About five hours. Your people will begin their attack at exactly 1700.'

He listened to the lieutenant's careful translation and saw Orel nod, apparently satisfied.

Seymour asked, 'Permission to test guns, sir?'

'Yes. Last chance. Any nearer to the enemy's patrol areas and we'd be inviting trouble.'

As the order was relayed to the gun positions, each one responded with a quick spurt of tracer, the stabbing flashes tearing across the dull sea like spears.

The others followed their leader's example. It would be too late when the raid began, and Devane had known boats to go into action only to discover that every gun was jammed. Vibration, sea air and careless maintenance had no respect for machinery.

Another Russian had come up to the bridge, a stocky, square-jawed captain of infantry who seemed to be enjoying the unusual experience more than his men.

He and Orel repeatedly examined their maps, and Devane had already noticed that they compared them with the chart on the table. They certainly did not take anything for granted.

'Aircraft! Bearing green four-five! Angle of sight two-oh!'

Binoculars and gun muzzles swivelled on to the bearing, and Devane held his breath as a small, lazy shape moved across the lenses and into a thin layer of cloud.

Orel gave a short laugh, and the interpreter said, 'Russian.'

'Disregard. Carry on the sweep.' Devane looked at Orel and smiled. 'Good.'

Orel shrugged and thrust his hands into his leather coat.

'Take over, Number One.' Devane walked to the ladder. 'I'm going below for a few moments.'

All at once he needed to get away from the frail atmosphere, the delicate balance between cooperation and downright hostility. In the deserted wardroom he sat with his back wedged against the vibrating bulkhead and listened to the swish of water past the hull. He went over it again, detail by detail. Plan of approach, observation, method, conclusion, *attack*. Just like the bloody tactical school.

He let out his breath slowly. It was really getting him down. Defeating his carefully constructed calm. What had the war done to him? He was like the cat on the wrong side of every door. Ashore, he was always frightened they were going to give him a job on the base or install him as an instructor at one of those training depots. And at sea, he could only think of getting over the operation, putting it behind him with all the others.

Devane stared at the locked cabinet below the pistol rack. He could almost picture the bottles inside. That would really give this Commander Barker something to complain about. The senior officer of *Parthian* arriving to do battle in a state of drunken stupor.

The voicepipe shrilled and Devane snapped, 'Yes?'

It was Dundas. 'Time to alter course.' There was a pause. 'Everything all right, sir?'

"I'll come up.' Devane sighed. 'Yes, everything's fine. And thanks.'

On the bridge Dundas snapped down the voicepipe cover and climbed up beside the wheel. What did Devane mean, he wondered? Thanks for what?

He heard Devane behind him, the shuffling feet as the Russians and the watchkeepers moved round in a crowded dance to let him through.

When he glanced at Devane, Dundas saw nothing to concern him. He looked calm and unruffled.

Over his shoulder Devane called to the interpreter, 'Tell them to stop worrying, will you? It's a piece of cake.' He grinned at Dundas. 'Let's see what he makes of *that*.'

Seymour, who had nothing to do until the flotilla went to action stations, watched each man on the bridge and tried to memorize every detail. It was something he had been teaching himself since he had first taken up journalism for a local newspaper. He wondered what they would say if they could see him now. The boat pounding across the water, dull pewter now in the dying sunlight, the men at their stations watching the sea and the sky, searching for the first hint of an enemy.

And the commanding officer, one of the Navy's real-life heroes, within feet of where he was standing. So confident, able to make a joke when everyone else must be tensed up like a coiled spring. Seymour's glance fell on Devane's hand, and he saw that it was gripped so tightly around a voicepipe that the knuckles were white against the tanned skin, as if it was taking all his strength to hold him there.

Seymour looked away, confused and troubled. It was like stumbling on a friend's secret, finding that all you believed was false.

Devane said, 'Starboard twenty, Swain. Steer north by west.'

Carroll's lamp clacked in time with his words, bringing the twin lines of MTBs round together on to the new course.

They were committed. From this moment it was all a matter of timing and faultless execution. Right now, as some of Sorokin's ships were bombarding enemy positions along the Crimea, and the fighter-bombers played havoc with ground positions, a submarine would be surfacing to put the first raiding party on the island. It was a backwater as far as the Black Sea battleground was concerned, but in a few hours' time it would become a small part of history.

Devane dragged his hand from the voicepipe and massaged his fingers.

Don Richie should be standing here, not me.

He saw Seymour watching him and made another effort. *It will soon be over.*

'Action stations, Number One. Go round yourself. Keep them on top line.'

Seymour relaxed as the alarm jangled through the boat. He was almost thankful. It was not good to steal another's secret.

7

ATTACK

'Go to the chartroom and check those calculations again, Number One.'

Devane wedged his elbows against the screen and trained his glasses beyond the port bow. It was supposed to be dusk, but the sea was already dark and vaguely menacing.

Dundas replied quietly, 'They seem all right, sir. I checked them just now—'

'Do it again!'

Devane could feel the lieutenant's resentment as he groped his way to the ladder. But it was all taking far too long, and the sickening motion created by the boat's dead slow progress for the past hour did not help.

Seymour said, 'Zero hour, sir.' He spoke very carefully, as if he was well aware of Devane's mood.

Devane moved his glasses another few inches. The little island was right there, blocking their path, or should be. It was unfair to take it out of Dundas. He was a damn good navigator, and the boat was lucky to have someone who had been so expertly trained in the merchant service.

He could feel the others crowded in behind him. The Russians, the bridge team, some spare hands with belts for the machine-gunners.

Dundas returned. 'It's dead ahead, sir. Four miles.' He

waited, expecting a sudden outburst. 'Commander Orel knows the place well, and his notes on the chart were a great help.'

'Good.' Devane lowered his glasses and rubbed his eyes with his knuckles. 'The raiding party should be ashore by now.'

If only the MTBs had radar, how much easier and safer it would be. On several occasions in the Mediterranean they had 'borrowed' the services of an American PT boat. All of their craft were fitted with radar. It had made the flotilla's cat-and-mouse chase amongst the Greek and Adriatic Islands far less of a gamble.

Someone moved up beside him, and without looking he knew it was Orel.

How must it feel, Devane wondered. If the Germans had invaded and conquered Britain he might be looking from seaward at the Isle of Wight and trying to imagine what was happening to his friends and relations in an occupied country. Maybe Orel was thinking of someone in particular.

Dundas said, 'If we receive no signal, sir, will we still go in?'

Devane swung on him and then said, 'I'm sorry I choked you off just now. Not deserved.' He touched his sleeve. 'I think not. No signal will mean that the sub withdrew without landing the raiding party. Her skipper probably knows better than anybody what the risks are.'

Orel leant forward, sensing perhaps from Devane's tone that the first optimism was beginning to fade away.

Devane turned towards him and then blinked as the Russian's features, the upper bridge and flapping ensign were suddenly illuminated by a vivid red glare. For a split second longer he thought that an enemy patrol had pinned them down with a star shell, or that some coastal battery had been tracking them with detection devices. But then came the explosion, crashing out of the glow like a thunderclap, and Devane knew it was something else.

The Russian interpreter was already explaining, but Devane said abruptly. 'The Russian submarine. She's hit a mine.'

As if a great hand had come out of the shadows to extinguish the glare, the sea became dark again.

Voices murmured and flowed down either side-deck, and Devane heard Seymour trying to restore order.

One thing, it was a quick death. Immediate. Like the bomb

had been for those people in the pub. Either the submarine had lost her bearings in the minefield or she had struck a 'drifter'. Either way, it did not make much difference now.

If the Russians had kept to their timetable, the raiders would be ashore. The only thing which was not according to plan was that the whole island would be on the alert.

He snatched up the microphone. '*Parthian*, this is *Merlin*. We're going in! Start the attack!"

He glanced at Pellegrine's shadowy outline. 'Full ahead all engines!'

The bows rose several feet as the MTB leapt forward with a roar of motors. But surprisingly it broke the tension, the sudden anxiety which the explosion had thrown at them.

Fingers closed on Devane's arm and he saw Orel staring at him, his eyes almost feverish as he shouted above the din of power.

The interpreter, who was still trying to stay on his feet after the violent increase of speed, shouted something, but Devane said, 'Don't bother!' He forced a smile and added, 'I think I *know* what he said.'

Orel was satisfied and relaxed his grip. When Devane glanced at him again he seemed as controlled and as impassive as ever. But for those few seconds the mistrust and the uncertainty had been left astern.

'Here comes the welcome!'

Red balls of tracer lifted as if from the sea and winged far abeam, and Devane thought he heard the heavier bark of artillery. But no tell-tale waterspouts shot upwards, and the tracer too stopped almost immediately.

Leading Signalman Carroll shouted, 'There's the signal, sir!'

Devane nodded and watched the drifting flares, two green over one white. The Russian raiding party might still be wondering what was happening, or if they would ever be rescued now that their submarine had taken a last dive. But they had fired the flares, and would not have much longer to wait before they knew they were not alone.

Boots scraped on deck, and Devane heard shouted commands as the Russians crowded forward on either side, weapons at the ready. It was to be hoped that the island's defenders were still confused, otherwise one good burst of machine-gun fire might sweep the soldiers overboard like rag dolls.

Orel was standing close beside the coxswain, peering forward with one hand resting on Pellegrine's shoulder. They were rushing headlong into shadow, and only Orel really knew what this place was like.

'All engines half ahead! Starboard fifteen! *Steady!*' Devane gripped the rail beneath the screen for support as the deck tilted over. 'Stand by to open fire!'

A solitary bullet thudded into the hull, and Devane found time to wonder who the marksman was. A startled sentry, most likely. A tiny island, well clear of the war's main thoroughfare, the sight of five MTBs rushing out of the gloom straight for the solitary inlet would be enough to terrify anyone.

Devane wanted to move round the bridge, to see if the other boats were reacting as planned. But he dared not take his eyes from the onrushing shadows, not for a second. They all trusted him. He must do the same for them.

'Grenades exploding to port, sir.'

But spray lancing over the flared bows hid the explosions. Devane saw a few dull flashes and imagined he heard the impartial stammer of automatic fire. Men were fighting out there. Hated enemies, with no quarter at the end of it.

Tracer flashed diagonally across the MTBs' approach and churned the sea into froth.

Devane shouted, '*Flares!*'

It seemed to take an age before the anchorage leapt into stark outline beneath the drifting lights.

It all seemed much smaller now, with no room for error or panic.

'Slow ahead port and centre! Half astern starboard!'

Devane winced as metal shrieked out of the gloom and ricocheted from the bridge.

'Stop starboard!'

He forced himself to remain upright as tracer hummed and whimpered overhead or streaked blindly out to sea.

'Slow ahead all engines!'

He pounded the rail until the pain steadied his racing nerves. There it was. Pale, wedge-shaped and blurred in the dangling camouflage nets.

More tracer ripped past the bridge and then hammered the hull like massive boots.

Without realizing he was shouting, Devane called, 'The bastards are on to us! Open fire! Knock that gun out!'

The bridge shook as the twin machine-guns on the port side rattled into life, joined by the Oerlikons' sharper note, and then the full onslaught from Walker's boat which was following nose to tail.

Devane looked round for Dundas, but he had already gone to rally his boarding party.

He heard a sharp exchange of light automatic fire, the wild whooping of the Russian soldiers as they tensed themselves for the impact.

But the E-boat's cannon had ceased firing, and Devane guessed that its crew had probably been wiped out in the first barrage.

'Easy, Swain! More to starboard!'

Devane saw a small boat drifting from its moorings, probably a dinghy, then felt the shudder as it was ground to fragments between the two hulls.

'All engines slow astern!'

He heard yells from aft as grapnels were hurled on to the enemy's deck.

One of the seamen holding the spare ammunition belts gave a sharp cry and fell to his knees. He was trying to speak, but it sounded as if he was drowning in his own blood.

Devane gritted his teeth. *Now.*

"All stop!"

As the motors died he heard the other sounds, gunfire and shouts, the stampeding boots of the troops, a grenade or two being hurled at some resistance on the shore.

He saw Walker's boat edging up to the E-boat's stern, more men with lines and wires jumping down on to her deck like pirates in an Errol Flynn film. Some of them had been fighting with German E-boats for years, but it was doubtful if any had been as close as this to one before.

Devane watched the feverish preparations to get the E-boat ready for towing clear. She was big all right. Standing high from the water with her torpedoes and stores removed she looked twice as large as her captors.

He saw Dundas appear on the German's bridge, his gestures, even his expression very clear in the reflected gunfire and flares.

Seymour called, 'There goes the second party of soldiers, sir!'

Mackay's boat was already gathering sternway as she reversed from some kind of pontoon. Her cargo of soldiers were scampering into the gathering darkness, machine-guns raking the shadows as they ran.

Carroll finished preparing his rockets. 'I can fire the recall whenever you're ready, sir!'

Devane waved to Walker's boat as she turned crabwise to receive a towline. He saw Walker's yellow scarf waving like a banner, and marvelled that they had all managed to reach this point without serious incident.

If they could move the E-boat under her own power that would really be something. But it was more likely the Germans had removed all her fuel before attempting any repairs.

Orel was thumping his interpreter on the shoulder to emphasize something, and even the flicker of automatic fire from the land seemed unreal and without menace.

Carroll hurried to a voicepipe and then said urgently, 'Sir! W/T have signal. *Most immediate!*'

Devane trained his night glasses on some separate flashes, high up to starboard. That must be the small hill he had seen on the chart. Men were creeping round even as he watched, trying to kill each other, hand to hand.

'Tell me.'

'Two enemy surface units approaching from north-east. Discontinue operation immediately.'

Devane took precious seconds to consider it. The signal was officially from Black Sea Fleet HQ, but it would have come through Beresford. That wasted time. Two surface units probably meant destroyers, and there would be more where they came from.

He picked up the microphone handset. '*Kestrel*, this is *Merlin*. Do you read me?'

He heard Mackay's harsh voice as if he were here on the bridge. 'This is *Kestrel*. Loud and clear.' There was a distorted chuckle. 'What'll we do?'

Devane ducked as something clicked against the side of the bridge. There were still a few Germans nearby, it seemed.

'Take over, Red. Recall the soldiers and supply covering fire. Tell *Harrier* and *Osprey* to take charge of the tow. Make good use of the darkness. It'll be a long, long day tomorrow.'

They had all heard the signal and were probably wondering what he might do. 'I'm taking *Buzzard* with me, got it?'

Mackay sounded grim. 'Roger.'

Seymour clung to the bridge ladder. 'Are we pulling out, sir?'

'Yes. Cast off from the E-boat. Tell Number One to stay there in charge. You take over from him here.' He swung round, dismissing the lieutenant from his thoughts. 'Bunts, call up *Buzzard*. Line astern on me. Fast as he can.'

He pictured the other MTB's commanding officer, the stolid, dependable ex-fisherman, Sydney Horne. He was no doubt comparing the odds. Two MTBs against two possible destroyers were hardly favourable. But if they were to give the raiding party and their prize more time, they would have to chance it.

'All gone forrard and aft, sir!'

'Very well. Slow astern all engines. Fend off forrard.'

Very carefully the MTB thrust through the drifting fragments of the dinghy. Smoke and vapour from the motors blended with that of explosions, and Devane could smell cordite, like the stench of death.

'All stop.'

Carroll reported, '*Buzzard* has acknowledged, sir.'

'Hard a-starboard, half ahead all engines. Stay close inshore, Swain, until Commander Orel indicates otherwise.'

The spokes gleamed in the glow of distant gunfire, and Devane thought he saw Dundas standing high on the E-boat's bridge, staring after his own boat as she continued to thrash clear of the inlet.

He heard feet dragging on the gratings and knew the dead seaman was being taken below. His name, what was it? It was suddenly important that he should remember.

Crookshank. That was it. A brief picture of a round, open face. A man he had not had time to know.

Seymour emerged from the chartroom. 'Commander Orel says that the course to steer is north thirty-five east, sir. We shall skirt the minefield and keep it on our starboard hand for the next five miles.'

'Thank you.'

Devane watched the glow astern, the sudden flurry of fire and sparks as the Russian raiders blew up another objective.

Crookshank, able seaman, a man who had just died, had already slipped from his thoughts.

'Bring her round, Swain.' He looked for Seymour. 'Check on damage, David. And ask the Chief about fuel levels. Just in case.'

As the MTB, with her shadowy consort close astern, settled on the new course, and some of the spare hands cleared away the empty magazines and spent cartridge cases, the Russian interpreter said gravely, 'You have done this kind of work before, I think.'

Devane looked at him, not knowing whether to laugh or weep.

'A few times.' He patted the Russian's arm. 'See if you can get me some coffee, there's a good chap.'

The lieutenant stared at him, mystified. 'Coffee? Yes.'

Pellegrine had heard the Russian's remark and pursed his lips with contempt.

A few times? My bloody oath!

'Pass the word to *Buzzard*. We'll stop and listen.'

The motors died once more, and as the boat began to slide abeam in a choppy upsurge Devane tried to consider their position from every angle.

The other MTB moved up until she was drifting some fifty yards clear, but without a moon and very little light she had lost her identity completely.

Every man who could be spared was posted around the boat with a pair of binoculars. Ears, eyes and experience were their best weapons now.

Devane licked his lips and tasted the coffee which the Russian lieutenant had managed to obtain from somebody. That was an hour and a half ago. If the report was correct, and the two German ships were on their way, the contact would be soon. All they had was agility and speed. Surprise was out of the question if the German captains knew the extent of the attack. They would very likely have radar. Devane stared into the blackness until his eyes throbbed. It made you feel vulnerable and naked. He could picture the two tiny blips on the German's scanner, the guns already trained round to blast them from the water before they could even see a target.

Seymour said, 'I've been round the boat, sir. All ready, guns and torpedoes.'

'They're feeling a bit low, I suppose.'

Seymour stared at him, surprised. 'Well, yes, sir.'

Devane wiped his glasses with a scrap of tissue. 'They would be.' It was always the same after a member of their tightly knit community had been killed. Their first loss in *Parthian*.

Orel's restless shadow merged with theirs. The interpreter explained, 'The commander wishes to say something.'

Devane trained his glasses again. Beneath his waterproof suit his body felt clammy and hot. Just to slip over the side and drift in that cool water.

He asked, 'What about?'

'The German ships are here too soon.' He faltered and rearranged his words. 'They could not have known, could not have been ready.'

Devane looked at him. Of *course*, it was so obvious he had not seen it. With Sorokin's forces throwing mock attacks at their other positions, it was unlikely the German naval commander would have had ships to spare, unless he had been warned of the attack. That was impossible, or the island would have been properly defended and waiting for them.

It was the Russian submarine they were after. They had probably known about her presence for ages and would not be put off by some vague explosion in the minefield. Whatever the Germans knew or guessed, it had all ended with the RDF station being blown up, for the enemy's radio link was in the same blockhouse.

Devane moved restlessly from side to side, vague shapes parting to let him through.

It was one hell of a risk all the same. Suppose the Germans did know about the MTBs and were coming hot-foot to destroy them?

He said, 'Tell Commander Orel thank you. It makes sense. How could they have known?'

Seymour sounded husky. 'We could be caught between the German ships and the passage home.' He forced a grin. 'Nasty.'

'Tomorrow they'll have every damn ship and plane looking for their E-boat. We've got to delay these two, no matter what.

Otherwise they'll pick us off one by one. Have you ever fought with a destroyer, David?'

'No, sir.'

Devane smiled. 'A destroyer is the only *ship* I'd really like to command. They used to make jokes about the Italian Navy in the Med. I did too, until I met one of their *Oriani*-class destroyers bows on. So we'll do this one our way. Check the chart and see if there are any navigation buoys hereabouts.'

Seymour nodded. 'There is, sir. Two miles to the north of this position. It's not in use, of course.'

Devane searched his flimsy plan for traps. It was likely the German ships had moved into the Black Sea before their army had reached a stalemate on the Eastern Front. With luck, their captains would be unused to the devious warfare of the narrow seas and the Levant.

He picked up the handset and pressed the switch. 'This is *Merlin*. At slow speed, take station on unused buoy, two miles to the north'rd. Silent routine.'

He heard Horne's brief acknowledgement, the immediate flurry of white foam from the other boat's screws.

To Seymour he said, 'Slow ahead. Direct the cox'n to steer for the buoy.' He clapped him on the shoulder. 'You've done your homework. I like that.'

He felt the boat tremble and respond to the thrust and triple rudders.

'Pass the word to all positions. Jerry *could* be playing our game.'

The machine-gunners swung their barrels in wide arcs, the long belts of ammunition trailing like brass snakes. Kirby, the leading torpedoman, would be making his last rounds with his assistants to ensure that if they got the chance to fire their fish would not fail or remain jammed in their tubes.

He wondered how far the E-boat had managed to get, and if the flotilla had received any other casualties.

'Coming up to the buoy in five minutes, sir.'

Devane nodded. Time was passing so swiftly. It seemed only seconds ago that he had given his orders.

He was tired, the strain had seen to that. It was so easy to let your mind drift, anything to avoid the reality and the menace.

Leading Seaman Priest's sturdy outline detached itself from forward of the six-pounder mounting, and with another seaman close on his heels he hurried towards the bows.

The starboard lookout said hoarsely, 'Fo'c's'le party ready, sir. Buoy in sight, starboard bow.'

'Dead slow. Steer for the buoy, Swain. A little port rudder to allow for drift.'

Pellegrine frowned in concentration. 'Got it, sir.' He leaned on the spokes, his lively wife momentarily forgotten.

Within ten minutes both MTBs were lying to on long slip ropes, with the gaunt navigation buoy swaying before their bows like a drunken bishop. It was covered with rust; a legacy of neglect, Devane thought. A relic of lost empire. The Czar's yachts had come this way to avoid the pitiless winters, and later the White Russians had fled to Turkey, to anywhere to escape the revolution's bloody fury.

Someone dropped a steel helmet on the deck and Pellegrine swore savagely.

Devane snapped, 'Who's that?'

'S-sorry, sir.' It was Metcalf. It would be.

Devane saw that he was holding some fresh ammunition belts, and wondered if he knew what had happened to the other seaman.

He said, 'Sound carries like hell, Metcalf. So find your place and stay in it.'

Metcalf nodded and backed carefully against the flag locker. He had expected the captain to blast him apart, but he had spoken to him quite calmly. Even Dundas, whom he admired, would have had a few sharp words for him.

Unaware of the awe he had aroused, Devane continued to search the darkness with his glasses. If he appeared to relax or not to care, others would soon follow his example. And then. . . .

'Sir! Port bow!' The lookout broke off, confused. 'Thought I saw a light.' He sounded relieved as he added, '*There*, sir!'

Devane steadied himself against the uneven roll of the deck. He had seen it, but without the lookout's quick report it could have been missed altogether. They might never know what it was. But it was probably a ship's dead-light momentarily unfastened and swinging open to the same motion which was tossing the MTBs about. It was strangely comforting to realize that even the Germans could become careless.

No time to inquire if Horne and his men had seen it too. Nor would he dare to use the R/T. But Horne would be watching his every move like a cat.

'What do you think, Swain?'

Pellegrine squinted in deep thought. 'They'd be on to us by now, sir.'

'Yes.' German E-boats had often used the old ruse of mooring to a navigation buoy off the British coastline. A radar operator in some old, overworked escort would see the blip on his scope, but because it was known there was a marker buoy in the vicinity he would notice nothing strange. He would see what he had expected to see. 'I think these Jerry skippers are in for a shock.'

Devane pushed his way to the other voicepipes and waited for the engine room to reply.

'Chief? This is the captain. Any second now. Full revs. And hold on to your boots.' He heard Ackland laugh. He sounded miles, not yards, away.

'Warn the fo'c's'le party, David. Slip the bow line the moment I sing out!'

The men around him tensed their bodies as if to test the weight of the enemy.

Devane climbed on to the gratings again and gripped the rail. There it was. Like the sound of a fast car, far away. But it was the roar of fans which drowned even the engines and racing screws as the ship, whatever she was, tore through the water. Moving from left to right. A copybook, diagonal attack.

'What the *hell*!'

A burst of red tracer ripped across the sea and vanished in the space of a second. Some bloody fool in Horne's boat had forgotten a safety catch and had fired by accident.

It was too late now.

'*Slip!* Starboard ten! All engines full ahead!'

The other MTB vanished astern in spray and smoke as Ackland threw open his throttles.

Devane held on tightly and watched the darkness which was parted by the high, crisp arrowhead of the MTB's bow wave.

A line of low trajectory tracer, which appeared to skim the water, tore past the port beam, and Devane pictured the alarm, the guns swinging round towards him.

'Port ten! *Steady!*'

Devane watched the double flashes, the vivid reflection against the other vessel's bridge screen.

Two shells exploded together, flinging up great columns of

water which seemed to stand for minutes like white spectres before cascading back into the sea.

Splinters whined overhead, and two more guns shot out their scarlet tongues from another angle.

Two pairs. Devane tried to fix the other ship in his mind.

'Stand by torpedoes!'

The whole of the hull seemed to be standing up on its keel, as if only the screws were holding it to the surface. On either beam the banks of broken water peeled away in two great white wings, and Devane wondered if Horne had managed to follow him yet.

Somebody gasped, ' 'Ere come the bleedin' flak!'

Tracer lifted and plunged towards them, and one of the machine-gunners twisted round towards the bridge as if pleading to open fire in return.

Devane watched the bright tracer, felt the deck tilt this way and that as Pellegrine expertly eased the boat in a tight zigzag towards the enemy.

Two more shells burst nearby, the water falling across the afterpart with such violence that two seamen were knocked to the deck.

Devane felt his eyes cringe in the searing light as a star shell exploded overhead, laying them bare to the enemy's guns and an immediate response in tracer and cannon shells.

Devane shaded his throbbing eyes. *'Open fire!'* There was always a chance of hitting a vital point. Luck, more likely.

The hull rocked unsteadily, and Pellegrine almost lost control as the boat was bracketed by two heavier shells.

There was no sign of Horne's boat. Devane wiped the sighting bar and tried to clear his mind of everything but the patch of shadow beyond the searing light. Darkness but for one jagged white moustache—the enemy's bow wave as he turned and charged towards them like a battering ram.

'Fire!'

The green and red tracers clawed at each other, then knitted together in a tight mesh until they ripped across steel and woodwork alike.

'Torpedoes running, sir!'

Devane yelled, 'Hard a-port!'

He screwed his mind into a tight muscle as he tried to count the seconds. Splinters shrieked and clattered everywhere, and he heard a man cry out, a high, desperate sound as the breath was torn from his body.

Missed. They had missed the target with both torpedoes.

The enemy was still turning, and Devane could hear the great thresh of propellers and the roar of fans as she tilted hard over in pursuit.

More waterspouts, more great bangs and cascading spray.

Devane gasped, 'Hard a-starboard! We'll try and cut across his stern!'

Another star shell lit the scene from sea to sky. A deadly, icy glare. As if they were already dead and did not recognize it.

A machine-gun jammed, and Devane heard the seaman cursing and yelling meaningless words as he tried to clear the stoppage. Forward of the bridge the six-pounder pivoted on its power-operated mounting, as if the boat was moving around it as it fired at the enemy's shadow with barely a pause.

Carroll yelled, 'We're losing way!'

Devane tried to listen, but needed to know little beyond the dropping bow wave as the revolutions fell and continued to fall. The engine room was in trouble.

He pulled himself across the shaking bridge to seek out the other enemy ship. But there was only one after all. It made him despair to realize that, but for Horne's careless gunner, and this latest setback, they might have won.

Seymour was shouting, 'Do we break off, sir?' He looked and sounded wild.

'*No!* Stand by to re-engage!'

The MTB wheeled yet again, more shells bursting dangerously close as she lost more and more power from her motors.

A towering column of red and orange fire shot up seemingly to the clouds, as if it was something solid and would never move again. It took just a few seconds, but Devane and his men saw their enemy for the first time. She was still charging in pursuit, but with half of her forecastle and her complete stern blasted away she was already ploughing deeper and deeper, driven down by the thrust of her engines.

In the glare of flames and exploding ammunition Devane saw the small shark's fin of the other MTB's bows far beyond the sinking ship, and knew that Horne had caught their attacker as she had turned for the kill.

'Slow ahead all engines. David, check with the Chief.'

Devane made himself watch the other ship in her death

agonies, and listened to her breaking up as she lifted her stern and started to dive.

Orel was watching too, peering into the night until the sea swallowed the broken hull and doused the last of the fires. Did he think it was all worth it, Devane wondered? A destroyer sunk, a submarine mined and lost with all hands, and an able seaman named Crookshank whom he had not found time to know.

Carroll said, '*Buzzard*'s calling us up, sir. *Do you require assistance?*'

Devane threw back his head and gulped at the air as if it was water in a desert. Around him men were peering at one another, dazed and bewildered by the closeness of death.

Devane said, 'Assistance, Bunts? I think we *all* need it!'

8

NEAR MISS

Devane wiped his face gratefully with a flannel dipped in warm soapy water. Torpedoman Pollard, who did secondary duty as wardroom messman, watched approvingly and said, 'That'll make you feel like ten men, sir.' He had a Newcastle accent you could slice with a knife.

Devane handed him the basin. 'Thanks.'

It felt strange to be idling along at a mere seven knots after the speed and chilling danger of the night. He stared beyond the stained screen. The sea was a darker blue and the sky devoid of cloud. From horizon to horizon there was nothing.

He listened to the occasional thump of hammers as the hands below deck dealt with another splinter hole in the hull's fabric. From aft and the engine-room hatch he heard the clatter of metal as Ackland and his men continued with their repairs.

And yet, in spite of the loneliness, and realization that at any minute they might be discovered by an enemy patrol, there was an air of acceptance, of resignation.

Ackland had been forced to stop the port screw altogether. An exploding shell from the German destroyer had damaged the shaft, and to force any more use from it might put it out of action for good.

Devane recalled the moment when dawn had opened up the sea around them. His feelings as he had ordered Horne to take his undamaged MTB to seek out and support the rest of the flotilla and their captured E-boat. As the senior officer of the flotilla it was arguable that he should have moved to Horne's boat and left Seymour to cope as best he could. Now as the boat moved sluggishly over the dark water he was glad he had stayed behind.

Merlin had taken enough. One man killed outright, and another, a young stoker, clinging to life by a thread, had made a deep impact on their small company.

They had expected to be pounced upon as soon as it was full daylight, had almost welcomed the need to hit back, no matter what the odds might be.

But now it was close on noon, and still nothing had happened. Just the painful progress, the boat steering almost crabwise in the water, so that constant changes of rudder and screws kept the helmsman busy. Apart from the lookouts, and a relay of men at the helm, most of the hands were engaged on repairs, snatching hasty meals of sandwiches and sweet tea, or merely sitting isolated and staring out at the empty horizon.

Seymour appeared on the bridge and examined the compass before saying, 'Stoker Duff's in a bad way, sir. Left thigh shot through. Tracer too.' He shook his head. 'Pity we can't carry a sick-berth attendant who can shoot as well! We could certainly use some expert help.'

Devane nodded, his eyes on the man at the wheel. Pellegrine was below with the wounded stoker. The coxswain was remarkable in many ways. His instincts about danger and the position or movements of an enemy in total darkness were uncanny. Now he was acting as ship's doctor, and doubtless he was good at that also.

Seymour removed his cap and pushed his fair hair from his forehead. 'What about the flotilla, sir? Do you think they're home and dry yet?'

'Depends on their speed. Whether they've had additional help from Ivan.' He did not need to look at his watch. He knew every minute on it since Horne's boat had dipped over the horizon like a minute insect. 'With Red Mackay making all the running, I'd say they've a better chance than most.'

They looked at each other. Each knew that but for their attack on the destroyer *Parthian* might have been decimated, or driven so far to the south that their fuel would have run dry.

It needed no words.

Leading Signalman Carroll moved up beside the helmsman. 'I'll take over, Jimmy. You get some char.'

Seymour nodded as the helmsman glanced at him for confirmation.

Devane looked at the sea as it slid slowly down the hull. They were a good team, he thought. Trusted and trusting.

He said abruptly, 'I'm going to the chartroom.' He had seen Orel and his lieutenant coming through the wardroom hatch and knew he could not face another stilted post mortem.

In the chartroom it was stuffy and humid. He leaned over the table, listening to the hull groaning around him, the restrained power of the motors.

He picked up the brass dividers and made a few swift calculations on the chart. Matchbox navigation, as Dundas called it. They had come a long way. Another hour. Provided Sorokin was still keeping his patrols at first-degree readiness, or that the enemy had not launched such a massive counter-attack the E-boat escapade had been forgotten.

Devane thought suddenly of his first MTB. They had been returning from an attack on enemy coastal convoys off the Dutch coast when they had begun to sink. Too many shell holes, too much damage from previous battles up and down the Channel; nobody really discovered. The senior officer of the flotilla had previously ordered Devane's skipper to make his own way home. He stood a better chance as all enemy attention would be focused on the others.

Abandoning ship had seemed unreal, because of the silence, but then, as the angle had increased and some of the men had begun to jump overboard into the bitter water, Devane had accepted what was happening to him.

He could remember without effort that first night, the faint glow of red lights on the life-jackets as the men drifted about, shouting encouragement to each other, searching for special friends.

An air-sea rescue launch from the RAF had discovered them late the following day. To sharpen their understanding of how close they had all been to death, the RAF skipper had told them he had in fact been looking for an aircraft reported shot down and afloat in the North Sea.

Only seven had survived the bitter cold and tempting numbness of sleep.

One had been Devane's commanding officer, who had said

flatly, 'I wasn't going to die like that! When I go, I'm taking a few of those bastards with me.' He was right. He was killed three months later.

Devane jerked upright as a voice yelled from the bridge, 'Aircraft! Aircraft bearing red four-five! Angle of sight one-five!'

The alarm bells jangled throughout the boat, and Devane ran for the ladder, his mind frozen and stopped like a watch as he waited for the game to begin.

Covers were ripped from the muzzles, which were still blackened from the night's fighting. Hatches and doors were slammed shut, and men groped for ammunition or jammed themselves firmly into their gun-shields and harnesses.

Seymour was training his binoculars over the screen. Without lowering them he said, 'Two, sir. Look like Ju 88s.'

The boatswain's mate said, 'All guns closed up, sir.'

Devane watched the two black silhouettes. So small, so slowly confident as they banked right over to reveal their twin engines and caught the sunlight on their cockpit covers.

Devane said, 'Tell the engine room what's happening. These beauties will take a good look at us first. But I'll lay odds they're calling up their chums right now.'

He added, 'Better move the wounded man to the wardroom. He'll have a bit more protection over his head.'

Pellegrine swung the spokes and cursed as the hull tried to drag the bows off course.

'Not to bother, sir. He's bought it.'

Devane rubbed his eyes and then searched for the two Junkers again. *Bought it*. So easily said. In England there would be another heartbreak, another telegram and, hopefully, a sympathetic letter.

He thought suddenly of the silent women in the hotel. Waiting for their husbands' medals.

No wonder Whitcombe had planned for the extra crew members.

'Here they come.' Devane wheeled round. 'They'll close from starboard. Stand by all guns!'

The two aircraft had settled down on a shallow approach and were wafer-thin above the water as they turned towards the slow-moving MTB.

God, how long they were taking. Devane heard cocking levers being pulled and the starboard machine-gunner whistling through his teeth as he depressed both barrels to hold the enemy in his crosswires.

Devane said, 'Get up forrard, David, and supervise the six-pounder crew.'

Once more their eyes met. Seymour did not need to be told why. Devane was sending him from the bridge in case the whole bunch of them were wiped out to leave the boat without an officer or a coxswain.

Devane studied the oncoming aircraft until his eyes watered. Coming out of the sun, as they always did. How many more times was he going to cross swords with them, he wondered? The Ju 88 had a formidable reputation as a fighter, a bomber and recce aircraft all in one.

As the planes drew closer they appeared to accelerate. Devane held his breath as the cannon and machine-guns stabbed out from the leader. He saw the shells and bullets flailing the sea like whips, then tensed as steel whimpered overhead and a great shadow roared above the mast, the twin engines deafening as the plane pulled up and away in a steep climb.

'Open fire!'

The Oerlikons, already trained to port, sent two lines of tracer searing after the aircraft, then swung round again as the second attacker tore towards them.

'Hard a-starboard!'

Painfully the MTB slewed round, the six-pounder hammering violently as if to outpace the machine-guns on either side of the bridge.

'Midships! Port fifteen! Steady!'

Devane had to stop himself from cringing as the Junkers 88 roared overhead, its pilot momentarily off balance because of their zigzag turn. He thought he saw smoke from the enemy's belly, and guessed the six-pounder had found a target. But these planes could take a lot of punishment. Devane knew that from long and bitter experience.

The aircraft were dividing, one climbing slowly, the other turning in a wide circle almost brushing the water. Devane saw the black crosses on the wings, could even imagine the thoughts of the two pilots. The MTB was alone but apparently not disabled.

Aloud he said, 'They'll come in from bow and beam. Just to test us. Hold your fire until the last hundred yards.'

He tore his eyes from the two black silhouettes and looked along his command. Gaunt, unshaven faces, red-rimmed eyes. The feverish light of battle. Toughened hands which had once wielded pens in an office or school, or had served bread to chatty housewives, like Carroll, who was now helping a lookout to drag more ammunition to the machine-guns. These were his men. Men their mothers and wives, sweethearts and friends would never see.

He saw Orel and his interpreter carrying a sub-machine-gun to the rear of the bridge and wondered where they had found it. Probably discarded by the soldiers when they had swarmed ashore, a million years ago.

Forward, squatting down behind the gun-layer and his mate, Seymour was pointing towards the low-flying Junkers. No, his parents would certainly not recognize *him*, the dreamer, the would-be writer.

Devane let the glasses drop to his chest as the two planes started their run-in, dividing the MTB's defences by their varied heights and bearings.

And what of me? She had wanted to hear from him. What was it really like?

'*Here come the bastards!*'

Seymour was yelling, 'Hold your fire! Easy, *easy*!' Like a man calming an excited horse.

'*Open fire!*'

The guns hammered into life, the tracers streaking away and crisscrossing the aircraft like a vivid web.

Brrrrrrrrrrrrrr! Brrrrrrrrrrrrrr!

Splinters cracked and thudded across the hull, and a shell ripped through the flag locker and exploded above the side deck. Devane saw Carroll puff out his cheeks and Pellegrine tug his battered cap more tightly across his slitted eyes as if to get better control of the wheel.

The six-pounder purred round and bracketed the second aircraft as it thundered across the sky, its great wings making it look like a bird of prey about to snatch them from the sea.

Brrrrrrrrrrrrrr!

More bullets and cannon shells ripped across the hull, and Devane saw a hole appear in the gratings within inches of his seaboot.

'Cease firing!'

Devane tore at his collar and wiped his face and throat with a piece of rag. The two attackers were turning away, like conspirators, as they prepared for another run.

Devane shouted, 'Report damage and casualties! More magazines, lively there!'

Men came from their stiff attitudes and stumbled to obey his commands. There was not one of them on deck who was older than twenty-five, and most were ninteeen or thereabouts. But as they readjusted their gun-sights and dragged at magazines and belts they responded like old men.

Devane licked his lips. They felt like parchment.

Two more attacks like the last one, maybe just one, and they had had it. It was like fighting a tiger with an umbrella.

He saw the seaman called Irwin tying a bandage on Orel's wrist, and the port machine-gunner playing with a crucifix which hung from his identity disc.

We're all equal here. So equal we'll be nothing in a few more minutes.

Devane shouted, 'Keep at it, lads. Wear the bastards down!'

It made him want to hide his face as he watched their efforts to rally to his words.

A thumbs-up from one, a broad grin from the six-pounder gun-layer, the tough leading hand from Manchester. Even Pellegrine was looking at him and nodding.

Carroll said in a hushed voice, 'Engine room, sir.'

Devane crossed to the voicepipe in two strides. So they were not even to have the last chance, that impossible gesture which had seen the end of so many battles.

'Yes?'

Ackland called, 'I can give you fifteen knots, sir.' He must have taken Devane's silence for disappointment. 'On all three shafts.'

Devane dimly heard the rising note of the aircraft as they turned towards the MTB once again. 'Thanks, Chief. Bloody well done. And they say there are no more miracles.'

Ackland sounded confused. 'Sir?'

'Never mind, Chief. Give me all you've got, *right now*!' He snapped down the cover. 'Hard a-starboard, Swain!' He felt the deck rising to the added thrust even as the wheel went over. '*Steady!*'

The leading Junkers seemed to swerve away as the MTB's wake broadened out on either beam in a rich white furrow. Fifteen knots was not much compared with nearly forty, but after their slow acceptance of the repeated attacks it felt like a new heart in the boat.

'On the first aircraft! *Fire!*'

Devane clung to the jerking bridge and watched every weapon which would bear, even Orel's short-range Tommy gun as it cracked out in unison.

Maybe the enemy pilot imagined the MTB had been shamming, although at these speeds it was hard to think clearly about anything. But Devane had seen the darker line in the plane's belly, the bomb bay doors wide open to put an end to the impudent boat once and for all. Their sudden increase of speed, made more impressive by the churned wash astern, must have unnerved the German enough to make him change his approach.

Devane saw the ripple of flashes along the fuselage, the spurts of bright fire from one engine as the cannon shells smashed into the exposed belly and wing like a fiery claw. Then the plane exploded, blasted apart by her own bombs.

One second it was still there, filling the sky, and the next there was a solid ball of fire. Devane could feel the force of the explosion and its consuming heat until the fragments were scattered across the sea and only the drifting smoke remained.

The other Junkers came in fast and low, but the attack was at arm's length, with only the machine-guns spitting through the drifting pall above their consort's remains.

A few bullets hit the hull and some whined overhead, then the Junkers altered course away from them and did not turn back.

Leading Signalman Carroll was training his glasses towards the starboard bow and exclaimed huskily, 'Here come the cavalry! No wonder the buggers made off!'

Devane clung to the screen and listened to the vague throb of aircraft growing stronger and stronger. Sorokin had kept his word. They had made it.

He stared at his hands on the bridge rail, mesmerized by the red streak he had left on the grey paint with his fingers.

Seymour pounded up the ladder and stopped as he saw the shock on Carroll's face. Then he ran across the bridge and caught Devane in his arms as he lost his grip and began to fall.

For a few seconds they stood like statues, words pointless, as three pairs of Russian fighters screamed overhead in pursuit of the Junkers.

Then Seymour said, 'Help me with the captain! He's hit!'

Devane stared at the sky. The pain was coming now. A hot, relentless probe, deeper and deeper.

He tried to hold on, to keep his mind from slipping away. He congratulated himself that he had recognized the disbelief in Seymour's voice. But now he knew that even their leader could break and die like the seaman named . . . it was getting confused. What *was* the man's name? He had died too. Here on the bridge. What was. . . .

Seymour lowered Devane to the gratings, aided by Ordinary Seaman Metcalf.

'Help me get his jacket off.' He tore open the clothing, only half his mind under the control of discipline and experience.

'Bunts, tell W/T to make a signal to base. Require medical assistance.'

Seymour looked up and nodded to Carroll's troubled face. 'I know the orders too. But make the signal anyway.'

Pellegrine stepped back from the wheel and tapped Metcalf with his boot. 'Here, boy, 'op up and take the wheel. North eighty east, and mind you hold it there.' He saw the astonishment in the youth's upturned face and the fact he had blood on his hands. 'You want to be a bloody officer? Well, take over!'

The stocky coxswain dropped to his knees and opened Devane's jacket before slitting his shirt with his knife.

Seymour said tightly, 'Lot of blood, Swain.'

Pellegrine's hands were already busy with a dressing. 'Yeh. And a lot of *man*, too, wouldn't you say, sir?'

The picture refused to become any clearer. It was like a steamy window. Devane lay flat on his back and wondered if he would vomit. He felt sick and dizzy, and he guessed he had been pumped full of morphia both on the passage back to base and since then in this place.

He made a feeble attempt to lift himself on his elbows, but weakness and the sudden reawakening of pain made him lie still again. Where was *this place*?

A square, low-ceilinged room, blurred and in part shadow. Like a dream sequence, made more so by the other bed on the far side of the room. It too contained a motionless form, and sudden panic made Devane believe he was in fact dead and looking at himself.

He stared at the ceiling until his head ached from concentration, and he tried to remember what had happened. But he could recall little, except vague pictures of groping hands, anxious, searching eyes.

Devane had seen plenty of men die, and had expected to go the same way on many occasions. But this experience had shocked him deeply. His helplessness, and the complete lack of feeling when he had been struck during the Junkers' final attack.

He flexed his hand and knew that his watch had gone. He had no idea how long he had been here. No understanding of anything.

A door opened somewhere and a white figure glided past the bed. It was a woman, a nurse, her eyes very dark above a kind of mask. She had bright red spots on her apron. Someone else's blood.

Devane moved his head painfully and watched her as she bent over the opposite bed. She was short and sturdy but surprisingly gentle as she turned the inert body on its side and examined some dressings.

Then without another glance she pulled the sheet over the bed and covered the body from head to toe.

She turned and walked towards Devane, slipping aside her mask as she did so. She had a round, almost Mongolian face, ageless, although Devane guessed she was in her early twenties.

She took his wrist and checked his pulse, her eyes completely absorbed as she looked at her watch and then put his arm down on the bed again.

It was so quiet he could hear her breathing, the soft squeak of starch as she bent over to remove the sheet and feel his dressings.

'Am I going to live?'

She did not understand a word. His voice brought no change of expression, and he had the sudden, mad desire to burst out laughing. It was completely crazy. Perhaps she was part of the nightmare. He would wake up at any second and discover, *what?*

She eyed him calmly and then pushed some hair from his forehead. Her hand was hot but very soft.

'Thanks.' He tried to smile. 'We don't understand a bloody word, do we? But I know you're helping me. I'm lucky. Not

114

like the young stoker.' His mind was straying again. 'Not like . . .' He saw her eyes move to the enamel tray with its jars and needles. She was going to put him out again. Desperately he gripped her wrist and said, 'Please don't do that! I'll be quiet, if that's what you want.'

She released her wrist without effort and looked at him impassively. Then she seemed to come to a decision and left the room.

A nurse who will not speak, and a body in the next bed who never can again.

Devane lay back and felt the sweat trickling down his legs. He was naked, but felt as if he were wrapped in stifling blankets.

Voices ebbed and flowed beyond the door and he thought he heard someone whistling.

Then he looked up and saw Beresford standing beside the bed, and realized he must have fainted or fallen into a drugged sleep. He could see past Beresford, the other bed was empty and stripped clean.

Beresford smiled. 'All right?'

Devane felt the despair giving way to sudden, uncontrollable emotion. 'Fine. Yes, I'm feeling great.'

He hated Beresford seeing him like this. Helpless, and so grateful for his being here that he could not contain his feelings.

Beresford squatted on a chair. 'I've spoken to the doc. You'll be up and about in no time.' He reached across to the table and held up a star-shaped piece of metal. 'See this, John? Jerry wanted you to have it. He made a damn good try to see you kept it too.'

Devane closed his eyes. 'Is it bad?'

'Should have been worse. This lump of Krupp steel must have ricocheted off something before it slammed into you. Otherwise. . . .' He did not elaborate.

Beresford continued, 'And in case you're worrying, the boats got back intact. Three killed, including your two, but otherwise it was a perfect operation. Everybody was hopping with delight!'

Delight. Devane thought of all those who had died in so short a time. Russians, Germans and three of his own.

Beresford said, 'Barker's arrived, by the way.'

115

Devane had to grapple with the name for several seconds. Commander Barker.

'What does he say?'

Beresford grimaced. 'Not much. He's a book man. A real gunnery type. He and I are going to get along like a house on fire. I don't think. But the Russians made a big show for him, so maybe he'll settle in.' He sounded unconvinced.

'Where *is* this place?'

'This?' Beresford looked round as if seeing the room for the first time. 'It's a really cushy billet. Fifty miles inland from Tuapse. A commandeered farm, now a field hospital for the army. There was a big flare up along the front while you were away, and there are about seven thousand casualties as a result. Quite a few of them seem to be here. You're getting the red carpet treatment, all on your own.'

'What about the other . . .'

Beresford glanced at the empty bed. 'Oh, him.' He shrugged. 'Search me.'

Outside the door someone coughed, and Beresford stood up.

'Must dash. Can't have your nurse getting stroppy. She'd have me for breakfast!' He became serious again. 'Everything's quiet. Red Mackay's half-stripe has been confirmed, so he's driving the flotilla until you return to the fold. Dundas, your Number One, is taking care of *Merlin*, and Ivan is gloating over the captured E-boat.' He touched Devane's shoulder. 'Take it easy, John. The war will still be there when you come back.' Then he was gone.

The nurse entered the room and studied him thoughtfully.

'Damn, I forgot to ask him how long I'd been here!'

Devane felt her hands on his dressing again, the hot stab of pain as she disturbed the wound. That star-shaped splinter must have struck him in the back, just above his belt. No wonder he had felt winded. It must have rammed into him like a steel fist.

The round-faced nurse bent over him, her expression intent as she snipped away the bandages with her scissors. Then, like a mother with a difficult child, she rolled him on to his side and started on the other end of the dressings.

She was so close Devane could feel her warmth, even her concentration as she folded away the soiled bandages until with a swift jerk she pulled the last piece free.

Devane gasped as the pain stabbed through him. Even the protective layers of drugs were not controlling it now.

He said thickly, 'You've got lovely eyes, did you know that?' He tensed his muscles to withstand the pain. 'I know, I *knew* a girl with eyes like yours. Her name's Claudia. We made love, but I think I love her. That's crazy, isn't it?'

Snip, snip, snip, the scissors trimmed a fresh bandage, and Devane felt the firm pressure of a new dressing across the wound he had never seen.

He added unsteadily, 'I don't suppose she even remembers me now. It was just one of those things.' His eyes were stinging and he could not understand why. 'Like the song, you know. Just one of those crazy things.'

She lowered him on to his back again and rearranged the sheet, her fingers brushing against his skin as if to calm him.

Devane murmured, 'Sorry to be such a bloody nuisance. You must have a hell of a lot to do with all those wounded soldiers out there.'

He watched her preparing a hypodermic needle but found that he had no resistance left in him.

She dabbed his arm and took it firmly in her grip, the needle poised like a dart.

Just for a moment she looked at him and then smiled.

'You are not a *bloody* nuisance, comrade, and my name is Ludmilla.'

Devane was smiling as the darkness closed over him once again.

9

ACT OF WAR?

Lieutenant-Commander Ralph Beresford watched Devane as he lowered himself from the camouflaged staff car and said, 'I still think you should have stayed in hospital a bit longer.' He forced himself to remain where he was as Devane released his grip on the car and swayed slightly until he recovered his bearings.

Devane twisted his mouth into a grin. 'They needed the bed.'

It was blinding sunlight, and the hammers inside his skull were worse than any hangover. The bouncing, lurching progress of the Russian car had not helped.

He turned stiffly and nodded to the two army orderlies. They both beamed at him and then drove back along the pockmarked road.

Beresford said, 'Barker's expecting you. The Russians have knocked up an office for him next to mine. He's a *captain* now, by the way.' He made no attempt to hide his dislike. 'He's nobody's fool, so be warned.'

Devane stopped and looked at him. 'Something's wrong.'

Beresford nodded. 'I checked up on Barker. He's got quite a record in Special Operations. A planner, not a doer exactly. A year or so back he organized a raid behind German lines in

North Africa. Some say it was to bag Rommel or one of his top generals.'

'I heard rumours about that. It was a shambles, I believe.'

'Yes. The Krauts knew what was coming and were well prepared. Our lads were wiped out almost to a man. Including a young commando officer. Barker's son.'

Beresford saw Devane's expression and exclaimed, 'Don't be sorry for him. *Captain* Eustace Barker is proud of the fact!'

They continued in silence towards the stark concrete bunkers with the oily, littered water beyond. Some of the warships were so knocked about it was hard to distinguish them from wrecks sunk in previous air-raids. Rusty metal, fallen gantries and rubble lay everywhere. Only the slender muzzles of AA guns and carefully sandbagged rocket launchers betrayed the vigilant defences.

Devane felt light-headed and concentrated on the patch of deep shadow at the mouth of the bunkers. As they moved into the shade he saw several seamen pausing to watch him, some to salute, the more confident to grin and wave as he passed.

Beresford said dryly, 'You will note that the pirates' rig has gone. All hands are in proper working gear as laid down in orders. Our Captain Barker made that one of his first priorities.'

Devane said nothing. He had been shocked to discover he had been in the field hospital for twenty days. During the past week he had been allowed to take short walks, usually with the aid of the nurse, Ludmilla. Her English was excellent, she had served as a stewardess in a Russian ship just prior to the war and had used the time to learn an extra language.

Devane thought of the makeshift hospital. The endless rows of cots and stretchers, the wounded soldiers, including many amputees, laid out with little shelter, like battlefield victims of a hundred years ago.

They paused and looked at the moored MTBs. No signs of scars, not even a bullet hole to betray that short, fierce raid.

As if reading his mind, Beresford commented, 'They've not had anything else to do but paint and polish.'

By the time they reached Barker's new HQ Devane was wondering if he was going to pass out. Dizziness came and departed in waves, each spasm leaving him sick and on edge.

Beresford knocked on the door and opened it for him to enter.

Captain Eustace Barker was standing against the opposite wall, as if he had been there for some time, watching, preparing for this moment.

Devane's first impression was of neatness and a bright-eyed alertness which seemed at odds with an officer who bothered about the sailor's rig-of-the-day in a place like Tuapse.

He was short and slightly built, but held himself so erect, his shoulders back as if on parade, that he appeared much taller. Barker was evenly tanned, biscuit-coloured, with very dark hair parted in the dead centre.

'Ah, Devane. You've arrived.' It sounded as if he meant to add, 'at last'. 'Take a chair. No sense in wearing yourself out on the first day, what?'

His eyes were very sharp. Like his voice, sharp and incisive.

Devane sat down carefully. 'Thank you, sir. They patched me up extremely well.'

He felt unreasonably angry with himself. For feeling so ill at ease with the spruce little captain, as if he was apologizing for being wounded at all.

'Quite. Well, it's behind you now. And we've not been idle in your absence.'

Devane held his tongue. He was too sore from the car journey to argue.

'Any flotilla anywhere must retain its individuality. Even a solitary rating in a foreign country must remember who and what he represents at all times. That's the way it was, and the way it will be as far as I am concerned.' He shot Beresford a quick smile. 'Right, Ralph?'

Devane relaxed slightly. It had started already. Barker's use of Beresford's name. To separate the regulars from the part-timers. God, he had imagined such stupid and harmful barriers had drowned for good at Crete and Singapore.

Barker had been out of the Navy between wars, axed like so many others in the service cuts which had left the country so ill-prepared. A Navy stretched beyond the limit and officered by hastily trained volunteers had welcomed back the forgotten regulars like a gift from heaven. Some, like Whitcombe, had done very well. But there were others who had used their arrogance to cover their own dismay at discovering that the peacetime years had left them too far behind to be of much use.

Beresford said evenly, '*Parthian* is at first-degree readiness, sir. The 'plumber' has managed to order some more spares, but in any case his workshop is pretty well supplied.'

'Quite. I have already spoken with *Lieutenant-Commander* Buckhurst myself.'

Beresford tried not to look at Devane. 'The captured E-boat is working up satisfactorily. We are sharing the maintenance with Captain Sorokin's staff, of course.'

Barker raised one eyebrow. 'I don't see why "of course", Ralph.' He sighed. 'But then I was not here when the actual decision was made to undertake a raid.' His clear eyes fixed on Devane. 'A raid which I still consider to have been an unnecessary risk.' The smile returned. 'However, we shall deal with that later. My first priority is to make the Russians realize we are here to perform specific tasks, some with, others without, their cooperation. In my opinion they would never have asked for our aid unless they were in real difficulties. Well, I'll not grovel to *them*, believe me!'

Devane said, 'It was my decision, sir. The Russians are fighting the same war as ourselves. Any extra losses to the enemy must help all of us, surely? Captain Sorokin has already said that the Russian forces will attack the Crimean peninsula in about four months' time. If the Germans continue to harry their convoys and shoot up their naval forces they'll be in no position to sustain an amphibious landing on the Crimea.'

Barker smiled brightly. 'Done? Lesson over? Good show. Well, I know your record, naturally. Plenty of *dash*. But experience comes in handy too, especially when dealing with the Reds.' He started to speak faster, Devane and Beresford apparently forgotten. 'I was in Odessa in 1919. A little T-class destroyer. I had plenty of chances to see what the damn Bolsheviks were like, and they've not changed, *believe me!*'

Devane watched Barker regaining control. This man was no figure of fun, no old-timer who filled his days examining ratings' uniforms and haircuts. This one was totally different. And very dangerous.

Barker added calmly, 'As it happens, I have been in regular contact with Admiralty and Chiefs of Staff. I have a mission in mind, and when it is out of the planning stage I will see that you are briefed.' His clear eyes moved between them. Like glass. 'No waste, gentlemen. No pointless risks. Everything must be planned to the last degree. It's my way.'

He moved to his desk and arranged two sheets of paper until

they were exactly in line. Then he said, 'There is the matter of Lieutenant-Commander Richie.' He glanced at Devane. 'A contemporary of yours, I think?'

Devane replied, 'Yes, sir.' Where would this lead?

'I thought so. It was all a beastly business of course. Bad for morale, especially at the beginning of *Parthian*, the creation of a new offensive.'

Beresford tore his eyes from Devane's face and said, 'Captain Whitcombe knows all about it, sir. It was decided—'

Barker said sharply, 'Please do not interrupt. Decisions can be wrong. Likewise, they can be reversed. I was taking part in an investigation before *Parthian* was sent to the Caspian, and before Richie decided to take the easy way out.'

'That's unfair, sir!' Devane struggled to his feet, ignoring Beresford's warning glance. 'He was a very brave man, with more than just decorations to prove it! I'm not defending what he did, but he must have had his reasons.'

'Do sit down, Devane.' Barker perched against the desk and folded his arms. 'I admire loyalty above all else. But blind loyalty I can live without.' He continued in the same unruffled tone, 'The investigation was over another matter. But for Richie's action it would all have been settled by now.'

Beresford asked quietly, 'May we know about it, sir?'

Barker smiled. '*That's* better. I did not ask for the assignment, but I have learned to obey orders without question. I dare say the matter may have been carelessly handled in its original stage, but *heroes*, the public's darlings, do tend to get away with murder, eh?'

Devane watched him, fascinated. Barker was actually enjoying it. The war, the Russian front, *Parthian*, everything else could wait. But he obviously had influence in high places. His casual dismissal of Whitcombe proved that.

Barker said, 'Lieutenant-Commander Richie's position is to be investigated. I have received a signal to the effect that the true facts of his death will be released immediately after the hearing.' He glanced from Beresford to Devane. 'You look surprised?'

Devane said, 'He was listed as killed in action. His past achievements demand that—'

'*Demand?*' Barker leaned slightly towards him, his hair gleaming in the bare lights. 'I think you are becoming a bit of a Bolshevik yourself!'

Beresford said quickly, 'I feel the same, sir. Richie's widow will discover what happened. Is that necessary?'

'She will be told, of course.' Barker thrust himself from the desk, as if bored by the discussion. 'Their lordships are having her flown out. It is her right to attend under the circumstances.' He did not elaborate.

Devane heard himself ask, 'Where is the inquiry to be, sir?'

'Port Said. Didn't I say?' He smiled again. 'I was probably interrupted, eh! Ralph and I will be going, naturally. You can't have a game without an umpire, can you?'

Beresford said, 'I think Lieutenant-Commander Devane should attend, sir.' His features were devoid of expression. 'His assuming command of *Parthian* might call for a few questions at any official hearing?'

Barker stared at him. 'You think so, Ralph?' He turned to look at Devane. 'You *are* excused from active duty for the present, so I suppose. . . .' He nodded. 'Very well. Make a signal to that effect. Lieutenant-Commander Mackay will be left in command, with Lieutenant Kimber from Intelligence to keep an eye on him in case he wants to win the war single-handed during our absence.'

He walked around his desk, apparently unwilling to sit down until they had left.

'Send in my writer. I have a dozen signals to dictate.'

Outside the door Devane leant against the cool concrete and took several deep breaths.

Beresford peered at him anxiously. 'Bad?'

'No, just stunned. Can he really go off like this and leave *Parthian*?'

Beresford took his arm and led him away from the door.

'Someone, somewhere is biding his time. Probably because of Barker's alleged operation. We'll see. But if you'd rather not go to Port Said, I'll fix it through the Russian doctor. I just thought . . .'

Devane shook his head. 'No. I'd like to go. If you hadn't stepped in, I'd probably have asked him myself.' He smiled bitterly. 'Not that he'd have listened to me.'

They walked down the deserted corridor in silence.

Then Devane asked, 'Do you know what the inquiry is about?'

Beresford did not reply directly. 'Richie was engaged in the North Sea a year ago. Dropping and picking up agents from

Norway. A very dicey job, I believe. It has something to do with that. And that's all I know.'

Devane saw Dundas hurrying to meet them and said dryly, 'Thanks, *Ralph*. How can Barker have served in 1919 in a destroyer, and have lost a son in North Africa, and still look so young?'

Beresford smiled. 'Will power and hair dye. Never fails.'

Devane walked towards Dundas, his mind still unable to face what had happened. He hardly felt his wound as he shook hands with Dundas. All he could think about was Claudia, which was even more unreal. He would be the last one she would want to meet.

Dundas was obviously delighted to see him. 'You look *fine*, sir! We'd all have come to see you, but Captain Barker refused leave beyond the base.'

They stood side by side on the jetty and looked at the moored boats.

Dundas said, 'I expect we'll be off again soon, sir.' It sounded like a question. 'I heard from the Russians that the Germans have stopped searching for their E-boat.'

Devane faced him. That was strange. Beresford had failed to mention that.

'How can they be certain?'

Dundas looked uncomfortable. 'Sorry, I thought you'd know. Captain Sorokin had an old motor launch taken to sea and scuttled near to the German minefield.'

Somehow Devane knew what was coming.

Dundas continued quietly, 'When we took the E-boat there were fifteen Germans on board, so we captured them as well. Sorokin's men made certain they were still aboard when the launch was scuttled, and wearing life-jackets. It wouldn't take a genius to discover the corpses were from the E-boat's original crew.'

Devane turned away, sickened. The Germans would discover the drifting corpses and some suitably collected flotsam and imagine their E-boat had tried to return to base and had hit a stray mine.

He remembered the lines of wounded soldiers at the field hospital, the little nurse who had spoken perfect English.

Sorokin had needed a secret. In his war there was only one way of keeping it.

Beresford opened the wooden shutters and winced as the sunlight gouged across his face.

'Phew! But at least they managed to find us a fairly good billet. What I know of Port Said, it's like trying to open an oyster with a bus ticket to get a decent room.'

Devane lay back in a cane chair and nodded. It was oppressively hot, and the drive from the airstrip had turned their car into a private kiln. At least in the room there was an illusion of coolness and shadow.

Through the partly open shutters he could see the masts and funnels which lined the waterfront, could hear the unending murmur of voices, street-cries and the occasional blast of a car horn.

Tuapse and its bomb-shattered dockyard seemed lost in distance and time.

Beresford closed the shutters and threw his khaki drill jacket on to a chair.

'Bloody hell, John, it feels like a homecoming.'

'My thoughts too.'

Devane watched his friend as he lifted a gin bottle, frosted with moisture, from a bucket of rapidly melting ice. *A homecoming.* After all they had done in the Mediterranean together, not that many miles away, the deaths, the moments of tragedy and loss, it seemed wrong to feel like this. Glad to be back.

He asked, 'When does this inquiry begin?'

Beresford sounded vague. 'They've had some sort of preliminary hearing. It will take a few more days. I think. We shall be the last to know, as per usual.'

Devane watched as he made two pink gins, large ones even by naval standards, and remembered Beresford's explanation about Sorokin's ruse to stop the enemy's search for the E-boat. He had been matter of fact, as only he could.

'You'd had a rough time, old son. Didn't want to deluge you with gloom. Barker was enough for one day, I thought.'

They had left it at that. For the moment.

Beresford sank down in a chair and plucked his shirt from his chest.

'Cheers!'

Devane moved his body gingerly against the chair. The scar

125

was healing well, but hurt like hell whenever he forgot to guard it against sudden contact. He had seen it in a mirror. It was livid and star-shaped like the steel splinter.

He wondered what the little nurse was doing. Probably tending more wounded troops. That small, silent room was likely crammed with sick and injured men now. They were strange people, almost impossible to know except for short, uncertain contacts. Like those he had had with Orel and the girl called Ludmilla. Perhaps even Orel spoke fluent English and listened to the background chatter of his British allies whenever he could. What were they suspicious of?

Beresford said, 'Richie's widow is being flown in today. She's got a room at *the* hotel. That's what they call it.'

Devane watched him, looking for a sign. But if Beresford had suggested his coming for some deeper motive he did not show it.

Up to this moment Devane had expected, even hoped, that she would not come. She might not want to. And with a war raging round the world it was more than likely the air transport might be withdrawn, or cancelled altogether.

He was deluding himself, clinging to the impossible dream. As usual. She was more than capable of handling these people. Often in the past he had seen her turn a man aside with the deftness of a skilled swordsman.

Beresford closed his eyes and tilted his head to swallow some more iced gin.

'Remember Korvettenkapitän Lincke?'

Devane stared at him, caught out by the sudden change of tack.

'Lincke. Of course. Why, has he been killed at long last?'

It was strange how a man's name could become as strong as the man, or a memory. Korvettenkapitän Lincke had first proved his ability in the Channel when in command of an E-boat. As soon as the dust of Dunkirk had settled, his name had begun to appear in intelligence packs, sometimes with blurred newspaper photographs pinned inside for recognition purposes. Shaking hands with Grand Admiral Raeder, or receiving an Iron Cross from Hitler himself, Lincke had lived a charmed life. A survivor like himself in many ways. It would be hardly surprising if his luck had finally run out.

Inevitably, their paths had crossed, and Devane had wondered if his enemy had known about him also. In the

Mediterranean Lincke had popped up, in command of an Italian naval unit in the Adriatic. For, if the Germans' allies possessed some of the finest torpedo boats in the world, they had for the most part lacked the leadership to make the best use of them.

Submarines had their 'aces', and in the world of fast motor torpedo boats and gunboats Lincke was high in the same quality.

Beresford did not open his eyes. 'Far from it. There were some dispatches waiting for me. Intelligence seem pretty sure Lincke's in the Black Sea.'

Devane said uneasily, 'Barker had better watch his step.'

But the joke fell flat. Lincke in the Black Sea. It was very possible. Especially if the German High Command had got wind of *Parthian* and its true purpose.

He added, 'It's too much of a coincidence. Lincke's arrival and Barker's proposed operation.'

Beresford looked at him. 'I agree. It's getting a bit personal. I also discovered that Vice-Admiral Talents, my overall boss, was at Dartmouth with Eustace Barker. I can smell the workings of the Old Pals' Act.'

Devane laughed. 'I'm glad I'm a simple soul.'

'You?' Beresford leant forward with the bottle. 'That'll be the bloody day!'

He stood up. 'I'm going to try and bribe my way into a shower somewhere. Failing that, a good woman.' He touched Devane's arm as he passed. 'Get your head down while you can. We assemble at 0900 tomorrow.'

Devane nodded, his mind dulled by the gin. Beresford's disclosure about Lincke did not fool him for a moment. Whether or not Barker's mysterious plans had anything to do with the German E-boat commander did not really count.

He must face it. Lincke was in the Black Sea for one purpose above all others.

Devane said it aloud without realizing it. 'He's going to get me, if he can.'

But Beresford had already left.

Devane poured another gin very carefully. He should feel flattered. If it had to happen, they had chosen the best one to do it.

He got to his feet, the gin untouched. Mabye that was why Beresford had let it out so casually. To give him a chance to stand down. To plead unfitness due to strain and the stress of constant action. Nobody would be able to deny him a relief, no matter what some might secretly say or think.

Devane pushed aside the shutters and allowed the sun to scorch his face and arms like a furnace.

If they thought that about him, they would have to think again.

For he was *not* like the others. *He* had nothing to lose.

When Devane, accompanied by Beresford, arrived at the shabby building where the inquiry was being conducted, he was astonished to see the familiar figure of Captain Whitcombe also present.

Devane exclaimed, 'You didn't say he would be here?'

'Oh, didn't I?' Beresford showed his pass to a sentry. 'It's all this secrecy, I expect. I never say anything nowadays, just to be safe!'

Devane strode into the shade and saluted. Beresford's explanation sounded as unconvincing as some of his others. Nevertheless, he was glad to see Whitcombe in some strange way. Although God knows why they had brought him from Special Operations for an inquiry which could have been completed in Whitehall.

Whitcombe beamed at him. 'You look well, John, damn well. Considering. How is it, by the way?'

Devane answered, 'Doesn't hurt much now. I was wondering—'

'Later.' Whitcombe took him aside as more officers arrived panting from the heat.

'I'm sorry about all this, for Richie's sake, and for his widow's, of course. But my coming out here will help *us* to complete our plans for the Black Sea strategy without attracting too much attention. Mrs Richie has the right, after the hearing, to claim the body. It's in the military hospital.'

Devane looked away. Until now he had imagined Richie was buried, probably at sea, like the men who had died after the capture of the E-boat. As he would have been if the star-shaped splinter had not been half spent.

What might it do to her when she was told? To know that Richie was lying in some iced vault while she had made love in a Chelsea hotel.

Whitcombe was watching him worriedly. 'Beresford's told you about Korvettenkapitän Lincke. My guess is that he was being sent anyway, as soon as the Germans picked up the news that Richie was on his way. You or Richie would affect Lincke in the same fashion.'

'I know.' He glanced at the clock above a military police-man's head. 'But before we go in, sir, is this inquiry really necessary, even to cover up our future operations? Richie was wrong to shoot himself, but it happens. Brave men should never crack under the strain, but they do.' He waved his hand towards the white and khaki uniforms. 'This is a farce.'

Whitcombe nodded to a messenger and headed for a side door. 'Cowardice doesn't come into it. Lieutenant-Commander Richie was already being investigated, and he knew it. He's well out of it by now, but we have to go through the motions.' He looked him directly in the eyes. 'So that we are not branded with the same mark as the Nazis!'

Devane turned to speak with Beresford, but he too had disappeared.

What the hell was Whitcombe talking about? He made no sense at all.

He saw a car stop outside the building to be surrounded immediately by a crowd of babbling onlookers and beggars. The car carried a Swedish flag, and two men left it immedi-ately. Their pale skins and neat briefcases put them miles apart from the sweating military policemen at the entrance.

'Take your places, gentlemen.'

The doors opened and Devane followed the others into the adjoining room. It could have been anywhere, but for the outdated fans and a native servant who was putting out ashtrays on a long trestle table.

The court consisted of an elderly commander, two lieutenant-commanders and a bespectacled lawyer from the Judge Advocate's department. At another table sat Whitcombe and Barker, the latter shining in a suit of white drill.

The two Swedish visitors were seated at yet another table, and were watching the members of the court settling down, arranging papers and clearing their throats.

Devane sat with his arms folded. He should not have come. Perhaps if he just got up and left nobody would notice.

The commander at the trestle table put on a pair of glasses

but looked over the top of them as he surveyed the room at large.

'Governed by the same rules of secrecy as before, this court of inquiry is reopened.' He nodded to the two Swedes and added, 'And may I offer my thanks and greetings to our, er, guests.'

Devane looked quickly over his shoulder but there was no sign of Claudia Richie.

The commander said briskly, 'Before we get down to the matter concerned in this inquiry, I have something to announce of great importance.'

He had everyone's attention now.

'This very morning, the Allied forces made several successful landings on the island of Sicily. Enemy resistance was overcome and all first objectives taken.' He looked at their faces and added dryly, 'The Royal Marines were, I'm told, the first to land yet again!'

If they could have cheered, Devane knew they would have done so. All the waiting, the setbacks and stunning losses in four years of war. This was the first step on the long way to victory.

Devane saw the commander glance quickly at the Swedes and wondered if the Sicily announcement could affect them in any way. Something to soften the pill, but for what?

The commander continued, 'The evidence in the case of Lieutenant-Commander Donald Jason Richie, Distinguished Service Cross and Bar, twice Mentioned in Despatches, Royal Naval Volunteer Reserve, is as follows, the facts having been verified by the sources contained in my report, and which out of necessity must remain a matter of secrecy.'

Devane could feel the tension around him, also the resentment against the two foreign visitors whose country remained neutral. It was a stupid resentment, but a natural one. Their presence was like an intrusion.

The commander must have sensed this. He continued, 'Our distinguished guests, Mr Winter and Mr Revelius of the Swedish committee for the investigation of welfare into the conditions of prisoners of war and enemy occupied territories, have played no small part in this investigation.'

Devane felt the resentment draining away like sand in a glass.

'On the date stated in the final report, Lieutenant-

Commander Richie was employed on a special operation on the Norwegian coast. He was in temporary command of a motor gunboat as it was considered more suitable for the operation than one of his own flotilla's MTBs.' He peered over his glasses. 'Members of the court will have noted that the motor gunboat was subsequently lost with all hands whilst attacking an enemy convoy off Ostend.'

That was why Dundas and some of the others who had served with Richie knew nothing about it, Devane thought.

The commander said, 'The operation was not completed but, whilst ashore with three of his men, Richie surprised a squad of six German soldiers and three civilians. Lieutenant-Commander Richie was well used to that kind of mission and managed to take all the Germans prisoner, one of his own men having been killed in the brief exchange of fire. It later transpired that the three civilians were Norwegians who were being taken into custody for interrogation.' He glanced severely around the room. 'Richie disarmed his prisoners but apparently made no effort to question either the German soldiers or the three civilians. Having ordered his two remaining men to carry their dead companion back to the landing place, he shot all nine men with a machine-pistol.'

Devane sat bolt upright as the quiet words plummeted into the room like grenades.

The voice continued, 'One of the Norwegians, who was in fact a member of the Resistance, managed to crawl away, and eventually crossed into Sweden for safety. From him, and as a result of more recent investigations, the facts have become fully documented.'

Devane saw Whitcombe staring across the room at him, his face like stone. Only Barker appeared calm and relaxed, like a man who has heard nothing about some terrible tragedy happening within feet of him.

The commander said, 'This is not the story of a brave man who has given so much for his country, one whose reflexes have been sharpened and honed to a point of military excellence. Nor is it something which because of his fine record should be swept aside and ignored. To do so is to condone the very things we have been fighting against for so long.'

Devane heard the murmur of voices flowing around him until it was silenced by a sharp rap on the table.

He could see it all. The unexpected confrontation, the

Germans caught off guard in what they probably considered a safe area. The Norwegians no doubt expected to be rescued, instead of facing the horrors of torture at the local Gestapo HQ.

Perhaps Richie had already passed the danger point, and the sight of an enemy, flesh and blood at close quarters, had been too much for him. But to disarm them, to gun them down like beasts, had been premeditated and not the deed of the moment. It was ironic that the men who might have been prepared to vouch for him were as dead as the Germans.

The commander folded a page on his file and signed it with a flourish.

'These are the facts and so shall they be recorded.'

He rose and replaced his cap. 'The court is dismissed.'

Devane stood up, his mind grappling with what he had heard. Richie's name was ruined. He must have known that Barker was on his way to Tuapse and once there would complete the investigation which would destroy him in the eyes of his command, *Parthian*. And that, he had been unable to bear.

Beresford was waiting for him, his eyes hidden behind dark glasses.

Devane asked harshly, 'You knew that too, I suppose?'

'Not all of it. Some I guessed. When I heard the Swedes were involved I knew it could not be kept secret.'

'Could not or *should* not?'

Beresford sounded surprised. 'For six Krauts and a couple of terrorists? God, I've shot more men in an afternoon, and so have you probably!'

'There's a difference!'

Beresford touched his cap in a casual salute. 'You could have fooled me.'

Military personnel were already putting up a larger table, carrying in more documents and resetting the scene for another service drama.

What was it, he wondered? A court martial? Someone's fingers in the mess funds, or a man drunk on duty?

He saw the servant laying out clean ashtrays even though the others were still unused.

Captain Whitcombe joined him and grunted, 'Let's have a noggin. I need it after that.'

Barker walked lightly towards them. 'Went pretty well, I

132

thought. No loose ends.' He shook his head gravely. 'Some of these fellows, I really don't know. Want to play God, it seems to me, eh?' He nodded to Devane. 'I'll talk with you later.' He nodded again. 'No loose ends. That's what I like to see.'

Devane murmured quietly, '*Bastard!*'

Whitcombe said uneasily, 'I didn't hear that. Oh, *damn*!' He turned as a lieutenant hurried towards him with something to sign. 'Won't keep you.'

But Devane was looking across to the other end of the corridor. With servicemen in all kinds and shades of uniform hurrying past her she stood out like a bright picture.

She was dressed all in white, so that her dark hair and eyes seemed to accentuate her poise, her defiance.

He saw the lieutenant leave Whitcombe and push through towards her, a book held out as if for an autograph.

Whitcombe explained heavily, 'That's the release permit for her husband's body.'

But Devane did not hear, he was already thrusting past the others, remembering that other time in the taxi when her defences had begun to crumble.

He said, 'Hello. It's me.'

She swung towards him, her eyes and mouth, even her body tensed as if to ward off an attack.

Devane took her arm and turned her to the wall, shutting out the busy people and the door of the courtroom.

She said, 'You did make me jump. I had no idea. In fact, I was just thinking. . . .'

He squeezed her arm gently. '*Easy*. You don't have to pretend with me. Just let me be with you.' When she neither looked at him nor spoke he added urgently, 'Please, Claudia, I'm not saying that to deceive or impress you. I—I thought, when I saw you in this terrible place. . . .' His voice faltered as she faced him directly.

'I hoped we might meet again one day.' She trembled as if it were freezing cold. 'Not like this.'

He watched her struggling to retain control. It was like a physical act, as if her mind and body were being possessed.

Then she said, 'If you could help. . . .'

Devane guided her towards the door. 'Let's get away from here.'

She said, 'Everyone kept apologizing, as if they were genuinely sorry. Don can't be buried at sea with naval honours because of all this. Not the "done thing" apparently.' Her chin lifted with sudden anger. 'He really messed it up for himself this time! And I thought it was because I said I was having an affair!'

Devane heard himself ask, 'Were you?' He added quickly, 'That was unforgivable. Don't say anything.'

A beggar loaded with cheap brass ornaments placed himself across their path, his teeth bared in a determined grin.

Devane said, 'Don't worry. They're not used to seeing girls like you these days. He probably thinks the cruise ships have started up again!'

But she did not smile. She turned and looked at him searchingly, the beggar and the crowded waterfront forgotten.

'I know it's very wrong. But in a strange way I'm happy.' She studied each feature of his face, as if committing it to memory. 'And I am very glad to see you. I hope it shows.'

Whitcombe paused at the top of the steps as a staff car pulled up for him.

Beresford followed his gaze and said, 'I suggested that he should come with us, sir. I seem to have done the right thing for once.'

The old captain muttered something and climbed into the car.

Captain bloody Barker's plan was almost foolproof. As safe as any of their crackpot schemes could ever be. He almost wished that he had been able to find a flaw in it before giving the signal to go ahead.

And the tall, khaki-clad lieutenant-commander with the unruly hair poking around his cap, with the lovely widow on his arm, was the obvious choice, and at short notice the *only* man who could carry it out.

There was a flaw, but not one strong enough to move the Chiefs of Staff. Even the PM had given the mission his blessing.

Whitcombe opened the file on his plump knees and frowned at the photograph of a smiling German naval officer. Korvettenkapitän Gerhard Lincke.

If Barker had thought of the plan, so too might he.

10

RIVALS AND LOVERS

Captain James Whitcombe stubbed out a cigarette, then mopped his face and throat with a crumpled handkerchief.

Outside the room, which had been loaned to him by the Army, it was pitch dark, and he could hear nameless insects hammering against the screens. In the sealed office it was stiflingly hot, like a Turkish bath, and some hissing pressure-lamps added to the discomfort. For some inexplicable reason the electric generators had failed, and Whitcombe knew he was getting too old for this kind of thing.

They had been at it all afternoon, going over aerial photographs, checking intelligence reports and listening to the local operations officers from Cairo.

He glanced at his two companions. Beresford, characteristically slumped in a chair, eyes slitted against the harsh lamps, his hair tousled. A keen and intelligent man, but one you would never know in a thousand bloody years.

As a complete contrast, Captain Barker was still as bright as a button, pushing ideas, blocking observations of which he disapproved and generally making a nuisance of himself. Even his voice, Whitcombe thought, it went on and on at the same level, toneless and inhuman. *Useless Eustace*, he called him under his breath.

But, like him or not, there was no denying the logic in his

plan. For months the Russian and German naval forces had been playing a cat-and-mouse game. Hitting a convoy here, attacking a shore position or supply dump there, with the casualities too often outweighing the value of each operation.

The Russians used their massive weight, while the Germans relied on agility and ruthless determination. It was a stalemate, and while it lasted there was no hope of a major military advance on the Eastern Front with the resulting drain of German forces in the west.

Whitcombe thought of that morning, the little commander's announcement about the Sicily invasion. 'Operation Husky', as it had been named in his secret files for so long. The pressure had to be maintained and increased. Mere people did not come into it. He tried to avoid thinking of Richie. A hero, a man who had done so much to improve the light coastal forces until they had become a powerful weapon. One slip had broken him, and soon he would be entirely forgotten. But he was not as much a casualty as a man who died under fire or by drowning?

Barker was looking at him fixedly, and with a start Whitcombe realized he must have said something.

'What?'

Barker smiled gently. 'It *is* late. We are all tired.' Except me, his voice seemed to imply. 'But we must decide. I, that is *we*, have a lot to do. The enemy might change his arrangements.'

Beresford leaned forward wearily and dragged a map across the table.

Barker eyed him confidently. 'A ship lies in a Rumanian port, safe from attack, protected more by a false neutrality than anything with real teeth. The Rumanians have encouraged a complete German occupation, I see no reason to excuse their actions or respect their non-combatant status. The Russians, on the other hand, have lost all their tactical bases in the Black Sea, except Tuapse, which could be immobilized any day if the enemy made a determined assault without regard to cost. If Germany holds the Crimea, I am certain she will use it as a springboard in the New Year.' He glanced severely at Whitcombe. 'The Germans occupy several good bases. Not content with these, they have others in Bulgarian and Rumanian territory.'

Beresford said, 'It makes sense, sir. Hit them hard through

their main support lines and the effect could escalate all along the coast. The German naval command would have to withdraw forces from the Crimea in case our attacks were part of a new pattern.'

Whitcombe nodded. Two to one. More if you included the people in London. Vice-Admiral Talents in particular. Barker's 'old chum'. He would see Barker in control of Special Operations if he could.

Barker sensed his victory. 'The captured E-boat will be able to enter the harbour without difficulty. A suitable diversion elsewhere and the use of some skilled personnel should make it a knock-out punch.' He pointed at the map. 'South-west from Tuapse and proceeding inside Turkish waters as long as possible. Then in and out, the job done.' He sat upright in his chair, his pale eyes challenging. 'Well?'

Whitcombe thought of Devane. He would be with the girl right now. Two more casualties, but he hoped that neither of them accepted it.

'What about a submarine?'

Beresford shook his head. 'None available, sir. Not small enough to get in there. Anyway, it's too shallow for a safe withdrawal. They'd pound her to scrap before she got half a cable.'

Barker smiled. 'Don't worry so much, James. If Devane is only half as good as they contend, he should be able to manage this one.'

Whitcombe retorted angrily, 'Don't patronize me! You've done a lot, but you don't know these people as I do. I was like you and all the others brought back from retirement, the "beach". Grateful at first, but ready enough to criticize all the reservists, the six-week-wonders. But now I know better, a whole lot better!'

Beresford murmured, 'Easy, sir. Nobody doubts that. Not anymore.'

Whitcombe nodded heavily. 'I should bloody well hope not. Young John Devane is the best, but he's over the edge. He knows it too, which doesn't help. We should have brought more boats into the area. *Wait and see*, that ought to be the Admiralty's damned motto!'

Barker sighed. 'It's settled then.'

The lights blinked and came on again.

Whitcombe rubbed his eyes and groped for another cigarette. 'I suppose so.'

'I'll draft the necessary signals.' Barker appeared to bounce to his feet. 'After that it will be up to me.'

Whitcombe regarded him curiously. 'And a few others.'

'About the German, Lincke?' Beresford seemed eager to cover up Whitcombe's contempt for higher authority. 'Do you think his presence means anything?'

Barker was already locking his briefcase. 'A coincidence probably, or a live wire to put some go into their naval flotillas in the Crimea. I understand that Klassman is still in command,' he shrugged carelessly, 'but maybe he needed a jolt too. Like others I could mention.'

He opened the door. 'In the morning then, gentlemen? Eight-thirty?'

Whitcombe glared. '*Nine!*'

They listened to his brisk, retreating steps, then Whitcombe said, 'Let's go to the Army mess and have a few drinks. That man really gets under my skin.'

'You'd never have guessed it, sir.'

Whitcombe grinned and then said, 'Keep an eye on Devane for me. This war isn't going to end tomorrow. We'll need him a lot more before that happens.'

Beresford smiled. 'Besides which, sir, you've made the unusual mistake of growing too fond of one of your glory boys, correct?'

Whitcombe sighed. 'Right. Trust you to realize that. You'll make admiral, you see. All brains and no bloody heart. It'll fit you like a glove!'

Devane opened the door and stood in the quiet darkness, listening, but hearing only his own breathing.

The hotel was small and scruffy, and but for the massive movement of servicemen to the new battlefields in Sicily he knew there would have been no accommodation left, even to sit down.

'Where have you been?' Her voice came out of the darkness. 'I was worried.'

Devane walked to the window and opend a shutter very slightly. It was hard to believe there was a great canal out there, ships and people, a lifeline from one sea to the next.

138

'It took time. But it's done.' He tugged open his shirt and tried to cool his skin beside the window. 'God, it's hot.'

She said, 'Come here. Tell me about it.'

He felt his way to the bed and sat down beside her, sensing her nearness, her warmth.

'I had to see several people. Luckily I know one of them from way back.' He tried to keep his voice steady. 'They've agreed to a burial at the military cemetery tomorrow. I've arranged for the Army padre to do it. Seems a nice chap. Comes from Taunton, would you believe?'

Her voice was husky, and for an instant he thought she was crying.

'You're good to me, John. I don't know what I'd have done.' Her hand reached up and touched his face and his chest. 'You know that, don't you?'

He looked down and saw her dark hair framed by a pillow. Her bare shoulders gave a faint glow, like silk, and he wanted to take her in his arms, to love her and to lose himself in her and tell her everything.

'I know that I love *you*, Claudia.' He groped for her arm and felt her stiffen.

She said, 'Sorry. It's the vaccination. Stings a bit.'

She gripped his hand and lowered it to her breast. It was hot and supple, and he could feel the nipple against his palm as she squeezed his fingers around it.

Devane bent over her and kissed her. 'This isn't just a passing thing. Not to me. I want you to accept that. If anything happens, I need to know you understand, even if you can't share all that I feel.'

Her hand left his and she touched his mouth, his eyes and his hair.

She whispered, 'I'm so happy.' She pulled him down and kissed him hard, her mouth opening to contain his, as if she wanted to make each moment last a lifetime.

He said softly, 'I shall be leaving tomorrow.'

'I see.' She struggled up and hugged herself against him. 'One night. Like the last time.'

Devane could feel the tears against his mouth as she said, 'But we're really old friends, aren't we?'

He lowered her to the bed again and threw his clothes on the floor.

'Neighbours, too.'

She clung to his neck, pulling herself up to him as he covered her with his body.

'You *must* come back, John. I need you so. If only . . .'

The rest was lost as they came together as one.

The room was small and square with a tiny window high up near the ceiling. It was freshly painted, white, like a sick room, or, in its spartan simplicity, a monk's cell.

Korvettenkapitän Gerhard Lincke lay on his back, fingers interlaced behind his head, as he stared unseeingly at the ceiling.

He disliked the smell of the fresh paint, but hated the dirt and the discomfort it caused far more.

He thought of the speech he would have to make that afternoon to the combined crews of his new command, *Gruppe Seeadler*. Seven sound boats, some with officers and men who were new to their élite service. He would probably make the same speech as usual. In Germany and Holland, in France and North Africa, Italy and Greece. Only the faces changed. They got younger.

Lincke thought reluctantly about his last leave, the one which had been cut short without explanation. The medical officer at Kiel had insisted he needed a complete rest, although Lincke had assured him he had never felt better.

He was not sorry to be back. This time it was Russia, but the enemy, like his speech, was the same. The thought made him smile, so that he looked even younger than his twenty-eight years.

His home was in the old town of Schleswig, and he had been shocked to find his parents so aged and, worse, disillusioned by their country's struggle against so many enemies.

Lincke had had two brothers. Hans, the youngest, had died at sea in a U-boat. Bernd, the oldest, a pipe-smoking infantry captain, had been captured after the British stand at El Alamein. He was sorry for his brothers, but had been embarrassed when his mother had burst out that she was actually pleased Bernd was a prisoner in England. At least he will be alive when this butchery is over, she had sobbed. It made him uneasy for her and the whole family if word of her criticism reached the wrong ears.

He threw his legs over the side of the bed and stood up in the centre of the room. He wore a white singlet and pale cream trousers. Matched against them, his fair hair and tanned arms and face made him look more like an athlete than a naval officer.

His uniform hung in a canvas wardrobe, pressed and ready. Lincke's faithful orderly, Max, saw to that. With its three bright gold stripes, the Iron Cross and the other decorations on one breast, it looked more fitting for a much older man.

On a small scrubbed table was a framed picture of his parents, dwarfed by the massive folder of secret information which he had carried with him from Kiel.

It was strange to learn that some of his old enemies from the Channel and Mediterranean were here also. He wondered if they loathed the Russians as much as he did. Their brutish soldiers, their coarse peasant women who screamed abuse even into the muzzles of a firing squad. Dirt and squalor in this vast terrain seemed even more depressing. Thank God his brother had been taken by the British and not on the Eastern Front, if half the stories of Russian atrocities were true.

He walked to the table and idly leafed open the folder. It would be like a clean canvas for him. He had the backing of the Grand Admiral and of the *Führer* himself. He would cause resentment, even hatred, but he was used to that. The war would be won. *Must* be won. The *Führer* had said so to him personally when he had hung the most coveted decoration around his neck in Berlin. Lincke was no puppet, and made his own decisions, but his meeting with Hitler had stayed with him, had inspired him beyond belief. Perhaps it was because of the different attitude. His admirals had praised him for his victories at sea. Lincke had, after all, sent one hundred and thirty thousand tons of enemy shipping to the bottom. With one *Schnellboot* that was no mean achievement. But they respected him as a weapon, whereas Hitler had made him feel like a man, a German officer.

He scanned the neat writing of the admiral's secretary, the brief comment about the British flotilla leader named Richie. *Dead.* But not in action. That was very strange. Perhaps they would soon learn more about it. When you fought a fast-moving war in little ships you needed to know your opponents far better than the details of weapons and endurance.

Lincke never believed in luck or coincidence. He had studied all the reports on the unexpected destruction of the torpedo boat escort to the Crimean convoy, the devastating attack launched by British MTBs which were not even supposed to be in the Black Sea.

One surprise was never enough. The same independent unit had attacked and seized a German *Schnellboot*, and even though it had managed to break free, only to be destroyed in their own minefield, it would not stop there.

If only he had been present when it had happened. He had questioned the idiot who had picked up the bodies and some fragments, but had learned nothing. Fools thought like fools. There was no sense in wasting more time.

Lincke had seven boats, with the authority to use the other light forces whenever he thought fit.

A page hung in mid air as he examined a newspaper photograph of Lieutenant-Commander John Devane. The new leader, but not a new name to Lincke. He was one of the British reservist officers who had caused so much amusement in Kiel in those first heady days of war and one victory after another.

People often made jokes at the expense of their enemies, usually to cover up their own uncertainties, he thought. They should have known better. An island race like the British had always relied on their amateur sailors. Dunkirk had proved that, but Drake and Raleigh had known it centuries earlier.

After the war it would be pleasant to obtain an appointment in England. Lincke had been a junior officer in the *Graf Spee* at the 1937 Coronation Review at Spithead. He could remember it vividly. The long lines of grey ships, the last great review the world would ever know. Among the foreign visitors had been many fine ships now sunk, like his own *Graf Spee* Even more, the British ones which had anchored nearby, ships like *Hood* and *Repulse*, *Barham* and *Courageous*. Now only their memories remained.

Privately, Lincke thought a shame that they were forced to fight the British at all. A total alliance against the Russians and the French, even the Italians, who were once allies and were now said to be deserting and changing sides in the wake of the Sicilian invasion, would stabilize the world.

He sighed. But that was hindsight. His immediate future was here in this miserable, war-torn corner of Russia.

The door opened, and Max, his orderly, servant and faithful guardian, peered in at him.

'They are waiting, sir.'

Lincke dressed deliberately and with care, examining his even features in a clean mirror to make certain his hair was tidy and did not bristle beneath the band of his white-topped cap.

Korvettenkapitän Gerhard Lincke, holder of the Knight's cross and Oak Leaves, and three other decorations, leader of the newly formed *Gruppe Seeadler*, was ready.

He frowned at his reflection. There had been something missing in the folder. What was it? He would send a signal about it. Devane troubled him. There was some clue or explanation which went beyond their old score.

He said, 'We have made this journey before, Max.'

The seaman stood aside to let him pass.

Lincke was an example to everyone, he thought, and he had known him for a long time. Often in the past he had imagined he might possibly die for Gerhard Lincke. Now, as he heard the assembled crews stamp to attention to receive their commander, he was quite certain of it.

Moored to the dockside, apart and slightly ahead of the smaller British craft, the captured German E-boat presented a picture of strength and power. A few shaded lights hung from the dripping concrete roof of the pen, so that the E-boat's hull appeared to glow eerily, the effect magnified by her strange interwoven camouflage of dazzle paint, blue and grey, with stark black stripes striking back from her bows like the markings of a tiger.

Commander Felip Orel moved slowly about the deserted bridge, opening a locker to check its contents, pausing to examine the compass, the torpedo sighting-bar, anything which was of interest but unfamiliar to him.

He could sense the two sentries on the jetty watching him. One British, the other one of his own men. How they symbolized their struggle, he thought bitterly. United because of a common enemy, divided by so much more.

It was past midnight, and in the bunker-like pen it was as silent as a tomb. Just the slap of oily water between the moored hulls, the occasional creak of lines and fenders. Down here, even the guns along the front were soundless.

Orel always found it easier to think clearly at moments like these. Even in the small, crowded hulls of his mixed collection of gunboats and motor launches he had trained himself to remain aloof when he needed to, or find privacy when there was none.

He reconsidered the proposed operation in the Rumanian port which Captain Sorokin had outlined to him that afternoon. It made good sense, but if things went against them the whole Russian force could be destroyed and the supply routes along the Black Sea coast left unguarded and open to attack.

The minds in Moscow still thought in terms of flotillas and squadrons, grand strategy and safe bases to keep a fleet in being. They should be here, Orel thought, especially in a few months' time when the winter sets in and the guns refused to fire and men froze at their posts.

He admired Sorokin for several reasons. His ability to keep ahead of the powerful staff in Moscow, and to stand up for his command whenever its achievements were criticized or doubted. He could even accept that some of the things which his superior thought necessary were wrapped up in the needs of war. Sorokin was often photographed in military and naval hospitals, shaking hands with wounded comrades, presenting medals to those who were dying of their wounds or for lack of proper care. Stern-faced, Sorokin had appeared in many a front-line newspaper, his camouflaged combat coat often smudged with the dried blood of those he had just visited.

Orel had seen him strip off that same coat to reveal an immaculate uniform underneath as he strode into his HQ to share champagne and caviar with his personal staff. An enigma, a hypocrite, it was hard to decide.

He thought too of the newly arrived British and what they must achieve together if the success of this operation opened up possibilities in the Crimea itself.

He had always understood that the British were different from his own people. Spoilt, over-confident and arrogant. And yet so far these failings had not shown themselves.

Orel gave a grim smile as he sat carefully in the steel chair where the dead German commander had once taken his ease. The British captain, Barker, was the exception. He was *exactly* what he had expected. A man who hid his irritation with an empty smile, who appeared to concede a point but never gave way on anything.

He slid from the chair and walked to the starboard side of the squat, businesslike bridge. She was a superior boat, he decided. With her three great Daimler-Benz diesels she could manage forty-two knots without difficulty, and four torpedoes and powerful thirty- and thirty-seven-millimetre cannon put her well ahead of the British boats.

If the enemy had seen through Sorokin's ruse they might be ready and waiting. He peered over the bridge wing at the newly painted insignia, the sea eagle with the torpedo in its claws. It had to look exactly like one of the German flotilla, *exactly*. His swarthy face hardened as he pictured the man who commanded the new *Gruppe Seeadler*. A German officer of great ability, but one who thought nothing of shooting hostages and burning coastal villages if the mood took him. Moscow had a complete file on Lincke, much of which had been gathered during his service along the Adriatic coast of Yugoslavia. A skilled and daring tactician. Orel's lip curled. But underneath all the bravado he was a true Nazi, a butcher.

He thought suddenly of Devane, his British counterpart. A hard man to know. On the surface he seemed friendly and genuinely eager to cooperate, but you could never be sure. Devane must have been picked for the command for reasons beyond his experiences afloat, his past victories. He was still away with Barker and the calm-voiced aristocrat named Beresford, the intelligence officer who spoke Russian like a second-year student. They kept their secrets well, so too would Sorokin.

Orel lowered himself from the bridge and walked aft, past the rails which ran along either side to carry the spare torpedoes and mines, until he was stopped by the guardrail across the stern. The resting British MTBs were in darkness, and yet he felt they were watching him like the two sentries.

Months and years of bitter warfare had hardened and tempered Orel more than he was prepared to admit. It had to be so. It was the only way to survive. He had lost many comrades and had also shared the agony of the family losses amongst his various commands until he had wondered if the war's brutal demands would ever end.

Towns and villages completely destroyed, old men and boys slaughtered by the advancing German armies, while their wives and daughters had been sent to Germany in cattle trucks to end their suffering in brothels and labour camps.

That was changing. Now the Germans were learning the despair of retreat. To drive them back until Russian soldiers were marching down *their* streets and repaying *their* cruelty in kind was all that mattered, and to make that possible was Orel's daily dedication.

To achieve victory many more would die. His gaze rested on the nearest MTB. Some might not know why, but the end would justify even the deaths of the innocent.

Orel turned his back, angry with himself that he had even doubted that fact, and groped his way to the brow.

The Russian sentry stamped to attention and banged his rifle to the ground. The British seaman dragged his heels together and watched Orel pass without interest. He only saluted his own officers anyway, and certainly not at night. He gave a great yawn. Bloody foreigners. Roll on my twelve.

Devane lay on his back, his face turned towards the shuttered window, outlined now by the dawn's strengthening light.

He had dreaded this morning more than any he could recall, and yet in some strange way he felt reborn and cleansed.

The girl lay pressed against him, her breast touching his, her touseled hair across his shoulder. He could feel her heartbeat, the warmth of her spine as he touched it with his hand. It must have been almost dawn when their combined want for each other had left them spent and totally exhausted. Perhaps they had hoped to hold back the new day, to repel the inevitable.

Devane felt her stir, her hand sliding across his chest, and was instantly reminded of their discovery, their love which each had believed was only a momentary need.

Now it was too late for doubt, and there was no chance of turning it aside even if they wanted to.

He turned his head and saw that her eyes were open, watching him, her lips slightly parted and moist in the pale daylight.

'I shall not go back to England.' She said it simply, as if, like their new-found love, it was past discussion. 'I'll wait. In Cairo perhaps. Until . . .'

He pressed her spine and sensed her awakening desire, rising to match his own.

When he said nothing she added, 'It will be nearer. Your Captain Whitcombe can arrange it. Anyway, they'll need all the space on the aircraft and ships until the Sicilian battle is decided.'

Devane smiled in spite of his despair at leaving her. She had it all worked out, and she was probably right about Whitcombe.

He said, 'You'd be better off in Devon. I'll know where to come when we pull out of—'

She touched his lips with her fingers. 'Shh. Careless talk. No, I'd like to stay here. Closer. Just in case you come this way again.'

He raised himself on his elbow and looked down at her.

'Closer? Eleven hundred miles as the crow flies.'

She watched his hand encircle her breast, her body moving restlessly.

'I wish I were a crow.'

He lowered his head and kissed her, knowing that he should go, knowing too he would crack if he prolonged their parting.

It was like having a terrible nightmare lurking in the background, with nothing he could do about it. He heard the traffic sounds below the window, someone whistling brightly and a far-off hoot of a tug.

She reached up and gripped him, and they gasped together as she guided him and drove away all resistance.

Later, as he dragged on his khaki drill uniform, she moved from the bed and touched his wound. Even that simple gesture made his head reel.

He turned and held her against him, knowing he was hurting her, but needing to grasp this moment.

He whispered into her hair, 'I never want to lose you, but. . . .'

She lifted her chin and looked at him steadily. Only her lower lip made her self-control a lie.

'No buts, John. We love each other. Whatever happens we must remember our luck. *Come back to me*, darling.'

And then, or so it seemed, Devane was an onlooker again, standing in the street and looking up at the hotel window. Their window.

She had opened the shutters only slightly and he could see just the pale line of her skin between them. She had been crying when the door had closed behind him but he had kept going. To return would have finished him. She probably knew that too. She seemed to understand him better than he did himself.

How long he remained in the street, oblivious to curious

stares and jostling servicemen, he did not know. He held on to her with his mind and his being. The things they had done to each other, the words they had never spoken.

Then Devane turned and stared at the waterfront, the awakening bustle, the smell of a war still to be won.

He walked quickly away from the hotel. But still the pain did not come. With sudden realization Devane understood why. He was no longer alone.

11

BARKER'S WAR

Captain Barker thrust his hands into the pockets of his reefer jacket, the thumbs protruding forward at matching angles, while he regarded the assembled officers.

'The plan of attack is virtually complete, gentlemen.' His pale eyes gleamed in the overhead lights. 'Our captured E-boat has finally been supplied with torpedoes, which seem to be sufficient. The remainder of the necessary equipment will be taken aboard in the next twenty-four hours.'

Devane sat to one side of the captain's desk and watched the other officers' reactions.

He had only been away from Tuapse for a matter of days. It felt much longer. But the bunker seemed more squalid, the surrounding bomb damage pathetic rather than defiant.

Barker was enjoying himself. His casual mention of torpedoes had brought a quick frown to Dundas's features. Barker had suggested that there should have been time enough to find the E-boat's original torpedoes which had been unloaded during her repairs and bring them back to Tuapse as well.

If there was any show of real enthusiasm amongst the officers it was one of eagerness to get the job done and be sent elsewhere to a war they understood, Devane decided.

They had all seemed genuinely glad to see him back as the flotilla's senior officer, and even Red Mackay had said cheerfully, 'Thank God I didn't have to take this lot to sea without you!'

Again and again Devane's thoughts returned to the girl named Claudia.

Already the distance between them seemed endless, their chances of meeting again almost a dream.

Barker snapped, 'It will be a hard one, gentlemen, but I want it to go like a clock! A lot will depend on timing and determination.'

Devane glanced at Beresford, who was slumped in another chair with only a tapping foot to show he was awake.

There were four other men in the room who knew the exact whereabouts of the target. A small Russian port called Mandra, some forty miles north of the Bulgarian border. With both countries completely under German control and influence, it was obviously a careful choice. The actual target was still shrouded in mystery.

He recalled what Beresford had told him about Barker's previous appointments, of his son's death in a raid which had been doomed before it had begun. It made him uneasy, and he hoped the rest of *Parthian*'s officers were not thinking as he was. Barker knew nothing of MTBs, other than what he had read or been told. His was a war of planning and local strategy. But there was no doubting his confidence. That and the fact he was out for another advancement, and possibly Whitcombe's job, were all they had going for them. Barker's toneless voice droned on and on, lifting only occasionally as he completed a sentence with a sharp snap.

Did he know about Claudia and the hotel, he wondered. Unlikely. Barker was a cold fish, a 'book-man', as Beresford had described him. He would have delighted in keeping them apart.

'And now the matter of distinguishing marks.' Barker glanced at his watch. 'I shall see that it is circulated immediately, but I want all boats to paint on a temporary pendant number forthwith. The time for stealth is over and of no value. The enemy will know *Parthian* is here, he will *not* know what we are doing.'

Devane found he was clenching and unclenching his fists. Barker was probably right, but why bother at this stage?

Barker was saying, 'The senior boat will be Number One, of

course,' he gave a thin smile, 'and the rest painted in seniority. Recognition between us and the Russian patrols is vital.'

Devane controlled his breathing with an effort. *Number One*. It was like having a target painted on the boat. There was enough to worry about without. . . . He shook himself angrily. He was overreacting. Counting his past operations and missions and matching them against the growing chances of disaster. He had seen plenty of others do it. He stared hard at the floor between his feet. *Not me. Not now.*

Lieutenant-Commander (E) Buckhurst said dourly, 'I'd like more time to go over the Jerry boat, sir. The Russian mechanics are fair enough, but still. . . .' He left the rest unsaid.

Barker regarded him coldly. 'Check it, certainly. But I should not need to tell you your duties.'

Surprisingly, Buckhurst smiled. He had considered Barker to be a bastard and merely wanted it confirmed in front of the others.

Beresford cleared his throat. 'We have invitations from several Russian messes, sir. I thought we might relax the non-fraternization at this stage.'

Barker stared at him. 'This is a combat flotilla on special operations. I do not have to spell it out, surely? The Reds have no love for us. They need us, which is entirely different in my book.'

Beresford nodded and said no more.

Devane guessed that some of the others had been getting on to Beresford about taking leave in the town and accepting invitations to dine with the local forces.

Barker squared his shoulders and looked around their faces.

'Return to your boats and tell your people. But I suggest you keep your pep-talks to a minimum. Some of the ratings seem pretty rebellious from what I've seen of them. Their records suggest they've occupied the detention quarters more than sea-going stripes!' He nodded curtly. 'Carry on.'

The officers left the concrete room and made their various ways back to the jetty. More than one of them paused to study the moored E-boat with her tiger stripes and eagle insignia.

Dundas fell in beside Devane. 'I'll be glad to get cracking, sir.' He spoke with feeling and unusual bitterness. 'This place gives me a pain somewhere.'

Devane glanced at him. 'I'll not be sorry.'

'Did it go well?' Dundas flushed. 'I—I mean at the inquiry?'

It was funny that nobody had spoken about Richie, or had tried to pry round the bald official statement. It was because others had decided, Devane guessed. Richie, right or wrong, hero or killer, was one of their own.

He answered, 'I only heard the end of it. But for the moment it's being hushed up. *Shelved* for the duration.'

Dundas said, 'His wife, er, widow, I wonder how she'll see it?'

Devane looked away. *I told him I was having an affair*, she had said.

The last night as they had laid entwined and breathless in each other's arms he had asked her about it.

She had answered without hesitation. '*You* were the affair. I invented it. Maybe I made it happen. Wishful thinking. But you were the only friend I ever heard Don praise. That meant one thing, he'd taught me that well in the past. He envied you. . . .'

Devane said slowly, 'I saw her after the inquiry.' Why had he said that? 'She took it very well.'

'Lovely girl.' Dundas could not drop it. 'He must have been mad.'

Devane remembered that Dundas had admitted his feelings for Claudia.

He said, 'We'd best check the boat. Then I'll go round the flotilla and end up with Hector Buckhurst in the *Jerry*.'

Dundas followed him down on to the MTB's deck. If they could just get through this operation and return to the Med, anywhere but here, he would try and see her again. With Richie out of the way, she might welcome a friendly face. Dundas had never forgotten. The way she moved. Her laugh, her refusal to let her husband talk down to one of his subordinates in her presence.

Lieutenant Seymour hurried after them. 'What about this stupid numbering of the boats, sir?'

Dundas grinned. 'It's so the enemy will know the men from the boys, David!'

Devane turned swiftly. 'Don't you ever let me hear you say that again, Number One! Now get on with your jobs, both of you!'

When Devane had gone below Seymour grimaced awkwardly. 'Sorry, Roddy. Should know when to keep my trap shut.'

Dundas touched his arm. 'Forget it, chum. I'll be a bastard when I'm in command too! He didn't mean anything by it. In one ear and out the other, that's my motto in this crazy regiment!' He watched the lieutenant walk away, his face clouded in gloom.

But Devane *did* mean something by his sudden anger. Was it the last mission which had shaken him so badly? The wound perhaps, the brutal reminder that death was always close by? God, they hardly needed reminding in MTBs.

A voice from the jetty made him start. He saw Barker peering down at him, his head jutting forward as he snapped, 'You've a rating aft without his cap on! You *are* the first lieutenant, I believe? Then see to it!'

Dundas saluted and kept his face expressionless. 'Aye, aye, sir!'

Inwardly he was fuming. First one telling off, then another. It was simply not his day.

Lieutenant-Commander Ralph Beresford leaned on the E-boat's chart table and looked directly at Devane. The hull was throbbing around them, the sound controlled and contained but adding to the illusion of a great beast about to be slippped from a leash. It was dusk outside. No more waiting.

'Well, how do you feel, John? Now that it's time to go?'

Devane scribbled another note on his pad and then sat back in the chair. He had been almost continuously in the German boat for two days, trying to get her measure, to thrust aside the sense of hostility. But she still felt unfamiliar, just as Barker's final plan lacked a sense of reality.

He shrugged. 'It'll be better when we get there.'

He tried to sound convincing for Beresford's sake. They had done a lot in the Mediterranean, but usually Beresford had been there with him, taking the risks, sharing the victories. Now he was being left behind at Tuapse. It would not suit him at all, especially as Barker seemed more eager to consult his superiors in far-off London than discuss his strategy with Beresford.

Devane added, 'It should be a quiet passage to the enemy

coast. If we're spotted we'll have to break off the mission anyway. No sense in stirring up the hornets in advance.'

They both smiled, remembering all the other times. The wild excitement, the despair at seeing friends fall and die, and vessels burn.

The captured E-boat, code named *Trojan*, was to enter the enemy-occupied port of Mandra and carry out a single-handed attack on a large supply ship which had been moored there for several months. She was the headquarters of the local German admiral, as well as the repair and mother ship for E-boat flotillas. She had probably serviced this very craft on arrival in the Black Sea, which helped to add to the strangeness of it all.

It was just the kind of operation which if properly executed would put *Parthian* right in the headlines, no matter what the security boys tried to do, and the effect on local enemy shipping would resound from one end of the Black Sea to the other.

Barker had said crisply, 'The spirit of Drake. None of this heavy-handed tactical nonsense. Straight in and fast away. Jerry will think twice before allowing his bases to become so scattered, eh?'

Only one MTB, Lieutenant Horne's *Buzzard*, now with a crimson number 4 painted on her hull, would accompany the E-boat as escort, and provide covering fire in the withdrawal from Mandra. It sounded dangerous, but no more so than some they had carried out before.

What Devane disliked and mistrusted more than anything was Barker's insistence that the E-boat should be crewed by selected officers and ratings from the rest of the flotilla. Horne, *Buzzard*'s CO, would be acting as Devane's second-in-command. He was very competent and experienced, and Devane guessed he had been picked specially just in case he himself should be killed. The third hand was a Canadian named Bill Durston, Mackay's first lieutenant. *To share the honour fairly*, as Barker had commented.

Pellegrine was to be Devane's coxswain, and likewise Petty Officer Ackland had charge of the E-boat's engine room. The remainder of the British ratings were mostly engine-room hands, while Barker had reluctantly conceded that the gunnery should be handled by a Russian contingent from the naval base. A total company of thirty-six officers and ratings, whereas the E-boat's normal complement was twenty-three.

Devane said, 'Provided we can get in without too much bother, we should be out again before daylight. Ivan can provide air cover for the home run to base.'

Perhaps Barker was right about urgency, but they needed more time to test the E-boat's reactions under all conditions. She was equipped with her own powerful forty-millimetre and twenty-millimetre cannons, but the replaced torpedoes, with hasty modifications, were Russian. Her full cargo of mines for the last part of the attack were also from the local armaments dump. What with that and her mixed crew she was one of the freaks of naval warfare, Devane thought.

Beresford gathered up his papers and prepared to leave. He said suddenly, 'Take care, old son. Do it your way. In the past few days I've come to believe that Churchill, Stalin and Hitler don't count for anything. This is Barker's war, and we're not allowed to forget it! So keep your head down.'

Devane guessed that Horne would be waiting impatiently to report that they were ready to get under way.

But he said, '*Parthian*, what will the rest of the lads be doing?'

Beresford swept his hair back and jammed on his cap. 'Oh, some sort of mock attack along the coast, I think. Captain Sorokin's got over his row with Barker, it seems. He had it planned as a Russian-led venture, not one managed and directed by our own gallant captain!'

Devane nodded, still troubled. 'Keep an eye on them, all the same. I'd trust Red Mackay with my life, but even he has to obey orders.'

Beresford grinned. 'Don't we all, chum. Leave it to me. You just take care of yourself.' He glanced round the brightly lit cabin. '*Trojan* indeed. Only *he* could dream up something so bloody obvious!'

Beresford held out his hand. 'I'm off then.'

Devane took an envelope from his pocket. He felt awkward without knowing why. But it was suddenly important.

He said, 'If anything goes wrong, would you send this letter for me?'

Beresford's eyes flickered down to it very briefly.

'Sure. I'll see that she gets it.'

Then with a nod he turned and clattered up the ladder.

Horne and Durston entered immediately. Horne banged his hands together and said, 'My own boat is loaded to the deck

155

beams with extra fuel. But with me aboard here with you, sir, my Number One'll not dare to lose contact!'

He gave a great guffaw. In spite of all his active service Horne still looked like a fishing skipper.

Durston grinned. 'Red sent me because he's glad to see the back of me!'

They looked at each other like conspirators.

Then Devane said, 'Make the signal.'

He glanced at the cabin and pictured the previous occupants. Maybe they had written their letters to their loved ones. *Just in case*.

He heard the Russian lieutenant mustering his gun crews and decided to leave him to it. Sorokin had picked him himself, and as he spoke very little English there seemed no point in useless translations. They all knew what to do. If they didn't, it was too bloody late now.

Devane thought of Orel and wondered how he felt about playing another support role.

Pellegrine touched his cap. 'All engines standin' by, sir.' He seemed smaller on the E-boat's bridge.

Devane smiled at him. 'They sound fine.'

The great Daimler-Benz diesels were throbbing more freely now. Soon to be moving again. New masters, a different flag, she would be indifferent to them all.

The signalman called, 'Signal acknowledged, sir. *Proceed when ready*.'

It seemed odd that the man was a stranger and not the familiar Carroll. Devane smiled. The ex-baker's roundsman.

Horne swore. 'God, there's some idiot coming inboard!' He sounded edgy, which was not like him at all.

It was Dundas, as somehow Devane knew it would be.

'Just wanted to wish you luck, sir.' He peered around the bridge as the shutters were slammed shut and the engine-room hatch swung down with a metallic clang.

'Thanks, Number One. Have the drinks set up. See you on Thursday.'

They shook hands and Dundas returned to the gloom of the concrete bunker.

'Tell *Buzzard* to start up.'

Devane walked to the rear of the bridge and watched their solitary escort vanish momentarily into a cloud of high-octane gas as she roared into life and thrashed clear of the jetty.

Mooring lines snaked aboard, and vaguely through the din Devane heard the crews of the other MTBs cheering their friends.

He saw Horne waving to his own boat as she continued to turn towards the bunker's mouth, and guessed he was probably more worried about handing over command to his number one than he was about a raid on some enemy port.

Lieutenant Durston had already gone forward and could be heard yelling at the seamen fore and aft as they prepared to cast off the final mooring ropes. His warm Canadian voice sounded strangely reassuring, Devane thought.

He thought he saw Barker and the lieutenant from Intelligence watching from the rear of the jetty, but forgot them as he ordered, 'Let go aft.' He craned over the side of the bridge. 'Slow astern starboard outer.'

The bridge began to shake, and somewhere a man said, 'You behave yourself, Jerry.'

'Let go forrard! Fend off aft!'

The jetty was sliding past very slowly, and Devane saw the seamen waving their caps from the MTBs as they moved towards the wider part of the dock.

'Stop starboard.'

Devane glanced around the bridge; the tense figures, the little pieces of fluttering bunting which were tied to unfamiliar voicepipes and switches to act as reminders. Barker would certainly not approve of those.

'Half astern port, half ahead starboard, wheel amidships.'

Big and powerful she might be, but she turned her one hundred and fifteen feet like a London taxi.

Pellegrine murmured, 'I can see the markers, sir.' He sounded slightly breathless, as if he had been running.

Devane patted his arm. 'She's all yours. Slow ahead, port and starboard outer.'

Around him men started to relax and move in their new surroundings. Wires and ropes were stowed away and the guardrails stripped to the minimum to give every gun a full arc of fire. Down in his engine room Petty Officer Tim Ackland was already busy amongst the glistening machinery, oblivious to everything but his job and the care of the three great diesels, which to him at least were beautiful.

Horne crossed the bridge, his broad figure muffled against the evening air in a duffle coat.

'We'll be clear of the dockyard and harbour limits in twenty-five minutes, sir.' He grinned. 'Don't want to end up here on a wrecked Russian, eh?' His eyes lit up briefly as a lamp blinked across from the MTB which was beating round to take station astern.

The signalman said, 'From *Buzzard*, sir. *We are following father.*'

Devane moved away as Horne replied, 'Make to them. *Stay close and learn how it's done.*'

Devane looked abeam, the town and the bomb damage were already masked in shadow, the worst scars hidden until tomorrow.

He removed his cap and let the breeze ruffle his hair. What was she doing now? Perhaps he had been wrong to leave that letter with Beresford. If he bought it, she would be made to suffer all over again.

'Starboard fifteen, Swain.' Horne sounded easier now. 'Follow the guardboat.'

Devane left them to it. They were all professionals here. They only needed him when the attack was begun.

Oh, Claudia, I love you so much.

'Sorry, sir, did you say something?'

Devane swung away from the screen. 'No, I'm going below for a moment. Take the con.' He had to fight to keep his voice level.

Horne watched him climb down from the bridge and waited for Durston to join him on the gratings.

'He seems cool.' The Canadian levelled his glasses on a half-submerged wreck as it slid past, a bell-buoy tolling mournfully like a dirge.

Horne grunted. 'Yes. He'll do me. The best.'

Durston persisted, 'This place we're going. D'you reckon we'll pull it off?'

Horne glared. 'For God's sake, go and rustle up something hot to drink. I'll *tell* you about bloody Mandra when we're back here again!'

The lieutenant strolled away, chuckling to himself, and Horne tried not to think about his own command following astern.

Pellegrine swayed at the wheel and kept his eyes on the marked channel and the will-o'-the-wisp light of the launch which was guiding him out.

As always he was weighing up his chances. They had a good team, but the E-boat was different. He pictured the necklace of mines around the decks, the extra drums of fuel, the torpedoes and magazines to feed the rapid-fire armament. A floating bomb. One mistake and his wife in Gosport could do what she bloody well liked. He frowned into the shadows. Not if he could help it.

The first hint of deeper water sluiced along the hull and raised the forecastle with a shudder. The engines responded with a deeper growl, and Horne remarked, 'We'll start the main engine as soon as we clear the harbour. That'll steady her down right enough.'

Pellegrine nodded, his mind elsewhere. Funny to think of Jerries up here. Their officers were always in a tangle too, he supposed. The petty officers in any navy were the backbone, without them the wardroom would be in a right potmess.

Below in the deserted cabin Devane sat with his legs outstretched, his ear within inches of the bridge telephone. He took out the star-shaped splinter from his pocket and turned it over in his fingers.

Then abruptly he stood up and climbed swiftly to the bridge.

He said, 'We'll test guns in thirty minutes.'

Horne was startled to see him reappear so quickly. Devane sounded completely calm, and if he had any misgivings about the mission he did not show them.

Horne said carefully, 'I was sorry to hear about Lieutenant-Commander Richie.'

'Yes.' Devane took out the star-shaped splinter and then sent it spinning over the side of the bridge. 'But that's all in the past. There's just us now. Right, Swain?'

Pellegrine showed his teeth. 'True, sir. Like all them other times. Us against the bloody world!'

Devane climbed to the forepart of the bridge and stared beyond the bows. Perhaps Lincke was out there somewhere. In Mandra maybe?

It had to happen one day, so why not there?

He tried to shrug it off. They had nearly lost the desert war because Rommel had become almost super-human in the eyes of the Eighth Army soldiers. If he let Lincke affect him in a similar fashion he could end up losing his life.

Torpedoman Pollard appeared with a steaming fanny of tea.

'Char up, gents!'

Pellegrine said sourly, 'I thought we'd got shot of you, Geordie!'

But Devane took the hot mug of sweet tea and was suddenly grateful. With men like Pollard and Pellegrine, Horne and Ackland around him he had a far stronger weapon than Lincke would ever possess.

Horne turned as he sensed Devane's presence on the bridge.

'About to alter course to south seventy west, sir.' He watched Devane's shadowy outline. 'Dawn will be up in about fifteen minutes.'

'Good.'

Devane moved to the forepart of the bridge, his feet and legs taking the E-boat's uneven plunge as she pushed across the low ranks of wavelets. No boat designed to move with speed and agility was expected to enjoy this painful crawl but, as Ackland was quick to remind anybody who was interested, fifteen knots was economical. Lost in the darkness astern, the smaller MTB was also suffering the enforced snail's pace.

Devane said, 'This is the nearest we shall be to the Turkish coast. Inform the lookouts. A punch-up with some patrol boat is the last thing we need.'

He had no worries about Horne's skill as a navigator. If anything, he was better than Dundas, and had proved in the past that he could almost smell the coastline before anyone else could spot it.

Horne said quietly, 'This is the first op I've done in the war where I've set off knowing there's not enough fuel to get me home again. I just hope Captain Barker and the Ruskies have it all worked out for a fuelling rendezvous. We'll be down to a cupful of diesel by then.' He shot a glance over the glass screen. 'My own boat back there'll be even harder to keep going.'

Devane nodded. He could trust Horne and Durston to keep their mouths shut about this extra hazard. But the seamen and engine-room ratings were not fools. They knew the score all right.

'We *must* conserve fuel. This time tomorrow we'll be in the thick of it. After that. . . .' He shrugged. 'We'll manage somehow.'

Horne chuckled. 'Most of the lads are too sick with the

motion to care. As for the Ruskies, they seem as happy as sandboys. They know their gunnery too. Just as well.'

Devane raised his glasses and moved them carefully from bow to bow. Black horizon, the sea confined to a few pale crests, and a jagged edge of spray from the stem. In minutes it would all change again. Blue sky and empty sea. The last part was the most important.

He thought of the long, endless day while they cruised closer and closer to the western end of the Black Sea. The nearer they got, the hazier the plan of attack and last-second alternatives seemed to become.

The seaman on the wheel stood to one side as Pellegrine appeared yawning and rubbing his eyes. He seemed to sense each alteration of course and trusted nobody but himself to handle it.

The watchkeepers changed, the gun crews removed the waterproof covers and checked their magazines. A leading torpedoman appeared from nowhere and began a methodical inspection of the starboard tube. To an onlooker it would appear as if each man had been aboard for years instead of hours.

Devane got his first glimpse of the MTB bouncing gracelessly astern. Cracking on speed for the final part of the attack would seem like a relief after this.

Horne followed his glance. 'She's lively. But I'll lay odds that my Number One'll heave a sigh when he's used up some of his fuel and to blazes with the return trip! Why the hell can't *we* have diesels like the Jerries? The fools who are supposed to be planning this war might at least spare a thought for the poor devils who have to put to sea in a mobile petrol drum!'

Lieutenant Durston lurched on to the bridge and squinted at the brightening sky.

He said brightly, 'Breakfast's ready.'

'*Aircraft!* Bearing red four-five! Moving right to left. Angle of sight two-oh!'

Horne leapt across the bridge. '*Jesus!*'

Devane raised his glasses and moved them deliberately across a filmy bank of cloud. Against it the tiny black dot appeared to be motionless. An insect pinned there in midflight.

'Call up *Buzzard*. Tell them—'

'She's seen it, sir.'

Horne breathed out fiercely. 'Good thinking. If my Number One had used a lamp instead of flags I'd have murdered him!'

'Dead slow all engines. Tell the Chief what's happening.' Devane concentrated on the little dot until his eyes throbbed. Even at this speed their wake could be seen for miles by some vigilant airman. The engines sighed and the deck swayed and wallowed more heavily.

'Aircraft's altered course, sir. Heading due south.'

Durston muttered, 'Anti-submarine patrol maybe. Too near land to be German.'

It will make no difference, Devane thought grimly. If the plane was Turkish the enemy would hear of their presence just as quickly.

Durston rubbed his chin. 'Hell, I wonder if the bastard's spotted us.' He had forgotten all about breakfast.

The lookout, crouched over his massive search-binoculars, shifted them slightly on their mounting.

'No change, sir.'

'Now what?' Horne did not look directly at Devane. 'Did he or didn't he?'

Devane let the glasses fall to his chest. They were all looking at him even though their faces were directed anywhere but in his direction.

It was his decision. *The independent command.* Press on, or abort now and hope for another chance later on?

A German pilot would fly exactly as this one was doing. He would remain on course, do nothing to show he had seen the two white wakes on the sea below.

He would make his signal later. *What ships? Where bound?* Devane could imagine the wires humming, some German staff officer being sent to report to his admiral.

But suppose it was a Turk? Unskilled in the craft of modern warfare, he might be too curious to stay away. On the other hand. . . .

Devane jammed his fist into his pocket and clenched it so tightly the pain helped to slow his racing thoughts.

He said, 'Disregard. Resume cruising speed in ten minutes. Inform *Buzzard.*'

Just like that. It was all it took to make a decision. One which might kill every man aboard within the hour.

He continued with the pretence. 'Now about breakfast. . . .' He saw them relax and grin at each other.

The skipper's not bothered. No panic yet. He could almost hear them.

Claudia had wanted to know what it was like. But how could he describe this kind of madness?

12

NO CHANCE MEETING

'Course north twenty west, sir,' Pellegrine's eyes glowed faintly in the shaded compass light. 'Revolutions for eighteen knots.'

'Very good.' Devane tugged at his jacket and shirt. With the steel shutters slammed shut, and all but the observation slits closed around the E-boat's bridge, the air was clammy and oppressive.

Lieutenant Horne stood just beside the coxswain, his thick figure rising and falling easily to the motion. His upbringing in lively drifters had seemingly left him untroubled by anything but a Force Ten.

Devane felt the tension around and below him. All the waiting, the hourly expectation of discovery or an ambush following the sighting of that aircraft had taken a toll of their nerves. On the last leg of the journey they had stopped engines while the spare fuel drums had been lowered outboard and forced beneath the surface until they had filled and sunk from sight. One empty diesel or petrol drum sighted by a patrol vessel would be more than enough to alarm the defences.

Some sort of argument had broken out between two of the Russians and some seamen. The Russian lieutenant, a round-faced, amiable-looking man called Patolichev, had stopped it simply by producing his automatic pistol and clicking the safety catch back and forth. The Russians had dropped the argument, and the British sailors had been too shocked by such unorthodox behaviour from an officer to push the matter further.

Horne said suddenly, 'I think we've made it, sir. We're less than twenty miles from the inlet. Even Jerry wouldn't delay an attack much later than this.'

Devane said nothing. Horne was worried. About the mission, or his own boat which was still following somewhere astern, he could not tell. He examined his own feelings. He felt surprisingly calm, as if his whole being was resting. Like a cat about to gather every ounce of skill and prowess to spring on its unsuspecting prey.

Devane wiped his face with a signal flag. He had forgotten nothing, as far as he could tell.

Thank God they were making better headway now, so that the sickening motion was gone. When he had started in MTBs Devane had often wondered why the German boats had appeared steadier and hard to hit with anything but rapid fire. The boat was cruising along at eighteen knots with barely any wash to betray her presence. Horne's boat would be lifting her bows and tossing the water aside in a great white moustache. Impressive and dashing, but it could be a dead giveaway.

The German designers had thought of everything. Pellegrine was able to steer the boat with the central rudder, one of three. The side rudders were turned outwards to an angle of thirty degrees. It improved speed and cut down wash and bow wave to a minimum. Simple, when you thought about it.

Devane said, 'Test communications. And post two more lookouts on the upper bridge.' He peered round in the gloom. 'Interpreter?'

'Here, sir.'

'Come and join me.' Devane was astonished at his own casual manner. Perhaps he was always like this and had never noticed it before. 'If we have to speak to a patrol, you'd better be ready with the loudhailer.'

The interpreter groped from the rear of the wheelhouse, and Devane heard Pellegrine mutter, 'Gawd, you again?'

It was Metcalf. Devane had left it to Beresford to select a convincing interpreter, but he had not expected to see the young seaman who had failed to get his commission.

Like most of the hands he was wearing a white sweater, the

165

nearest thing to a German's sea-going gear, without actually wearing the uniforms of dead sailors.

Metcalf gripped the bridge rail and said fiercely, 'Ready, sir.'

Horne called, 'Communications tested and correct, sir. All guns loaded.'

Devane peered at his luminous watch. Even that was German. *Soon now*.

Metcalf must have taken his scrutiny as uncertainty and whispered, 'Will I have to speak, sir?'

'Not likely. There'll be a challenge, and provided the Ruskies have got it right, we should be able to flash the correct reply.' He tore his mind from the mental picture he had formed of the little port, Mandra. 'Feeling all right, Metcalf?'

Metcalf shivered. 'Yessir. Fine.' It was true. He had never felt better. All the way from Tuapse, through the day and night, as he had listened to the others swopping stories of their conquests ashore, of their officers, or simply about their homes, he had been thinking of this moment. It might be his last chance. Even the other seamen had studied him with more respect once they had discovered he could speak German. Metcalf could speak three languages as it happened, but the others could wait for the present.

Devane forgot the young seaman at his side as Horne yelled, 'Port lookout reports a light at red four-five.' It sounded like a question.

Devane snapped, 'Alter course. Steer north thirty west.'

It would take only minutes to make up for the alteration of course. But to steer straight past the mysterious light would be inviting trouble. If there was an enemy patrol lying off shore he would soon spot the British MTB's wash etched against the black horizon like a playful dolphin.

'Who's the lookout?'

Horne answered promptly, 'Able Seaman Tomkins, sir. One of my chaps. He's red-hot.'

The rating at the voicepipe said in a hushed tone, 'Lookout reports the light again, sir. Low down. Could be a torch.'

'Torch?' Devane crossed the bridge and wrenched open one of the steel shutters.

As he levelled his powerful night glasses he heard Horne say, 'Fisherman, most likely. Fouled a net.'

Horne should know. But whoever it was would probably

have a radio. Two unlit craft passing so near might make him nervous. It was like the Turkish aircraft all over again, except that now they were within an hour of their objective.

The rating at the voicepipe said, 'Another flash, sir.'

'Could it be a buoy of some kind?'

Horne said, 'No. I checked the chart before we increased speed.'

'Fine on the port bow now, sir.'

'Slow ahead all engines.' And let's hope the MTB is awake and doesn't run up our backside.

'All slow ahead, sir.'

Devane bit his lip. 'Bunts, get aloft to the searchlight. Train it on the bearing and when I give the word. . . .'

The signalman grinned. 'On me way, sir.'

Devane rested his back against the signal locker and felt the pain of his wound stab at him like fire. He remembered the hotel room. The shutters. The girl's softness against the scar.

'Warn all guns to stand by.' What was the matter with him? Instinct, some latent warning?

'Ready, sir.'

'Searchlight!'

The beam cut across the sea like something solid, pinning down the other vessel and transforming her into solid ice.

Horne murmured, 'Fishing, right enough!'

Another voice yelled, 'Launch alongside!'

'Bloody hell!' Devane jumped to the voicepipes. 'Full ahead!'

With her great engines roaring, the E-boat crashed across the water like a battering ram. Devane saw tiny figures mesmerized and unreal in the unwavering beam of light, and a tiny patch of colour beyond the fisherman's battered hull.

A grey tripod mast, the glint of steel. A patrol boat. It was probably a routine search of local Rumanian vessels, as much to break the boredom as anything.

Horne shouted, 'Open fire, sir?' In the reflected glare he looked wild. Like a stranger.

'No!' Devane wheeled round and seized Metcalf's arm. 'All set, my lad?' He saw the youth nod jerkily. 'Steer round the other side of them, Swain!' He gestured sharply at Horne. 'Reduce speed. Twelve knots.'

Horne said hoarsely, 'But if they fire on *us*, sir?'

'I know!' Devane could not keep the rasp out of his tone. He

did not have to be reminded of the lethal necklace of mines around the deck, the torpedoes and all the extra ammunition. Horne should not need telling either.

The engines sighed into a throaty rumble, the throwback from the bows surging alongside like a mill stream.

Devane wanted to run to the upper bridge and look for *Buzzard*. But he dare not take his eyes from the oncoming boats. He had to trust men he barely knew, like Harry Rodger, the MTB's number one who was in temporary command. One slip now and they could be blown to fragments, or at best crippled.

Devane said, 'Call him up, Metcalf. *What ship?*'

A German E-boat, new to the Black Sea, would make a challenge without hesitation. They were well away from the main combat area, and one of their own was already carrying out some specified duty. He listened to Metcalf's voice, harsh and distorted in the loudhailer. When he rested his hand on his shoulder he could feel his whole body quivering. But it was not fear. Devane could see his features clearly in the searchlight's blue glare. He was wildly excited.

Devane said, 'Alongside, starboard side to. Warn Lieutenant Durston. Get the fenders ready, we'll grapple if possible.'

Pellegrine eased the wheel over so that the fishing boat, with the low-lying launch tied alongside, seemed to pivot round on the end of the beam.

Devane said, 'Tell the W/T office to listen for any squawks from the Jerry. We'll lob a depth charge under his keel if he tries anything.'

Horne yelled, 'Stop those Russians from jabbering!'

Metcalf lowered the loudhailer. 'No reply, sir.'

'Not to worry.'

Devane levelled his glasses and watched some German seamen shielding their eyes from the searchlight as they lowered rope fenders over the side. The suddenness, the casual challenge, each had played a vital part. The next three minutes were critical.

A heaving line snaked across the disturbed water and was caught deftly by a German.

Devane looked quickly across the two hulls towards the horizon. It was playing tricks. It had to be. It looked paler already. He could not afford to hang about any longer.

'*Boarders away!*'

A whistle shrilled, and even as the E-boat surged alongside the smaller craft the first seaman leapt across the slit of trapped water.

A shot cracked out, and the searchlight above the bridge exploded like a hand grenade. Above the throbbing engines Devane heard the Canadian lieutenant's voice, the sudden clatter of automatic fire, then complete silence.

Horne exclaimed thickly, 'Both boats taken, sir. The Ruskies shot down a few by the look of it. Bastards.'

Devane nodded. Who did he mean? 'Take charge of the patrol launch!'

Durston could not hear him and he seized Metcalf's arm again. 'Go across and tell him to follow us in. Disable the fishing boat and leave her.' He saw the MTB's bow wave surging out of the gloom and breathed out tightly. 'And tell Lieutenant Durston from me. Fast as he can, right?'

Metcalf nodded, barely able to speak. 'Y-yes, sir.'

Devane found he could even smile. 'You did well, by the way. Now off you go, and keep your head down.'

Pellegrine chuckled, 'Better watch out, sir. 'E'll 'ave your job otherwise!'

Horne came back, breathing noisily. 'All secure, sir. But I'm afraid Bunts has bought it.'

They both looked up as a thin black line ran down from the upper bridge searchlight mounting. When daylight came that stain would be red.

'Cast off.' Devane strode to the ladder. 'I'm going up. See that the flags are hoisted for the final run in.'

Horne watched him climb up the short ladder and heard him snap open the voicepipes. He could see it clearly in his mind. Devane outwardly calm, risking his life on the exposed upper bridge to guide his little flotilla through hell if need be. Sharing his position with a dead signalman whose name he had never known.

As the light filtered towards the land to separate sea from sky, shore from shadows, the flags were hoisted to either yard. The white ensign to starboard and the blue and white Russian flag, its star and hammer and sickle emblems standing against the dull sky like the signalman's blood.

A searchlight, already feeble in the dawn light, swung across the water and hesitated above the three approaching boats.

From another bearing a lamp blinked out a curt challenge, and just as quickly a reply was flashed by Durston's unexpected command. Devane found time to realize that the signal was different from the one he had been instructed to use. Fate was still watching over him.

He licked his lips, his mouth suddenly like ashes.

'Full ahead all engines! *Start the attack!*'

Beresford sat down in a corner of Captain Barker's office-cum-operations room and watched his superior as he peered intently at his coloured chart. There were counters and little flags on it, strips of coloured tape to denote local minefields, tiny pencilled signposts of reports which awaited confirmation.

Beresford sighed. The whole of the Black Sea's naval strategy condensed into one small room. Barker showed no sign of tiredness, and beneath the glaring lights his neat head looked glossy and well groomed.

It would soon be time. Beresford glanced at the clock. He pictured the MTB and the captured E-boat, Devane and other faces he come to know as friends.

Barker looked at him. 'Did you discover anything from the command bunker?'

'I saw Sorokin and his staff, sir. It all seemed spot on.'

'Spot on. I do wish you would confine yourself to the English language!' But Barker's tone lacked its usual severity. His mind was busy elsewhere.

Beresford added, '*Parthian* has regrouped as ordered, sir. Lieutenant-Commander Mackay is taking the four boats on a sweep to the west sector.' He hid a smile. He had almost called Mackay 'Red'.

'Hmm. Lieutenant Kimber should be here too.'

'I left him with Sorokin, sir. Our link with the Russians, just in case things get a bit hectic later on.'

'*Things* will soon change, be assured of that.' Barker looked around his little HQ. 'I shall have my own staff, communications, intelligence, operations, everything I need. I'm not playing messenger boy for the Reds, believe me!'

Beresford did not know what had brought this on, nor did he care. Had he been with Devane he would have felt differently, part of it, win or lose. He tried not to look at the clock again. Damn bloody Barker and his empire building.

He said gently, 'This command may even warrant an officer of flag rank, sir? An accelerated promotion for you, perhaps?'

He had expected Barker to bite his head off, or at least to scoff at the idea. But Barker nodded gravely.

'You may be right. I would certainly not shirk the responsibility.'

The telephone jangled and Beresford lifted it swiftly to his ear. It was Kimber, the poker-faced intelligence officer.

'Everything is quiet, sir. Sorokin has received several reports about the diversions. The Germans are running a fast convoy towards Sevastopol. They are bound to be expecting an attack on it. I gather that Commander Orel is in charge. He's got some gunboats and a couple of heavy support craft.' He lowered his voice as if others were nearby. 'The Germans are using F-lighters unfortunately.'

Barker snapped testily, 'Is this a private conversation?'

Beresford put down the telephone and smiled at him. 'The diversionary attack is under way, sir. But Kimber has discovered that Jerry is using F-lighters.' He saw the shutters drop behind Barker's pale eyes and added, 'F-lighters are fairly fast and carry heavy armament. They also hump cargo, so they are in fact both convoy *and* escort. Another worrying factor is that they are too shallow draught for a torpedo attack. I've run up against them in the Med.'

Barker walked to another wall map. 'Well, I *know* that, Ralph. You're not the only one with combat experience!'

Beresford turned away. *You lying little bastard. You hadn't a bloody clue!*

The door opened and Lieutenant Kimber entered the concrete room, his face pale and tired.

Barker glared. 'Why are you here?'

'Captain Sorokin thought I should be with you, sir. He will keep us informed.'

'See?' Barker turned to Beresford. 'Secrecy. Tell us nothing. Damn Bolsheviks!'

Kimber laid some counters on the coloured chart. '*Parthian*'s approximate position, sir.'

Barker leant over the chart. '*Merlin*, what the hell is *she* doing?'

Kimber shifted uncomfortably. 'Sorokin requested that a boat be detached to search for the crew of one of their aircraft

171

which has ditched, sir. Lieutenant Dundas in *Merlin* was at the end of the patrol area and so the nearest. I thought—'

Barker said sharply, 'You *thought*, did you? That makes a bloody change around here!' He swung on Beresford. 'I instructed Mackay to stay in position, I ordered him to remain in his sector until after the attack on Mandra was completed! Well, did I not?'

Beresford felt a touch of anxiety. Barker was really worried about something. There was sweat on his upper lip and he seemed unable to keep still.

'You also ordered *Merlin* to patrol on the flotilla's extreme westerly flank, sir. She would be the obvious choice to search for survivors. If you like, I'll go and speak to Sorokin myself —' He got no further.

'No. I want you here.' Surprisingly, he began to hum quietly to himself, his fingers tapping in time against his thigh. 'Ring Sorokin's operations staff and find out all you can about enemy movements.' He stared at the clock. 'Well, Devane will be in position about now.' He could not resist adding, 'Provided he has not forgotten how to obey orders too!'

Beresford spoke to the officer he had already met at the Russian HQ, his mind automatically sifting details, but his attention still fixed on Barker's busily tapping fingers.

He said, 'The attack on the German convoy has begun, sir. No reports of damage or casualties yet, but it seems as if the Germans were expecting it.'

'What about *Parthian*? Is Mackay still in his sector?'

'South of the Crimea the weather has closed in a bit, sir. Sea mist, poor visibility.'

'I did not ask for a weather report!'

'Lieutenant-Commander Mackay has retained radio silence, sir. As ordered.'

'Yes. Yes, I see.' Barker's hum rose and fell like a disturbed bee. 'Keep that line open. Any news of *Merlin* and. . . .' He shut his mouth and returned to the chart table.

Beresford gripped the telephone so tightly that he thought it might snap. It could not be. Surely not even Barker would set up Dundas's boat as the bait for Lincke? He shook himself angrily. He was too tired, too rattled to think clearly. It was ridiculous. He tried again, his eyes moving to the nearest wall map.

German coastal forces *had* to be drawn away from the

Rumanian port of Mandra. The Russians had mounted a spirited attack on a legitimate target, except that the target would be more capable of hitting back than a handful of merchantmen. After *Parthian*'s previous successes, an old hand like Lincke would be looking further afield, searching for flaws, taking counter-measures.

Beresford realized he had started to sweat. It was unnerving. Barker had foreseen this possibility but had sent Dundas to the extreme boundary of the so-called safe patrol area. Safe? In the Black Sea? He must be raving mad.

If Lincke took it upon himself to investigate, *Parthian* would be in the vicinity. Beresford thought about it soberly. He could see it exactly. The MTB with the new number 1 painted on her hull, like a bone to a terrier as far as Lincke was concerned.

But things had gone badly wrong. A plane had ditched, and Dundas had been requested to make a search for its crew. As the Russians were laying on such a massive attack to draw the fire from Devane, it was the least they could do.

Barker snapped, 'Anything?'

'No, sir.'

Beresford did not dare look at him. Barker would know that every minute was taking Dundas further and further away from his consorts. And Barker could do or say nothing about it without betraying himself and showing what he had planned.

Kimber was on the other telephone, still fuming at Barker's onslaught.

'Russian Intelligence reports that the attack on Mandra has begun.' His eyes lifted to the clock. 'Allowing for the delays, they should be clear away by now.' Or dead, his voice seemed to suggest.

Beresford watched Barker's shadow as he moved another little counter on his chart. Perhaps that was how his son had died in the crazy attempt to capture a German general. It made Don Richie's crime seem like a joke.

He thought of the letter Devane had given him, the one which lay in his safe.

Come on, John, fight your way home. Just like the other times. It's not just us who need you now.

The telephone came to life against his ear, and he could feel Barker looking at him.

Beresford said, 'Dundas has picked up faint radio signals.

Probably from a life-raft. He passed the information on R/T to a Russian patrol boat before heading off to investigate.'

Barker stared at him for several seconds. 'Good. Fine. Dundas should be able to get a fix on it and return to *Parthian*'s sector without further delay.'

Beresford licked his lips and watched the colour returning to Barker's face.

It was true. All of it. Barker had staked out Dundas like a goat for a tiger.

Even Barker could not hide the relief, the knowledge that Dundas would be within call of *Parthian*'s boats once he had found the luckless airmen.

Beresford wanted to hurl the telephone at his complacent, arrogant head.

In every theatre of war men were dying right at this and every moment. Hundreds of them, maybe thousands. And what of the ones who counted each hour as another reprieve, he wondered. The first soldiers on the prongs of a raid on an enemy's position, the ones who rarely lasted. Others who covered the retreats and waited for death to root them out. Were they being used by men like Barker?

He stood up angrily, the telephone hot against his ear. In the end there were no victors. Only survivors.

Some one hundred and fifty miles west of the cramped bunker where Barker and Beresford waited for news, the motor torpedo boat code named *Merlin* idled like a ghost ship through a swirling maze of mist.

Lieutenant Roddy Dundas recrossed the open bridge and trained his glasses abeam in a hopeless attempt to find the horizon or the sky. It should be dawn, and but for the eerie mists which passed through the gun mountings and rigging like pieces of torn shrouds they would surely have sighted something by now.

The feeble distress signal was intermittent but identifiable as the kind used by airmen in rubber dinghies, something for searching vessels to home on. When the sea got colder the signal was the margin of life itself.

He swore under his breath. The boat felt different. Like a hotel where all the old guests have departed. Able Seaman Irwin, boatswain's mate, was on the wheel, not the redoubtable Pellegrine. There was an excellent artificer looking after the motors, but not a patch on Petty Officer Ackland.

Leading Signalman Carroll murmured, 'I reckon we'll see something soon, sir.'

Dundas grimaced. 'Hope so.'

It was comforting to have Carroll anyway. He peered at his watch and wondered how Devane and the others were managing. Should have started by now. It was always much quicker than you believed it would be. Minutes, when you had imagined it was an eternity.

Dundas thought too of the letter he had seen on Beresford's desk before he had locked it away. Her name and a box number. So their meeting had not been casual. He felt the prick of resentment behind his eyes. He was being stupid, but could not help himself. That was the trouble in small ships. Too much watchkeeping, too long hours with only the memories to keep you company.

It was no use trying to ignore it. No good to keep saying it was hopeless. He had only spoken to her a few times at flotilla parties in England. God, how he had envied Richie. And now Devane had taken over.

He heard men shifting their feet on deck, the creak of a gun mounting as the muzzle was swung from side to side.

Suppose Devane did not make it back? He tried to repress the wild idea. He would go to her and explain. She might. . . . He swung round as Lieutenant Seymour appeared on the bridge.

'I've been all round, Number One.' Seymour grinned. 'I suppose I should call you "sir" as you are temporarily in command.'

'*Right*.' Dundas turned away and added, 'Sorry I snapped, David.'

'Is it the temporarily bit you dislike?'

'I'd like to read that book of yours, when you write it.' He felt foolish, idiotic. Seymour had done as much as anyone. There was certainly no cause to take it out on him. 'And discover what you think of all of us.'

Carroll said, 'Sparks reports another signal, sir. Same bearing.'

'Thanks.' Dundas banged his hands together. 'I wish we could pile on some revs, but we might overshoot or run the poor buggers down in the water.'

'Who'd be a high-fly boy, eh?' Seymour yawned. 'Hope the SO's all right.' He glanced to the forepart of the bridge. 'He's a real character, is our John Devane.'

Carroll, oblivious to Seymour's mental picture of Devane, the one he would eventually put in his book, and to Dundas's hurt and resentment, added, 'Signal's very strong, sir.'

Dundas sighed. 'Get up forrard, David, with three good hands. Have a scrambling net and a grapnel ready. I'll stop everything when you pass the word.' He gave a rueful grin. 'Bloody Russians. I just hope they're grateful, that's all!'

Seymour clambered to the deck, nodding to the machine-gunner on the port side, and knowing the man was concealing a lighted cigarette beneath his duffle coat.

Characters, characters; there were almost too many to cope with.

He walked carefully forward, his feet slipping on the wet deck as the MTB pitched uneasily in a quarter sea. It was humid and clammy. In an hour or so it would be sunny again.

He saw Leading Seaman Priest by the six-pounder and beckoned to him.

Priest grinned through the mist. 'Net an' fish 'ook ready, sir!'

Seymour clutched the rim of the forward hatch and knelt down, his eyes on the drifting mist. The seamen watched him curiously, glad of something to break the boredom.

Priest asked, 'D'you think there'll be some mail waitin' when we get back, sir?'

Seymour smiled. 'Don't tell me you're in more trouble at home?'

He stiffened as he saw the incredulous expression on Priest's face. When he swung round again he felt as if his heart and lungs were being crushed in a vice.

A small breeze had lifted the mist very slightly, so that it floated above the dull water like a canopy.

And there, almost dead ahead, her black and white stripes stark against the sea, was an E-boat.

Seymour was twenty-two years old and had seen enough action to prepare him for almost anything. And yet he was unable to move, as if he was under some sort of spell.

Small pictures flashed through his mind, apprehension and despair, and the chilling understanding that this was no chance meeting in the mist.

It was all in a split second, and yet his mind was able to record each part of it. The yellow dinghy lashed to the E-boat's side, two dead airmen still dangling towards the water like puppets. The trap which they had sprung.

Something snapped inside him and he twisted round on the wet deck, his mouth shaping the words, the warning, even though it was too late.

Then came the cannon and machine-gun fire, crashing into the slow-moving boat like iron flails; flames, smoke and wood splinters ripping through the air, engulfing Seymour, stopping him and hurling him to the deck.

He dimly realized that Priest was running towards the six-pounder, that a seaman called Nairn was rolling over and over, his clothing smoking and then blazing before he vanished over the side.

Seymour managed to lurch to his feet, the agony closing around him, tearing his face and body like claws as he tried to stagger aft.

He heard someone screaming and screaming, the sound scraping his skull until he collapsed against the six-pounder's shield and tried to press his hands over his ears.

In those terrible seconds Seymour knew that the screaming was his own, and it occurred to him he could not shut it out, for both of his hands had gone. Then, mercifully, all sound and pain stopped.

13

THE BRIGHT FACE OF DANGER

Lieutenant Horne exclaimed thickly, 'I just *don't* believe it!' He stared across the port side of the bridge as a wedge-shaped spur of land swept abeam. 'They must be fast asleep!'

A seaman at the voicepipes said, 'Better if we hauled the flags down, eh, Swain? We might get clean up to the ruddy front door!'

Pellegrine tucked his jaw firmly into the neck of his sweater and concentrated on the shifting patterns beyond the bows where the inlet's sheltered water jostled with the sea.

Unlike the seaman, he knew quite a bit about Devane. If only half was true it seemed unlikely he would begin an attack under false colours. Personally, the coxswain could not have cared less if they had entered the inlet with a Portuguese ensign. All he wanted was to get on with it, then find the open water again.

'Stand by!' Devane's voice sounded clipped in the voicepipe. 'Port a bit, Swain.'

Pellegrine moved the spokes and strained his eyes through the observation slit. He was not sure what he had been expecting, and after all all the ops he had done he should not have had any room left for surprises. At the briefing,

Lieutenant-Commander Beresford, 'his lordship' as the lads called him, had told them about the German supply and HQ ship which must be destroyed at all costs. She had originally been named *Potsdam*, a cargo liner of some twenty thousand tons which in peaceful times had traded between Hamburg and the South Americas.

Pellegrine had studied some pictures of the ship, old ones showing her in her peacetime livery.

Now, as she loomed through the shadows at the far side of the inlet, he could not imagine how she had managed to pick up her moorings without running aground. She was huge, vast like a block of tenements, so that the pale blobs of houses dotted about the hillside beyond seemed insignificant by comparison. •

He found that he was sweating with anticipation. The engines were growling confidently at half-speed, the bow wave rolling away towards the shore to port and rocking some sleeping fishing boats to starboard. Surely to God someone would sound the alarm?

He heard Devane again as he said, 'Signal Durston to increase speed and take the lead.' His voice grew louder as he lowered his mouth to the tube. 'Boom ahead. Prepare for some excitement.'

That was all. No doubts, no uncertainty.

Pellegrine wiped his fingers on his sweater and took a firmer grip on the wheel. To the seaman at his side he said grimly, 'If I catch one, you take over on th' double, got it?'

The man nodded. 'What if *I* get clobbered, Swain?'

'Then we'll both sit on a bleedin' cloud and watch the rest make a potmess of it!'

On the platform bridge above the wheelhouse Devane watched the German launch sliding ahead, some vague shapes crowded in her open cockpit. Lieutenant Harry Rodger in the MTB had dropped well astern, but for all the interest being shown after their brief exchange of signals they could have gone in line abreast with a band playing, he thought.

Two Russians hurried to the forepart of the bridge and cocked their sub-machine-guns. One of them was using the dead signalman to steady his gun.

Devane lifted his glasses and examined the great wall-sided HQ ship. She looked as if she was never intended to move again. Catwalks and derricks, pontoons alongside, even a tug nestling against her fat flank as if for succour. She was damn big.

'Slow ahead all engines.'

The enemy would be expecting them to reduce speed about now while the boom was opened. He could see it well in the strengthening light. A long line of buoys, no doubt with anti-torpedo nets strung between them. There was no chance of a submarine getting in. She would hit bottom in no time.

Thank God Durston had managed to seize the local code-book before the German launch crew could fling it overboard. He saw the sudden blink of a hand lamp, the responding flicker from the great ship's upperworks.

Faintly above the engines he heard a clatter of machinery and saw the boom begin to open, a shaded blue light bobbing on the end of the unmoving part.

He cleared his throat, then said sharply, 'Stand by, torpedoes! Signal Durston to remain in the boom entrance. We'll pick him up as we leave.'

The blue light was passing them now, they were already through the line of buoys. It was no longer a suggested attack, another crackbrained operation, nor was it next week or the day after tomorrow. *It was bloody now!*

Devane gripped a stanchion, his eyes watering with concentration as he tried to estimate the range and exact bearing of the target. Not that he could miss. Provided the Russian torpedoes worked properly, and the detonators and pistols functioned, that the torpedoes did not nosedive to the bottom and blow off the bows. . . . He had to smother his racing thoughts, to accept the inevitable.

A searchlight swept across the inlet, even fainter now as the sky continued to brighten. It seemed confused until it settled on the launch by the open boom and rebounded to the two fluttering flags above the approaching E-boat.

A single shot echoed flatly around the inlet, and Devane heard the shell hiss almost apologetically above the E-boat. Fired on a fixed bearing, probably because the gun-layer, hauled bodily from his bunk, still did not understand what was happening.

Devane shouted, 'All guns, *open fire*!'

His words were drowned by the instant crash and rattle of gunfire. It was as if every finger on every trigger had been tensed and waiting for hours for this second. Tracer cut the retreating dawn aside and tore across the water and into moored craft like liquid fire. Smoke, then flames belched from one of the anchored vessels, and Devane saw more tracer, its trajectory almost flat on the water as it cracked past him and burst along the shoreline to add to the confusion. That was Rodger in *Buzzard* doing his stuff, his relief as great as everyone else's. The fear and shock would come much later. For the lucky ones.

A launch loomed beyond the flared bows, and Devane saw light flood from its wheelhouse as figures stumbled on deck to be met by the terrifying clatter of machine-guns and cannon fire.

One of the Russian seamen whooped gleefully and poured a full burst from his Tommy gun into the launch as they thrust past. The lights went out, and the scrambling figures dropped and lay still as the big forty-millimetre raked it from aft and turned it into a furnace.

Devane pressed his face to the sighting-bar, knowing that Horne would be copying his every move. Just in case. Steady . . . steady . . . steady now.

Tracer lifted from the shore at long last and shrieked overhead like hornets. Splashes and violent bumps alongside showed that some German gunners were finally alert to what was happening.

'*Fire!*'

Devane felt the deck kick slightly, saw the brief splashes beyond the bows.

'Torpedoes running, sir!'

'Hard a-starboard! Revs for twenty knots!'

Vaguely from one corner of his eye Devane saw the British MTB tearing past, the sea boiling aside from her upraised bows like solid snow. A searchlight settled on her, but vanished as one of Rodger's Oerlikons smashed it into oblivion with a long burst of tracer shells.

The explosions were merged into one, but in the roar of the E-boat's diesels and the maniac clatter of gunfire almost unnoticeable. It must have taken the Germans a long time to work the *Potsdam* into her carefully dredged moorings, and she was dying just as slowly. Great white columns shot up her side, hurling pontoons, small boats, catwalks high into the air. When the torrents of water cascaded down again the wreckage came too, pockmarking the anchorage with leaping fountains of spray.

Devane felt a shockwave boom across the inlet, winced as it lifted the deck beneath him and pushed Pellegrine's control momentarily off course.

Fire, smoke and columns of sparks were already rising above the great ship, blotting out the town, quenching the ferocity of the tracer and explosions as the MTB curtsied round, tearing the water apart as she fought with rudders and screws to get clear from the danger.

Both of Rodger's torpedoes also exploded on target, the smoke rolling and twisting with a scarlet centre as the devastation continued.

Devane felt steel hacking the deck, saw the Russian seaman thrown hard across the dead signalman as bullets hammered across and through them into the dense smoke.

Another series of explosions burst vividly across the inlet, joined instantly by another, even greater one, as fire reached something vital deep in the *Potsdam*'s hull.

'Dead slow all engines!' Devane had to gasp out the order twice before Pellegrine heard and repeated it. 'Stand by to pick up the party from the launch! Incendiary grenade as we pull clear!'

More savage crashes and explosions which made the hillside show itself clearly as if it was bright sunlight instead of early dawn. When Devane darted a glance astern he saw a great black shadow rising through the smoke, like something from a nightmare. Higher and higher, shining now in the reflected flames. He recognized it as the ship's bottom and keel as she continued to capsize, her full length rocked constantly by internal detonations.

As if to defy being overwhelmed by the inrushing water the keel exploded outwards. It was as if a great fiery fist had smashed right through the dying ship. Devane imagined he could feel the searing heat even as he watched.

Bullets whined and cracked around him. The second Russian seaman had vanished, overboard, or dragging himself to safety, Devane did not know.

Stooping figures ran doubled-over towards the port bow as the launch emerged from a wall of smoke.

'All stop!' Devane pounded the rail. This was the most

dangerous moment. Come on, for God's sake. *Shift your-selves.*

He saw Durston clambering up last, ducking as a seaman hurled a grenade into the disabled launch. Splashes too, as the German crew abandoned their craft and started to swim for the shore. Machine-gun fire spattered amongst them, from the Russians or some of his own men, Devane could not see.

The grenade exploded prematurely as the launch bobbed clear, burning and crackling fiercely, a solitary corpse sitting in the cockpit as if to await his own cremation.

Devane ducked down as tracer swept across from starboard. Bright green balls, lifting gently and then tearing towards him with frightening speed.

He felt the deck buck and kick, heard someone cry out in agony as the torrent of cannon fire tried to hang on to its target. More tracer slashed out from forward and aft as the Russian gun crews accepted the duel, the vivid reds and greens locking with each other and making the towering pall of smoke glow like a volcano.

Devane shouted, 'I'm coming down! Half ahead all engines!'

Time to go. No living thing could last up here much longer.

The dead Russian, arms and legs entangled with those of the signalman, had blocked the oval hatch by the ladder. Splinters cracked against the hull as it started to forge ahead again, and Devane heard the deeper bark of artillery. No shells fell nearby, so he guessed the frantic gunners were mistakenly firing at one of their own returning patrol vessels.

He clambered down the vertical ladder to the deck beside the wheelhouse. His ears cringed as one of the twenty-millimetre cannons swung on extreme bearing and fired at a shadowy boat which was already sinking from their first attack.

He saw the man staring through his sights, his eyes like yellow stones in the reflected fires. If Devane had not thrown himself clear the man would have continued to fire right through him.

Devane wrenched open the steel door and almost fell into the bridge.

Horne yelled, 'Mining party ready, sir!'

A stray bullet whined through a slit in the shutters and ricocheted around the enclosed bridge like a maddened hornet.

There was a hard slapping sound, and a seaman fell dead at Devane's feet.

Devane stepped over him and swept paint chippings and broken glass from the chart table as he peered down at the madly vibrating bearings and figures.

He jabbed the chart with his dividers. '*Here*. Alter course now. Steer north thirty east. Fifteen knots.'

He waited for Horne to shout to Pellegrine and inform Ackland in his engine room. Everyone had to know what was happening. Devane had learned it the hard way. In the past it had not been unknown for the whole bridge party, skipper, number one, coxswain, the lot, to be wiped out in one go. It left the boat to forge ahead out of command, with nobody else knowing what to do or when to do it.

The hull shook violently to a near-explosion, and Devane saw the falling water cascading down the front of the bridge and through the open slits, as if the boat was plunging to the bottom.

He shouted above the din, 'Ten minutes! Then start the drop!'

Horne stared at him fixedly, oblivious to the noise and the savage cracks against the hull.

'It'll take too long! They'll pin us down as soon as it's daylight!'

Devane replied sharply, '*Do it*. The mines will keep the local shipping held up for weeks.' He turned away. 'Signal *Buzzard* to take station astern.'

The mention of his own boat seemed to steady Horne, and he barked off his orders without further argument.

'Casualties?'

A seaman by the voicepipes, his forehead speckled with red droplets from flying glass, called, 'Six, sir. All dead.'

A dull boom shivered around the hull and continued to follow it as the E-boat headed along her new course.

Devane knew it was the HQ ship finally surrendering to the onslaught of internal explosions. The shallow inlet had helped to contain and expand each one beyond measure, and he guessed that half of the waterfront would also be in ruins.

Six dead, the seaman had said. Looking back at the smoke and leaping fires it was a marvel anyone had come through.

At the prescribed position on the chart the mines were released over the E-boat's stern at regular intervals. With luck

184

they might bag a German warship or supply vessel, but even if they caught nothing the delays and shortages their presence would cause would more than make up for it.

'Last one, sir!'

'Very well. Increase to twenty knots.' He ducked as a shell screamed over the bridge and burst far out to sea. 'Zigzag, Swain. Make that twenty-five knots until *Buzzard* has finished her part.'

The MTB only carried a few mines, but carefully laid they might still bring home a catch or two. The Rumanians' faith in their German landlords would be badly shaken after this, Devane thought grimly.

The deck swayed this way and that as the E-boat turned and forged towards the bright water. The land astern and on the port quarter was still blurred, concealed in smoke and an intruding layer of morning mist.

But there was a coastal battery somewhere which was wide awake and out for revenge.

Another shell burst to seaward, throwing up a thin column of spray, to be followed almost at once by another. Fired from a slightly different bearing as the German gunnery officer tried to trap the runaway E-boat in crossfire.

'*Buzzard* has increased speed!' Horne gulped as a shell exploded on the surface within half a cable of the MTB. But she was already opening her throttles, a smoke container spewing out a dense tail to further confuse the artillery spotters.

Horne shouted, 'Get the hell out of it, Harry!'

Pellegrine said, 'Don't think your Number One can 'ear you, sir!' He was actually grinning.

Devane heard a faint abbreviated whine and pressed himself against the side of the bridge. The explosion seemed to be somewhere else, nothing to do with them, and for an instant Devane thought the MTB had received a direct hit.

In the next second he felt himself lifted from his feet, the whole wheelhouse and bridge deck bursting upwards and outwards, flinging bodies about, knocking them senseless, while others groped like blind men as smoke and sparks belched amongst them.

Devane realized his hearing had gone in the explosion, but as it returned he regained his feet, his eyes stinging and burning as he tried to reach the forepart of the bridge.

There was smoke and grit everywhere, and the diesels sounded as if they too were in terrible agony, rising and dropping in a succession of roars.

Devane slipped and almost fell on a sprawled body. It was the seaman with the cut face, his eyes fixed and angry as he stared up at Devane while blood pumped between his outflung legs as if it would never stop.

'Must slow down! She'll break up!' Devane was almost sobbing as he gripped the voicepipes and realized for the first time he was alone. There was smoke coming from two of the voicepipes as if it was being forced through by a pump.

'*Jesus!*' Devane dragged the engine-room telephone from its clip and pressed it to his ear. Nothing. He jabbed his thumb on one of the communications buttons, but instead of attracting Ackland's attention it blew the little switchboard to fragments.

'Right then, me lads. What's all this then?' It was Pellegrine, his voice husky and slurred like a drunk as he climbed painfully to his feet, shaking off broken woodwork and severed wiring as he peered around at the chaos. He saw the dead seaman and grunted, ' 'E was supposed to take over if *I* copped it!' He peered short-sightedly at Devane and bared his teeth. 'You okay, sir?'

Devane nodded. To see Pellegrine's brick-red face, to know he was not alone, almost tipped the scales.

He answered shakily, 'Yes. Near thing. I'm not sure what. . . .'

He watched a frail figure swaying through the smoke, pausing only to vomit as he saw the staring corpse at his feet. It was Metcalf.

Devane said, 'Take the wheel. I'll give you a course—'

Pellegrine blew his nose violently into a signal flag. 'Compass 'as burst, sir.'

Devane saw the young seaman staring at him, his face white with shock.

'Take it anyway. Try to keep the boat from chasing her tail.' He turned to Pellegrine before the youth could protest. 'Get aft. See what you can do. Fetch help.' He winced as another shell exploded brightly on the port beam.

'Where the hell is . . . ?'

The thickset coxswain gestured beyond the flag locker. ' 'Ere, sir.'

'Get going, Swain. Find the Chief.' The words were tumbling out of him.

Pellegrine picked up his battered cap. 'I'll deal with it. Mr 'Orne's in a bad way, sir.'

Devane picked his way across the broken deck and upended gratings. There were two more dead men. One British, the other Russian. Apparently unmarked, killed by blast or shock, they sat side by side and watched him as he moved past.

Horne lay in one corner, his leg pinioned by a steel plate which had been folded round it like wet cardboard by the force of the explosion. The shell must have passed through the fore deck and burst deep in the hull. If only the engines would stop. They were coughing and roaring intermittently, shaking the whole hull with each revolution. But the boat was slowing down. Not from Ackland's doing. She was going under.

Horne opened his right eye and blinked it several times. The other side of his face had been torn away. No cheek, no eye. Nothing.

Horne whispered, 'My boat okay?'

'Fine.'

He felt Horne groping for his hand and stooped lower to hear him. He must have been hit in the side too. He was bleeding terribly. Dying.

Devane gripped the man's rough hand and squeezed it. 'You did bloody well.' He held him against the side as he tried to free himself. Not that he could. He was already as weak as a child.

Horne looked at him. 'It's over, isn't it?'

His voice was so clear and calm Devane was barely able to answer.

'We're getting out.' He heard feet sliding and crunching through the destruction, Torpedoman Geordie Pollard's voice as he yelled for more hands to come to the bridge. 'You just lie still.'

Horne's eye watched him gravely. 'Over for me, I meant.'

Devane bent over him, their hands locked together as his body shook with uncontrollable sobs.

Horne whispered fiercely, 'Take hold, sir. People are coming. If they see you give in, what chance do they have?' He waited for Devane to face him and added, 'Back there'—he took two painful breaths—'when the shit started to fly, I was the one who nearly cracked up. But you knew, didn't you?'

Devane nodded brokenly.

'Well then.'

Lieutenant Durston lunged through the smoke and gasped, 'I've told the Chief to stop engines, sir. The pumps are bloody useless. We're taking water fast. Did I do right?'

Devane reached out and closed Horne's eye. Then he gently removed his hand from the ex-fisherman's grasp and stood up.

'You did right. Tell the cox'n to muster hands, starboard side. Be prepared for ditching.' Another explosion shattered the stillness but it no longer mattered. 'Lieutenant Horne has just died.'

'God Almighty.' Durston stared at the dead man, then at the shattered bridge. 'You were damn lucky, sir.'

Devane looked at him despairingly, knowing the worst was over. That Horne had saved his sanity. Perhaps it had helped him to die without fear?

He replied, 'I know that now.'

Metcalf called from the wheel, '*Buzzard*'s coming alongside, sir!' He sounded dazed, as if nothing could ever harm him again.

Devane walked to the door and wrenched it back. The gunfire had stopped, and the land was completely hidden by the endless bank of smoke. But there was an airfield less than twenty miles away. They must not waste time. He glanced at his weary, filthy men, the wounded propped between them as they listlessly watched the MTB surging alongside.

Here was Petty Officer Ackland, soaked in oil, almost unrecognizable until he smiled at Pellegrine, his friend.

Devane heard himself say, 'Well done, Chief. Did you get all your people out?'

'Didn't lose one, sir.' Ackland stared along the pitted, listing deck. 'Jerry or not, I'd have liked to get her back to base.'

Lieutenant Patolichev moved up to join Devane and Durston. He hesitated and then held out a black cheroot to Devane.

'Good fight, *da*?'

Devane looked past him and watched the MTB making fast, the busy purpose of the seamen as they carried or dragged the wounded and shocked sailors to their own boat.

Durston hesitated. 'You coming, sir?'

Devane did not hear him. He studied the sinking E-boat, the

two ensigns still hanging from her stumpy mast. Here, he had nearly broken. But others had lost far more.

He heard steps behind him and somehow knew it was Lieutenant Rodger.

Devane said, 'She's sinking fast now. No need for a demolition charge.' He turned and looked at the lieutenant. 'Get us out of here.' He saw the man's gaze dart to the blackened and punctured bridge. 'You're in command now.'

He followed Rodger across to the other boat and watched the two hulls, the old enemies, drift apart.

As the MTB's screws thrashed the sea into lively froth Devane climbed to the bridge, the unlit cheroot still in his mouth.

Alone, in spite of the men around him, Metcalf sat on a vibrating hatch cover and stared at the E-boat as she dipped further and further, the sea flowing towards her bridge as if the water was moving uphill.

He had been there. On that bridge and at the wheel. The captain had trusted him. Even the grumpy old coxswain.

The MTB gathered speed and headed swiftly away from the land. Astern of her the sea was empty once again.

Captain Barker stood in the dead centre of his office, his severe features fixed in a rare smile. The smile weakened as Devane entered the room and waited for Beresford to close the door behind them.

Being here was almost the worst part, Devane thought. Incredibly, the passage back to Tuapse had gone without incident, and even the carefully prepared rendezvous with a force of Russian patrol boats and aircraft had worked like clockwork. The sea had remained calm, so that a quick stop to take on fuel from an adapted tanker, while the watchful fighter-bombers had snarled overhead, had been completed undisturbed.

At any other time he would have been jubilant, the success of the operation rising to soften the hurt, the pain of those who had died in battle.

He was so fatigued he felt like dropping to his knees, and yet he was afraid of what sleep would bring to torment him. All the way back to Tuapse he had kept busy, too busy to give time to whatever it was which awaited him. He had not even sought the solitude of the MTB's wardroom, had not washed or shaved. The longest part of the journey had been right here in Tuapse. The walk from the jetty to this office. The other MTBs had been at their moorings, their companies waving and cheering as he walked past them like some returning warrior. Hector Buckhurst had pumped his hand, and Beresford had fallen in step beside him, as if to cushion him from the welcome.

Nothing had made much sense until Beresford had said gravely, 'Before you see Captain Barker, John. *Parthian* was out to help with the patrols. Your own boat ran into a Jerry.'

They had both stopped dead as Devane had swung towards him.

'What happened?' Devane had gripped his arm fiercely. 'Tell me!'

Beresford had described the incident with brief clarity. The signal from the ditched airmen, *Merlin*'s search through the sea mist, and the last part when the MTB had been pounced upon by the E-boat.

Beresford had finished with, 'It could have been a whole lot worse, John. By rights they should all have bought it. But a Russian submarine surfaced in the vicinity, quite by accident as it turned out, she had battery trouble, and she whistled up air support. The Jerry raked *Merlin* from bow to stern and then made off like a bat out of hell.'

Together they had walked to the small dock which was like the bottom half of the letter L. Buckhurst's mechanics and artificers were working busily on the dried-out MTB, but the signs of the encounter were starkly visible. Without leaving the jetty Devane could see the splintered mahogany planking, the dark stains where men had been cut down by flying metal.

As he stared at the boat he had listened to Beresford's even tones as he described the aftermath. Lieutenant David Seymour very badly wounded, a seaman named Nairn missing. The helmsman, Able Seaman Irwin, critically wounded, who had died on the way back to base.

'I must see David.' It was all he had found to say.

Beresford had led him away from the dock. 'Roddy Dundas has gone to the hospital with him. They can do wonders these days.'

'He was going to be a writer, did you know that?'

'Everyone did.' Beresford had forced a smile but it would not hold.

'No hands, you say. Poor David.'

Now, as he stood beneath Barker's glaring lights, he could still not accept it. He felt bitter and cheated. All he had thought about was the attack on Mandra. Yet while it had been going on David had been crippled. It would have been fairer if he had died.

Barker said crisply 'Good to see you back! God, the whole place is talking about it. The HQ ship destroyed and at least two warehouses of military equipment blown up as well. I wish to high heaven I had been there to see it! There are strong indications that the German commandant of the base, a rear-admiral no less, was killed in the raid!'

Devane looked at him emptily. 'I'm glad of that.' He ignored Beresford's warning glance. 'We lost a lot of good men. Lieutenant Horne was one.' He wanted to look at the ground but did not dare in case his control broke. 'He saved my life, did you know that?'

Barker's smile looked unreal. 'How could I? But the job was *done*, and that's the main thing.' He rubbed his hands together with a dry sound. 'We'll drink to it later on. It's a bit early for me just now.'

Devane said, 'Not for me. I think I shall probably get very drunk. After I've discovered what happened to *Merlin*, that is.'

Barker turned and fiddled with some signals on his desk. 'Bad busniess. But it happens. Two boats meeting. One always has to be the first to act. Pity it wasn't ours.'

'It was Lincke. It must have been.'

Barker thrust his hands into his pockets and pouted. 'Well, we can't be certain.'

Beresford said, 'I think we can, sir. Russian Intelligence insist he was sighted in the area. On his own too. Unusual.'

'Very.' If only the tiredness would let go. Devane tried again. 'We need more boats. We must have support.'

'I've been telling Ralph here the same thing.' Barker tried to relax. 'A proper staff, minds working as one to—'

They jumped as Devane slammed his hand down on the chart table. 'I said boats, not bloody desk warriors, *sir*!' He stared at his own hand, grimy with oil, with another man's blood. The dirt of war.

He hurried on without waiting for Barker to recover. 'I hear the Germans have got F-lighters now, and probably more E-boats. Well, if they can get reinforcements, and God knows they're fighting us and the Russians on two fronts as it is, surely we can get some?'

He moved restlessly to a wall chart and stared at it unseeingly.

'It was Lincke. It's got his stamp. He's worked it all out for himself!'

Barker said sharply, 'The operation at Mandra was a complete success. If indeed Lincke's attack on *Merlin* was planned, it hardly makes up for the destruction of their Rumanian support base, does it?'

'Lincke won't care.' Devane looked at Beresford. How much did *he* know? 'He's out to destroy *Parthian*. It's personal to him. So we must get replacements. The medals can wait, in my opinion.'

Barker said smoothly, 'You're tired. It's been a great strain for all of us.'

Devane smiled. 'I apologize, sir. That was thoughtless of me. Now, if you don't mind, I've things to do. Letters to write, a report to be completed.'

'In that case,' Barker seemed momentarily at a loss, 'you had better carry on. I shall draft a signal to the Admiralty immediately.'

Devane stood in the doorway, the room swaying before his eyes.

'More boats, sir. This is only a beginning. Lincke never gives up. I know him like I know myself.' He jammed his stained cap on his head. 'Well, I don't give up either.'

The door slammed and Barker stared at Beresford as if he had just heard some terrible obscenity.

Beresford said quietly, 'Let it drop, sir. He's had about all he can take. You can't go on forever, mission after mission, and still be expected to say "sir" in the right places.' He watched Barker's face set for a new argument. 'The raid was a knockout. The end justifies the means. It must. Otherwise . . .'

Barker sounded ruffled and unconvinced. 'It wouldn't have done in my day, I can tell you.' He smiled brightly. 'Enough said. Get Kimber. I must word my dispatch very carefully. This'll make them sit up and take notice.'

Beresford walked out of the office, but paused outside the smaller one used by the flotilla's senior officer.

Devane sat at the table, his face flat on his forearm, his cap lying on the floor nearby. He must have been near collapse even when he had been asking about Seymour and the others. It was the first time Beresford had ever seen him give in like this and he felt strangely moved.

He crossed to his safe and unlocked it very quietly. Then he took out a full bottle of Scotch and a glass, pausing only to ensure that the sealed letter was still there.

He put the whisky on the opposite side of the table and said softly, 'Best medicine in the world. I'm just sorry it's all I can do for you, old son.'

Then, just as carefully, he closed the door and walked away.

14

DRIFTER

The two motor torpedo boats drifted about half a cable apart, their weapons and upperworks like burnished copper in the strange sunset. There was a late breeze, but not enough to break the regular swell into whitecaps, so that the water appeared to be breathing, lifting each boat without effort before moving on towards the shadows.

Devane rested his elbows below the screen and stared at the horizon. Waiting and listening. Hoping for an unwary enemy. The deadly game which never ended.

He heard the men on watch moving below the bridge, the occasional snatch of conversation, but few laughs. Ever since the raid on the Rumanian anchorage and the destruction of the enemy HQ ship Devane had shifted from one boat to the next in his small flotilla. So that he would get to know his command better, and they him. Or was he deluding himself? Perhaps he needed to stay aloof and at arm's length, dreading the personal contact which had brought him so near to cracking when Horne had died.

This was *Harrier*, Lieutenant Willy Walker's boat. But in the fading light it could have been almost any MTB anywhere. Oiled weapons, dull paintwork, faces searching the horizons, the skies, each other.

Merlin was still in dock at Tuapse, and Devane was thankful that Dundas was with her, and away from him. It was something he felt but could not explain.

He glanced abeam at the other boat as she lifted and dipped in a web of her own phosphorescence. *Buzzard*, with her scarlet number 4 painted on her spray-dappled hull. How quickly time passed, how soon the faces became blurred. Harry Rodger was in command of *Buzzard*. Did he still expect to see Horne on his bridge, hear his step on the ladder during the night watches? Horne had died nearly two months ago. It did not seem possible.

Weeks of patrolling, boredom and the occasional carelessness which had been shattered by the nerve-stopping clatter of cannon fire or the searing glare of the enemy's star shells.

Along the Eastern Front the two great armies had stirred, as if each dreaded the merciless grip of ice and slush which the winter would soon bring to torture them.

Dog-fights by day, the clouds blinking to artillery duels by night.

But at sea the war was different. Searching for scattered convoys, rounding them up and escorting them to safety. Hunting the enemy's light forces, exchanging rapid fire, then fading into the night even before a kill could be confirmed.

The news of the Allied landings in Italy at Salerno had changed little here, Devane thought. They had become too involved with their own restricted war, and from their isolation had grown a fanatical and ruthless determination to seek out and destroy the enemy at every opportunity.

Goaded by Captain Barker, *Parthian* had been switched from one sector to the other, so that sometimes it was hard to know which the British seamen hated more—Barker or the enemy.

They had had successes along the way. F-lighters sunk in a fight which had been at less than twenty yards range. Two heavy transports stalked and torpedoed within a mile of a safe harbour. This boat had shot down a German bomber, Mackay's had sunk two converted gunboats and a lighter filled with oil.

And each move made by *Parthian* seemed to be matched by Lincke's *Seeadler*. The Germans had become very adept at using a single E-boat to cause panic amongst a Russian convoy, then, while the escorts struggled to restore order, Lincke's striped E-boats thundered out of the darkness and painted the sea with fire and livid explosions. A small fragment of a very big war, one which might barely warrant a mention on the world scene, but to the officers and men of *Parthian* it was very real indeed.

Devane thought of Claudia, as he often did during moments of illusory peace like this. She had written twice to him, but her letters had been vague, devoid of the warmth which had filled him with hope. She was in Cairo. A friend of her dead husband had pulled strings and had got her a job at some regimental office.

If only he could see her. He had written to her, but what was there to tell? She knew better than many what their war was about. To describe it would seem like enjoyment, but to stay silent was a lie.

Perhaps she had found someone else? Devane felt the familiar pain as he allowed the thought to hurt him again. And why not? A moment of love in some cheap hotel was hardly an offer for a girl like Claudia.

He heard Walker step up beside him, saw his familiar yellow scarf pale against the water abeam.

'All quiet, Willy?'

Walker sucked on an unlit pipe and nodded. 'Might get a sniff tonight, sir. Jerry's been pushing storeships into the Crimea. Getting jumpy about Ivan making an attempt to retake the bloody place, I expect.'

Devane removed his cap and ran his fingers through his hair. The enemy-occupied coast was only forty miles away. Soldiers and equipment, airstrips and camouflaged field guns. All facing south and east. Waiting for it. Dreading it.

To the north the German armies were in retreat, but contesting every foot of the way. Only here, in the Crimea, the hinge of the war, were the Germans holding fast. If the Russian army could force the strait and gain a beach head on the peninsula, the whole front would crumble. It said so in all the reports, and Barker's little coloured flags left no room for doubt.

But the Russian high command still seemed unwilling to use the Allied successes in Sicily and Italy for that final, necessary pivot. They spoke of next year, or waiting for the coming winter to wear down the last German resistance, their dwindling stocks of fuel and supplies.

Even the air felt different, Devane thought. Cold at night,

and it was not yet October. The boats too were feeling it —leaks, wear and tear, shortages of spare parts—and Buckhurst was full of complaints and moans which he was normally loath to express in front of Captain Barker.

Barker's promised expansion had made a modest beginning. A couple of lieutenants for his operations section, another engineer to assist Buckhurst's department, and some spare ratings for the boats themselves.

As Pellegrine had dourly commented, 'All we want is a few Wrens an' it'll be just like bloody 'ome!'

But no more boats had been earmarked for the Black Sea's forgotten war. They were needed elsewhere. In the Med, where it was rumoured that German resistance would stiffen once the Allied advances in Italy were contained or slowed by bad weather. In the Channel too they would already be preparing for the big one. The invasion of Northern Europe.

Walker sensed his mood and added quietly, 'D'you think we'll get a chance to finish here soon, sir?' He gestured disdainfully beyond the corkscrewing bows. 'Let the pongoes fight it out. Leave us out of it.'

Devane smiled. 'It will *have* to be soon. The Germans have not been getting naval reinforcements lately. They're like us. Jumpy.'

He thought suddenly of his visit to the military hospital to see David Seymour. The Russian medical staff had been gravely confident that he would recover from his wounds. Not until Devane's visit was over had a senior doctor told him that Seymour had tried to kill himself.

In some ways that was no worse than seeing him. Shrunken, eagerly peering at his visitors as Devane and Mackay had stepped into the small, crowded ward.

It had been difficult not to look at the bandages where his hands had once been, to search for the youthful confidence which he had always shown in the past.

Now he was on his way home. To what?

Devane said, 'We'll do a listening-watch for a while, then sweep to the nor'-west. Maybe some of their coastal craft are on the move. Might bag one if we're lucky.'

So casually said, but that was how it had to be. If you thought too much about the Seymours of this war you'd be ready for the chop yourself.

After this patrol he would be returning to *Merlin*. Dundas

was feeling Seymour's loss very badly. Blaming himself. He had been in command. The blame always rested there, no matter how unfairly.

Barker had promised a new officer for *Merlin*. Somebody from the Levant, another misfit probably. Barker never let up, ignoring their dislike, overcoming every objection. As they hardened to the unceasing patrols and close-action attacks, he seemed to thrive. One seaman had said that Barker was too scared to walk alone at night in case one of the lads did for him. Maybe they needed men like Barker, Devane conceded. You did not have to admire him.

He pushed Barker and his command bunker from his thoughts and said, 'Not much visibility tonight, Willy. I think we'll move in now. We can still rendezvous with Red Mackay at the end of his sector as arranged.'

Walker showed his teeth in a grin. He understood. Impatient to move, frightened of no decision rather than the wrong one.

'I'll pass the word.'

Alone again, Devane wiped his night glasses with some tissue, already damp in cloying air.

Two torpedoes, twenty-two young men, some very young, and the power and grace of a thoroughbred. No wonder they were never short of volunteers.

'Ready, sir.'

Devane hesitated, Beresford's quiet briefing intruding into his thoughts. 'What was that about lighters, Willy? The intelligence report before we sailed?'

'Which one?' Walker grinned again. 'Oh, the gen about some steel and cement being moved eastwards along the peninsula by barge. Not exactly our style, surely?'

Devane stooped and thrust his head and shoulders beneath the canvas hood above the chart table. He waited, allowing his eyes to become used to the tiny shaded lamp. He could feel Walker watching him, the other men on watch becoming interested.

There it was. The crisscross bearings of an enemy minefield. A ship sunk there, another old wreck marked right on the edge of the field. Walker was right, of course. Cement and steel for gun emplacements were important to the enemy, but Orel's gunboats and some fighter-bombers might be more useful for the job of sinking the barges.

But if there *were* some barges on the move. . . . He peered fixedly at his watch, the hands and numerals glowing like tiny eyes. And if they were sunk somewhere inside the minefield it would play merry hell with enemy coastal movements and force them into open waters where Sorokin's destroyers might have better luck. A handful of E-boats would be at a disadvantage for once, just as *Parthian* had been when beyond the reach of air cover.

He stood up. 'Lay off a course, Willy. We'll head for the south-westerly tip of the minefield, line abreast. Fifteen knots. Tell *Buzzard* what we're doing. The rules are the same. We know that anything between us and the land is one of theirs, right?'

Walker took another twist around his neck with the yellow scarf.

'You're the boss, sir.'

As the last margin of copper melted into the horizon the two MTBs quivered into life and they turned towards the hidden land, their progress betrayed only by twin lines of choppy foam.

Walker's young first lieutenant bustled across the bridge and leaned on the chart table, his buttocks and legs protruding from the cover as he laid off the course to contact the enemy coast.

His voice was muffled as he complained, 'Bloody mines all over the place, Skipper. Is this necessary?' He had obviously not got used to having the senior officer on the bridge.

Devane said quietly, 'We're in the cement business, Number One. You just get us there!'

Walker chuckled. 'Hard luck, Ernest. I'll put in a good word for you!'

As his first lieutenant lapsed into embarrassed silence beneath the canvas hood, Walker added softly, 'He could be right of course, sir. Nasty spot to get jumped if the coastal batteries get a fix on us.'

Devane looked at him calmly. 'Through the minefield, into the shallows, then along the coast, fast as you like. If you were the Jerry commander, what would *you* do about it?'

Walker sighed. 'Whistle up *Seeadler*. Is *that* what you want, sir?'

Devane nodded, his mind suddenly very composed. 'We'll not get a better chance. But if the bloody barges have gone, or never intended to come anyway, I'll think again.'

Walker shrugged. 'What could be fairer?'

They looked at each other as the first lieutenant called, 'Steer north thirty-five west, sir.'

Devane said, 'Action stations, Willy. Let's go and put down some strong foundations!'

He watched the immediate response of men around him and from the guns on either side of the squat bridge.

I have to keep pushing. It's my purpose for being. Our reason for staying in this damned stretch of sea. The others can doubt my judgement, hate my guts for stirring up the nest again, *but I must do it*.

He felt his stomach muscles contract as the final reports rattled through voicepipes and wires.

Two MTBs and two more patrolling to the east. Insects stinging the beast into fury and retaliation.

He licked his lips and stared through the dappled screen. But no sentry ever won a war by standing still.

'Enemy coast to starboard, sir!'

Devane levelled his powerful glasses and strained his eyes above the lively spray from the bows. He felt the boat turn slightly, the matter-of-fact way which the coxswain acknowledged another change of course. It was ridiculous, but he almost expected to hear Pellegrine's gruff voice.

Walker stood beside him moving his glasses in a small arc as he searched for the land.

He drawled, 'I hope you're right, Ernest. I can't see a bloody thing!'

Several men chuckled and the boatswain's mate gave one of the machine-gunners a nudge. A good bunch, Devane thought. They knew each other like friends from way back. And yet a year or so ago some of them had probably been at school. Now they were all veterans. Walker's own special team.

Devane asked, '*Buzzard* on station?'

Walker grunted. 'As far as I can tell. I daren't use R/T or even a lamp. If the coast is only a mile abeam, I think it might make trouble!'

Both boats had earlier cut their speed down to a little more than steerage way. The sounds still seemed deafening, the surge of water along the sleek hull, the occasional smack as the bows lifted and fell on an off-shore roller.

But ashore, with any luck, such noises would be lost in wind and sea, and the average soldier's total disbelief in anything which floated.

Devane recalled the time that his own boat in the Mediterranean had come almost gun to gun with a German tank. They had been following the North African coastline, searching for supply lighters, landing craft, anything. Instead, as they had moved parallel with two great banks of sand, they had seen it, motionless and obscene. One of the much-vaunted Tigers. And even as the MTB's cannon and machine-guns had raked its armour like fiery darts the great gun had begun to swivel, the sleeping animal disturbed. One shell from a Tiger would have put paid to the mahogany hull there and then, and with all hands breathing a sigh of relief Devane had speeded out of immediate danger.

A tiny incident, a fragment of war. Something which made all the rest endurable.

There were some who actually enjoyed it. Usually they were beyond help. Maybe Don Richie had been one of those?

Walker said tersely, 'Starboard lookout reports machinery noises, sir.' He turned and stared at Devane. 'I *know*, he must have ears like a damned bat!'

'All engines stop. Silent routine. Pass the word to the Chief.'

Everyone froze as the motors sighed away with a final defiant shudder. A few hands moved to restrain clattering signal halliards, and Mecham, the boat's number one, ducked to catch a pair of parallel rulers as they skidded from their rack.

Devane wedged himself in the forepart of the bridge and turned his head from side to side. They were all doing it, like a group of blind men trying to find their bearings.

'Got it.' The first lieutenant jumped lightly on to the gratings. 'Starboard bow. Low down.'

Walker nodded approvingly. 'Well done, Ernest. You're not as stupid as people think.'

Devane ignored the banter. He knew how shallow it was, but how vital it could be. They were all tensed up. They had to restrain themselves, like wolves at the smell of blood.

The coxswain muttered, 'It's a pump, sir.'

Walker clapped his first lieutenant on the arm. 'This must be the place. Machinery, pumps.' He became very calm just as swiftly. 'Stand by. Gun action. Tell Leading Seaman Kirk to have his flares ready.'

Devane made himself look away from the muttering noises. Where the hell was Rodger's *Buzzard*? No sign of a wash or of a deeper shadow against the dark water. Sweet damn all. He could feel his teeth grinding together, but the fact he was aware of his anxiety helped to steady him.

Lieutenant Ernest Mecham, the number one, said casually, 'My bet is that they'll be sitting ducks. The work has to be done in the dark. They'll not be expecting us to pop up!'

Devane found time to note the change in the young officer's attitude. All the way over and through the minefield he had barely been able to hide his apprehension. Maybe he had had cause to fear the anchored mine, and even the knowledge that the boats were of too shallow draught to be affected could not hold back some terrible memory.

But now, probably within range of an ordinary army rifle, he was outwardly relaxed.

Walker had his mouth to the engine-room voicepipe. 'Ready, Chief? All the lot when I give the word! Home for breakfast!' He was grinning as he snapped down the cover.

Suddenly Devane found himself wishing he was back in his own boat, with Pellegrine and Ackland, Carroll and cheeky Geordie Pollard. Dundas too, who had had the worst end of the stick in some ways. Who had served with Richie, but had been the one to find him with his brains blown out. Now he was learning all over again with a new senior officer. Yes, he wished he had their faces around him now. Here he was in control, but an outsider, excluded.

A voice said sharply, 'Boat, sir. *Port bow!*'

Binoculars and gun muzzles swung quickly on to the rough bearing, and Devane saw a blurred shape, probably end-on and almost lost against the dark backcloth.

The vessel was moving very, very slowly, although it was hard to estimate the true speed when set against the MTB's crablike drift.

'Stand by!' Walker glanced at Devane for confirmation. This was Devane's show, but the MTB was his command.

Devane blinked to clear his vision. Experience gathered in a thousand encounters was more valuable than mere eyesight. That tell-tale wisp of white froth as the darkened vessel's engines increased speed, the sudden change of shape as her commander tried to sheer away from the low shadow on the water.

'*Now!*'

As the motors roared into life and the boat reeled round in response to the helm, Devane saw the other vessel shining like a boy's model as the flares burst above it. A trawler, her fishing days long past, and now a small part of the German navy.

'*Open fire!*'

Devane clung to the jerking, vibrating bridge as every gun which would bear ripped the darkness apart in a mesh of livid tracer.

Cannon shells speckled over the trawler's tall bridge like fireflies, turning the wheelhouse into a furnace and lopping off the boat's thin funnel like a dead tree.

There was a solitary gun mounted in the trawler's bows, and Devane saw men falling and dying even as they tried to train it round on their attacker.

Searchlights swept over the water, crossed and passed by the trawler. Maybe they would not depress to a target so near to the shore?

Machine-gun fire joined in the clatter of *Harrier*'s on-slaught, and Devane saw short, stabbing bursts from beneath the enemy's blazing bridge. Somebody had managed to train a Spandau on the onrushing MTB, but it was like trying to stop an elephant with a boat-hook.

'Hard a-port!' Devane shouted to Walker above the noise. 'Barges, Willy! There, coming down the safe channel!'

Round in a tight circle, her guns still hammering the armed trawler until she was burning fiercely from stem to stern, the MTB plunged across her own wake as the three long lighters appeared again in the drifting flares. Astern of them, but unable to offer much assistance, was another trawler, a local escort for the cargo of cement and steel supports.

'Depth charges!'

'Steady as you go, Swain! Pass that bastard to port!'

Men ducked and yelped as steel hammered the side of the bridge and whined across the water. Someone was shooting back, and Devane guessed that the burning trawler was making them a fine target.

Walker's gun crews knew their work well and, as the first lighter was deluged in tracer and half blinded with smoke, depth charges were released within yards of her blunt bows.

The shockwave slammed the MTB like a train, but the

lighter was already capsizing as the next set of depth charges were off-loaded near the second deep-laden craft.

Devane turned his head as a hand plucked at his duffle coat, simultaneously the boat's coxswain gave a sharp cry and buckled to his knees. As the man's fingers slipped from the spokes the first lieutenant pushed another rating to take over and bring the boat back under control.

Devane turned his gaze to the last of the careering lighters, but his mind still clung to the icy realization that a bullet had passed through his coat and had missed him by an inch.

Walker yelled, 'Swain's dead! Fetch Nobby Clark!'

Devane watched the cannon shells exploding savagely along the lighter's ugly deck and ripping through a small wheelhouse perched right on the stern like a sentry box.

Somebody yelled, 'Here comes bloody *Buzzard*!'

A seaman dragging a new belt to the starboard machine-gun gasped between his teeth, 'Late as bloody usual! 'Alf of 'em come from Chatham, so what can you expect!'

Surprisingly, with the smoke and ear-splitting clatter of automatic weapons, and the gleam of the dead coxswain's blood below the wheel, they could still manage a laugh.

A depth charge exploded astern, the tall column of water shooting straight up like a geyster. When it fell, the third lighter was still there, pounding along at about six knots, the boxlike hull punctured in a dozen places and a small fire going on her forecastle. But she was afloat, whereas the other two were almost gone, the great weight of their cargo slewing them round in the safe channel while the water seethed with bursting air bubbles and smoke.

Devane tore his eyes from the second armed trawler. She was shooting wildly with her bow gun, but it was too old and slow for such a target.

He shouted, 'Get after that barge, Willy! One more wreck in the channel should do it!'

With her men frantically reloading and clearing stoppages from their weapons, the MTB went about yet again, her motors labouring and bellowing as they fought against the rough handling.

Devane said, 'Signal *Buzzard* to engage that trawler.'

The signalman yelled hoarsely, 'From *Buzzard*, sir. *Unidentified craft closing from the south!*'

Devane looked at Walker. 'Quicker than I thought.'

Walker nodded grimly, his eyes slitted against the smoke which was streaking back from the MTB's six-pounder like steam. 'Here we go then!'

The last pair of depth charges, at minimum settings, almost blew off the lighter's stern.

Devane could even hear the destruction above the sounds of the motors and gunfire, as one shaft and propeller tore loose and some of the cargo began to fall apart and thunder through the hull.

Walker lowered his glasses. 'That's it. They're abandoning her. Don't bloody blame 'em!'

A star shell burst far out over the minefield, and Devane guessed that a local artillery battery had been roused. He watched *Buzzard* tearing across the water, balanced perfectly upon a knife edge of white foam. But the trawler was taking no chances. She was steering away on a diagonal course, which with luck would bring her under the cover of the shore battery.

'Break off the action, Willy. Signal *Buzzard* to take station astern of us. We're getting out.'

'*Buzzard*'s acknowledged, sir.' The signalman sounded dazed. 'From *Buzzard*, sir. *Am reducing speed. Underwater damage.*'

'Bloody *hell*!' Walker's face glowed as another star shell mushroomed against the clouds.

Devane looked past him. The unidentified craft which Rodger had sighted should be here by now. Or they might see the exploding shells and tracer and imagine the Russians were conducting a commando raid. Either way they might stay out of it.

'Tell *Buzzard* to maintain speed *while he can*.'

Whoooosh. . . . Bang!

A big shell exploded well abeam, hurling a column of spray towards the clouds and leaving a pall of smoke above the water.

Walker grinned. 'Poor shooting.'

Devane nodded. It should get poorer as the fires and the drifting flares died in the water. No artilleryman could hope to knock out a small MTB except with a miracle.

Walker added, '*Buzzard*'s managing to keep up anyway. Probably collided with a wreck and stove in a few planks.'

Another star shell burst almost directly overhead, the eerie, glacier light mesmerizing them with its power.

Walker snapped, 'New course, Number One. We'll head south-east. I don't want to get clobbered now!'

Devane felt the seaman next to him stiffen. 'Sir! Dead astern!'

Devane pushed past him, his eyes aching from the drifting flare. Two high-explosive shells burst about half a mile away, but had they been alongside Devane knew he would not have cared.

How perfectly the other MTB showed her lines in the hard glare. Almost every detail, from her small mast and tattered ensign to her squat bridge. He could even see the heads of the men behind the low screen.

Between the two boats the sea was like black glass laced with silver, but all Devane saw was the tiny, bobbing dot which lay in direct line with the other boat's stem.

He shouted, 'Call up *Buzzard* on R/T!' He swung round as Walker ran to see what was happening. 'Tell them there's a "drifter" dead ahead of them!'

Feet skidded on the wet gratings and Devane heard the sharp exchange between Walker and his telegraphist. And all the while he kept his eyes on the little glistening dot, fading now as the star-shell merged with some clouds.

Walker snapped, 'Full ahead! Starboard fifteen!' His eyes still reflected the dying flare as he said harshly, 'No sense in risking the boat!'

Then came the explosion. One great searing flash with a red centre, and the other vague, more distorted sounds as fuel, ammunition and depth charges detonated as one huge bomb.

Like the flare, the explosion was extinguished with terrible suddenness, snuffed out as if the MTB had never existed. For what seemed like endless moments pathetic fragments of wreckage continued to fall in a great circle, and a few tiny flames burned on the sea itself until they too vanished.

Walker's boat cruised round the place where Rodger's first command had hit a drifting mine. But there was not even a life-raft left to mark the place.

The signalman broke the silence, his voice very loud in the bridge. 'W/T had just spoken with *Buzzard*, sir.' He looked over the screen as if he still expected to see their consort following astern. 'Then it 'appened, sir.'

Walker looked at Devane. 'Return to base, sir?'

'No. We'll rendezvous with *Kestrel* and *Osprey*.' He could sense their hurt, their resentment. Hatred even. As if he had killed that MTB himself with his bare hands. 'Remain at action stations, just in case those unidentified vessels put in an appearance. Lieutenant Rodger might have been mistaken.'

Walker said quietly, 'But he's dead, sir.'

Devane nodded. 'And so is your coxswain. So let's get on with it, shall we?'

He walked to the forepart of the bridge again and found that he was holding his breath, keeping his whole frame tense, until slowly at first, then out of discipline and routine, the others responded to their tasks.

Before it had been different. He had never questioned the whys and the wherefores. You did your best and tried to stay alive. But a whole MTB's company wiped out, and the coxswain killed at his side, the bullet touching his arm in passing like a taunt. *Not your turn. Not yet.*

'Have a mug of kye, sir.' It was Walker again, his voice normal and level.

'Thanks, Willy. A kind thought.' He held the hot mug to his lips and watched the sky over the rim. 'Near thing that time, Willy.' What had he meant by that?

Walker nodded dully. 'And then there were four.'

15

NOBODY LIVES FOR EVER

Lieutenant-Commander Red Mackay had been leaning against the dripping wall of the bunker. He straightened up as Devane left the operations room.

'Everything okay?' He sounded worried.

Devane shrugged, holding back the tiredness with an effort. 'Yes.' The fact that Barker had listened to his patrol report and the loss of *Buzzard* without any sort of criticism had only just occurred to him. 'Next of kin will be informed.' How often had they all heard that?

Mackay fell in step beside him. 'You did a good job, putting down those barges. I've heard a buzz that Ivan has already bagged a couple of ships which were trying to skirt the minefield.'

'It's *not enough*, Red.'

Devane hardly realized he had spoken aloud. It was what Beresford had told him just over an hour ago when a Russian harbour launch had guided them back into the concrete pen. What Barker had hinted at but not hammered home as Devane might have expected.

Any doubts about Lincke's activity in their sector had been stamped out. But what was worse was his apparent skill and ability to foresee each plan they produced and then thrust his own counter-measures into action before anyone guessed what he was doing. He had known about the three barges and their value to the battered army emplacements on the peninsula. But, whereas Devane had seen them as bait, he had used them as a distraction. His own E-boats had made a sweep along the Russian patrol lines and had destroyed two warships and a heavy transport almost at the gates of Tuapse itself.

'Lincke outguessed me, Red, right down the line.' In spite of his bitterness he could feel a reluctant admiration for the man he had never met. 'He can run rings round the Russians, and now he's taunting *us*, wearing down our guard, our vigilance. German naval forces here are outnumbered two to one by the Russians, everyone knows it, but pride prevents Sorokin and his staff from admitting it. That's why *Parthian* was brought here to Tuapse. To even the score. Skill for skill.' He turned and slammed his hands together, the sound echoing around the concrete roof like a bullet hitting flesh. 'What can we achieve with four boats? I need another two at least, and that's if we can stop the Germans from catching us on the hop again.'

Mackay forced a grin. 'Hell, you weren't *caught*. A drifting mine is just bad luck. You know that. We've seen a few.'

They walked on again, each lost in his thoughts.

Then the Canadian said, 'If only we could catch the E-boats in the open. We could at least cripple *Seeadler* and give Orel's old gunboats a chance.'

Devane thought of Barker, sitting at his desk, his head on one side like a watchful bird. He had seemed more pleased at the confirmation that a German flag officer had died in the shattered *Potsdam* than he was prepared to admit. His own opposite number perhaps?

Devane said, 'The boats won't take a hard winter here. We must have replacements, to give the hulls *and* the men, a breather.'

They stood above the little dock and looked at the repaired *Merlin*. Devane saw Dundas glance up at him and then hurry towards the brow. He had been talking to a lanky officer in blue battledress. Seymour's replacement, no doubt.

'I'll leave you then.' Mackay rubbed his stubbled chin. 'I'm going to take a bath. If I can find one.' He blurted out, 'They may offer you another command. It's on the cards, it must be. With the landings in Italy, the big flap at home as to if and when we'll invade France, they'll need experienced leaders as never before.'

'What's up, Red?' He smiled gravely. 'You want my job here?'

But Mackay refused to be deflected from his course. 'If you stay with *Parthian* we *might* just come through this one. If you go, and who could blame you with your record, I reckon that bloody Lincke will have us for breakfast.' He stuck out his chin. 'I've said my piece. Bill Durston, my Number One, told me how you held them all together during the raid on Mandra. And he's not easily impressed, the big-headed bastard. The fact is, and no matter what Captain Barker imagines, we're out of our league here. This is an army war. We're just a necessary nuisance.'

Devane nodded. 'I've no intention of going, Red. Not unless they order me out of here.'

'That suits me fine.' Mackay gave a great grin. 'One for all.'

Devane watched him stride towards his own boat and wanted to call after him. But what was the point? He had known it from the moment that Don Richie's death had been revealed to him. There was no easy way out.

Dundas saluted as he walked slowly down the brow. 'Good to have you back, sir.' He looked tired, as if he had not slept for days. 'This is the new third hand, Lieutenant Chalmers.'

Chalmers also saluted, the movement of his arm and hand stiffly mechanical, as if he was saving his strength. He was tall and angular, very tanned, with a hawkish face and a pair of bright blue eyes. At a guess he was about twenty-five.

He said, 'Transferred from the base at Alexandria, sir. My last boat bought it during the Sicily invasion.'

Dundas said quickly, 'He's been in hospital, sir.'

Devane held out his hand. 'Glad to have you. What's your first name?'

Chalmers answered softly, 'David, sir.'

'I see.'

Devane tried not to look at Dundas. The lanky lieutenant had the same name as Seymour. His grip felt hard, like a glove. Without dropping his eyes Devane guessed that Chalmers had been badly burned. Now he was back to be retested, like some of the others.

'Well, David, get to know the boat, then see Lieutenant-Commander Beresford about local operations, right?'

The blue eyes watched him curiously. Relief, despair, it was hard to tell.

Dundas interrupted, 'There's been some mail, sir. I've put yours in the wardroom.' He fidgeted with his buttons. 'I was sorry about *Buzzard*.'

'Yes. Bloody waste.' He nodded to Pellegrine whose brick-red face had just appeared around the side of the bridge. 'Hello, Swain, how are things?'

Pellegrine grimaced. ' 'Ad a letter from the old woman, sir. If she's not up to somethin' I'll give up me pension, so 'elp me.' Then he smiled. 'Still, that can wait, eh, sir?'

Devane lowered himself down into the small wardroom, a twin of the one he had just left. Except that it was cleaner, and there was a smell of fresh paint everywhere.

He took down the letters from the rack and examined them. Two from his mother, a bill from Gieves and . . . he hesitated as he saw her writing on the last one.

Deliberately he threw off his waterproof coat and cap and then poured himself a large glass of brandy. Someone, probably Dundas, had left it ready for him.

His mother would understand, he thought vaguely, and in any case. . . . His hand shook as he opened Claudia's letter and allowed his gaze to hang on the first line.

My darling John. . . .

When Dundas entered the wardroom half an hour later he found Devane sitting us before. Crumpled and unshaven, the bottle near his arm, the glass of brandy untouched.

Devane looked up at him, wondering how his voice would sound when it eventually came out of his mouth.

Nothing had gone, everything was as he had dreamt and prayed. She loved him. She had cried when she had received his letters. There was a lot more too which he would read and re-read.

'All right, sir?'

Devane nodded. 'Not much changed in Dorset. My mother has been busy knitting socks and balaclavas for sailors, and Dad is still running the business—' He saw Dundas look at the other letter. 'Everything's fine. Now.'

Dundas sat down as if a wire had been cut. 'I—I'm very glad, sir.'

It hit Devane like a fist. Dundas had nobody. He was an orphan and had been put through his original training for the merchant service by an uncle who had let his obligations lapse as soon as Dundas had established his cadetship.

All these weeks and months while he had clung on to his hopes, Dundas had only dreams to sustain him. The sight of Claudia's letter had put paid to those too.

Devane pushed the bottle across the table. 'Join me in a drink, Number One. I'm afraid I'm back to plague you again.'

Dundas stared at him and then reached for another glass. 'We've all missed you, sir.' The glass hovered momentarily in mid air. 'And I'm damned sorry about what happened. To David. To the others.'

'You'll get over it. You must. Anyway, I've recommended you for a command of your own.'

He saw the astonishment and the gratitude in Dundas's eyes and was glad he had told him.

He added quietly, 'Tomorrow can wait. Today you and I are two of the "few", and that's important. It's all that matters.'

My darling John. Was he wrong to hope? The bullet which had passed through his sleeve, was that to warn him not to hope for too much?

Devane swallowed the brandy and felt its warmth. For the first time in many months he was drinking because he wanted to enjoy it. Not because he needed it as a shield against himself.

What had Willy Walker said? *And then there were four.*

Well, if necessary, they would be enough.

'Where the hell are we going?' Devane clung to the door of the army staff car and tried to prepare his body for each jarring wrench.

Beresford grinned. 'To Captain Barker's villa. You've not been before?'

'Never been asked.'

Devane watched the feeble glow from the shuttered headlights swing past some fallen trees and two lounging sentries. The whole area to the east of Tuapse was in the hands of the army, and he guessed the soldiers were used to this and every car on the rutted track.

He remembered the journey from the hospital after he had

been wounded. And the other time he had gone there to see Seymour.

Only the boats and the concrete pen with the sea beyond were real.

The roads which thrust inland meant nothing.

He asked abruptly, 'What's all this in aid of, Ralph?'

Beresford glanced at the Russian driver and said quietly, 'Ivan is going all out for the big push.' He spoke more easily as the driver began to hum to himself. '*Parthian* is going to take part.' He shot a quick glance at him. 'I think Barker's been scheming for something of the sort since he arrived.'

Devane accepted the sparse information calmly. Before, he would have been on the edge of his seat. Suspicious, apprehensive, waiting for the bad news. Could her letter do so much for him?

He said, 'Another raid, is that it?'

Beresford smiled and lit a cigarette. 'Piece of cake to you, John. No bother. You've changed, you know. Maybe you've got your second wind?' When Devane remained silent he added, 'Anyway, the Russians will go through Jerry's defences like the proverbial steamroller. But Barker needs us there, if only to put on a show.'

Devane thought about it. It would certainly explain Barker's reception after *Buzzard*'s loss. His mind had been elsewhere. Planning another operation.

'We can't do much with just the four boats.' Devane looked at his companion. Beresford was more guarded than usual. 'Are we getting reinforcements at long last?'

Beresford replied, 'Don't think so. Nothing in the pipeline. But then you know the top brass. We'll be the last to hear.'

The car butted between two collapsed gates and turned into a small courtyard. It was a low-roofed villa, built probably for some party official. Now it was Barker's.

'One thing, John.' Beresford touched his arm as the car quivered to a halt. 'Go easy with Barker. He's been a long time on the beach, remember? He'll do almost anything to help his career in the future.' He gave his arm a quick nudge. 'D'you follow, old son?'

They climbed out into the darkness as the car moved away. The place smelt of damp and the countryside. But you could still hear the faint murmur of artillery even here.

'*Parthian* is supposed to be my responsibility. I'll have to hear what's expected of us before I can give any assurances, Ralph.'

He had expected Beresford to pass it off with a laugh or a casual comment but he was deadly serious.

He said, 'Barker will get you replaced if you kick up a fuss. Don't kid yourself on that score. He didn't care a fig about Richie, so why should he about you?' He sensed his words going home and nodded slowly. 'You can't say what you are thinking, can you? That nobody else in *Parthian* could cope?'

'Rubbish. Any one of us might get killed any day. . . .' But in his mind he could hear Mackay's voice seeking that very reassurance.

Then Beresford gave a chuckle. 'Barker's a book-man. He doesn't understand about experience won in combat. If you've got the rank, you do the job. It's his religion.'

Devane was not sure what he had been expecting, but as they were guided through two doors and a blackout curtain he was almost blinded by the glare of bright lights and the uniformed figures who crowded a long room.

White-jacketed stewards or Russian orderlies bustled amongst the officers with trays of glasses, and somewhere there was lively music and a clatter of dishes.

Beresford grinned. 'Well, well. Most impressive. Here he comes. Remember what I said.'

Barker was tiny in stature when compared with some of the Russian naval and military officers whom he had invited to this unusual gathering. But somehow he seemed to shine and rise above all of them as he strode to meet the two lieutenant-commanders.

'Good show. Right on time.' He ran a quick glance over Devane's uniform. 'You *could* have worn a bow tie, but still. . . .' He swung round as one of his new operations officers whispered over his shoulder.

Barker snapped, 'Sorokin's here.' He tossed back a glass of champagne and placed the empty glass on a passing tray.

Sorokin stood in the entrance while two orderlies stripped off his shabby coat. As he turned to the lights his dress uniform and medals transformed him into an impressive figure.

He nodded to Barker and his officers and glanced casually around at his own colleagues and subordinates.

He seemed satisfied, and took a glass of champagne before saying in his thick voice, 'Commander Devane. You did some

214

brave work, my staff tells me. Pity you lose a little ship, but. . . .' He gave an eloquent shrug.

Barker rocked forward on his toes. Even so, his chin barely reached Sorokin's shoulder.

'Which is why I was gratified to hear that your people are almost ready to attack.' It sounded as if he was about to add, 'at last'.

Devane watched carefully, realizing that this meeting was no mere gesture, any more than Barker's words were to pass the time. Barker wanted Sorokin to understand that he was already fully conversant with the prepared plans, that he was trusted by the chiefs of staff in London.

Sorokin beamed. 'I would have told you the full details later, naturally.'

Barker's pale eyes flickered. 'Naturally.'

Beresford said, 'The fact is, it's going to take a lot of organization if the Russian army is to cross the Kerch Strait from the mainland to the Crimea. To support such an advance, the army will need constant supplies, unimpeded convoys both across the Strait and down from their positions in the Sea of Azov. Commander Orel's gunboats and support craft are familiar with those waters of course.'

Sorokin's great head swivelled towards him. 'You are saying that the Germans will forestall such a landing? That Comrade Orel's forces will not,' he searched for a word, '*withstand* the German flotillas?'

Barker said curtly, 'Nobody wants your attack to fail, Captain Sorokin. Least of all your, er, Admiral Kasatonov, I imagine.'

Sorokin seemed to falter at the mention of his superior's name.

Devane watched the game pass again to Beresford who said smoothly, 'Captain Barker has a plan, sir. A commando raid immediately *before* the main assault across the Kerch Strait.' He gave a winning smile. 'I hasten to add that the men involved would be your own, sir.'

Sorokin breathed out slowly. 'And what would be the object of this *solitary* deed?'

Barker moved in. 'Up to now, *Parthian* has been employed well, but only as an extension of your overall command, so to speak.'

Sorokin blinked. 'So to speak?'

Barker hurried on, 'With the result that my small force is being whittled down instead of being retained as a single, vital weapon.' He gave a slight cough. 'Which I am sure your chiefs of staff would agree with mine was the intended object, right?'

Devane took another glass from a tray and listened with amazement. Four MTBs, and Barker was discussing them like a cruiser squadron. But it meant that the Russians were worried, far more than Sorokin had ever admitted. Until now.

Sorokin spread his big hands. 'That has some sense.' He nodded ponderously. 'I can understand.'

Barker rocked back again on to his heels, his hands characteristically wedged into his reefer pockets with the thumbs protruding.

'*Parthian* will execute the raid which I planned. Four boats, under cover of night and with *certain* help from your patrols, a landing force of some one hundred trained men, and we can cause such confusion and disruption behind the main German defences it will give your assault every chance of success.'

Sorokin's jaw tightened. 'Not possible. My people have fought and died, starved and suffered to win back our country and crush the fascists once and for all!'

Other officers nearby had stopped drinking and talking to watch the unmatched confrontation.

Barker waited impatiently. 'Orel does not have the right vessels at his disposal. I do.' He removed one hand from its pocket and brushed an invisible speck from his sleeve. 'Furthermore, if Korvettenkapitän Lincke, who is not unknown to you I believe, throws his E-boats amongst your landing craft and supply ships at the moment of attempting to retake the peninsula, your whole campaign may have to be curtailed.'

Devane waited for Sorokin to explode, or smother the little captain who was not even bothering to hide his self-confidence.

But Sorokin bit his lip and then said, '*Parthian*, as you call it, will draw Lincke away, is that what you are saying?'

Devane tensed. He should have seen it coming. It was not such a bad plan, provided they could get more MTBs, and that Lincke did not have ideas of his own.

Barker turned and looked sharply at Devane. 'My study of Lincke's past behaviour leaves me in no doubt as to his intentions. Lieutenant-Commander Devane here has met with him before, and will back me up.'

216

Devane stared at him. He could recall exactly how Barker had scoffed at the remotest possibility of Lincke's new vendetta with *Parthian*, and more particularly, with its new senior officer.

It reminded him too of what Beresford had told him about Barker's ignorance on the F-lighters. If the war lasted that long, Barker would be an admiral yet.

'And where is this place you intend to launch your attack?' Sorokin sounded dangerously calm.

'My team is working out the final details with the intelligence people. I cannot say too much. We have had reason to believe that the enemy is getting information already from certain Russian prisoners.' He eyed him blandly. 'Security is everything, as you will appreciate, I'm sure.'

Devane put down his glass. He did not even notice he had emptied it.

It was incredible. Sorokin had backed down. If Barker's raid failed, the enemy would be roused and ready for a major attack. If he was refused permission to carry out his plan, the Russians were in worse trouble. Lincke's flotilla and the other collection of small naval units would see to that.

Beresford said almost humbly, 'I am empowered to assure you, Captain Sorokin, that everything will be done to help your raiding party achieve success.' He hesitated, gauging the exact moment. 'The place we have selected is largely occupied by Russian soldiers who chose to change sides when the German armies were advancing. I would think that your men would have plenty of reasons for—' He got no further.

Sorokin's champagne glass shattered in his grip and yet he was oblivious to the pain, to the droplets of blood which ran down the front of his impeccable uniform.

He exclaimed fiercely, 'Those *swine*! Those soft-bellied scum!' A vein throbbed on his forehead as if his whole face was overheating. 'So they are on the Crimea!' He stared down at Barker's impassive features for a long moment. 'Then you shall have your wish, Comrade Barker!'

He swung Barker around by his elbow and bellowed to the room at large. Soon everyone was clapping and cheering, and an infantry major was throwing glasses into the air with crazy abandon.

Beresford explained in a loud whisper, 'He is telling them that we, his allies, are going to stand shoulder to shoulder against the common enemy.' He grinned. 'Very melodramatic, although I think our captain is still smouldering at being classed as a comrade!'

Devane said, 'What about his plan? Is it really any good?'

Beresford turned and studied him calmly. 'I've no idea. But it could shorten the war on this front.' He let his words sink in. 'It's what you came here to do, remember?'

Devane noticed Lieutenant-Commander (E) Buckhurst on the far side of the room, one arm around a cheering Russian. It was probably as far as any of them could see. Get it over. Return to a navy they understood, or thought they did.

Beresford added gently, 'Barker wants you with him when he finalizes the plan with his chief, Vice-Admiral Talents.'

Devane stared past him, seeing Dundas and the new lieutenant with the burned hands and the pain in his eyes. Seymour trying to kill himself before his life had really begun. Metcalf excited beyond fear as he had shouted in German through his loudhailer, and all the others in *Merlin* and throughout his little flotilla.

'So he's here too?'

Beresford lowered his voice as Barker pushed through the crowd, his face stiff but pleased all the same.

'No. The admiral is in Cairo. Well, are you on?'

Devane looked at his hands as if he expected to see them shaking. It was all decided. There was no point in fighting the inevitable.

Barker joined them and snatched up a full glass of champagne. 'Damned Bolsheviks!' His eyes moved just briefly to Beresford, like a question.

Beresford nodded. 'Next stop Cairo, sir.'

'Good. For one moment I thought. . . .' Barker's old brisk manner returned. 'Get it laid on. Mackay can take command here. No sea-time for *Parthian*.'

As Barker hurried across to meet another senior Russian officer, Devane said, 'You've known right from the start, haven't you? Just as you must realize that *Parthian* stands no chance at all if we hit real opposition.'

Beresford shrugged. 'Some I've known, some I've had to guess. It's my job, just as it's yours to lead, no matter what the odds might be. It's never been any different.'

'It hasn't, but I thought *you* were different. I was wrong. You use people, they don't matter to you.'

Beresford grinned uneasily. 'Here, steady on. Somebody's got to do it.'

'Why didn't you tell me how Dundas got jumped by Lincke? Tell me that Barker had set up my boat, knowing that Lincke would go after it, thinking it was me? Did you bloody well imagine I wouldn't work it out for myself?' He looked round the room, hating the faces, the laughter. 'David lost his hands because of it.'

'We don't know for certain. You're guessing.' Beresford watched him anxiously, then persisted, 'But you *will* come to Cairo?'

'You even used Claudia, didn't you? You knew I'd go, if only to see her.' He did not conceal his contempt. 'It's partly true, but I *need* to see her, more than ever now. It'll probably be the last time. But tell Barker not to worry. I'll get Lincke. Or he'll get me. Now I'm going back to the base.'

As he turned on his heel Beresford called after him, 'You're just tired, John.'

Devane took his cap from a Russian servant. 'Not tired. *Sick!*'

For a long while, Beresford stood staring at the blackout curtains as if he still could not believe what had happened.

Barker crossed the room again. 'Trouble?'

'No.' Beresford sighed. 'Nothing I didn't ask for.'

Barker did not hear him. He stared at Sorokin's broad shoulders, sensing the excitement his proposed attack had roused.

He had shown them. Others had doubted him after his son had been killed. But he had *known* that given the right moment he would make them all sit up and take notice.

Vice-Admiral Talents was flying specially to Cairo to see *him*. It would be the end of Whitcombe and his kind, and about time too.

He glanced severely at Beresford and said, 'You look a bit shaky, Ralph. Go to the heads and stick a finger down your throat if need be. I will not tolerate any of my officers being the worse for drink in front of the bloody Russians!'

Beresford smiled wearily. 'I'll remember that, sir. I really will.'

Outside in the cool, damp air Devane watched a few pale stars.

My darling John. The words hung in his mind as if she had spoken them from the shadows.

He saw a staff car jerk reluctantly towards him.

He was going to see Claudia. Tell her exactly what she had come to mean, what they would do. . . . He hesitated with his hand on the car door. But there *was* no future now. He shook himself angrily. *What did you expect? Nobody lives for ever*.

The little villa was soon out of sight, and the sea was waiting for him. As usual.

They sat opposite each other at a small table in the English Tea Shop. The name of the café and its mock-Tudor beams were bizarre when set against the screened windows, the arguing Egyptian traders in the street outside.

Neither of them noticed the contrast, nor the curious stares of some women at another booth.

They held hands across the table, speaking only occasionally as they studied each other as if for the first time.

She said quietly, 'I knew you would come. If I had gone back to England I would have missed seeing you.' Her hand tightened around his fingers. 'I love you so much. We must not be sad.'

Devane thought of the flight to Cairo, the new barrier between him and Beresford. He had waited for *this* moment only. Seeing Vice-Admiral Talents, going over the usual aerial photographs, shaking hands with anonymous staff officers, it had all been a part of the enforced waiting. Now they were here, together, and he could not find the words to tell her how he really felt.

He smiled, and watched the moisture on her upper lip, the way the humid air held a small dark curl across her forehead. She was lovely, and he wanted to throw aside the table and its ridiculous cakes and clutch her body to his. Tell her his fears. Of his longing for her which made the prospect of dying more terrible than ever before.

'And I love you, Claudia. How have you been getting on?'

She shook her head. 'It is an office job which I do for the garrison. Easy when you have had to help run an estate.'

Her throat quivered and Devane felt her nails dig into his hand.

'Dear old Dorset. I wish to God we were there now,

220

together.' She pushed the sudden sadness aside. 'Tell me about you, and your work.'

Quite suddenly he found himself doing just that. The café faded away, the street sounds became non-existent. Only her face stayed with him as he told her what had happened to Sydney Horne, Harry Rodger and the others. Some of them she had met when Don had been alive. His 'warriors', he had called them.

Then she said, 'After this visit here, you're going back to something special, something really dangerous.' She smiled gravely as she studied his features. 'I *know*. Careless talk costs lives. So does war, my darling. Just tell me this. Is it extra bad?' Her grip tightened again. 'You know what I mean.'

He looked at the table, barely able to answer. Like that time with the dying Horne whose remaining eye had compelled him to go on, to resist the urge to break down completely.

'It'll not be easy.'

He recalled the admiral's narrow features, another Barker almost. No, there would be little chance of any extra boats. No, they could not obtain even one fitted with radar, not yet anyway. Which implied that it would have been too late anyway.

Devane said, 'When I got the chance to come to Cairo I was of two minds.' Still he dared not look at her. Until he had finished. 'I—I thought it would be unfair to you, after what you've already endured. In a way it was selfish, I see that now. I needed you so badly I thought only of myself when I agreed to come. In a day or so I'll be gone. Even that I could bear if, if I thought. . . .' He looked up, his voice pleading. 'Don't you understand? You're the one person I love, the one I can't bear to hurt. Yet when I do one I cause the other.'

She said gently, 'We shall be together again soon. We must.' She watched him steadily. 'Remember the night in that little pub? We knew then. If you asked me to marry you, I would, right here and now if it were possible.' She freed her hand and reached up to touch his face. 'We are married now, as far as I'm concerned, my darling.'

'If anything happens—'

She put her fingers on his lips. 'Don't say it. It shall not happen.'

She stood up slowly and smoothed her dress. When she looked at him again there was a new light in her eyes, something almost desperate as she whispered, 'We can go to my room now. It's hard to sit still and kill time when I *want you so badly*.' She thrust her hand through his arm, just as she had that day in London. 'It's not far. I share it with another girl. Her husband is with the tanks.' Her voice shook. 'We console each other.' Her step quickened and they were out in the dying sunlight. 'But she'll be away by now.'

He looked at her. 'I must be dreaming.'

'I'm being sent home quite shortly.' She turned her face away from him. 'So when we meet again it will be Devon.'

'I'll remember.'

'You'd better.'

'If you see my mother and father, tell them—'

She shook her head. 'We'll tell them together.'

They arrived at a medium-sized house which had been broken up into apartments for the duration. Once it had housed the family of an army officer, now it had a shifting population. Clerks for the garrison, officers on transit, lost souls in a world at war.

The room was quite spacious, and the paler outlines on the walls where pictures had once hung were disguised with cheerful rugs and shawls from the local traders.

She closed the door behind them and stood with her back against it, her breasts moving quickly as she appeared to listen.

Then she said, 'Gone. We're alone. It's ours until I tell her differently.'

She came to him eagerly as he held her tightly. Only when he unbuttoned her dress and let it fall to the floor did she exclaim, 'Let's not waste a moment. I want you.'

Later, as they lay on the bed, the room in strange shadows from the window, she murmured, 'That was so wonderful, my darling.' She propped herself on one elbow and looked down at him, her hair touching his throat while her hand explored his body, then holding him until his longing was aroused again to a point of madness.

He made to rise and pull her down on the bed, but she rose above him, her slender body etched against the ceiling like a living statue.

'No, my captain, stay a prisoner.' She straddled him firmly, her hands on his shoulders, her voice lost in whispers as she lowered herself to contain him and repeat their act of love.

Totally exhausted, their bodies and limbs entwined, they lay still again to await the dawn. Another day of discussion, of meaningless talk, while he thought only of her, the dragging minutes and hours until he would join with her once more.

He pushed some hair gently from her face. She was asleep at last, her head on his chest, her breast moving steadily against him. At moments like these she was more like a wanton child than a woman. Full of desire, yet vulnerable. Full of ways to make a man lose his self-control, his inhibitions, in the fashion of her love-making. There would, there *could* be nobody else for him.

Devane touched her spine and felt her snuggle closer, but she was still asleep. He cupped her breast in his hand and whispered, 'I shall come back, somehow. I don't know how I'll manage it, but I will.'

Then he too was asleep.

Twelve hundred miles from the room where Devane lay with the girl pressed beside him, his adversary, the man he had never met, stood below the window and contemplated the dawn. It was cold and without promise. Damp, like the accursed country.

Korvettenkapitän Gerhard Lincke watched the sky and listened to the far-off wail of a siren. The Eastern Front never rested for long, but Lincke had taught himself to keep his mind clear of unnecessary diversions. He would inspect the whole of *Gruppe Seeadler* this morning. There was no substitute for routine.

He heard the girl moan in her sleep and turned to look at her, at her nakedness, and the way her hair hung over the side of the bed.

Lincke had taken her to his bed not from lust or affection. It was just another part of his routine. Necessary, although in her case unsatisfactory. She made love like an animal, and had cried several times. She was an interpreter, described as Polish. But Lincke had checked her record sheet. She had been born a Russian, and had lost her parents and family in the revolution. She had the features of an aristocrat, the mind of a slut, he thought.

He shivered and stood back from the window. Today the new admiral would come and inspect the naval forces here. He would replace the one killed in *Parthian*'s attack on the

Potsdam. Lincke gave a tight smile as he recalled how some of his brother officers had seemingly expected him to be enraged by such an impudent attack in his territory.

Quite the reverse. Lincke had been seeking the last clue in the pattern of events. He knew that Devane commanded the handful of motor torpedo boats named *Parthian*. He had studied his background, and now knew him better than some of his own subordinates.

He thought of the coming Russian offensive. It could not be delayed much longer, and it must commence before winter closed its grip. It was to be hoped that the new admiral was better than the last one or the senior captain who had been sent from Odessa temporarily to assume command. A useless object. Lincke could feel his anger rising again. The man had kept moaning about the great ships which were now no more. Even the mighty *Tirpitz* had been attacked by midget submarines within the safety of a Norwegian fjord and was out of service. He should have realized that it was a small-ship war. U-boats, fast patrol vessels, with young minds to command them.

Lincke had been to the local field HQ to examine some photographs of Russian supply vessels. On the way he had seen a firing squad unhurriedly shooting a dozen or so ragged figures. They had fallen into a long trench, almost grateful it seemed for the reprieve from suffering. Partisans, a brutal-looking SS lieutenant had explained. They had been interrogated fully. No further use.

Lincke had little time for savagery of the SS, but accepted it. All information was useful. How you got it was not the fighting-man's concern.

The thought still troubled him, and he walked over to the bed and looked down at the girl.

In the grey light she looked almost beautiful. The White Russians must have been mad not to see the inevitability of revolution.

Lincke never considered the possibility of Germany losing the war. It was out of the question. But should any of these patriots or traitors, whichever way you saw them, fall into enemy hands, God help them.

He stood stock still, suddenly ice-cold. All that work and study of useless intelligence material and it had been right there in front of his face. It was lucky none of his subordinates had thought of it first. He almost laughed aloud. It was so devious. So British.

The girl stirred and opened her eyes. For a moment she was startled, even frightened. Then she reached out and stroked his skin. It was like ice.

She murmured something but Lincke ignored her. His heart was beating faster as he considered the possibility of his discovery. A Russian pilot had been shot down and captured. They had found some maps on him. No doubt the airman had been taken to see the SS slaughterhouse. That should loosen anyone's tongue.

Lincke considered the idea of telling his new superior but discarded it instantly. *He* commanded *Seeadler*, not some admiral who knew nothing of these people.

His second-in-command could inspect the boats today. Max would drive him to where the Russians were quartered, the ones who wore the uniforms of the Reich.

Time was running out fast. If Lincke knew it, so would the man Devane. He had stayed alive too long to be a fool.

Lincke stooped down and touched the girl's bare shoulder, amused at the pathetic way she moved her body to please him.

But his need of her was gone. There was work to be done. He pushed her away and shouted for Max, his orderly.

When the door burst open and Max, dishevelled in a watch-coat, a Luger in one huge fist, peered in at him, Lincke said calmly, 'I need a bath and a shave.'

He noticed the way Max kept his eyes averted from the girl's nakedness. That too sharpened his humour. It was going to be a better day after all.

'Max, we are going to lay a trap for the Englishman.'

'Yes, sir.' He thrust the pistol out of view. What a man. You never knew with Korvettenkapitän Lincke.

Lincke watched him cheerfully, then patted his thick forearm.

'*Yes*, *sir*. That is all you say. Even to the jaws of hell if necessary, eh, my fine seaman?'

He left the room, laughing.

16

CAT AND MOUSE

Lieutenant Dundas climbed on to the gratings in the forepart of the bridge, staggering and waiting for a suitable handhold to steady himself.

'Signal received from Russian escort commander, sir. He is withdrawing as ordered.'

'Very well.' Devane rubbed his eyes and peered abeam. But the escorting warships had already melted into the darkness.

He noticed how Dundas's breath drifted above the screen, and felt the rawness of neck as his collar rubbed against it. The first week of November. He could feel it in his bones and blood like a threat. Or was it a touch of the usual nerves?

'Signal *Kestrel* and tell Red to check the launches and make sure they're on station. Time enough later on to play silly buggers. But, until we hit the land, I want a tight formation all way.'

He leant against the corner of the pitching bridge, his ears and senses taking in the labouring motors, throttled down to slow speed, the sluice of the sea against the hull and the boat's sluggish response. Packed with fuel and extra ammunition, depth charges and spare machine-guns which Barker had borrowed or bribed from the Russians, the MTB felt heavy in the water.

November. Four months since he had taken over command

of *Parthian*. It seemed an eternity. It was as if all the rest, even Horne's death, were a working-up for this last operation. Not weeks away now, but a matter of hours.

As they had prepared the boats and trained for a hit-and-run assault on the Crimean shoreline, Devane had waited for news of his enemy, Lincke. There had been practically nothing. A few sighting reports from Russian air patrols, but they could have been wrong anyway. The Germans had a lot of small craft working the coastal waters. The famous 3rd Minesweeping Flotilla had made a name for itself over and over again in its unfamiliar role as an attacking force rather than a defensive one. They had supported the German army, run stores and evacuated wounded, and had bombarded Russian positions on the notorious 'death mountain of Noworossisk'. Lincke might have been with them. Then again, he might already know or guess what *Parthian* was doing. Biding his time, as they had done while they had waited for the order to attack.

The fact that Sorokin had sent his four fastest and most modern launches to carry the one hundred Russian shock-troops proved how much he valued Barker's plan.

Devane thought of the men around him and the others in the flotilla. He heard Carroll humming softly to himself, a lookout whispering to the boatswain's mate, who chuckled as he got to the point of his joke. Lieutenant Chalmers was aft, checking the depth charges. Soon he would be on the forecastle, doing the same with Leading Seaman Priest's six-pounder. He never seemed to rest or sleep, as if he was driven by some terrible urge or memory.

A seaman had the helm, and he guessed that Pellegrine was below in his mess, preparing himself as he always did before an action. A real old sweat. Money and paybook in an oilskin pouch. A small flask of rum in one pocket, a spare bulb for his life-jacket lamp. Ready for anything, was the coxswain.

He heard Leading Seaman Hanlon say sarcastically, 'Come on, la, what's up with yer? You're like a spare part at a bleedin' weddin', you know that?' His hard Liverpool accent seemed at odds with the Black Sea, Devane thought. He was probably having a go at Ordinary Seaman Metcalf again. Those two seemed to hate each other more than the enemy.

Dundas came back rubbing his hands. 'All checked, sir. Boats on station. Feels a bit lively. We may be in for a blow.'

He knew that Devane did not need telling. It was something to say. To contain the innermost thoughts.

Four MTBs making a tight box formation, with the launches close astern. Eight low shapes heading towards the land. The escorting vessels had turned away in good time to avoid being detected. Orel's supporting gunboats were closing in from the south-east, like the jaws of a trap. If Lincke took the bait, Orel would catch him. If he did not, the raid would cause enough panic anyway to help the main Russian thrust across the Kirch Strait.

'Time?' Devane moved to the opposite side to look for Mackay's boat.

'Two minutes to midnight, sir.' That was Carroll, ready and on the ball.

Devane considered it, as if he could still see the plan, the neat lines and cheerful flags on Barker's plot-table.

The point of attack was a small niche in the coast named Suzrov, some twenty miles north-east of Krasnoarmeisk. It was a safe part of the peninsula as far as the enemy were concerned. There was an extension to the minefield, some difficult shoals inshore, and lastly, the area was known to be zeroed in for two artillery batteries. The latter were controlled by a RDF station which the Germans had positioned in a bombed building which had once been a church.

A straightforward attack. They had done it several times in the Med and in the Adriatic.

Pellegrine's untidy shape appeared on the bridge, and he grunted as he took over the wheel.

'Course, north twenty west, Swain.'

Dundas peered at his watch. 'Action stations, sir?'

'Yes. Most of them will be there already anyway.' It was always the same. Not easy to rest when you most needed it, with only three planks of mahogany between you and the sea.

Someone gave a little cry as the sky was bathed in deep red. Later, much later it seemed to the watching sailors, they heard the sullen rumble of guns. Miles and miles away, a night attack had been disturbed or scattered. Or a sentry had allowed his nerves to change shadows into advancing enemies.

'Two minutes past midnight, sir. *Parthian* at action stations.' Then the age-old chestnut, 'Enemy coast somewhere in the vicinity.'

Devane smiled and shrugged his shoulders deeper into his waterproof suit.

It was so easy, in spite of the danger, to let your mind drift. Like a man will fall asleep quite happily and freeze to death, or a motorist will doze off at the wheel of a fast car. It was always there, waiting to tempt him. Claudia's arms around him, pulling him closer, their words lost in each other's hair as they had fought off the daylight. The last moments also were only too stark. Breaking the contact, turning away to the street where a car had waited to carry him to the airstrip. He had looked back just once. Now, in retrospect, it was like a still-life painting. The pale house and the clear sky. The girl in the doorway shading her eyes to see him, to hide the tears.

By now she would be in England. In Devon again. But his mind refused to accept it. She was still there, in that quiet room, waiting for him.

A dull thud jerked him back to the present. A hatch slammed shut. Or a man falling headlong as the boat caught him unawares.

Dundas hovered by his elbow. 'I'll get down aft, sir.'

Devane saw that Chalmers had come to the bridge. In a stunt like this one, it would be safer to have Dundas working with men he knew and who trusted him. Chalmers could take over the bridge if his CO bought it.

'Warn the engine room. Minimum revs in about ten minutes.' He could feel the towel which he had tucked around his neck getting damper with spray, or was it the sweat of fear? He realized Dundas was still there. 'Something wrong, Number One?'

Dundas fumbled with his coat and the heavy pistol-belt he had donned.

'Good luck, Skipper. In case. . . .' He sounded awkward. 'You know.'

Devane was moved. 'Keep your head down.' He felt shocked by his own words. What Beresford had often said. It sounded like a betrayal. They had barely spoken since that evening, and then on matters of routine.

'One more time.' Devane looked at Chalmers, but he was standing a hundred miles away, or could have been. Searching the darkness ahead. Poised, taut like a spring. Maybe he heard those same words when his boat had been blown up at Sicily. He knew their true value.

Pellegrine shifted his seaboots and muttered, 'What wouldn't I give right now for a few jars at the Nelson, then back 'ome for a bit of the other.'

Metcalf, who was acting as spare hand on the bridge, asked, 'The other what, Cox'n?'

Pellegrine glared at the darkness. 'Gawd Almighty!'

Carroll and some of the others laughed, and Dundas said, 'No bother there, sir.' Then he climbed down and disappeared aft.

The minutes ticked past and still nothing happened. The sea's motion became less violent, and Devane knew it was because the land was creeping out on the port bow to shield them from open water. But no flares burst overhead, no tracer ripped past their slow approach to destroy their puny challenge.

'Dead slow. Tell the first lieutenant to keep a close watch astern for the launches.'

Orel had handpicked his men. Men who knew the coast. Some perhaps who had lived there, who would be waiting for victory, yet dreading what they would discover.

Another dull glow lit up the sky, but with a difference. The bottom of it was black and uneven, something solid.

'Enemy coast ahead, sir!' No jokes this time.

'All guns stand by.' Devane licked his lips. They felt as if they were glued together. *Come on, Jerry. What the hell's got into you?*

The motors sounded louder now, and he wondered if anyone on the shore had heard them yet. Guns manned and pointing at *Parthian*, at him. The local airfield alerted so that even the survivors would be strafed into oblivion.

Devane thought of Lincke and was suddenly calm. It did not matter how either of them felt. They had to prove something. To settle a score which had already cost too many lives.

'Here come the launches, sir.'

Four low shapes. Like long predators, darker then the water which held them, as they overtook their escorts and swept towards the shore. Not even a sound or a glint of metal to betray them. It made them all the more sinister.

Devane had seen the soldiers, tough and hard-faced, being mustered to collect their various weapons and equipment. The other Russians who had changed sides because of the old

230

hatred left by the revolution would find no mercy or quarter there.

A seaman said fiercely, 'God, how much bloody longer?'

Pellegrine snapped, 'Silence! As long as it takes, see?'

Devane readjusted his night glasses. In a matter of hours the big push across the Kirch Strait would begin. Russian troops on the Crimea for the first time since the big retreat when hundreds of thousands of men, Russian and German, had frozen to death.

Once across the minefields which the enemy had laid in the strait, and on to the peninsula, it all depended on planned support and no shortages of ammunition, and men to replace the casualties.

Far to starboard a flare burst against the clouds. But it was over the land and no immediate threat. Devane saw the familiar faces suddenly clear and pale in the light. Men he had come to know and respect.

Another flare, even further to starboard. Someone was getting nervous, or suspicious.

Devane heard the sudden splutter of water as the boat's outlets were forced deep into the sea by the off-shore swell. Like a nervous animal scenting danger, when there was none to see.

The port machine-gunner nestled more firmly against his twin guns and repeated over and over, 'Come on, yew bastards! Let's be 'avin' yew!'

The six-pounder moved very slowly from bow to bow on its power-operated mounting, and Devane could imagine the tough leading hand behind it, the 'skate' from Manchester who had been with Seymour when he had been cut down. He wondered if Priest was thinking of his women and his brawls ashore now.

Another shadow loomed above the water, and Devane knew they were as near as they could expect to get. They would have to stop and take stock of their bearings soon. Once again he was amazed that it had been so easy. Perhaps on this part of the Crimea the troops felt safe. A secure distance from the real front and the savagely contested strait.

Carroll said in a whisper, 'The Ruskies *must* be ashore by now!'

Devane could picture them creeping up into the rugged darkness with their weapons out and ready. A knife for the

231

throat of an unwary sentry, grenades for the weapon slits and blockhouses, burp-guns and mortars for the real work.

A launch glided past and Devane let out a slow breath. It was empty. At least twenty-five heavily armed men were ashore and undiscovered.

The tension was unbearable, and when something metal clattered across the engine room Devane thought for an instant it would make the machine-gunners overreact with a burst of tracer.

A second launch moved abeam, and Devane saw a figure waving a white flag or a handkerchief as he passed.

Chalmers said bitterly, 'He's well out of it.'

Devane turned his head to look at him when the whole bridge and fore deck lit up with a single explosion. It came from high up, and for a moment longer he thought they had been tracked by a shore battery. Then he saw the flashes along the shoreline, sharp and deadly, as grenades were flung into dugouts and bunkers. The first explosion had barely died when it flared up again with livid brightness. Great flames leapt towards the clouds, and Devane saw what he guessed to be blazing fuel running down a slope like molten lava.

'Starboard ten. Slow ahead all engines.'

The deck vibrated confidently, and Devane smelt the high-octane as Ackland opened his throttles with great care.

There was a lot of firing now, small-arms and light automatic weapons which seemed to fan out from the landing point, the progress marked by little stabs of fire and the occasional bright star of a grenade. A mortar was brought into use, and Devane heard the dull crump of bombs exploding further inland, the slow response from a German artillery position until it too was bombed into silence.

All hell will be let loose now. Devane watched the flashes and listened to the brittle clatter of machine-guns. A tall, tree-shaped burst of flame lit up the land and the water's edge where one of the launches was trying to stay in position, and Devane guessed that the raiders had blown up the RDF station.

'Twenty minutes past midnight, sir.'

'Very well. Remind me at the half-hour, Bunts.'

Across the water, Devane heard a grinding roar of tracks, magnified by the sloping wedge of land. Tanks or troop-carriers rushing to the scene, but still a long way to travel.

'There's supposed to be a road of sorts at about red

four-five. Any armour will come from the town. We'll have the advantage over them.'

Chalmers said quietly, 'For a while anyway.'

The raid was spreading in both directions, and Devane could imagine the alarm changing to terror as the defenders heard Russian voices like their own right amongst them.

The killing would be terrible. Devane found himself thinking of Richie. He would have enjoyed this, had he lived. The blind, white-hot anger which accompanied the slaughter and made men do things they might have believed impossible. Courage or madness? It was hard to tell.

An explosion, very near the water, rocked the hull, and Devane heard fragments falling on the deck and splashing alongside.

'On helmets, everyone!'

Pellegrine steadfastly ignored the call. He had never been known to wear a 'battle bowler' as he called it. Nor would he.

The raiders must have discovered another fuel dump, for that too was blazing fiercely, and some of it was running down to the sea's edge to make a small fiery barrier.

Metcalf said, 'They're throwing supplies into the fire, sir.'

Devane lowered his glasses, sickened. Metcalf was mistaken. In the powerful lenses he had seen the kicking bodies, some of them burning like torches as they were hurled into the river of fuel. He heard someone retching helplessly and was glad that he at least had not become so hardened that he could watch human beings burned alive and stay unmoved.

'Time, sir.' Carroll sounded hoarse.

'Right. Make the signal for recall. Tell *Kestrel* by R/T to execute phase two.' He heard the men moving about, grateful to have something to do to disperse the terrible spectacle amongst the flames.

The boatswain's mate said, 'Still, I suppose if it was *our* country an' they was fighting for the Nazis—'

'Hold your noise, *damn you*!' Chalmers' face was staring and wild in the reflected glare. 'You don't know what it's like!'

Devane said sharply, 'Easy, David. He didn't mean it like that.'

Chalmers stared at him like a stranger. Then with a great effort he said, 'Couldn't help it. Should have been ready.' He bent over as if he were going to vomit. 'I saw my chaps die like that. We were swimming. The boat had gone by then. We were

233

making for a destroyer which had been hit by a bomb but was still afloat. As I swam I could hear the burning fuel coming after me.' He pushed his knuckles into his mouth. 'I could *hear* it!'

Carroll called, '*Kestrel*'s acknowledged, sir.' He was unwilling to intrude on Chalmers' despair.

Chalmers stood up very slowly and turned his back to the land. Then he said simply, 'The fire took all but three of us.' He seemed perfectly calm again.

Devane touched his arm. 'Go aft and relieve the first lieutenant.'

As Chalmers made to leave the bridge the boatswain's mate blocked his path.

'Sorry for what I said, sir. No 'arm intended.'

Chalmers looked at him and then replied, 'I know. I'm the one to apologize.'

Pellegrine pouted like an enraged pig. 'I dunno, I really *don't know*!'

Metcalf asked in a whisper, 'What, Cox'n?'

'Tomorrow, that what. It's me birthday!'

Devane thrust his hands deep into his jacket as the green flare exploded to recall the raiders to the beach. Pellegrine had judged it perfectly. It had been a near thing. He shook himself from his apprehension. What did it matter anyway? The boatswain's mate was probably right the first time.

But he thought of the burning, frantic shapes, of their agonized screams which he could hear in his mind if not in his ears, and knew that it did matter. Very much.

Carroll said, 'First launch loaded and away, sir.'

Devane nodded. Mackay and Willy Walker in *Harrier* were already moving out to open waters. *Merlin* and *Osprey* would screen the final withdrawal.

After that it would be a matter of a few hours before they knew if Barker's ruse had worked or not.

Dundas appeared on the bridge. 'Ready to move, sir.'

'Very well.'

Thank God Dundas had enough sense not to question him about Chalmers, a man who should never have been sent back to this kind of warfare. He had been scarred too deeply to forget or·to recover.

Star shells exploded across the glittering water, but the cloud was low and the smoke too dense for them to be of any use.

'New course, Roddy. Jump about.'

He saw another launch gathering speed as it throbbed past. There were a lot of bandaged heads and limbs in that one. As he watched he saw a corpse rolled over the side and left to float astern like so much rubbish.

We shall never understand the Russians, he thought. Not in a thousand years.

'Last one clear, sir.' Dundas watched him guardedly. 'No casualties to us.' He grinned as the relief took hold. 'Makes a change.'

Devane looked up as another star shell exploded directly overhead.

'And if Orel's gunboats are in the right place at the right time, we should keep it that way.'

It was an easy lie, an expected one. Before Pellegrine's birthday arrived, *Parthian* would be badly mauled even if the ruse had worked.

But at least it would be over. For the lucky ones. The few.

'Ready to take up new course, sir. North seventy east. *Osprey* on station astern.'

'Carry on. Increase revolutions for twenty knots.'

The land had already dipped into the shadows again, but here and there a fire still flickered, and a pattern of sparks circled above the beach where men had perished for their treachery. Or their beliefs.

Devane settled himself in his corner. So now we wait.

Captain Barker stood with his heels together, hands in his reefer pockets, and surveyed his operations room. It was considerably larger now that he had had a wall removed and an adjoining store transformed into an extension of his command post. The lights were very bright, so that the charts and wall maps, coloured markers and flags stood out like parts of a pattern.

A seaman was collecting empty teacups, and Barker's new officers were by their telephones, sharpened pencils and signal pads within easy reach.

Only Beresford looked out of place. He was slumped at his own table, his chin resting in one hand, his hair tousled as if he had just got out of his bunk, Barker thought.

Barker snapped, 'The attack must be working. We'd have heard otherwise.'

A telephone jangled loudly and was snatched up by one of the lieutenants. He spoke carefully in Russian and replaced it.

'From Russian HQ, sir. The first attack across the Kirch Strait has been launched. Heavy fighting reported.'

Barker glared past him at the massive concrete wall as if he expected to hear the ferocity of the battle. But the strait was a good one hundred and fifty miles from the bunker.

Beresford stirred himself. 'Orel's six gunboats will be in position to support *Parthian*.' He looked at the clock. 'I wonder what Lincke makes of all this?'

'He'll not be in the strait, be certain of that.' Barker's pale eyes gleamed. 'Even if he suspects Devane's raid is a sprat to catch a mackerel, he can't afford to ignore it.'

He swung round as the telephone interrupted him. '*Well?*'

The lieutenant spoke for several seconds and then covered the mouthpiece with his hand.

'It's all a bit confusing, sir. I—I don't really know what's going on.'

Beresford was on his feet and over to the other table in one movement. He snatched the telephone from the lieutenant's hand and spoke rapidly.

Then he put the handset down and said, 'That was Captain Sorokin himself.' His voice shook momentarily and then he recovered. '*Parthian*'s attack worked. The enemy has started to move men and armour along the coast before the main Russian assault.'

'*Well?* Spit it out, man!' Barker's face was suddenly deathly pale.

Beresford said in the same quiet tone, 'Sorokin's been removed from his command. He just told me. By order of Admiral Kasatonov. He's in disgrace.'

Barker sounded dazed. 'I don't see what that has to do with *us*?'

'You don't?' Beresford walked to the brightly lit plot-table. 'The admiral is withdrawing the bulk of Orel's covering force. He says he needs it at the strait. Hard opposition. You know the story.' He glanced at the motionless lieutenant. 'I'm not surprised you couldn't understand. I think Sorokin's drunk, or halfway there. But he *tried* to explain. Orel has left two of his gunboats. The rest are already running for the strait as fast as they can go.'

Barker stared at him. '*Two?*'

'Yes, sir. *Two gunboats.* They might as well have taken the bloody lot.'

Barker rubbed his eyes. 'Now. Let me think.' He began to hum busily. 'This is where it counts, eh, Ralph? Thinking caps on, what?'

The rating who had just entered with a fresh tray of tea stood stock still, as if he could sense what was happening.

'We must not overreact, Ralph. *Seeadler* may also be heading for the strait, had you thought of that?'

Beresford ignored him. To Lieutenant Kimber he said flatly, 'Make a signal to *Parthian.* Get it off immediately. Top priority, and never mind what the Russians say, *do it.* Tell *Parthian* that Orel's covering force has been withdrawn. Two supporting vessels only are in vicinity.'

Barker said sharply, 'That's unnecessary! Totally so. We don't know—'

'We don't *know* anything, sir. I just want John Devane to get a chance to run for it.'

'Run? Is that what he'll do?' Barker was barely able to control his agitation.

Beresford kept his eyes on Kimber who all but ran from the room with his signal pad in one hand.

'Of course he won't. But he's got to be told. To have a chance, no matter how slight.'

Barker swung round and saw the rating with his tray of teacups.

'Don't stand there gawping, you useless idiot!' He was almost screaming. 'Get me Russian HQ on the telephone *at once!*'

The other door was opened by a sentry and Sorokin lurched into the harsh lights. He was crumpled, and his uniform coat was unbuttoned and stained. He was obviously very drunk, and yet in spite of it he held a kind of power which was both compelling and pathetic.

He saw Beresford and nodded. 'I come to you. I come to say sorry. That is not an easy thing for me, but I am dirty. Ashamed.' He forced out the last word very carefully, determined Beresford should understand.

Beresford said gently, 'Here, sir. Sit down.'

He gestured to the stricken seaman with the tea but Sorokin shook his massive head and slumped down heavily. He dragged a flask from his pocket and drank for several seconds.

Then he said thickly, 'They are sending me to a new place.' He grinned and the effort made him look incredibly sad. 'Siberia probably, my friend, *da*?'

Beresford said, 'What happened?'

'Nothing. Politics. Enemies. What is the difference? Maybe you are to blame, for being here, for being seen as my friends?'

Beresford said sadly, 'I understand. About *Parthian*, sir. . . .'

Sorokin tried to rise but fell down again. 'I gave a last order. There is another gunboat in the base. It was just repaired.' He looked up, his gaze suddenly firm. 'You take it. You go and help your friend. There is only few men on board.' He dragged an envelope from his breast pocket. 'Here is authority.'

Beresford said quietly, 'It is two hundred miles. Even if we leave now we will never reach the rendezvous. Already it may be too late.'

'No matter.' This time he did get to his feet. 'Your friend will know you have tried. And I will not feel like a traitor.' He looked at Barker but did not see him. 'I shall go.' He gripped Beresford's arm like a vice. 'Leave now.'

Then he lumbered towards the door and they heard his dragging footsteps until they were lost in the murmur of Buckhurst's generators.

Barker said abruptly, 'God! I've never seen anything like it! No pride in the man!'

Beresford opened his drawer and took out a pistol. As Kimber reappeared he said, 'Muster all the spare hands and march them to the dockyard. Give the OOD this authority to board the gunboat. Take all the medical gear you can find. Steal it if need be.'

Barker interrupted sharply, 'I'm not sure I am hearing you correctly, Ralph!' He looked at their intent faces. 'Take a Russian gunboat, to do what, for God's sake?'

Beresford clipped his pistol-belt in place and answered, 'I am a good officer, sir. If you order me to stay here, to do nothing after putting *Parthian* in a position without support, to leave your people to be *wiped out* to prove some idiotic theory, then stay I will. But by God I shall make certain everybody knows why I stayed. You can say goodbye to promotion after that!'

Barker looked as if he had been punched in the face.

He exclaimed, 'How *dare* you!'

Beresford eyed him coldly. 'Then I'm leaving. Now. It may be a useless gesture, but I'll feel cleaner. We all shall.' Except you, his voice seemed to imply.

They turned as the telephone shattered the tension.

The lieutenant who had just come out from England stammered, 'From Russian HQ, sir.' He was staring at Beresford. 'Their troops are on the peninsula and pushing inland.' He swallowed hard under Beresford's cold stare. 'Intelligence reports that *Gruppe Seeadler* has been sighted heading northeast from Balaclava.'

Beresford nodded. 'Thank you. So Lincke was not where we anticipated. He intends to jump *Parthian* from astern.' To the startled lieutenant he added, 'Make a signal to *Parthian* to that effect.' He walked to the door without another glance at his superior but something made him turn. He said softly, 'Add to the signal. *Keep your head down.*' But his voice broke. '*Old son.*'

The door grated shut and they all stared at Barker.

Barker was humming tunelessly. He said suddenly, 'I must draft a signal to Vice-Admiral Talents. To tell him about the great success of the raid. But for it, the Russian attack might never have begun.'

He glanced at his brightly lit command, but this time nobody was looking at him.

17

SUNSET

'Ease down to fifteen knots.' Devane dabbed his face with a towel and winced. His skin felt raw from the spray which came buffeting back from the bows. 'No sense in shaking ourselves to bits.'

Around him binoculars and gun-muzzles probed the darkness, the men saying nothing as they strained every sense to get a first hint of danger. There was a choppy off-shore swell which pitched the boat about, adding to the discomfort and the noise.

Lieutenant Chalmers seemed to have recovered completely from his sudden outburst, and was standing aft by the twin Oerlikon mounting, his arms folded, as the deck quivered and plunged beneath him.

Dundas emerged from the chartroom and said, 'We may have missed them, sir.'

Devane pictured his four MTBs strung out in pairs, the Russian launches managing as best they could somewhere astern. Their part was over, the killing done until the next time.

Devane said, 'We'll stop soon and listen. You never know.'

Feet clattered on the wet gratings, and Carroll called, 'Signal from W/T, sir. *Most immediate. Russian covering force* Romeo *is withdrawn. Two vessels only in your vicinity.*' He hesitated, then finished, '*Russian attack has begun. Ends.*'

Pellegrine stared hard at the black water beyond the bows. '*Ends?* It's a-bloody-'nough!'

Devane stood quite motionless, allowing his brain to translate the stark signal into reality. What the hell were the Russians playing at? Did they know that Lincke's E-boats were already in the strait, harrying the Russian troop transports, and no longer constituted a danger or a possible target?

Dundas muttered, 'Of all the luck!'

The boatswain's mate asked, 'Fall out action stations, sir?'

Devane thought rapidly as he felt the tension moving away, the dangerous air of relaxation growing about him.

'No.' He spoke sharply. 'We're not out of the woods yet.' He heard the quick whispers, could picture the meaning glances. *The skipper's over the top. Round the bend.* Well, they could think what they bloody well liked.

He swung round. 'Number One. Signal *Osprey* to fall back and cover the launches. Remainder of *Parthian*, line abreast. They know the drill.' As Dundas groped his way aft he added, 'After that, R/T silence. Not a whisper.'

Chalmers climbed into the bridge and listened to Dundas's clipped words over the R/T link.

He said, 'We might catch the Jerries with their pants down. That'll make a change.'

Devane gripped the wet screen and turned his head slowly, silently cursing the chorus of sea and wind.

No operation was perfect. But this was going badly wrong. Why should Orel's gunboats pull away? Certainly not without very firm orders from above.

'*Osprey*'s acknowledged, sir. Andy Twiss will *love* being lumbered as an escort!'

Devane barely heard him. The signal had sounded different. Like Beresford, and yet. . . .

Carroll said tersely, 'Another signal from W/T, sir. *German E-boats closing from south-west.*'

Dundas jumped for the voicepipes. 'Bloody hell!'

Devane remained by the screen, his fingers numb from the force of his grip.

'That all?'

Carroll said quietly, 'It finishes, *Keep your head down, old son.*'

'Thanks, Bunts.'

Devane released his hold very gently. It was almost better

this way. Like the inevitable moment when the cell door opens and the prisoner knows there is no reprieve, nor ever was. Or the last time a man hears the dawn chorus before the firing squad smashes him to oblivion.

He said, 'Stand by to alter course. Steer south sixty west. Signal *Parthian*, Bunts. Hand-lamp.'

He heard the swift clack . . . clack . . . clack of Carroll's shuttered lamp. The other boats would have monitored Beresford's signal, would have known they would get the order to turn and fight. It was what they had come for, Russian help or not. Now that was out of the question. Even the two remaining gunboats were in the wrong position and could not assist. Except to search for survivors.

'Acknowledged, sir.' Carroll's voice was a whisper.

'Very well. Execute. Warn the engine room to be prepared for maximum revs.'

The three hulls turned gracefully, their stems rising and then spewing foam as they recrossed their own wakes. Line abreast, each one shining in spray, facing an invisible enemy and with each turn of their racing screws taking them further and further from aid.

Devane wiped his glasses for the hundredth time and pressed them to his eyes. God help Andy Twiss if the enemy arrived before he had rejoined *Parthian*'s dwindling strength. But to use a lamp or R/T over this shortening range was like committing suicide.

Devane tried to find some small comfort. The sighting report could be mistaken. It often happened. Perhaps it was not *Seeadler* anyway. It would be just like Barker's lot to dramatize everything. But the comfort evaded him.

Dundas murmured, 'How many, d'you reckon?'

Devane moved the glasses carefully and tried to cushion them against the lurching screen.

'Half a dozen. Maybe more if he's scrounged reinforcements.' He stiffened, his mind locked like a jammed machine-gun. But it was only a deeper shadow in the swell.

Dundas grinned uncomfortably. 'Is that all? Piece of cake.'

Devane wanted to look at his watch but asked, 'Bunts? Time check.'

'Five minutes past one, sir.'

Soon. Even allowing for their alteration of course and speed. It must be. Stealth was the only thing they had left.

'Stop engines. Warn all hands.'

The motors rumbled away and Devane felt the deck slide forward and down, the screen press against his dripping coat, as the boat lost way.

'Well, Swain?' Devane glanced at Pellegrine's battered cap. It was all he could distinguish in the darkness. 'Don't let me down now.'

Pellegrine rested on his spokes. 'Should 'ave sighted our launches by now.' He shifted uneasily. 'I just 'ope Mr Twiss don't mistake *us* for Krauts.'

Carroll murmured, 'I'm ready with the lamp, Swain. No bother there.'

Pellegrine continued to listen. *No bother there.* But the commanding officer of the MTB which they had detached to escort the Russian launches had been an actor. Pellegrine grimaced. It would be just our luck if he saw this as his greatest role.

Metcalf whispered, *'There! Engines!'*

'What? Where?' Pellegrine sounded angry that the young seaman had heard something before him. 'Probably *Osprey*.'

Devane listened, the sound slipping into his head like a whisper. As if it had been there all the time. As if. . . . He shook himself angrily.

'Stand by!'

It was no mistake. The regular *thrum . . . thrum . . . thrum* of heavy diesels. He could see them clearly as if they were already right here and it was broad daylight. The squat bridges, the long low hulls, that familiar air of menace.

Dundas murmured, 'Andy Twiss must have stopped too. Thank God for that.'

Pellegrine called, 'No, sir. There's another MTB out there too. Starboard bow.'

Devane bit his lip hard. Twiss had probably gone back to round up a straggler or to take one of them in tow. Maybe even to lift off some wounded soldiers. The E-boats were closing fast astern. Just as they would have been on *Parthian* but for Beresford's signal.

Dundas said, 'I'll call up *Osprey*, sir. Andy might hold them off until we join him.'

Devane peered at the luminous compass. 'Negative. They'll cut us up piecemeal. This is our one and only chance, can't you

243

see that? *Osprey*'s lookouts may spot the danger in time.' His tone hardened. 'It's what they're for.'

Dundas stared at him, his eyes making deep shadows in his face. 'But he'll not stand a bloody earthly!'

Devane lowered his glasses. 'Get aft and send Chalmers up here. Gun action. Depth charges if we get the slightest opening.'

Dundas nodded jerkily. 'Yes. I see.' He was groping for the bridge ladder when Devane called him back.

'It's the only way. Do you imagine I wanted it like this?' It was suddenly important that Dundas should understand. He needed him to.

Dundas faltered, one foot in the air. 'I'm just glad I don't have to decide, sir.'

'*You will*, Roddy. You will, one day.' But his words were lost as the night split apart in a galaxy of flares and tracer shells.

Lurking like assassins in the shadows beyond the blinding flares, the three MTBs started their motors and moved slowly towards the brightly lit arena. In the centre of the crisscrossing balls of tracer, and pinned down by the enemy's flares, the isolated MTB was already increasing speed, snarling round to face the E-boats which had burst out of the night, their onslaught timed to the second.

A low shape rippled past the savage exchange of shots, and then burst into flames as cannon fire transformed one of the troop launches into a pyre in a moment.

A seaman behind Devane swore fervently, and was probably thinking of the other Russians those same men had burned.

Chalmers was here now, glasses levelled, cap tugged low over his hawklike nose, as he snapped, 'Six E-boats. Moving right to left.' This time he did not even blink as another explosion painted the sea like blood. 'There's the leader. Red-four-five.'

In the angry glow the tiger stripes were even clearer, Devane thought.

'*Osprey*'s stopping and on fire, sir!' The boatswain's mate sounded as if he was at a firing range. 'Two E-boats closing her, starboard side to.'

How puny the stabbing flashes looked against the heavier scars of tracer. Twiss's boat was almost stopped, and was being raked by the enemy without mercy. But Twiss's gunners were still firing back at a range of some twenty-five yards. The two E-boats which were thrusting towards him no doubt intended to finish it and blow the bottom right out of the MTB.

Now or never. Devane raised his voice. 'All ahead *full*! *Open fire!*'

In a tight arrowhead the three hulls raced from the shadows with every gun which would bear ripping into the circling E-boats and churning the sea into a white froth.

Above the clatter of machine-guns, the heavier bang of Priest's six-pounder, Devane heard the mounting roar of motors and imagined Ackland and his assistants being tossed about the engine room like rag dolls as the boat tore across the swell like an avenging devil.

'A *hit*! Got the bastard!' Another voice, cracked with anxiety. 'Watch that one! *Jesus Christ!*' Then the terrible thud and shriek of metal as the German gunners at last realized that *Osprey* was not alone.

Devane peered abeam and saw *Harrier* butting into the lead, Walker's yellow scarf whipping out above the screen like a lance pennant as he charged to the attack.

Tracer flashed over the bridge, and Devane heard the clatter of falling rigging and the ping of splinters against a gun-shield. Somewhere a man was croaking for help and a machine-gunner was swearing at his loader as he fumbled to serve the smoking breeches, oblivious to everything but the need to keep firing.

The E-boats had split into two sections, their long hulls gleaming in the fires as they tilted hard over to screws and rudders.

One of them had stopped dead, smoke gushing from aft and tiny figures slipping and falling in crossfire as they tried to find safety.

'Tell *Kestrel* to finish that one!'

Devane turned swiftly as bullets fanned past the bridge. Mackay's *Kestrel* came bouncing across the torn waters, guns blazing, barely leaving enough room to cross the damaged E-boat's stern as he lobbed his depth charges alongside.

Two more E-boats were coming head on through the smoke, but one swerved aside as she collided with the capsized hull of a Russian launch. Men were floundering in the water but vanished, their screams stifled as they were sucked bodily into the racing propellers.

The E-boat which had hit the half-submerged wreck veered

away, engines coughing and roaring, a signal lamp already flashing urgently to its leader.

Devane yelled, 'Steer straight for him!'

He felt nothing as tracer lifted from the oncoming E-boat and then tore down towards him. Priest's return fire plus a forty-five degree onslaught from Walker's gunners were enough. The leading E-boat swung away, guns still firing without a break as her commander sought to rally his formation.

Chalmers yelled wildly, 'Three of us to four of them now, the sods!'

A tremendous explosion lit the sky, and with shocked horror Devane saw Twiss's boat blasted apart, the torpedoes adding to the destruction as a passing E-boat dealt the death blow.

Devane turned away, unable to watch the pieces of hull and men dropping amongst the churned wakes of the antagonists.

He must hold on to Chalmers' words. The odds were better. One E-boat sinking, another damaged and out of the fight. But for the Germans' attention being riveted on Twiss and his launches, they would have stood no chance at all. Twiss, the actor who had intended to play the parts of the admirals after the war. Like Seymour, whose book would have been about them and their war.

He shouted, 'Nuts to starboard! Tell Red to watch his quarter!'

Devane heard Carroll using the R/T, the insane rattle of guns as Briton and German tried to knock out the resistance, just long enough, seconds even, to make the kill.

Chalmers yelled, '*Harrier*'s in trouble!'

Devane touched Pellegrine's hunched shoulder and felt him flinch. Expecting a bullet. 'Close on *Harrier*.'

He saw the tracers lifting and intertwining, brilliant green and cruel red, clawing and then ripping into wood and metal, flesh and blood.

A gunner shouted wildly, 'Got the bastard!' Walker's six-pounder must have raked the enemy's bridge even as the two boats charged headlong on a converging course. Coxswain, officers, cut down in a scythe of splinters and tracer.

Metcalf paused, gasping, as he hauled more ammunition to the machine-guns, and cried desperately, 'They're going to collide!'

246